## PRAISE FOR THE WAR WITH NO NAME SERIES

beguiling

"*Mort(e)* catapults the reader into a wild, apocalyptic world . . . A strangely moving story."
—*The Washington Post*

"Marvelously droll . . . This novel is all kinds of crazy, but it wears its crazy so well."
—*Slate*

"With poignant flashes of a morality tale, this debut novel makes us rethink our relationship to all of Earth's creatures (since they may someday turn on us)."—*Time Out New York*

"An epic science-fiction thriller . . . *Mort(e)* will stick with you long after you close the pages." —Tor.com

"Repino crafts achingly real characters from housecats and doggies, and gets you sympathizing with both sides of the in-equation. This is a perfect example of the power of pulp, wild adventure for domesticated humans."
—KQED Arts

"Read this novel and you will never look at your pet the same way again."
—Daniel H. Wilson, author of *Robopocalypse* and *Robogenesis*

"Robert Repino's *Mort(e)* is, page after page, an infectious tale."
—Electric Literature

"Excellent . . . The entire series is one of the most unique concepts in contemporary science fiction."
—*Inverse*

"Fantastic . . . Well-drawn characters and emotional heft are hallmarks of this unusual series about the power of myth, love, and redemption in a dangerous time."—*Publishers Weekly*, Starred Review

# MALEFACTOR

Books by Robert Repino
*Mort(e)*
*Culdesac*
*D'Arc*
*Malefactor*

# MALEFACTOR

## A NOVEL FROM THE WAR WITH NO NAME

## ROBERT REPINO

Published by
Soho Press, Inc.
227 W 17th Street
New York, NY 10011

Library of Congress Cataloging-in-Publication Data

Repino, Robert, author.
Malefactor : a novel from the war with no name
Series: War with no name ; book 3

1. Science fiction. I. Title
PS3618.E76 M35 2021 | DDC 813'.6—dc23  2021019986

ISBN 978-1-64129-374-7
eISBN 978-1-64129-099-9

Interior illustrations by Kapo Ng and Sam Chung
Wolf illustration: PO11/Shutterstock
Praise page: Naj Ativk/Shutterstock and Freevector.com
Interior design by Janine Agro, Soho Press, Inc.

Printed in the United States of America

10 9 8 7 6 5 4 3 2 1

*For my family*

"There is no fate that cannot be surmounted by scorn."

—ALBERT CAMUS

"We keep the wolves outside by living well."

—ANGELA CARTER, *THE COMPANY OF WOLVES*

# INTRODUCTION

**B**Y THE TIME the humans finally figured out that the War with No Name had begun, it was already too late.

For centuries, the Queen of the ants planned her revenge on humanity, breeding giant Alpha soldiers that would rise from the earth and attack without warning. But she did more than merely destroy. She created a new race of beings by using her strange power to uplift the surface animals. Before long, all the pets, livestock, and wild beasts became sentient, able to think, to walk upright, and to remember the cruelty of man. They became eager crusaders in the Queen's holy war.

It took nearly a decade to reduce humanity to a handful of scattered outposts and nomadic tribes. The humans' only hope was their bioweapon known as EMSAH, a powerful countermeasure that frightened even the Queen. In the face of this threat, the animals retook the land and built a new society. After it was over, they tried to forget the war. They tried convince themselves they would not make the same mistakes that had led to it.

Despite her immense power, the Queen could not make the animals forget everything. And so, the pit bull Wawa was haunted by dreams of her days in the fighting ring, battling for her greedy master. The bobcat Culdesac recalled his nameless brother, murdered and butchered by hunters. And the war hero Mort(e), a former housecat, could not stop wondering what happened to his friend, his only love, a dog named Sheba.

Through Culdesac, the Queen kept her eye on Mort(e). As did the dwindling human resistance, whose prophet—a child named Michael—had foretold that Mort(e) would find Sheba one day, and destroy the Colony. Mort(e)'s decision to begin this quest set into motion a new phase of the war, one that threatened to wipe out everyone, animal and human alike.

The prophecy, however, was a lie, another trick that the Queen played on the humans. But Mort(e) could not be stopped. He *forced* the prophecy to come true. He found Sheba and killed the Queen. Nothing would get in his way.

The cat and dog fled into the wilderness, hoping that the war was behind them. They became farmers, raising wayward Alpha soldiers like cattle. The humans and the animals tried to rebuild together, founding the holy city of Hosanna based on the teachings of the Prophet Michael. A new era had begun.

Meanwhile, the remnants of the Queen's empire began to rise again—a fail-safe triggered by her death. Portents of her return appeared in different forms. Reports of bizarre creatures in the forests and streams. A giant spider menacing the beaver settlement of Lodge City. And, the most dangerous: the Sarcops, a race of amphibious monsters. All the experiences of these creatures—their desires and fears—were channeled through their leader, Taalik, chosen by the Queen herself to fulfill the destiny of the Colony.

By then, Wawa the pit bull had become the chief of security in Hosanna. In response to Lodge City's request for help, she sent a husky named Falkirk, a veteran of the war. Nikaya, the leader of the city, suggested they reach out to some neighbors for help: a cat and a dog with experience in "taking down large insects." And with that, Mort(e) and Sheba's quiet time as ranchers came to an end. Mort(e) hated it. But Sheba, now facing the world for the first time, could not resist going on an adventure. Nor could she ignore the husky, the first canine she had met since before the war, when she'd had a litter of puppies with the neighbor's dog. The memory of those pups lingered, compelling her to find out if there was more to life beyond their quiet farm. As the battle loomed, she decided to take on a new name for herself: D'Arc. A name fit for a warrior.

It soon came to light that Nikaya had tried to control the spider, hoping to use it against a community of bats who threatened her stranglehold over Lodge City. Before going to prison for her crime, she witnessed the interlopers defeat the spider and rescue her people. But in doing so, they triggered Taalik's war with Hosanna. The Sarcops could sense the creature's death from afar. In retaliation, they enacted a swift vengeance by destroying the city's dam and flooding the city.

In the aftermath, the prophet was dead, Mort(e) was arrested for his murder, and a cult of human fascists called the Sons of Adam tried to seize power. To make things worse, the Sarcops issued an ultimatum. To complete their destiny, they needed someone who had communicated directly with the Queen, someone who had seen the world through her eyes. Only a person with that vast knowledge could unlock an ancient secret that would allow the Sarcops to survive. That person was Mort(e).

Like all of the Queen's plans, it was a trap, designed to annihilate the humans, along with the ungrateful animals who had betrayed the Colony. Mort(e) and D'Arc managed to stop it, but at a terrible price. Wawa sacrificed her life to save them, along with so many others. The Sarcops retreated. Hosanna barely held on.

Now battle-tested, D'Arc decided to forge her own destiny. In the wake of all this destruction, the government in Hosanna insisted on sending out a lone ship, the *al-Rihla*, to contact other settlements left behind in the war. D'Arc joined the expedition as the senior expert on Alpha soldiers. Though brokenhearted at her departure, Falkirk focused on his duty by taking command of the airship *Vesuvius*, which would keep an eye on the restless wolf packs that surrounded the city. Mort(e) agreed to help rebuild the dam, alongside the beavers, the best architects in Hosanna.

Nearly a year has passed, and peacetime brings with it the illusion of security. But the war still lives in the hearts of those who survived it. It flows with the blood. This is the Queen's design, an endless cycle of conflict that will purify the world and pull in all those who sought to escape it, no matter how far they've run.

# PART I

# WINTER

# CHAPTER 1

## THE STORY OF MERCY

**T**HE WOLVES BOUNDED through the snow, kicking it behind them in enormous white clumps. Mercy's paws burned from the cold. Then they went numb, and it felt as if she were flying over the white expanse, her snout pointed toward the scent of fur and flesh, so thick she could swallow it. The trees shook with each step. Their bare branches wobbled against the white sky, the sun no brighter than the full moon. All around her, her sisters and brothers, her cousins, her entire family sprinted beside her. Their breath steamed from their mouths. Her ribs brushed against one of the hunters, sending warmth to her pounding heart. Everywhere, heads bobbed. Tails hung low and stiff for balance. The fastest runners breathed the hardest. *Hehh-uh-hehh-uh-hehh-uh.*

This would work. It had to work. The pack would live.

The necklace she wore bounced with each step. It held a single yellowed fang. The sharp end kept spiking her in the chest, a sign that she was still alive. That this was not a dream.

The scent of prey lingered like a fog. The pack growled as one when they passed through it. Their voices made the earth rumble.

Too many of her people had died to bring her to this moment.

Her brother, her parents. A litter of pups. Her former mate, whose name they no longer spoke. The wolves who colonized this land, moving south in the wake of the great war. Their spirits watched her now. She could feel their breath in the bitter wind.

Her lungs burned as the pack reached the top of a hill. Cresting the ridge, the wolves poured down the other side. The gravity pulled Mercy along. She had never run so fast.

They found the hoof prints at the base of the hill. Mercy noted the loping, relaxed strides of a herd of deer. But as the pack overtook the trail, the hoof marks drifted farther and farther apart as the deer broke into a full sprint. Panic. Desperation. Mercy could smell both.

The trees thinned into a clearing. She spotted the deer. Dozens of them, with their white tails. A meal for every hunter. The pack would drive the prey into the thicker snow, where their hooves would become stuck.

All the wolves' snouts pointed toward the closest victim, a thin, weak buck with the antlers of a male half his age. This one would fall first. Mercy's tongue flopped out of her mouth as she imagined twisting the deer's neck until the bones crackled.

She jockeyed toward the front. Her new mate led the way. Wex, they called him. Wex the Cruelblood. His jaws snapped at the deer's legs, taunting him. It riled the other hunters. They barked at him, urging him to kill. To paint his fangs red.

The deer slowed. Soon his life would belong to the pack. Wex would make it quick. Not out of sympathy, but because there were so many others to kill. A bounty they had waited for all winter.

Mercy's mind cleared. Only her senses remained, allowing her to focus on the musk of the deer's fur. The hooves denting the earth. The snow whispering beneath her feet.

The pack must live.

• • •

THE DAY BEFORE, Mercy saw a human for the first time. And he was beautiful.

She was returning from a patrol on a bitterly damp and overcast afternoon. The clouds were heavy with snow, ready to unburden themselves. Winter had dug its claws into the earth and would not let go. Like any other predator, it claimed its territory. It fed on the weak. It laughed at those who made plans for the warmer months. Spring was never promised to anyone.

Two other wolves joined Mercy on her patrol. Wex's bodyguards. They made sure she did not go far. She was the only pregnant female in the pack this season. All the other females miscarried or gave birth to stillborn litters. Everything depended on Mercy bearing children this year. To make sure she fulfilled her duty, her sister, Urna, stayed behind. Wex's orders. He would let Mercy venture into the woods for her daily routine. But if she ever tried to run away, Urna would die. And it would not take long for the marauders to hunt a mother and her newborn pups and force them to rejoin the pack.

Maybe it would not matter. With the food running out, Urna's ribs had begun to form tiny ridges in her fur. Her hair fell out in scraggly lumps. Her deprived brain began to fail her. Urna's father had named her after a plant that grew here, a miniature sunflower with yellow petals extending from a black circle in the middle. As the flowers died out, so too did Urna's fragile mind. One time, she forgot where the den was. Another time, she pissed too close to a puddle and ruined a fresh supply of water.

Ever since Wex took over the pack and declared Urna the omega, Mercy tried to sneak food to her when she could. She fought off the others when they picked on Urna. She bided her time. A future awaited, a future without Wex and his traitors. And so Mercy kept fighting. She kept moving forward. She kept dragging Urna with her, even when her sister wanted to give in.

On this day, the patrol found something. Strange tracks and an abandoned campsite, coated with a scent that none of them recognized. Not a large war party. Not wolves at all, but intruders nevertheless, trying to sneak through Mudfoot territory. Mercy needed to tell the others.

Still, the patrol had failed to find anything to eat, which mattered far more than some trespassers who made a wrong turn. The elk and deer had long since abandoned the area, ever since the leaves stopped growing. The land had gone sour less than a year before. Nothing but dead trees, turgid streams. A smell of metal in the air. The river browning into a liquid copper. Sometimes Mercy wanted to scratch the scent out of her nostrils.

As Mercy approached the den, a great howl went up. The scouts had spotted her. The patrol howled in response. Their mournful call let the pack know that they returned with nothing. To acknowledge the bad news, the pack responded with a meandering song that lingered until the wolves ran out of breath. It called on their ancestors, the first Mudfoot to arrive in the valley, to help them. To show them the way. Or to simply stay dead if they had nothing useful to offer.

Near the entrance to the den, a strange creature stood on its hind legs, tied to a dead tree, with rope creasing his wrists and ankles. Mercy stopped. It was a human. A *man*. After years of listening to stories of their cruelty, she expected a human face to be a terrible thing, all fangs and snout, dripping spit and snot. But no. This man leaned his head on the bark, eyes closed, and sighed out each breath. His face was smooth, like a stone in a stream. A tattoo covered everything from his forehead to his chin, forming a mask. A wolf face, permanently inked into the flesh, with the fangs bared around his lips. His shiny black hair fell to his collarbone. An elegant animal too perfect to devour.

A wolf pelt hung over his muscular shoulders. At the base of his neck, the dead wolf's scalp formed a hood to protect him from the cold. It even had the pointed ears. His tunic and pants were fashioned from deerskin, judging from the smell, and the notches in the knees suggested at least a season's worth of wear and tear. On his feet were a pair of flexible leather boots, bound with twine that crisscrossed the ankles. Mercy had heard of these humans. The Toqwa, they were called. Rejected by the city of Hosanna, they lived like the animals, using their tattoos to identify themselves. She assumed they had all died out. After all, how could humans survive out here, surrounded by enemies, without the protection of their walls and their guns?

One of Wex's henchmen, a wolf named Jape, circled the tree on all fours. Jape had probably never seen a human before either. He was too young. And so he needed to show that this man did not scare him. As he made his way around the captive, Jape gave him an occasional sniff. The human continued his meditation.

Crawling closer, Mercy lowered her head and slid her chin along the dirt, to show that she posed no threat. That she knew her place. Despite the show of respect, Jape snorted at her. She was not supposed to be here. As the pack leader's mate, she needed to be at Wex's side.

With Jape looming nearby, Mercy sniffed the man. Beneath the pelt he wore, she could detect his strange scent: rank and oily and salty. She heard that humans leaked water from their foreheads and armpits when they ran. The man's eyes opened, the irises such a dark brown she could hardly see his pupils. He watched her until a movement nearby caught his attention.

Urna emerged from the blackness of the den. Despite her limp, she stubbornly trotted to Mercy, her tongue wagging. Her paws seemed enormous compared to her withered legs. A tooth had fallen out days earlier, the first of many. She had showed it to Mercy and asked if she should put it on a necklace as well. Mercy told her to throw it away.

Urna passed too close to Jape. As always, he slashed at her.

She recoiled with a yelp. Before it could escalate—and for an omega, it always did—Mercy put herself between them. With a series of barks and snarls, Jape warned Mercy that one day she would not be around to protect her crippled sister anymore. Mercy responded by scraping her nails in the dirt. It meant that he would be dead long before that happened.

Once the shouting died out, Mercy nudged her sister with her snout. She pawed the earth, carving a line that pointed directly at the human. It meant that she wanted answers. Urna yipped, her tail wagging. *Follow me*, it meant.

They took the trail around the edge of the den. Years ago, this mountain was covered with trees that would burst into green clouds come spring. Ever since the flood and the curse it carried, the last healthy trees grew on only the highest parts of the slope. The birds had already figured it out. The wolves, not long after. But the Mudfoot could not fly away.

At the end of the trail, the sisters found more humans—four of them. Two women, two men, all with identical wolf tattoos on their faces. Young and fit, like the one tied to the tree. Pale skin reddened by the wind, bronzed and tightened by the sun. They knelt in a single row, with heavy rope binding all their wrists together. The wolves surrounded them, but would not get close. They didn't know what to do with creatures like these.

One of the women leaned forward, and something round and pink poked over her shoulder. It was a baby, wrapped in cloth, strapped to the woman's back. Mercy had heard that human babies did nothing but cry. This one eyed the wolves with a line of drool hanging from its bottom lip. A few of the wolves growled and barked in response. Some of them became so frenzied that they bounced on the balls of their feet, shouting each time. *Death! Death! Death!*

It was easy to spot Wex among the smaller wolves. When he stood on his hind legs, rising high above the crowd, the shouting grew quiet. Tails lowered. Snouts dipped to the ground in deference to the pack leader. This was one of the rules Wex had imposed since taking control. When he stood on two feet, the others remained on all four. When he spoke, the others listened.

Long ago, before Mercy was born, all of these wolves lived as their ancestors had for generations—ever since the First Winter, when the ancient wolves formed a pack for the first time. And then one day, as the older ones liked to tell it, everything changed. Something in the water did it, an alien substance implanted by the Queen of the Colony that rewired their brains and added bulk to their bones and muscles. And yet the Change never really fit with such a perfect race. They could now speak the human language—but the wolves already had one. The way they flicked their tails or showed their teeth could convey all the meaning and nuance they needed. They could run on two legs, though using all four was always better. They could build or destroy with their front paws, though their teeth could do the same. Some of the wolf packs changed further, becoming like the humans and their animal pets. Several clans even followed the Colony's orders to forsake hunting forever. The ants showed them how to raise crops, and just like that, hunters became farmers. They seized entire towns, lived in houses. Some even learned how to drive cars.

But the Mudfoot held on to the old ways. That was how they survived, and how they would continue to survive, even to the Last Winter.

Wex was stuck somewhere in the middle. He could not resist painting his face and fur with splashes of white, yellow, and red, the way some of the rival clans did. He wore a necklace made of broken deer antlers. He gave orders in the human language, even when forbidding the others from doing so. And he took wolves as slaves. Including Mercy.

When he spotted her, Wex sauntered over, patting one of his lieutenants on the head as he passed. The young wolf wagged his tail in response. Wex could offer affection, but only on a whim. Only for show. Moments like this revealed the poor health of the pack. Mercy noticed the protruding hip bones, the sores that would not heal, the severed ears, the missing teeth, the broken legs that never properly mended. And in the midst of this, Wex the proud warrior strutted about, fat and painted like a female bird.

"You wish to see the humans?" Wex asked her.

She barked yes.

"My mate," he said. He motioned to her belly. "You bring the future. And so do I."

Urna exhaled loudly through her nose. She did not like it when Wex touched her sister.

"We caught them near the Whiskers," he said. It was his name for the bend in the river. "They tried to cross. We surrounded them."

Though the pack needed food, they could not eat this prey. Not yet. They needed to show off their prize.

"We give them to the Mournfuls tomorrow," he said. The neighboring pack. It would curry favor, maybe stop the Mournfuls from taking more territory. A generous wolf was a strong wolf. For the right price, the Mudfoot could regain access to the reservoir. They wouldn't have to survive on the polluted river anymore.

"We will keep their leader," Wex added, pointing toward the den where she saw the first man, the beautiful one. "We feast on him. He talks too much."

*Yes*, Mercy thought. *He talks too much.*

A distant howl made dozens of ears perk up. From their seated positions, the wolves craned their necks and bellowed in response. Despite his annoyance with the interruption, Wex joined in. His enormous chest expanded, and his necklace jingled.

The howl was an alarm. Scouts approached, bringing more news. The den responded with a soothing song. *We are here*, it said. *We are with you.*

And then, the humans let out a howl of their own. As if they could not help themselves. They tipped their heads to the sky and wailed.

"Stop!" Wex said. He howled again. "Stop it!"

He picked out one of the humans and backhanded him. The man fell to his side. Even with his mouth bleeding, he continued to howl.

Mercy nudged Urna. *Do they always do this?*

Urna continued to shout with the others. It was her way of saying that she did not know.

The wolves greeted the scouts at the mouth of the cave. Upon seeing Wex, the scouts raced around in circles. They barked; they snapped at tails. Even the old one named Mockler, who walked with a limp, worked himself into a fury. Soon the other wolves joined, forming a whirlpool of fur and fangs. This movement was a warning, meant to show that invaders had encroached into Mudfoot territory. The snapping meant one thing: food. Deer. Maybe an entire herd.

One by one, the scouts faced northwest, where the sun began its descent in the bleak gray sky. Mockler was the last to face the right direction, and that was only after one of his cousins elbowed him. Soon they all barked at the horizon, not merely in excitement, but anger as well. Even the other wolf clans had left them to their fate in this poisoned earth. For deer to cross the border was the greatest insult. Wex barked louder than the others. *Rip them all open!* he shouted. *Rip them apart!*

"You're making a mistake!" a voice said.

The howling died out. It was the human who spoke.

"Death awaits you over that hill," the man said. No smile, no hesitation. Just a statement of fact.

Wex marched over to the man. Instinctively, the others crouched lower—except for Mercy. Urna whimpered beside her. *Get down!*

"Death, you say?" Wex asked.

"I see red fangs dripping with blood," the man said.

"Those are *our* fangs you're seeing."

". . . and antlers, piled to the sky."

"Yes! We bring them here for you."

A few of the wolves laughed. They stopped suddenly when the man howled, the kind that wolves let out when they passed the spot where their loved ones were killed. The sound of it tore at Mercy's heart. She had howled in the same way for far too many of her people in the last year. Even tied to a pole, beaten and starving, this human could reach inside of them all. He could sing their language.

Wex gripped the man's jaw in his enormous hand. He turned the man's head to one side and then the other, as if examining some prize. "Where do you come from?"

"The forest," the man said. "Like you."

"Like us. You wear wolf skin. Like a human trophy hunter."

The human flicked his chin toward Mercy. "She's wearing a wolf tooth."

Everyone turned to Mercy. She tried to crouch so low that she would sink under the ground.

Still holding the man's face, Wex raked his claws along the cheek. The human did not flinch. Four red lines extended from his ear to his lips, slicing through the tattoo. Blood spilled onto his chest and disappeared into the collar of his tunic. One of the skinnier wolves made a move for it, his nostrils flaring. Then he thought better of it.

Wex licked the blood from his claws. "Do not be fooled by

this one," he said to the pack. "Talks like a wolf. Tastes like a man."

"Dregger helped us once," the human said. "We came to help him."

"Dregger is dead," Wex said. "I'm in charge now." With that, he dropped to all four paws. He could shift quickly from one role to the other, and he needed the others to know that.

Wex bucked and yipped and wagged his tail. All of it together meant that they would hunt. They would kill. There would be blood. Food. Life. The future. The others joined in again. Together they became a rolling wave of fur. One of the weaker ones fell. He squealed as the others trampled him. He got to his feet again, dazed but still hypnotized by the war chant.

Mercy felt Urna leave her side. The others let the omega dance with them despite her low status. In the melee, she could snap her jaws and bat the others with her tail all she wanted.

In the breeze, Mercy detected the scent of blood. She locked eyes with the human. His tongue slid from his cracked lips to lick the wound on his cheek. And for a moment, it appeared that he wanted to tear himself from his bonds so that he could sing and dance with the wolves. So he could howl with them. So he could kill with them.

AS THE PACK prepared for the hunt, Mercy tried to drag Urna along. Urna whimpered at first, knowing full well that she risked a beating. Mercy yipped at her again, slapping her paws on the dirt. *Come on!*

Wex interrupted by biting Urna's tail until she rolled over in submission. Jape followed by clawing at Urna's leg. She screamed and ran off. That settled it—Mercy's sister would stay behind, as she always did. If she behaved, they would bring her some antlers to chew on. Mercy could hardly blame Wex for not letting her sister join them. In the last big hunt, Urna had given away their position, letting a fawn escape. Later, she got lost, and Mercy spent the night searching for her. If Urna spoiled this hunt, the other wolves would almost certainly kill her.

The pack set out in an unusual predawn search. Mercy took her place at the front alongside Wex. Whereas Urna always ate last, Mercy would eat first. She needed it, as she was too thin for a mother expecting pups. Sometimes, the others would insist that she take their share. *Eat!* they would bark at her. *Get strong and fat!* She insisted that she was fine. But then, unable to resist any longer, she would bury her face in the warm, steaming flesh and rip it free of the bone. Once she became stuffed with meat, she would lie in the grass and wait for her pups to kick and dance inside of her. New life. The future, ready to burst forth.

In the darkness, Mercy glanced behind her to the glowing pairs of eyes that floated above the ground. The vapor puffing from the wolves' breath blurred her vision. The fastest way to the north took the pack across the old train tracks and through the valley where Mercy had formed her first memories. She and Urna would race along the riverbank while the older wolves kept watch. In those days, all the wolves, even the meanest hunters with broken limbs and scars on their bellies, played with them as if they were pups themselves.

These days, the depths of the valley were unrecognizable, ever since the flood had brought its dark water to poison everything. The grass had died out, leaving only frozen earth. A stench rose from the river. At night, the scant moonlight reflected off the surface. Some of the wolves wheezed at the scent. Wex barked for them to stop.

They came across the musk of deer in a grove of dead trees. The bucks had passed through here, scratched themselves against the rotting bark. Tufts of fur clung to the broken branches. An act of defiance against a weakened pack. No one respected the Mudfoot anymore, not even their food supply.

One of Wex's soldiers—a young biter named Toth—grabbed the tuft of fur and tried to nibble on it. Another wolf named Perl deftly snatched it away. The two tussled for it. When Wex came close, they dropped the fur, tails on the ground. An offering to the leader. Wex ignored it and walked away. Toth grumbled at Perl. *See what you did!*

The first snowflakes fell shortly after. Mercy caught a few on her tongue. Snow could mask the scent they were tracking. It would also force their prey to leave tracks. Wex urged the pack to move faster. He snorted, a signal that he detected something close. Mercy smelled nothing. Most likely, Wex was faking it to get the wolves running, to keep them warm. For all his faults, this was what he was good at.

And yet. That human with the black eyes. The strange, hairless face, like the skin of a ripened fruit. He warned them to go no farther. After nearly a year of uncertainty, he seemed more certain than anyone.

Mercy raced to the front again. She would not bark—it would give away their position. Instead, she nipped at Wex's hipbone. He flinched, but kept moving. She did it again. *Stop!* each bite said. *We must stop!*

Wex lunged at her, gripping her rear leg in his jaw. When she tried to break free, he bit harder without breaking the skin. Enough to remind her that he enjoyed the advantage. That he could kill her on a whim.

The other wolves surrounded them. None of them bared their teeth. They didn't have to.

Whimpering, she pawed at the earth, in the direction of the den. *We must go back!*

A quick snort from Wex. It meant no.

*But the . . . human! He said . . .*

She pulled her leg free, only to find herself pinned in the cold snow. Wex's hot breath made her ear twitch.

"Humans lie," he said. "*We* speak the truth."

He pressed his paw to her fang necklace. The point of it broke her skin. A bead of blood welled from the puncture wound, going cold as soon as the wind hit it.

"Here is truth," Wex said. "Remember who you are. Or your sister will feed us. As will your pups, if they prove too weak. Like your last mate."

He let go. She rolled quickly to all fours. The surrounding pack created a circle of warmth. Snowflakes melted as soon as they touched her hot fur.

Wex had nothing else to say. He continued walking. The others waited for Mercy to follow alongside him. Even Jape gave her an extra moment to gather herself. And so she went.

To keep her mind off the cold, Mercy held the fang on her necklace in her mouth. Her tongue slithered around its shape. Wex spoke only of the days to come, yet he forced her wear this symbol of the past. She was a mercy dog, after all.

EVER SINCE THE flood, Wex had kept the pack alive.

Most days, Mercy hated him for it.

Wex was among the first wolves to migrate here after the Change. With the humans gone and the forest overtaking their cities and towns, wolf clans from the north seized the open territory. The ant overlords welcomed them. The other animals knew to stay out of their way.

Dregger was the leader in those days. He made the decision to come here when so many of the clans panicked. Some of the wolves were so terrified of the Change that they gnawed their own hands off. Like a good wolf, Dregger could imagine the future. He worshipped it, as a leader should. He understood that the future was the only thing that was real, and thus saw opportunity in a land that cried out for new predators. The deer and the elk were migrating too. Like the wolves, they wanted no part of the war, no matter what they may have owed the Queen for the gifts she gave them. Unwilling to trust the humans who once hunted them, they would take the risk of living in the wild. Which meant they would contend with hungry packs, eager to conquer.

Mercy and her sister were born shortly after. They grew quickly. In those days, Mercy went by the name Roka. A hunter's name. Though she had parents, the entire pack raised her, as they did for all the young ones. The elders admired her instincts, her ruthlessness in singling out the smallest and weakest prey to pounce on. One day, the matriarch of the clan died when a deer hoof smashed her skull. Dregger needed a new mate. He chose Roka without hesitation. She was ten—old enough to take her place among the great mothers of the Mudfoot. Later that year, she bore him two strong pups.

The pack grew. Its newfound territory expanded. Other wolves feared them. Especially the clans that adopted the humans' ways, the ones who made peace, signed treaties, built new towns. The Mudfoot refused to join their Lupine Confederacy. The pack elders regarded it as a foolish human invention, a sad imitation of the Sanctuary Union government in Hosanna. Sitting in committees, bickering over votes, forming cheap, temporary alliances. Politics was beneath their species. Only the gonneys—the fake wolves who had lost their way—would participate in such a thing. No rule of law, no sense of fairness or justice, could sway the Mudfoot from keeping to their traditions. New lines on a map could not hem them in, nor could threats from Hosanna, nor the other wolves, nor the bears. Their reputation as outlaws spread so far that the dogs in Hosanna crafted legends about them.

Then the flood came. Roka was on a hilltop when it arrived, wrestling with her pups, Rove and Herc, both names chosen by Dregger. Roka stopped when she sensed the earth rumbling,

while the young ones nipped at her paws. *Play with us, Mama!*
A strange breeze brushed against her face, carrying the scent of
death. And then the black waters coursed through the valley,
overtaking the river, scorching everything like liquid fire. The
grass withered. Leaves fluttered from the trees. Fish bobbed to
the surface of the water and gathered in scaly clusters on the
edges of the river.

Unaware of the danger, her pups barked at the deluge. They
tried to outdo each other.

*Look at me, Mama!*

*No, Mama, look at me!*

They thought it was a game. Rove got so excited that he pissed
freely as he hopped around. Watching these oblivious children,
Roka knew that a terrible reckoning had come.

Much like the pups, the older wolves could do nothing but
pin their ears and bark at it all. As if they could tell the deluge to
reverse course and go back to the human city.

It did not take long to figure out what had happened. Word
got around—even among enemies. Far to the north, the humans
spent years blocking the river to harness its power. The dam
burst, thanks to some pointless conflict between the city and a
race of aquatic creatures. Hybrid beasts from the war. Hunters.
Like wolves with gills, some said. The conflict was the humans'
fault. Them and their animal pets, who could never survive a
day without their former masters telling them what to do. In
the midst of it all, the humans destroyed their own dam. Always
destroying, these humans. Never building anything that would
last. The resulting flood engulfed an ancient chemical plant, a
place the humans had abandoned. The waste and debris traveled
south into Mudfoot territory and poisoned everything.

The elders called it the Damnable. A judgment from someone
else's god.

No one from the human city—not the leaders, not their animal friends, no one—ever bothered to check on what had happened. The wolves became casualties in someone's dirty war.

Some of the wolves wanted to flee the valley. But rival clans surrounded them on all sides, enforcing the same border the Mudfoot established themselves. For years, intruders caught in the valley would never see their home again. Thus it was easy for the other wolves to hold a grudge. Who knew what kind of disease the Mudfoot carried in their blood, they asked. What if it was contagious? What if it was EMSAH or some other human invention? And so, when the Mudfoot went begging for safe passage through their neighbors' territory, the answer was no.

With the entire river polluted, the animals needed to rely on rainwater. And yet even this could prove lethal if the puddle formed on contaminated ground, or if the water trickled from the leaves of a poisoned tree. Within a month, the pups died, followed by the older wolves. Some fell asleep and never woke again. Many others convulsed and gagged while their families circled them, whining and helpless.

Others endured bizarre, painful side effects. After eating contaminated deer meat, Urna went from a brave hunter to a confused, doddering animal. For three days, she shivered and vomited. Roka brought her food, stayed with her. She groomed her sister, licking her fur incessantly. During those long nights, she lay over Urna's shaking body and howled. No one answered.

That summer, every pregnant female miscarried or failed to conceive. Dregger could do nothing to stop it. They could move anywhere in the valley, or maybe punch through the blockade and reach safer ground. It would not matter. The rot lived inside them now.

While he tried to negotiate with their neighbors, the others grew restless. Fights broke out over what caused the miscarriages. Wex and his brothers blamed Dregger, claiming that his weakness, rather than the dark water, had somehow poisoned the pack.

The coup happened quickly, almost like a second flood. One day, Dregger led the hunters on a patrol. Somewhere in the woods, they cornered him, tore out his throat. They mounted his head on a pike in front of the den. When Roka saw it, she took Rove and Herc and ran into the forest as fast as she could. But Wex's allies were waiting. Jape and the others seized her, pinned her to the earth. They dragged the young ones away.

Once again, Roka howled into the night. And again, no one answered.

In the morning, Wex appeared. He sat facing her, propped on his front paws, hindquarters on the ground.

"Dregger was weak," he said. "Weak blood. No choice."

He rarely spoke in the human language. She assumed it was out of shame this time. As if some other person confessed to his crime.

Wex handed her a necklace. A leather strap, with one of Dregger's fangs attached to it. Roka snorted in disgust.

"You are the strongest female in the pack," he said. "Join me, or we all die."

"Then we die."

He snatched her by the neck. Roka did not resist.

"You are ready for death," Wex said. "But who protects your sister, then?"

With his other paw, he lifted the necklace to her. "Take it."

Whenever a pack leader fell, their mates were forced to carry with them some token of their past. This was the price of holding on to the old ways.

"Your name is Mercy," Wex said. "For that is what I give you. We breed new warriors. The future. We save the Mudfoot. You and I."

The elder wolves always said that mercy dogs served the

noblest purpose of all. Then they would change the subject to something else.

Roka slipped the necklace over her head. In that moment, amid a dying forest, she promised to stay alive. So that she could kill him.

THE WOLVES BOUNDED through the snow, kicking it behind them in enormous white clumps.

The trees thinned to a clearing.

Mercy saw the slow deer. Their tails bobbing. The black eyes on the sides of their heads, expressionless.

Wex raced ahead of the pack. In the snow, the hoof tracks gave off a scent so thick Mercy could swallow it. These deer trespassed on their land. Not a handful of them, but their entire herd. Their last mistake.

*I see red fangs, dripping with blood*, the human had said. Yes. They all did.

Wex grabbed hold of the slowest deer, gripping the hind leg in his mouth. The deer bucked, pulled away. A hoof smacked Wex in the skull, but the enormous wolf pressed on.

And then, like a wave, the deer at the front of the herd jumped at the same time. Mercy saw their antlers rising over the others. As the herd moved forward, they all leapt over some object that Mercy could not see until it was too late.

A trip wire.

She jammed her paws into the snow and slid. Her feet dug in so deep that they ripped out the earth. The wolves behind her collided but kept moving.

*No!* she barked.

But with Wex in the lead, they ignored her. The deer he attacked—the bait, Mercy realized—jumped over the line. Wex never saw it. He hit the wire at full speed, right at his knees, and let out a piercing shriek that no one had ever heard before.

Mercy skidded on her side and came to a stop at the wire. A metal line, definitely human made. As more of the wolves struck it, the wire vibrated against her body.

More screaming.

A pile of wolves lay a few feet in front of the wire. The wolves in the rear rushed to their fallen comrades. Jape stood on his hind legs, clutching his broken left paw with his right. Wex was face-planted in the snow, his front paws snapped at such a horrifying angle that they appeared to be severed.

A film of blood dripped from the wire into the snow and immediately froze.

Mercy turned to the deer. The herd split into two groups, forming a lane in between them. Someone behind her growled, but it sounded more like a question than a threat.

Four bucks charged through the opening at full speed. Along with the horns on their heads, they each wore armor fashioned from antlers, becoming a wall of spikes thundering toward the wounded wolves.

Jape stepped in front of the Wex to protect him. For all his faults, he remained loyal. He died first. The bucks mowed him down. A sharpened antler opened his throat, shooting out a red mist that speckled the lead buck's face. The stag did not even blink.

The entire herd spun around and stampeded toward them. The wolves tried to scatter. Mercy dodged one stag. Another, following close behind, zeroed in on her. He lowered his head. Before she could get out of the way, an ice-cold antler cut into her shoulder and snapped off.

Lying on her side, Mercy saw the other wolves fall under the oncoming hooves. As the deer ran, the bottoms of their feet glistened bright red against the snow. With her paw, Mercy tried to stanch the wound on her shoulder. She bit down to fight through the pain.

The herd wheeled around again to finish off the ones still remaining.

"Run," someone wheezed.

As she clamped her paw on the wound, she scanned the bodies.

"Go!" the voice said, coughing. It came from the battered husk once known as Wex the Cruelblood. One of his eyes was missing. Even now, he knew that she was the future of the Mudfoot. She could not die here.

The sound of the hooves got her moving. With her injured shoulder, Mercy ran on two feet. A few others fled beside her, gliding over the snow on all fours. She knew their names. Uri. Knuckle. Cloy. None were brave, only lucky.

The hoofbeats continued behind her, along with the snorting from the stags. As she reached the trees again, the sounds died out. She stopped. A few of the deer waited nearby, daring the wolves to retaliate. Behind them, the remaining stags walked into the mass of bodies in the clearing, a mound of fur and limbs with a growing border of red that melted the snow.

One of the deer leaned over a fallen warrior, opened his mouth, and bit hard into the flesh. He tore away a bright pink chunk of it. No longer interested in the survivors, the others joined in the feast. The deer had sharpened their teeth into fangs. Mercy could only imagine the tool they used. They bit into the wolves again and again, peeling away the meat as their snouts glistened red.

Another stag remained, still as a statue. A breeze shoved him. He readjusted his feet while keeping his gaze on Mercy. He opened his mouth, displaying a row of perfectly carved fangs. "No more hunt," the stag said in a nasally voice. "No more Muddy Feet." He made a show of walking away.

Unlike the wolves, the deer ate their meat in silence, and without so much as a glance or a nod between them.

Mercy headed for the den. She needed to find Urna. They would run from this place. And most likely die together.

MERCY'S STOMACH SNARLED as she made her way through the snow. The wound in her shoulder burned until she could not feel it anymore. The frayed nerve ending fizzled out in the cold. On either side of her, tired wolves tried to keep the pace, leaving tracks and a white mist behind them. They must have wondered how a pregnant female could move so quickly. The thought amused her.

Wex was dead. They could speak freely in any language they chose. And yet no one said a word. They were all shattered. The deer had turned their own instincts against them. Wolves formed into packs, but a pack could be broken so easily, leaving only desperate savages.

Mercy barely knew the wolves who trudged alongside her to the den. Some had joined the Mudfoot after Wex's mutiny. Two others—a pair of brothers named Mag and Quick—fought alongside Dregger when the clan first migrated here. To stay alive, they fell in line when Wex took control, like everyone else. Since then, they could hardly look Mercy in the eye.

An old one hobbled behind them: Carsa, another female who lost her pups after the flood. When her last one died, she spent weeks gnawing at her paws and legs until they bled. Dregger tried to intervene. To get her mind off things, he let her lead the next hunt. A generous wolf was a strong wolf. Carsa tracked a fawn for miles before making the kill on a barren hilltop. She hummed like a pup while she chewed the meat. After a couple of weeks, the wounds on her paws were completely healed.

A fourth one Mercy recognized: Creek, an orphan. Old enough to hunt, young enough to not understand how things once were. He was fast, which meant that the older hunters were always screaming at him to be more cautious. In the battle with the deer, Creek had broken his tail. It bent painfully in the middle and hung to the side. Mercy could feel it in her own tail as Creek waddled from side to side with each step. This injury could help him to grow stronger and wiser, if he lived long enough.

The rest of them she knew by smell, mostly. Before long, she found herself in the lead of this sad pack. Though they were all going to the same place, she was now the highest-ranking member. As long as she carried her young ones, no one could touch her.

On the plateau, the dirt gave way to loose stones and boulders. A howl went out from the den. It came in waves. A question. *Good news or bad?*

The weary pack waited for Mercy to respond. She did not answer, which was the worst answer of all.

At the mouth of the den, three guards stood watch. Behind them, the human remained tied to the tree, a faint grin parting his lips, dried blood on his face and neck. The sentries let Urna run past them to greet her sister. They knew Mercy was the leader now, yet would not acknowledge it.

Urna yipped and danced around to show her relief. *What happened?* she barked.

*Death*, Mercy grunted.

Soon, all the wolves barked and yelped and tumbled about— their way of acknowledging that they were still alive. Other guards arrived. The news spread. A few lonely howls went out, all off-key and quavering.

While Urna pestered her with questions, Mercy trotted past the commotion and went straight for the human. He seemed ready to meet her.

Crouched before him, she sniffed at his legs, taking in his salty scent once more. The man's nostrils flared. He smelled her as well. She wondered if he was mocking her.

Urna watched from a distance with her feet tucked in and her belly on the earth.

Behind Mercy, the random shouts and cries at last coalesced into a single howl, loud enough to hear for miles. A song of mourning for their lost leader.

Amid the noise, Mercy rose to two feet and faced the man. The wind draped a few locks of his black hair over his face. He shook it away. She noticed then that the claw marks on his cheek had somehow healed, leaving pink indentations crusted with dried blood. His tattooed mask now had scars of its own.

He, too, howled like a wolf, indistinguishable from the others.

"You did this," Mercy said in the human tongue. It felt so strange. Urna whimpered at the sound of it. She seemed to forget that Wex could no longer stop them.

The man stopped howling. "No. I tried to warn you."

"How you know?"

"I see what is to come."

"You see future?" Mercy said, snickering. She motioned to the rope around the man's wrists. "You see this too?"

"I did."

The howling grew louder.

"Why you here?"

"I'm looking for something. I came to your clan for help."

"Why help you?"

"Because I'm the only one who can help *you*. Like I said: I see what is to come. What is to come is all that matters to a wolf, is it not?"

Mercy glanced at Urna. Other wolves took notice of her standing on two legs, talking with the human. They continued howling anyway.

"You're a mercy dog," the man said, nodding to her necklace. "The only reason you're still alive is because of your children. Once they come out, your enemies will have no use for you."

"You know our ways. Good for you."

"Don't act like there isn't more."

With a tilt of his head, he motioned for her to come closer. She leaned in. Urna rose to her haunches, ready to strike if this man somehow broke free.

"There *are* no children, are there?" he said, his voice no louder than a breath. "You were the last hope. The last hope for the last clan of true wolves. And now that's gone."

Urna leaned closer, her ears twitching. Mercy was certain her sister could not hear, which came as a relief. Even Urna did not know the truth: Mercy had miscarried over a week before. The Damnable had taken away her children. Her claim to power rested on a lie. And any day now, the entire pack would know, and they would tear her apart for it.

Mercy pinned her ears to her skull. This human could see inside of her mind and her body. Her instinct told her to rip his throat out while she still could and to share the meal with her sister.

"You're trying to survive today and maybe tomorrow," the man said. "If we work together, we can make sure you never have to worry again. I've seen it. I've seen your pack rising from the ashes of this place. Calling on all true wolves to join them."

"True wolves," Mercy said. "Like you."

"Like me," he said.

She waited for him to blink, but his eyes remained fixed on her.

"You say Dregger helped you," she said.

"He gave us safe passage a long time ago. Probably kept it quiet. I don't blame him."

"Who are you?" she asked.

"Call me Augur. Of the Toqwa pack."

"Humans have no packs."

"We are not humans. We are hunters. Keepers of the forest. Like you."

"You from Hosanna."

"No. Hosanna is the enemy. I come from the hills, out there. I wanted to find the great Dregger. I was willing to settle for Wex. But now I see that you are the one."

With the pads of her fingers, Mercy touched the newly healed scars on his face. Soft pink ridges. He did not flinch. She pulled her hand away to sniff her nails.

"We have the ability to heal," Augur said. "That's what your people need, isn't it?"

"Need food."

"Yes. And you could eat us, I suppose. Live a few more days. But I offer you something more."

"Speak, then."

"Someone is coming. An heir to the Mudfoot. A wolf-child. For you to raise as your own. He can bring all the packs together. He can destroy Hosanna."

"Where?"

"He arrives by sea."

This human mocked her after all. They were cut off from the sea, thanks to the blockade.

"I know what you are thinking," he said. "We can't get there. The recon units will see us."

"Yes."

"We know where their base is. Not far from here. Take that out, and you can make it."

Mercy turned away from him. The howling around her at last subsided. Several of the wolves went about jostling and sniffing at one another. Urna flattened herself on the ground, not wanting anyone to notice her presence.

"You'll need help," Augur said. "You'll need *us*."

Mercy willed herself to see into the future, as this human claimed he could. She saw nothing but a scorched landscape, littered with polished bones. This path she had walked for so long came to an end here.

She dropped to all fours and let out a quick bark. It summoned the two brothers, Mag and Quick. They were a unit. One day they would distinguish themselves. Until then, they shared a single name.

"Let them go," Mercy said. When the two brothers hesitated, she growled: *Do it!*

The wolves undid the human's bonds. It took a moment—the knots proved stubborn, and the two brothers grumbled at each other's mistakes.

Urna whined. *Are you sure?*

Mercy ignored her.

"Roka," Urna said. It was the first time Mercy had heard her old name since Dregger's death.

In a deliberate movement, Augur slid down the pole to a sitting position, then rolled onto his back. The submissive pose. A sign of respect and trust that a human would never do. The wolves pawed at him.

Urna spoke her old name again.

"Don't call me that," Mercy said.

# CHAPTER 2

―――――――  ■  ―――――――

# A BEACON OF LIGHT

(UNOFFICIAL) LOGBOOK OF THE SUS AL-RIHLA
JANUARY 15
WEATHER: LIGHT BREEZE. OVERCAST. MODERATE SWELL.

0630 ASSIGNED AS AN EXTRA HAND TO ENGINEERING CREW.
COMPLETED REFIT OF WIND TURBINE.
0900 SCIENCE TEAM MEETING. BLOOD RESULTS ON LATEST
SPECIMEN STILL PENDING.
1257 NEW SIGHTING REPORTED. 34.6, -74.8.
1325 CAPTAIN CONFIRMS NEW HEADING. INTERCEPT COURSE.

PERSONAL HEALTH: GOOD. THIRD DAY IN A ROW WITHOUT SEA-
SICKNESS.

HE BOW OF the *al-Rihla* dropped into the oncoming wave. Gripping the railing, D'Arc felt weightless until the boat crashed into the surface. Her legs buckled. Salt water sprayed all over her fur. She shook it off like a typical dog. One of the humans on deck chuckled when he saw it. The humans always liked pointing out the things the animals did that they found cute.

The boat ascended again on the next wave, so high that for a moment, D'Arc no longer saw the water, only the overcast sky. She was ready for the impact this time, absorbing the shock, bracing for the cold. She straightened herself. With her free hand, she lifted the binoculars and peered into the clouds.

She felt the engine slow. The captain would give chase only for so long.

"Come on," D'Arc said. "Where did you go?"

As the engine eased, she heard a hissing sound approaching. Dead ahead, a gray curtain descended from the clouds, disturbing the surface of the ocean. A few seconds later, the first icy drops splashed against her snout, making her blink. Winter rain. Too warm to freeze, but so cold that the droplets pelted her fur, numbing the skin underneath. D'Arc glanced at the deck, where the crew members fled for cover. Harlan, one of the human scientists, zipped his yellow slicker. Behind him loomed the security officer, a bear named Moab who did not approve of these excursions.

On the bridge, Captain Vittal waited with her hands folded at her belt buckle. The raindrops obscured her, though her bright blue jacket and cap remained visible. At her side, the ship's pilot, a dog named Koral, struggled to keep the wheel steady.

D'Arc faced the wind and rain again. Her muscles tensed when she saw something—a black dot streaking through the clouds.

D'Arc pointed at it and barked. Koral spun the wheel. The engine kicked again. D'Arc held on as the boat accelerated.

"I see it!" Harlan said, a huge smile splitting his red face.

The flier descended farther. D'Arc wiped the lenses of the binoculars with her thumbs. When she looked through them, she could make out the general shape: round body, black armor plating, transparent wings beating at a near-sonic speed. A winged ant. One of the only live ones that anyone had seen since the war.

Though confused by the rain and possibly injured, the ant

became a majestic black angel cutting through the storm. The ants that D'Arc raised herself could never do this. They loved their daily walks through the forest. They loved feeding time. The most adventurous ones, like Juke and Gai Den, splashed in the stream like puppies. They would have loved to fly.

Shaking away the memory, D'Arc waved her arm at Koral, begging him to go faster. The engine revved another notch. The weightlessness brought on a wave of nausea, strong enough to make her drop to one knee. She leaned over the side, facing the foamy water as it slammed into the hull.

"Hey, Mountain Girl," Harlan said. "I thought you were over the seasickness!"

Mercifully, her gut settled. She wagged her tail in relief. "Why don't *you* try standing out here?"

"No thanks," Harlan said.

As always, Moab did not react. The rain dripped from her thick brow and from the tip of her enormous nose.

"Holy shit, look!" Harlan shouted.

D'Arc turned. The ant descended until it skimmed the surface in a great white splash. The wings kept flapping as the ant corkscrewed. It landed on its back, legs twisted over its belly,  the antennae broken. The rising waves hid the body, then revealed it again.

"Harlan, get your people ready!" D'Arc said.

As the boat approached, D'Arc put her hands in the air to tell Koral to slow the engine. She guided the boat so that the fallen ant bobbed along the port side, where a crane could retrieve it. D'Arc followed the body as it scraped against the hull. On the way, she grabbed a telescopic boat hook that leaned on a cleat. She reached the pole to the ant and latched on to a joint in its leg. The science team swarmed around her. Two humans held out their own poles, using them to pin the ant to the side of the ship.

"Drag it toward the crane," D'Arc said.

Despite the rain, the entire crew stood on deck. Everyone wanted to see. The gawkers made room for Moab's team. The security guards lined the gunwale, all aiming rifles and readying to fire the moment the ant so much as twitched. Early in the expedition, Moab had let everyone know that she hated these missions. Even the half-eaten, stiff-as-a-board carcasses they found before this one put her on edge.

At the bottom of the crane's arm hung four heavy chain loops, fashioned solely for this purpose. While the boat swayed, D'Arc and Harlan fastened the loops around the ant's body. While bobbing in the water, the insect resembled any other piece of debris they encountered. One of the brittle wings crumpled against the metal.

"It's ready!" D'Arc said. "Take it up!"

The machine lifted the insect. The body went stiff as the water dripped from its exoskeleton. Everyone gasped. The rifles raised, their barrels tracking the crane as it swung over the gunwale. D'Arc met the creature as it hovered over the deck. She was the first to touch its cold shell. The bristly hair tickled her palm. The rain, the wind, the shouting people—all of it vanished for a moment. She was at her ranch again, riding on Gai Den, wearing a straw hat to shield her face from the sun. The other crew members remembered these creatures as the enemy. She remembered them as part of her youth, a fact that would always separate her from the people who survived the war.

The crane lowered the ant to the deck. Moab ordered her soldiers to make space. "Back away," she said. "Keep your distance."

"Let's get the measurements," D'Arc said.

Harlan was already on it. He dropped the tape at the abdomen and unrolled it to the mouth. "Nine feet, five inches." He moved on to the diameter of the abdomen and the length of the legs, calling out each number. One of his human assistants recorded each one while shielding her notepad under her raincoat.

D'Arc placed her hands on the ant's upper body. This Alpha was shaped all wrong. The thorax bulged out like a camel's hump. And the jaws barely covered the opening of the mouth. Judging from its condition, the Alpha could barely feed herself, let alone attack. So much time had passed since the Colony had collapsed. These last few stragglers, so lost without their Queen, did not even realize that they had become obsolete. For all D'Arc knew, this misshapen ant was the very last of her kind.

She ran her fingers over the ruts and dents and scars in the ant's armor. Thousands of stories, all etched into the tough skin of this abomination. "Where you been, girl?" D'Arc said. "What've you seen?"

"Jesus, she's *talking* to it," one of the humans whispered. Harlan shushed him.

Captain Vittal exited the bridge. Given her small stature, the crew gave her room to see. D'Arc detected a poorly concealed revulsion in the captain's expression. Like all the humans, she most likely witnessed one of these creatures killing the people she knew and destroying the places she would never see again.

"I need forceps," D'Arc said. Harlan's assistant handed them to her. She clamped the metal onto the antenna and lifted it from the deck. "No buildup," she said. "This ant still cleaned herself."

"No acid port in the abdomen," Harlan said. "No defensive claws. A scout, maybe?"

"A regular Alpha could scout just fine. I don't know what this thing was expected to do."

With the forceps, she peeled the mandible away from the ant's mouth.

"No signs of any illness," she said. "You'd think that—"

The jaw snapped shut with an audible click, snatching the forceps from her hand. Before she could say a word, an enormous furry paw grabbed her shoulder and wrenched her away. She landed flat on her stomach. The rifles unloaded. She covered her ears as the guards fired. The shockwave punched her in the chest. Feet scurried away. Voices shouted orders.

"Stop!" Captain Vittal screamed. "Stop it!"

"Hold," Moab said.

D'Arc rolled over. The bear towered above her. A few feet away, Harlan uncurled himself from the fetal position. The Alpha leaked fluid from multiple bullet holes. The rain washed some of it away. Pieces of shell lay scattered about. One of the legs had skittered to the railing.

Moab crouched to meet D'Arc's face. The bear sighed. "The next time you bring one of these on board, I might just let it eat you."

Moab had taught D'Arc a saying from her people: *What is bravery one minute is foolishness the next.* She spared D'Arc the lecture this time. Instead, she helped D'Arc to her feet.

"You have your specimen," Vittal said, her jacket now completely soaked. "Do what you must with it. Then throw it overboard."

The captain headed for the bridge. Moab gave D'Arc a disapproving snort before moving aside.

"You heard her," Harlan said. "Let's get this over with."

D'ARC ARRIVED AT the mess hall long after the last call for chow. The red night lights had already switched on. The engines slowed. The ship would go virtually silent until sunrise, save for a few people playing cards or filling out reports on the day's activities.

Two sailors occupied the far end of one of the tables. A human and a cat. D'Arc had forgotten the human's name, though she often saw her smoking on deck late at night. She was middle-aged, former United States military judging from her tattoos and crew cut. One of Moab's security personnel. She and the cat often lingered in the mess hall, arguing politics, trading war stories. The woman would laugh at her own jokes and the cat would sit there, stone-faced. They glanced at D'Arc, gave her a nod. Then they continued their conversation.

The woman lowered her voice. Not that it made a difference. "Ninety-six hours," she said.

"Ninety-six," the cat repeated.

"Ninety-six."

D'Arc poked her head over the counter to find a human named Kang kneeling in front of the cupboard, with both of its metal doors hanging open. Kang had migrated from China to California many years earlier and was one of the few people to make it across the country during the war. On the *al-Rihla*, he was both head cook and an engineer responsible for maintaining the solar panels. Everyone on board served multiple roles.

D'Arc waited for him to notice her presence. But he went right on counting the bags of black beans by tapping each one with his finger and mouthing the number. He wrote the amount in his notepad before moving on to the sardine cans. Ever since the resupply at Golgotha Base a few days earlier, Kang needed to get creative to store all the new foodstuffs. Stovetops and oven racks served as shelves. The walk-in cooler was stuffed so tight that someone said it resembled a game of Tetris.

"You know why that's the time limit for a rescue?" the woman asked the cat.

"No."

"Because that's the record for a person lost at sea with no supplies. After ninety-six, they call off the search."

*Okay*, D'Arc thought. *She's Navy. Maybe a Marine.* Like so many of the humans on board. *Makes sense.*

Kang wrote another number in his notebook. D'Arc got his attention with a light bark, almost like a sneeze.

"There you are!" Kang said. With some effort, he got to his

feet. "Don't worry. I got you." He opened the door to the refrigerator and grabbed something from the shelf, an object wrapped in tinfoil. As he brought it over, she could smell it: bean protein rolls flavored with Worcestershire sauce. Her tongue found its way out, dangling over her chin. He handed the food to her, then pulled it away when she reached for it.

"You know it's against the rules to serve you this after the mess hall closes," he said. "You snooze, you lose."

"I wish I *had* been snoozing." She had spent the last few hours performing an autopsy on the ant. In the lab, the organs and limbs were now spread out and labeled. She left the assistant to store them in the cold locker.

Kang gave her the food. "Find anything good?"

"Learning is always a good thing, right?"

He eyed her. "I guess that's why we're out here."

She lifted the tinfoil to her nose and inhaled. "Thanks for dinner."

"What dinner? You don't know me; I don't know you."

D'Arc walked by the woman and the cat as they began debating whether a dog could survive for more than ninety-six hours at sea.

"Dog would shit himself," the woman said. "Lose most of his hydration that way."

"Depends on the breed," the cat objected.

The woman laughed. "Whoa, I'm not touching that with a ten-foot pole."

The two stopped and whispered as D'Arc exited. They knew who she was, and they were probably wondering what she found, and why the *al-Rihla* had gone so far off course chasing these insects. The question came up a lot lately. She figured the answer was obvious. That did not stop people from asking.

D'Arc's bunk occupied a tiny sliver of space in a long hallway. She slept between two women. Verasco on top, Anderson below.

Both served on the laundry crew this evening, which gave D'Arc some privacy. The rules of the ship separated the crew by gender but not by species, which meant the various crew members often traded gossip late into the evening. The humans liked to ask silly questions about how different species had sex. They would squeak and snort with laughter before D'Arc could finish her answer. She could not figure out if they meant well. This vessel had a guiding principle: *No one above the other.* Everyone, from Captain Vittal to the people who cleaned the toilets, was expected to leave the old rules behind, as well as the war that overthrew them. These women may have genuinely believed that their banter helped to fulfill this ideal. And yet, every time, it reminded D'Arc of her place on this ship. She was an outsider. An oddity. It couldn't possibly be any different.

After coming of age on a sprawling ranch, the adjustment to a two-by-seven-foot bunk as her only private space still proved challenging despite many months at sea. If the Old Man ever saw her stuffed into this cubbyhole, he would have snickered at her change in fortune. "What are you doing out here?" he'd say. "Smells like human in this tin can."

D'Arc slid the curtain aside and lifted the mattress. Underneath, a row of compartments stored her toiletries, her vests and boots, and some random personal items, including her logbook. She grabbed it, dropped the mattress into place, and crawled into bed. Above, the scabbard of her sword hung duct-taped to the bottom of Verasco's bunk. She had positioned it in such a way that she could unsheathe it while lying flat on her back.

She opened the logbook at her last entry. Marking the page was her medallion with a raised image of St. Jude, patron saint of lost causes. A gift from Wawa, the Chief of Tranquility, whose recommendation got her on board the *al-Rihla*. Wawa believed in her, and in the mission. But here, D'Arc lay staring at her terrible handwriting, wondering if she should have somehow learned to be happy at the ranch. She could have tamed her curiosity. She could have been grateful for what she and the Old Man had built together. She could have found meaning long after the last of the Alphas died, long after she was too old to go on some foolish adventure. She could have done all those things if she had listened.

"Oh, stop it," she mumbled. She belonged here, no matter how much she missed home.

She checked her watch and wrote another time stamp for January 15.

**2235** AUTOPSY COMPLETE. REPORT DUE TO CAPTAIN VITTAL AT 0630.

On the last page of the logbook, she found a map folded in four. She opened it. On the translucent paper, a dark line traced the path of the *al-Rihla*, as best as she could determine in her navigation class. The line went from the mouth of the Delaware north to Maine, where they encountered an extended family of black bears. That day, the senior officers, along with the security personnel, took the patrol boat to the beach. The crew watched with binoculars while the ship anchored. As D'Arc heard later, the bears' leader told Captain Vittal that his people were claiming all of the former human settlements in the "cold country," as he called it.

"We mean you no harm," the old bear said. "But there is nothing for you here." As a peace offering, Vittal left them with a copy of the Prophet's sayings and a pack of rechargeable flashlights. The elder bear did not thank her.

From there, they skimmed the coast of Nova Scotia and Newfoundland. At every stop, they discovered the same thing. The earth had reclaimed the towns and cities. Only a few crumbling ports remained. The people in this part of the country lived like the bears did: foraging for food, forming into small nomadic groups, bartering for essentials. No one had seen a human in years. As the weather grew colder, the bears withdrew to their dens, and the flocks headed south as if the war had never happened. By the time the *al-Rihla* reached the southern tip of Greenland, a silence had fallen over the land. There was some discussion about continuing across the Atlantic. But Vittal had her orders: stay close to the American coastline, don't stray too far. Later missions would find out what happened to Iceland, the British Isles, and all the rest.

To flee the encroaching winter, they headed south to Bermuda, where they discovered a thriving community of rats, the largest fauna on the island. The rats knew the ship was coming, thanks to a flock of swifts that patrolled the seas. The *al-Rihla* spent a week there, gathering information, establishing an alliance so that ships could use Bermuda as a way station for an eventual trip to Africa. Few of the humans on board could hide their disappointment at the news that none of their kind survived on the island. The rat matriarch swore that the humans left on their own after a series of attacks from the Alphas. There was no way to tell if she was lying.

"These rats seem *awful* fat to me," one of the crew members remarked at dinner. Nevertheless, the Bermudans were generous hosts, donating supplies and food. They even gathered at the dock and waved goodbye as the *al-Rihla* lifted anchor.

The ink on the map then went directly west from the island to the newly formed landmass of Golgotha, the former nerve center for the Colony. At least three crew members served there during the great battle. The place still felt like a graveyard. No beach, no hills, no flora of any kind. Only an expanse of brittle gray rock. For years, the scientists tried to grow crops there, but the Queen had built it as a bunker, not a quaint farmland for mammals.

When they made landfall, Harlan, who specialized in botany, lifted a small chunk of the earth to his mouth and licked it like a cat. "Completely dead," he declared. "Like plastic." The texture of the land made D'Arc think of that first night on the island with the Old Man, watching the bonfires stacked with the bodies of Alpha soldiers. A blurry image, filled in mostly by Mort(e)'s stories rather than her own memory.

The soldiers stationed there gave the crew a tour of the catacombs that would take another lifetime to map out. Following the lamps embedded in the dirt, they visited the nurseries and cupboards and underground highways. Thanks to the ventilation shafts, the air tasted surprisingly fresh. Though she spent many years here, it appeared more alien than anything D'Arc had ever seen. She wanted to feel something as she dragged her fingers along the sides of the narrow tunnels. After all, the humans never stopped talking about the time before the war, an eternal vault of the past that they could reopen whenever it suited them.

D'Arc had no vault, only a few faded memories. Mort(e) insisted that this made her lucky. It certainly allowed her to conceal her identity. It allowed her to shed things, to move forward. It shielded her. It was why she was here.

On her last morning on Golgotha, D'Arc got a reminder of the *other* reason why she was here.

It began with a siren blaring from the Golgotha barracks. Bleary-eyed soldiers formed into ranks. The artillery maneuvered into position, aiming at the sky. A second siren on the *al-Rihla* called the entire crew to their battle stations. Someone ran screaming through the bulkheads: "Not a drill, people! Let's go!"

D'Arc strapped on her sword and took her position in the 50-mm gun turret. It required a crew of three to feed the shells. Anderson fired the gun while D'Arc and a German shepherd named Buck handled the ordnance.

A few others stood by the gunwale and pointed at something above. Anderson saw it too. Her thick triceps flared as she pointed the barrels at a high angle. "Oooh, I gotchoo," she said.

When D'Arc saw the ant zipping above, she nearly dropped

the ammo belt in her hands. Mort(e) had told her about the Alphas with wings, the airborne shock troops sent to destroy the settlements infected with the EMSAH syndrome. She could tell right away that this Alpha was dying. Her body hung from the beating wings. The legs dangled. When the ant arced closer to the ship, D'Arc saw that one of the limbs had been sheared off at the top joint. The antennae flailed, much like the ants on her ranch did when they needed to be euthanized. If this ant had traveled over the flat surface of the water for days, then the sudden appearance of an island filled with people and machinery must have startled her.

The Alpha looped around the island, its orbit sinking lower each time. She did not seem to notice the row of soldiers in her path as she scraped the earth. The soldiers toppled out of the way like bowling pins. The Alpha dropped again, this time tumbling end over end before skidding to a stop. The legs curled into a crisscross position.

The lead biologist, a man named Wilson, asked D'Arc to join the other scientists as they performed an autopsy. No one knew where the Alpha came from, though the scouts spotted her heading west. She could have come from as far away as Africa, for all they knew.

The presence of this creature alarmed the humans the most. A few of them suggested burning the body before it attracted any others in the area. D'Arc needed to contain her excitement as she compared this dead specimen with the ants she raised on the ranch. She could tell that her knowledge made them nervous. While wearing their surgical masks, they at first listened eagerly as she went over what she knew about the ants' eating habits, the way they moved in columns, the way they explored new territory. "Juke used to tap her antennae on something," D'Arc said, "then she'd poke her head up like this." She mimicked the movement. The doctors squinted at her coldly.

"You *named* them," Wilson said, his mask puffing outward.

"Well, yeah. Juke, Sugar, Anansi . . ." She trailed off when she noticed them all watching her, this animal, siding with the monsters that had destroyed everything they knew. Noticing their discomfort, she pivoted to body parts and behavioral patterns again. Wilson thanked her for her input.

The next day, as the *al-Rihla* continued its journey, another Alpha streaked across the clouds. The ship changed course, trailing the ant until she dropped from exhaustion and splashed down. Another autopsy confirmed that she had traveled a long distance, attracted to something so seductive that she kept flapping her wings until she died.

Twice more the *al-Rihla* altered its course to pursue the ants. The captain did not disclose the new heading to the crew. Using her compass, D'Arc figured it out anyway. At their current direction, they would make landfall close to where they started, somewhere south of Hosanna.

All this effort to move forward, to have a new adventure, and the war with no name called her back to her homeland. D'Arc was too tired to get angry about it. She would save that for the morning.

JANUARY 16
WEATHER: NO WIND. PARTLY CLOUDY. MODERATE SWELL.

0600 PREPARED NOTES FOR SCIENCE STAFF BRIEFING WITH CAPTAIN VITTAL.

PERSONAL HEALTH: STABLE. SOME NAUSEA IN THE MORNING.

CAPTAIN VITTAL INSISTED on conducting her big meetings at the bow of the ship, usually before first light, no matter the weather. Closed-door meetings made the crew nervous. And standing on the bow, with the sky brightening around them, the waves passing below, reminded them of why they joined this mission. "It puts things in perspective," she always said. "And it keeps people awake."

Dressed in her long rain slicker, D'Arc was the only nonhuman on the science team. Harlan worked in agricultural botany. Cooper was as an oceanographer for a British oil company before the war. Irele was a professor of biology in Nigeria. Wilson wrote a paper on cockroaches for his dissertation, making him the best expert on insects they could find. Their assistant, Madigan, furiously scribbled notes as the wind made her fingers turn pink.

Moab the bear stood guard near the bridge. When the new shift of crew members loitered nearby, she told them to move along.

The captain was waiting for them when they arrived. She wore a black overcoat that must have belonged to someone much taller. The sleeves draped over her leather gloves. Her graying hair fit snugly beneath her white cap. If all had gone according to plan—if the war had never happened—she would have been an astronaut by now. Everyone on the ship, including the animals, acted as if they shared in her would-be accomplishment. She still owned a NASA patch that she displayed on her desk. It would be a long time before anyone considered going into space again. For now, an entire world awaited, as it did for the explorers who came before.

When the science team assembled, all bundled in their parkas and sniffling, Captain Vittal got right to the point. "Tell me about the Alpha," she said.

They turned to Wilson. With his hood cinched over his face, only his dark brown eyes were visible. "Ma'am," he said, voice muffled, "the ant we found is not an Alpha."

"What is it, then?"

"It's a drone."

"A drone."

"A male."

"Male ants and female ants swarming about. What could that possibly mean?"

Wilson objected to the term *swarm*, arguing that they found only a few individuals so far. Harlan sighed at Wilson's quibbling.

"Drones have one purpose," Wilson said. "To mate. But none of the females we found seemed to be in any condition to mate. And this male had an extremely low sperm count."

"Ah, so he is like a middle-aged man, then?" Vittal asked. She allowed them a moment to react. Only Harlan chuckled, then immediately stopped.

"All it takes is one sperm," D'Arc blurted out.

Wilson glared at her. Ever since the first Alpha appeared over Golgotha, Wilson faced immense pressure to explain what the hell was going on. He made no secret that he did not believe her stories of running an Alpha ranch. During the autopsy, he barely acknowledged her presence, treating her like an extra pair of hands instead of a fellow crew member.

"The scientists at Golgotha have not detected any activity for years," Wilson said. "This could be some misfiring in the ants' brains. These insects are going senile. They weren't meant to live this long—"

Vittal silenced him by lifting her hand. "I want to hear from the big mouth," she said.

Since she was hiding slightly behind Harlan, D'Arc did not realize at first that the captain was addressing her. Harlan moved aside to make room for Vittal. Madigan flipped a page in her notebook.

"You're the one who lived with these things. For years, yes?"

"Yes."

"You told me you called them your girls."

If she were a human, she would have blushed. "My ladies, that's right."

"What do *you* think?"

The weight of it overwhelmed her. The Old Man so rarely asked her opinion on things, believing that he protected her by making decisions for the both of them.

"The Alphas only respond to a leader," she said. "Once they're drawn in, they follow orders. Or they mimic what the leader does." D'Arc described how she and the Old Man—she didn't give his name—lured a platoon of Alphas with their pheromone, then sealed them in a pen. Before long, the confused insects looked to D'Arc as if she were their queen.

Vittal folded her hands and walked to the railing. "The supply ships won't leave Golgotha for another two weeks. We're the only ones who can warn Hosanna."

D'Arc felt the others stiffen at the news.

"But there's a storm coming," Vittal said. "We'll have to go through it. *If*, that is, you think it's worth it."

They turned to D'Arc. A few months earlier, a storm off the coast of Canada nearly capsized the boat. She could tell that they wanted her to say that they shouldn't bother, that the ants were merely going through their death throes.

She couldn't do it. Even while picturing the beaches in Cuba, the rain forests of the Caribbean, she couldn't do it. "It's worth it," she said. "Something is happening."

"That's what I thought."

Vittal dismissed them. "Except for you," she said to D'Arc, who stood still while the others filed past. A strong wind blew open D'Arc's coat. She covered herself and waited for the captain to speak.

"Do you have something to say to me?" Vittal asked.

"Ma'am, I apologize for speaking out of turn."

"Not that. I'm talking about the reports of insubordination."

D'Arc's tongue fell out of her mouth—her default panic switch. Her tail lowered.

"The doctors tell me you've failed to report for your physical for weeks," Vittal said. "Which I would be tempted to overlook if—*if*—you had not already told them you were ill."

"Ma'am, I was seasick, that's all."

"Seasick. And I see you're wearing a nice long coat despite being covered in fur."

D'Arc said nothing. She wanted to be back in the examination room with drone's body parts scattered about.

"I used to run a dog shelter in my hometown," Vittal said. "The first of its kind there. I think that's what got me this job."

D'Arc was so desperate that she looked to Moab for help. The bear fiddled with the bandolier on her chest, uninterested in their conversation.

"I know dogs," Vittal said. "And I know you need more than a physical." She glanced at D'Arc's midsection. D'Arc immediately placed her hands over her stomach.

"Who's the father?" Vittal asked. "All the dogs on board are neutered, so it couldn't have been one of them."

D'Arc nearly collapsed. She lowered her head and let out a low howl that ended with a long wheezing sound, like some broken machine. For weeks, she had bottled her terror inside of her. It crept out in the open now. It no longer belonged solely to her.

"I'm sorry, Captain," she said. "I'm so sorry."

Vittal put her arm around her.

"I swear I didn't know when I came aboard," D'Arc said.

"It's okay."

"No, it's not. I've jeopardized the mission."

"Look at me."

D'Arc raised her head. A few crew members stood behind Moab, trying to see what was happening. Moab shooed them away.

"This *is* the mission," Vittal said. "Life is the mission. Remember, this ship is the prototype. We have to test it. Even if that means building a nursery."

"No one has to go out of their way for me."

"Ah, but they do," Vittal said. "It is through these acts of kindness that we will rebuild. We have to be a beacon of light in the darkness, guiding the other ships home. That's what Chief Wawa told me once. And she gave you her highest recommendation. She knew all the good you did with those ants. Empathy will save us. And forgiveness. Not conflict. Not punishment."

D'Arc thanked her. Vittal signaled to Moab that she was done here. The bear could go about her usual routine of growling at people who were out of place.

"You still have a job to do," Vittal said. "You will do it as long as you are able, no more. Understand?"

"Yes, ma'am."

"I hope the father was handsome," Vittal said. "I'm sure the other female canines would love to hear all about it."

D'Arc imagined the other dogs gossiping, sniffing her, rubbing her belly, asking what names she'd pick. For the first time, that prospect seemed like a good thing. A natural thing.

The captain let her go. D'Arc clumsily thanked her again and headed for the mess hall. The breakfast bell would ring at any second. Kang would joke with her about arriving on time for once.

To the east, the sun bubbled on the horizon, peeking under a gap in the clouds. It was a new day in the new path D'Arc had chosen. The unknown, expanding around her in every direction, wider than any sea.

JANUARY 17

WEATHER: UNSEASONABLY WARM. HEAVY RAIN. WINDY.

PERSONAL HEALTH: FAIR. (RELIEVED.)

0920 AL-RIHLA ENTERS THE STORM.

• • •

UNDER AN ASHEN sky, the deck of the ship tilted one way, then the other, shifting the angle at which the rain fell. In the filtered light, the ocean became the color of iron, foaming white at the peak of each wave. The wind took all the noise of the ship—the engines, the shouting, the sirens—and tossed it out to sea. The crew members formed a line at the stern. A few feet away, a mass of twisted metal marked where the main turbine had once been, before the gale tore it from its base. The turbine sat half-submerged behind the ship, still connected by wires and cables. The engineers had managed to get a chain around it. The crew—every last one of them—stood ready to reel it in.

Wearing soaked gloves and a heavy parka, D'Arc gripped the chain and wondered if she was somehow to blame for all of this. They could have continued south. They could have let Golgotha send the warning to Hosanna. They could have continued their mission. She had learned so much in her time here. All of it could be lost so quickly. And if that happened, no one would even know that she was here, at this moment, trying to hold in her vomit as the ship bobbed in the waves.

Only a few minutes earlier, D'Arc had been lying in her bed, writing in her logbook. Though the boat swayed, the storm was a distant rumbling. All nonessential personnel were ordered belowdecks for the duration of the storm. She imagined climbing out of the hatch the next morning under the bright sun, the puddles on the deck the only clues of what happened. When the alarm sounded, calling all hands, D'Arc was so startled that she grabbed her sword and raced to the exit.

She felt silly with the weapon strapped to her back and her logbook soaked in her pocket. Luckily, no one seemed to care.

She could sense their fear in the way their knuckles whitened against the chain, the way they gawked at the turbine as if staring incredulously at a severed limb.

A human officer leaned into the wind, holding his visor over his eyes as he walked the length of the chain. So stubborn. He probably thought that this gesture gave everyone hope.

"Get ready!" he screamed. The howling gale nearly drowned him out.

At the front of the ship, one of the engineers signaled him by waving her hand.

"Now!" he said. "Pull!"

D'Arc dug her feet into the deck and put her weight into the chain. To her surprise, it moved so fast that she nearly tumbled over. A woman in front of her slipped, and the officer raced to her spot and pulled the chain until she got to her feet again.

Like some strange flower, the turbine grew over the stern of the ship, its petals bent. Along with the engineers, Moab the bear waited at the railing to help steady the base. Another tug from the crew lifted the turbine a few more feet.

Something in D'Arc's stomach moved—a terrifying sensation until she remembered what it was. *Wait till you hear about this day,* she thought. *Wait till I tell you all about this. You won't believe it.*

Maybe her children could hear her thoughts. Why not?

A collective scream at the stern caught her attention. The turbine, having cleared the railing, toppled onto its side. The engineers tried to peel the windmill away from the starboard gunwale. But the propellers, now suspended over the side, caught the breeze and began to spin. As the boat tilted in that direction, it leaned directly into the path of an oncoming wave, a wall of dark water that rose higher than the bridge of the ship. D'Arc lifted her hand, as if that would stop it.

The water crested the gunwale, rolled along the deck, and

slammed into her so hard that it lifted her from the ship. She closed her eyes. Through the icy water, she heard a scream muffled by air bubbles and a sloshing in her ear. She flailed, hoping to catch something to hold her on board. But gravity no longer applied here. She ascended into the foam, tumbling and spinning. The salt water singed her nostrils and scorched her throat. Panicked, she swung her arms until she felt her body lifting again, toward a dull light.

She surfaced with a desperate gasp. The waves lifted her, dropped her. Lifted, dropped. Her jacket formed a lily pad around her. She gripped the hem of the nylon and flopped it over the water, forming a brief air bubble that helped her to float. Kicking her legs, she turned in a circle while the rain fell on her face, colder than the ocean.

A domed object bobbed in the water. It was a lifeboat, hurtled from the deck and capsized. She paddled to it, embracing the stern.

The clouds hung so low they nearly touched the surface. A heavy fog blotted out everything.

The *al-Riḥla* was gone.

# CHAPTER 3

## THE GRUMPY BEAVER

ORT(E) TOOK HIS usual place at the corner stool and rested his knobby elbows on the bar. The brim of his specially fitted baseball cap concealed his eyes. At this time of day, with the winter sun setting behind the Hosanna skyline, the patrons filed in three or four at a time. All beavers as usual, with Mort(e) the only cat. They worked together, helping to rebuild the dam that had burst many months earlier. His ears flicked at the chatter and the clinking glasses that marked the end of another long day on the river.

Without asking, the bartender delivered Mort(e)'s usual drink, a catnip and mint concoction, steaming hot. He swallowed the first gulp right away. It washed out the taste of salt water that always plagued him when he got nervous. Mort(e) called the drink an Archer, naming it for the raccoon who perfected the recipe during the war. Months earlier, he bullied the bartender into including it on the menu, though Mort(e) was the only one who ever bought it. The rest of the patrons drank an awful fermented honey soup flavored with wood chips. A Lodge City Special, they called it. Or LC. In the afternoons, they boiled the drink in enormous pots. The sweet fragrance wafted to the river, signaling the end of a shift on the dam. The beavers would often sing when they smelled it. They sang at every damn thing, especially now that their time here was drawing to a close. In a few weeks, after finishing their work, they would return to Lodge City. By the spring, the dam would create an enormous pond and nature preserve. It would partially wash away at the end of the summer, like all beaver dams did. Unlike stubborn human designs, the beaver dam could adapt to the land and the climate. And then, in the fall, the Lodgers would return to start anew, creating a permanent relationship between the two cities.

In the other corner of the room, three female beavers hummed in unison while a male patted his tail on the floor and slapped his little hands on a homemade drum. Later that evening, on the third or fourth round of drinks, the patrons would supply the lyrics, unprompted. They couldn't help themselves.

A few of Mort(e)'s coworkers acknowledged him by lifting their mugs. Mort(e) did the same in response. When they turned away, and he was sure no one was watching, he peeked out the greasy window into the street. It was why he was here. Some of them knew. The rest knew to leave him alone after a day spent hauling logs and drilling holes.

Like many streets in Hosanna, the cracks in the sidewalk allowed aggressive weeds and shoots of grass to claw their way out. Faded graffiti on the walls demanded equal rights for canines and an end to the occupation of wolf country. The flood had emptied this neighborhood of its residents. Only the beavers lived here these days. They built their lodges near the river because the sound of the water reminded them of home.

In the last few weeks, however, some visitors had arrived. Humans, all male, at least a dozen of them. They took over an apartment building and immediately sealed the entrance to the parking garage with a chain-link fence. They wore secondhand coats, re-soled boots, and patched jeans, like most of the humans in Hosanna. From the rooftop, they spent hours scoping out the dam with binoculars. The city government had made an effort to repopulate the areas lost to the flood, but these interlopers acted more like soldiers on some kind of recon. They didn't smell right. Then again, humans never did.

Right on schedule, the gate to the parking garage swung open, its chain links scraping against the battered asphalt. Two men stood guard on either side. They wore caps and amber sunglasses to conceal their faces. The shorter one, wearing fingerless gloves, cracked his knuckles. The other tried to warm his hands with his breath.

The show was about to start.

"Refill?" the bartender asked.

Mort(e) slid his cup toward him. The beaver topped it off, then set the clay pitcher on the stove to keep it warm.

Somewhere near the end of the block, the horn of a truck sounded. Mort(e) winced. *Couple minutes early*, he thought.

A dark-green trash truck with enormous tires lumbered into the window frame. The compactor in the rear of the truck was sealed shut. Something was inside. Definitely not garbage. No, this required a hydraulic metal door to protect it. Mort(e) sensed something, something that pulled him toward it. Not a scent exactly, more of a gravitational force. True, the humans most likely smuggled weapons. The gangs all over Hosanna needed them to protect their turf. But these humans ran this operation on the ass-end of town. If they sold arms, no one seemed to buy any. Nothing troubled Mort(e) more than not knowing.

The truck stopped and reversed into the entrance while the guards waved the driver inside. That was the cue. Before the truck could roll into the driveway, a beaver turned the corner and waddled right into its path. Through the glass, Mort(e) could hear the humans shouting, "Whoa, whoa, stop!"

The beaver walked with a cane. He wore a pair of goggles that extended a full five inches from his face like little telescopes.

Though Mort(e) could not hear, he knew that this fat rodent was asking for directions to the Grumpy Beaver. Exasperated, one of the guards pointed toward the bar. The beaver continued hassling them, his hands flailing. He must have launched into one of his rants about how the neighborhood was changing, and how different things were in Lodge City.

*Come on, Castor*, Mort(e) thought. *Don't oversell it.*

Now both humans pointed at the bar, trying to hurry the nuisance along. Castor continued yapping. He tapped the side of his head, maybe telling them that his old mind didn't work like it used to. With the beaver out of the way, the humans waved the truck in and closed the gate.

A few sips of Archer later, Castor entered through the front door. A great shout rose up, as it always did. He was their leader, the one who guided the Lodge City beavers to greatness. The patrons broke into song. Castor tossed the cane to the older beaver who had lent it to him. He removed the goggles and replaced them with his regular glasses. Each of his comrades greeted him by touching noses, a ritual that lasted a full nine minutes before Castor finally took a seat beside Mort(e). A mug of LC sat waiting for him. Castor sipped it, then plucked one of the pieces of wood out and gnawed on it with his enormous buck teeth.

"Wanna talk now or later?" Mort(e) said.

"Now. Before they ask me to sing."

Castor always asked Mort(e) to join in. Mort(e) always said no. It had become a joke between them: Mort(e) would pretend that he hated the beavers' music, though they both knew that it had grown on him.

"What did you find?" Mort(e) said.

Castor held out the goggles. "These things are amazing. I could see the serial number on the registration card. Two six. Zero nine. Seven eight."

Mort(e) sighed. "That's the one."

They both knew what it meant. Through his contact at Tranquility, Mort(e) found out that the same truck had been reported missing in the flood. These humans may have salvaged it. Nothing surprising there—all sorts of junk and debris gathered near the mouth of the river. It would take years for scavengers to pick it all clean. But a piece of hardware this valuable would not have been written off so easily. If the humans didn't simply find it, then they could have stolen it and then altered the records, especially if they knew someone on the inside. Either way, Mort(e) could not rule out the involvement of the Sanctuary Union in all of this.

"Where does that leave us?" Castor asked.

"Same as always. On our own."

A drunk beaver—Castor's nephew, Kerdigan—stumbled over to them and clapped Castor on the shoulder. "Two weeks!" he shouted. "Two weeks to go!"

"Two weeks, that's right," Castor replied.

"Hey, hey," Kerdigan said. "Did I tell ya? I named my kit after you."

"I thought you had a girl."

"Yeah! Castoria!"

Kerdigan turned to his comrades and shouted the name. They shouted it back. The band changed tune, and the entire bar started a new song.

"Congratulations," Castor said.

Mort(e) figured that Castoria was as good a name as any for a female kit. By his last count, there had been four D'Arcs and three Shebas born since he'd left Lodge City.

Castor thanked Kerdigan and sent him on his way.

"So we can't go to Tranquility because we don't trust them," Castor said to Mort(e). "We have to do this ourselves."

"*I'm* going to do it."

"Don't give me that."

"I've snuck into places like this one," Mort(e) said. "Besides—"

"Are you about to tell me that this is your fault again?"

"Yes. Because it is."

"It's not! Now let's come up with a way to do this together. Okay?"

To stop himself from saying anything else, Mort(e) chugged the rest of his Archer and slammed the mug onto the bar.

"I told you I lost people under my command," Mort(e) said.

"Not this again."

"Did I tell you their names?"

Castor set his drink on the bar. "No."

"That's right. Because you are the master over someone who has told you his story." As he said it, he heard it in the voice of his old captain, the bobcat Culdesac, whose story he never learned.

Mort(e) swiveled toward Castor. But after he stopped, the room continued to spin. A sharp smell of salt water made his nose twitch. The bitter taste filled his mouth, shriveling his tongue. He tried to lean on the bar, but his hand slipped from the counter, slamming his elbow into the wood. Castor became blurry, like a mossy rock in murky water. Soon, the entire room became submerged. The beavers' voices traveled to his ear in gurgling noises, like the gasps of a drowning person.

"Mort(e)?" Castor said, his voice like bubbles rising.

Mort(e) tried to plant his foot on the floor. His knee buckled. He slipped from the stool and collapsed. His hand landed next to his face. With his declawed fingers, he pawed at the wood floor.

When the floor fell away, Mort(e) knew that he had started dreaming again. He didn't fight it this time. The seawater pooled around him and then lifted him from the bottom of the ocean. A faint light penetrated the surface above, painting everything around him blue. The beavers' humming died out in the deep. A new sound emerged: a clicking and screeching, the song of the Sarcops who ruled this place. The fish-heads. He could understand their speech. No point in translating. The words summoned him. At last, he took in a breath, and the briny coldness poured into his throat and vented through gills on his neck. This was home, for as long as it would last.

WHEN HE AWOKE, Mort(e) recognized the ceiling with its white tiles and a mold stain in the corner. He remembered the thick drapes covering the windows. The tattered flag of Venezuela on the wall right next to an amateur oil painting of Simón Bolívar. The mahogany desk with a coffee cup filled with pens. A lamp with a green shade that provided the room with warm light.

He inhaled. The air felt dry. He lifted his hand to his throat to feel the gills. They were gone. When he tilted his head, Dr. Marquez appeared, wearing his usual khaki slacks and white doctor's coat. The man brushed his fingers through his salt-and-pepper hair, which conveyed either relief or exhaustion. Ever since the encounter with the Sarcops, Mort(e) still visited Marquez once a week. The doctor studied animals who had used the translator and the effects that still lingered in their brains. Sometimes he ran cognitive tests, but mostly he sat there and listened to Mort(e) talk. About the war, about his new life with the beavers. Sometimes, if Marquez asked nicely enough, Mort(e) would talk about D'Arc. He would imagine her staring out at the sea under the stars, and before long it would feel like another hallucination.

"Where did you go this time?" Marquez said.

"The sea again. Cold Trench." Mort(e) motioned for the pitcher of water on top of a liquor cabinet. Marquez filled a glass and handed it to him. As he did so, another set of footsteps sidled up to the couch where Mort(e) lay. They belonged to Castor. The beaver leaned over to touch noses with Mort(e), then reconsidered and backed away.

Mort(e) forced himself to sit. His head swam, and he cinched his eyes shut until the room steadied.

"Did you taste salt water?" Marquez asked. "Before the episode began?"

"Yep."

"How long has this been going on?" Castor asked.

"Please," Marquez said, "give him a moment."

"No, it's okay," Mort(e) said. Until then, the beaver knew only that Mort(e) still visited Marquez on occasion to run some tests. Nothing more.

"Remember last month, when I said I was taking a few days off?" Mort(e) said to Castor. "I was here. Well, my body was here. My mind was off on another adventure. Under the sea."

"What are you talking about?"

"I'm going crazy!" Mort(e) said.

"It's the translator," Marquez said. "It taxes the brain." He illustrated this by squeezing his hairy-knuckled hands into fists. "The damage is degenerative."

"That means it's getting worse," Mort(e) said.

"I know what it means," Castor said. "When were you going to tell me? You want to pick a fight with these humans, and now you tell me you're going senile."

"Pick a fight with what humans?" Marquez asked.

"Oh, great," Mort(e) said. "Tell each other all my secrets, why don't you? My stool samples are in the fridge. Let's break those out."

Castor told Marquez about the humans. They were organized, armed, secretive, transporting large objects with stolen vehicles. Whatever they smuggled, it triggered Mort(e)'s episodes from afar. He could feel its power calling to him, throbbing in his brain.

Marquez spun around to Mort(e). "Are you sure you are not imagining any of this?"

"My nephew went snooping around their building," Castor

said. "A couple of weeks ago. They found his body the next day, way downstream."

"I told him to do it," Mort(e) said, eyes on the floor. "It should have been me."

"I am sorry to hear this," Marquez said. "But whatever this is, it is a matter for Tranquility now."

"Tranquility's in on it. We ask them to inspect the building, and then the humans move their trucks to another location. We tell them that the building is unregistered, and then the next day it magically appears in their records. We show them a dead body, they say it's an accident."

"So you take this into your own hands?"

"What difference does it make? Either way, I'm your next cadaver."

Marquez motioned for Mort(e)'s glass. He refilled it and handed it back.

"Oh, wait," Mort(e) said. "I'm your *last* cadaver. All the other translator users are dead. I'm still hanging on for some reason. You'll have to find a new hobby."

"You can insult me, you can keep punishing yourself," Marquez said. "But don't tell me I see you only as a specimen. You have been coming here for months. You are my friend."

"See!" Castor said. "I told you you have friends."

"Quiet," Mort(e) said.

Marquez turned to his liquor cabinet again, opened it. "I can increase your dosage."

"Forget it. I'm sick of the side effects."

"What side effects?"

"The pills make me irritable."

"Oh, what's that like?" Castor said.

Ignoring them both, Marquez pulled a brown pill bottle from the shelf and handed it to Mort(e). "Take two the next time you feel a spell coming on."

"They're coming on faster these days. I'm telling you—those humans have something dangerous."

"Your stress level is not helping things."

Mort(e) attempted to stand. But when he wobbled a bit, Marquez reached out a hand to steady him. Mort(e) batted it away.

"Are we still on for next week, Doctor?"

"You cannot run away from this," Marquez said. "Let me bring you to the hospital. They have better equipment, more staff—"

"No. There's no time for any of that."

Marquez rubbed his temples. He must have known Mort(e) was right. "Next week, then."

"If I'm still around," Mort(e) replied.

He walked out.

"You'll still be around!" Marquez shouted after him. "We are not done yet!"

Outside, the street lamps were all dark, thanks to another scheduled blackout. A few candles and lanterns flickered in the windows of the neighboring buildings. A fierce wind whipped along the brick wall, slapping him in the face. When the sound of it finally stopped ringing in his ears, he heard Castor scrambling behind him, huffing and puffing, keeping an eye on him while maintaining distance. Soon, another breeze drowned him out entirely, leaving Mort(e) alone in the dark.

AT DAWN, MORT(E) offered to reinforce the inner edge of the dam. This meant tying a rope to his waist and rappelling to a spot near the surface of the water, where a recent storm had shifted some of the logs. There, he hammered the pieces into place and sealed them with a special glue that smelled like a Lodge City Special. It was dangerous work that the beavers had put off for a few days. But it allowed him some time to himself while the rest of the laborers gossiped and sang their songs about lodges and rivers. At lunchtime, a cook's apprentice at the Grumpy Beaver delivered a pot of insect stew, pungent with boiled cabbage. Mort(e) got in line, filled his bowl, and ate by himself while dangling his legs off the side of the dam.

When the workday ended, he waited for the beavers to disperse before climbing to the top of the dam and uncoupling his harness. Castor knew better than to wait for him. When Mort(e) got into one of his moods, there was little point in inviting him out to the pub.

With the sun tilting to the ground and the shadows stretching out, Mort(e) made his way to one of the abandoned buildings in the neighborhood—a hotel that would never host guests again. Yellow tape sealed the entrance, and a laminated sign announced that Tranquility had condemned the building because of water damage. They planned to implode it later that year.

Mort(e) ducked under the tape and walked across the lobby. A layer of dust coated the tiled floor, and a brown line on the wall indicated the high-water mark of the flood. The last of the sunlight leaked in through the grimy windows. Mort(e) climbed the stairs to the fifteenth floor. There, he opened the door to the penthouse suite with its gleaming white rug, enormous mirrors, and a hot tub from which the water had long since evaporated. The kitchen had marble countertops and a shiny steel sink and refrigerator. A little capsule of the decadent days before the war, all to himself.

He camped on the balcony and surveyed the city. Vehicles moved along the riverfront, far to the south of the dam. Lights in windows blinked on as the sun sank deeper behind the buildings. A fresh batch of graffiti tarnished the walls of several government buildings. This time, an image depicted a dog and a wolf shaking hands under the slogan STAND BY YOUR TRUE BEST FRIEND. Another painting showed a dog breaking its leash and heading away from Hosanna and into the forest, presumably to join some wild pack. *Dumbass dogs*, Mort(e) thought. *Always talking a big game about rebellion.*

Nearby, the growing pond at the base of the dam reflected like a giant sheet of glass. Nature was slowly retaking the city of Hosanna, and this new body of water would only accelerate the process, slowly transforming concrete and steel into mud and moss. A small victory for the natural way of things. Perhaps the only thing Mort(e) created that was worth preserving.

He opened his backpack and pulled out a pair of binoculars and a notebook. Peering through the lenses, he settled his gaze on the apartment building near the bar, where the humans were engaged in their nightly ritual of patrolling the perimeter. Two guards stood watch on the roof, two more waited in the lobby, and a fifth stalked the alley behind the building. Mort(e) tracked them in his book, noting the length of their shifts, what weapons they carried, and any insignias on their jackets or vests that would indicate rank. He called the short, stocky one the Waddler. A skinny one became Slinky. The older one, who sometimes appeared to give orders, was the Jerk. The others would share a cigarette and talk after he left, and Mort(e) imagined them goofing on him, maybe doing an impersonation.

The singing at the Grumpy Beaver grew louder. On the high notes, the guards would spin their heads in the direction of the noise. Over the past few months, Mort(e) had learned that some humans went to great lengths to show empathy with the animals. Sometimes they would go so far as to claim that they trusted animals more than their own kind. With these strangers, however, he recognized the permanent astonishment, the resentment, the disgust with this new world. These guards remembered the days before the war. If they had lived this long, they must have killed an animal at some point. They must have hated the terrible things they did to survive. How could these humans ever really forgive? Why would they want to?

Right around the time that the Jerk took his usual smoke break, a beaver stepped out of the pub and walked toward the hotel. Mort(e) raised the binoculars to his eyes. It was Castor, carrying two mugs.

"Aw, shit," Mort(e) said.

The guards stiffened when they spotted him. They tapped their earpieces as they alerted each other to a potential intruder. The Jerk dropped his cigarette. But as Castor got closer, they relaxed. A tubby little beaver posed little threat. By the time Castor reached the hotel lobby, the Jerk had retrieved his cigarette and continued to smoke. Mort(e) made a note of it.

Castor needed a breather after climbing the steps. Mort(e) remained in place, watching the bright ember of the man's cigarette.

"Learn anything new this evening?" the beaver asked.

"Not much. Same routine as before. Shift change coming."

Castor joined him on the balcony and set the drinks on the floor. They poked their heads over the railing and watched. Mort(e)'s drink had gone cold, but he appreciated the gesture.

Castor plucked a piece of wood from his drink and chewed on it like a wad of tobacco. "I'm going to regret saying this, but I talked to Grissom at Tranquility."

Besides Marquez, Grissom was the only person at Tranquility they trusted. The former assistant to Chief Wawa, Grissom supplied them with gossip and news from the wolf territories and beyond. Once in a while, he gave them reports about the *al-Rihla*'s progress. But it was never enough, only status updates and checkpoint confirmations. Nothing Mort(e) could hold on to.

"Go ahead," Mort(e) said.

"Grissom says the inspectors approved the dam. They say it's sturdy enough to drive a car over it."

"So?"

"So guess who asked about it."

Mort(e) lowered the binoculars.

"That's right," Castor said. "Our human neighbors even asked about weight restrictions."

"Who are they?"

"They're refugees. Hosanna is trying to take in as many humans from the frontier as possible."

"Refugees, my ass," Mort(e) said. "What kind of refugees have bodyguards?"

"Well, that's how they're listed in the records. The wolves even gave them safe passage."

"And nobody found that suspicious. Good job, Tranquility."

Mort(e) leaned on the railing and sipped his drink. If these humans planned to smuggle something out of here, crossing the dam into New Jersey made perfect sense. The other bridges were too conspicuous, manned by the best soldiers. In contrast, Tranquility maintained only a small garrison on the Jersey side, and the humans could shoot their way through if they had not already bribed someone. Once they made it onto one of the old highways, no one would catch them. And the records would merely list them as another gang of nomads who decided to move on.

"What day do they open the dam to traffic?" Mort(e) asked.

"Week from Sunday. At dawn."

"All right then. They're coming to us. We have to stop that convoy."

"We don't have to do anything," Castor said. "We could let them be on their way."

"They killed one of yours."

"We don't know that for sure. And besides, I don't want to lose anyone else. Not when we're about to go home. Not when we . . ."

Mort(e) glared at him. "Go ahead, say it."

Castor needed a sip first. "Not when we have so much to do back home."

"Right, so much to look forward to," Mort(e) said. "Unlike me."

Castor cradled the cup on his lap. "I wish there was something I could do."

"There is. Help me."

The beaver shook his head. "Dr. Marquez told me that being fixated on a single thing might be a symptom of your condition."

"You should have met me ten years ago," Mort(e) said.

On the street below, the patrons of the Grumpy Beaver started a chant. Their slapping tails echoed among the buildings.

"I'm running out of time," Mort(e) said. "Trying to make the most of it."

"Are you trying to get yourself killed?"

"No."

Castor took another drink, keeping his eyes on him.

"I'm *not*," Mort(e) said. "Oh, if you only knew some of the kooky thoughts kicking around in my head."

"Try me."

Stalling, Mort(e) licked his paw, raked it across his face. "I never wanted to believe in the prophecy about me and Sheba. About how we would be together. And now it's the only thing keeping me alive. I'm not trying to treat every day like it's my last. I'm treating it like it's the day she comes back."

"My mother was right. The Three Goddesses brought you to Lodge City for a reason."

"If that's true, then your Three Goddesses messed everything up."

"No!"

Mort(e) flinched. The beaver almost never raised his voice.

"You said you were supposed to be dead by now," Castor said. "The translator was supposed to finish you off. But you're still alive. Why is that?"

"Marquez thinks that the fish-heads did something to me. Maybe they repaired some damage."

"Aha! So if you never came to Lodge City, you never would have met the Sarcops."

"Oh, shut up."

"They must have given you that gift for a reason! They saw some good in you!"

"The prophecy, the goddesses, the fish-heads. Pick whatever fairy tale you want."

Mort(e) peeked over the railing. More humans appeared on the rooftop for the scheduled shift change, with Slinky, the Jerk, and the Waddler swapping out for Bozo, Dum-Dum, and Meat. Mort(e) called out their names as they arrived.

"Meat?" Castor asked.

"Look at him! He's a pile of meat!"

The man took his spot and waited, his thumbs hooked into his sagging belt.

"I'll talk to my people," Castor said. "We'll, um . . . we'll probably help. If they find out I said no to you, they won't like it."

"Thank you."

"But you need to do what Marquez told you to do. And at the first sign of trouble, we're out."

"Fine."

Castor took his mug. "Need another?"

"No. I'll be fine. I'll see you in the morning."

Castor left. A few seconds later, Mort(e) tracked his movement as he walked to the bar, where he rejoined his comrades for another round, maybe two. They were a family, united by blood and destiny. And they did not have to wait for a prophecy to come true to spend their evening together.

Mort(e) turned his attention to the apartment building once more. Any minute now, the human he called Meat would urinate off the side of the building, giggling all the while. In fewer than thirty minutes, Bozo would begin his smoke break. Mort(e) would sit here, alone, and record everything until the sun rose again.

# CHAPTER 4

## THE STORY OF NIKAYA

ATURDAYS WERE FOR hauling guano out of the bat caves. A big scoop, they called it. At sunset, when the bats went foraging for the night, Nikaya headed for the caves, rolling a wheelbarrow containing a shovel, a headlamp, rations, and a tin of tobacco for a brief smoke break. Though she could smell the guano from anywhere in the camp, the thick stench at the mouth of the cave always made her gag, the same way it did on her first day. Even in winter, with the trees bare and the ground as hard as cement, the scent latched on to everything, a constant warning to stay away. A reminder that she deserved to die here, in a prison that did not even have a name.

A guard trailed behind her. A male badger named Geller, dim-witted and coarse, but packed with muscle, and with canine teeth that could tear meat and tendon from a bone. He and his brothers handled security at the garrison. The bats paid them in food, lodging, whiskey, cannabis, whores. As the runt who could not follow simple orders, Geller got stuck watching this old beaver. Boring work, yet easy. He did not bother to remove the rifle strapped to his shoulder. Nikaya would not run. And the longer she worked, the faster that idea would slip out of her mind. On a good night, she would haul out nearly a dozen loads, each one heavier than the last.

Before she could enter the cave, Geller placed his paw on the front of the wheelbarrow. She stopped. He snatched the tin of tobacco, sniffed it. With his filthy fingernail, he dug out a hunk of leaves and stuffed them into his pipe. He lit it and inhaled, making the leaves smolder. Two jets of smoke shot from his nostrils, the scent briefly masking the guano. Nikaya wanted to correct him—pipe smoke was best puffed from the mouth so the flavor could settle on the tongue. The badgers always needed to show off, and this one wanted to send a message. Tonight, Nikaya would get one smoke break rather than two. With a team of scouts stationed at the garrison over the last week, tonight's work would require a few extra trips. No time for lollygagging. In the morning, her knees and hips would feel like rusted hinges. Her thighs and arms would burn. They would give way under her weight if she stood too quickly.

While Geller made a show of enjoying the tobacco, Nikaya did what she would always do at this time of day. Without moving her head, she made note of the nearby barracks, where the badgers slept. She saw paw prints in the mud, and used them to count the number of guards. She guessed twelve, maximum. The same number as before the scout bats arrived. The guards changed shifts at dawn, noon, dusk, and midnight. They made the mistake of letting her see that. She saw the embers of the campfire, barely glowing in the darkness. A small creek snaked beyond the weapons shed. Farther away, a single guard pissed in the latrine while his lamp swung from a nearby tree branch. Framing all of it was a mountain bristling with pine trees, powdered with snow on top.

The mountain allowed her to figure out where she was. She knew this forest. It was she who named the hills and rivers and ponds, not these bats, nor their badger allies. Nikaya and the city she founded had brought order and prosperity to this region. The bats knew that, having once made their home there. One day, Nikaya would escape from this place and into the open arms of the forest. Once she reached the river, they would never find her again. Because even an old bitch like her could swim. Oh, the weight of all these years would melt away. She would float. She would fly. She would dive, then rise again. These many months of labor made her tired, but also made her stronger. *The water flows.* And it would wash the scent away.

"Better get to it, Your Highness," Geller said. "Big scoop today." He tried and failed to blow a smoke ring.

Nikaya donned the headlamp and flicked it on. The badger's pupils shrank in the light. Nikaya gripped the handles until her calluses crunched into the softer flesh underneath. The wheel squeaked, echoing off the walls of the cave. The overpowering stench of bat shit surrounded her. In less than a minute, the entrance to the cave lay far behind, a dim glow that soon vanished. She was alone.

THE SHOVEL GREW heavy, and the muscles stiffened around her spine. Her tail dragged behind her, so caked in mud that she would not be able to clean it properly until the spring. She leaned on the shovel each time she wheeled out a load and dumped it in the latrine ditch. The badgers would use the manure as fertilizer and fuel later.

Though she hated what her body had become, she had not felt this strong in years. Each day here scraped away the fat that had congealed around her waist. When she first arrived, the badgers joked about how bloated and lazy she had become. She swore to them that she was too old and frail to work hard labor. As a punishment, they cut her rations, giving her only enough food to survive. Still, she refused.

And then, one night, a new shipment of booze arrived from

Hosanna. The guards got drunk, deserting their posts to run about the forest, shouting at the moon. Seizing the moment, Nikaya ran for her life, faster than she had ever run before. But they were waiting for her. It was all a ruse to catch her in the act.

"Looks like Her Highness is stronger than we thought," Geller said. Nikaya said nothing. Instead, she took the shovel and got to work, if only to avoid listening to their scummy voices. Badgers were never funny, no matter how hard they laughed at their own jokes.

On this night, many months later, Nikaya passed the time by singing the songs from Lodge City. Partly because they soothed her, partly to annoy Geller. Visitors to the city often remarked that the songs all sounded the same: a low humming for harmony, the tails beating the ground for percussion, and lyrics that were always about the warm lodges the beavers called home.

> *We will meet again*
> *In the darkness,*
> *Where you and I*
> *Will be the only light.*

After the third load of guano, she no longer had the strength to beat her tail, nor the breath to sing a full line without gasping. Even worse, there were no others of her kind to join her. The songs were meant to be sung in a group. One beaver singing alone was the saddest sound in the world.

"Why is that, Nana?" her granddaughter once asked. "*Why is it so sad?*" Little Nikki, named after Nikaya. She spoke with a lisp and was a stronger swimmer than the males. She carved little beaver dolls out of chunks of wood left behind by the tree cutters. She made a whole family of them. A mother, a father, two kits—

"No," Nikaya said to herself. Not this again. No wallowing in the past. She was getting out of here. Better to think of something to keep her angry. The rage made her feel young again. It restored feeling to her numb feet and loosened the stiff joints.

With a grunt, she lifted another shovelful into the wheelbarrow.

Yes, it was better to think of when she first arrived here. That always got the blood pumping. The bats had arrested her in front of her family, her people, and hauled her away in a tornado of wings and skin and fur. She screamed for them to let her go while the wind howled in her ears. They dumped her in a clearing and flapped away, tossing about the leaves and dirt. When Nikaya opened her eyes, a line of badgers waited for her. Stupid creatures with long snouts, black stripes extending from their stubby ears to their cheekbones. The space between the stripes was painted a snowy white. Each of them had rings of skin on their biceps where they shaved their fur. There, on the pink flesh, they carved crude tattoos, hieroglyphs from their worthless language.

The leader, a fat one named Zuck, read aloud her sentence in stilted English. The bats would not even face her. Instead, they had these mercenaries do it for them. "For crimes against Nature, you are hereby sentenced to punitive labor for a period of eighteen seasons."

"This is not a Sanctuary Union facility," she told them. "The Hosanna Charter does not recognize this jurisdiction. You have no right to hold me here."

They whipped her.

"My people will come for me!" she screamed. "My Watchers will put your heads on spikes!"

None of it was true. Her people had left her to her fate. The bats tricked them. They even tricked Castor, her son. He would not speak to her before they carried her away. But he must have known why she did what she did, why she tried to eliminate the bats once and for all. It was to protect Lodge City, the only refuge for her kind. Those ratwings would destroy it all, if given the chance.

"Mother, I wish you wouldn't use that word," Castor often said.

When she fell silent at last, Zuck went through the trouble of reading the statement again. "The work you do here will be important," he said, rolling the paper into a tube. "Every day, you'll know that you made the world a better place."

With welts blooming under her fur, Nikaya repeated the mantra in her head. *The water flows.* Lodge City could never die. Not as long as she lived.

Which she did.

And now, shoveling shit again, her regret and anger sharpened her senses. After so much time spent as a ruler, she had become an animal once more, sniffing the wind for traces of danger. Every new movement of the guards, every break in their routines caught her attention. She knew all their names, their habits, the sounds of their voices. Daily, she probed their weaknesses. Soon, she would put it all together. She would vanish from this place. In a rage, Zuck would turn the whip on his brothers. And then someone would use the whip on him. The Great Cloud of bats would tremble knowing that the heart of Lodge City still thumped in the woods.

At the end of her shift, with her knees aching and her throat wheezing, the sky changed color from black to purple. She dumped the last load with Geller trailing behind her. He would escort her to the gutted school bus that served as her prison cell. The rear door hung open, welcoming her once more. With the windows barred, the door served as the only entrance. The badgers covered the bus with graffiti, mostly symbols of horny females wiggling their hips. For their part, the bats often shat on the roof of the bus when they returned from the cave, a reminder of Nikaya's war crimes against them.

The walk to the bus provided her best chance of the day to scope out the campsite. As usual, a trio of badgers played cards by the fire as they waited to start their next shift. Inside the cabin, two more badgers guarded the supplies and armaments. Unlike the bats, who foraged for everything, the badgers needed to haul in their own food. They would restock soon. Another weakness to exploit.

Without tilting her head, Nikaya spotted an ax leaning against the cabin wall. Beside it, someone had left a carving knife embedded in a split log. More tools she could acquire, should the opportunity arise. She kept track of every sharp instrument and blunt object in the camp. If she got free of her cell, and found herself stumbling in the dark, she would find the nearest one and aim it anyone who tried to stop her.

As she imagined driving the head of the ax into Zuck's snout, a frantic screeching sound filtered through the trees. A panic signal, meaning *follow me, now*! She'd last heard it on the day she ordered the Cloud expelled from Lodge City, the day she became their enemy, according to the bats. But they knew damn well that they viewed her as an enemy long before any of that. She'd merely struck first. All these years later, the screeching still rang in her ears, like spirits reaching out from hell.

The noise was getting closer. Geller grew tense. He shoved her forward. "Get in your cell." She heard the keys jingling on his belt. Another mistake on his part—she knew each lock that the keys opened.

"Let's go," Geller said.

A fluttering overhead, followed by a breeze. A branch swayed. In the slowly brightening morning, it took a moment to realize that a bat hung from it, his wings wrapped around him. He panted. He shivered. No—he trembled.

She knew this bat.

Two more of them circled the tree. The bats clutched

the branch on either side of their comrade. The screeching changed pitch from a high squeal to a lower chirping. An annoyed tone. She knew some of it. None of the guards had figured out that she could speak Chiropteran. None of them gave her the credit. It was another miscalculation that would cost them their lives.

*Why?* one of the bats asked.

*Danger*, another said. The bat in the middle kept his beady eyes on Nikaya as he argued with the others. His name was Gaunt. He was there the day they took her away. The day they destroyed what she spent a lifetime building, something a rat with wings would never understand. That day, Gaunt had mocked her. He'd ordered her silenced. And now, amid his other noises, Gaunt uttered a panicked squeak, again and again. *Wind. Wind now. Wind!* It meant fly. Fly away, as fast as they could, as far as their strength could take them.

Geller's palm shoved her again. "I said get in your cage, Your Highness."

She could not afford to argue. Something important was happening. She got inside. The door shut behind her. The key scraped against metal as Geller locked her in.

She waited near the slatted windows and listened. Several times, the bats left their perch and flew in circles, squawking and whining, the pitch going so high it made Nikaya wince. This was how they argued, all movement and chaos. She followed what she could. Danger was coming, they said. *Danger close. Danger here. Danger. Death.*

*Can't be!*

*Yes, true. Wind. Wind now.*

Soon, the entire cloud joined them. Their voices blended into one another. Nikaya could no longer understand. But she did not need to. They were screaming for help, for someone to save them, like so many doomed peoples before them. This is why the beavers would prevail. They awaited no messiah. They could count only on themselves.

In a great whoosh, the bats poured into the cave. By then, the eastern sky blazed with the sunrise. Another day was beginning. At last, a day different from all the others before it.

THE BADGERS WERE not without mercy. On the morning after a big scoop, they typically let Nikaya sleep late. She would need it. Upon returning to her cell, she would find a pot of bush tea waiting for her, along with a salad stuffed with greens, fresh water, and a roll of tobacco. They would toss in a fresh log of maple or birchwood so she could sharpen her teeth—without it, her bright orange incisors would protrude from her mouth in a matter of weeks. She hated herself for being so grateful for all of it, but some days this small feast seemed a great bounty. If she weren't careful, the badgers' random moments of generosity could break her as easily as the crack of their whips.

In a matter of minutes, she had licked the salad bowl clean. The water was nearly depleted, the teapot empty. Her belly continued to grumble, demanding more. She imagined the smoke taking solid shape in her mouth, somehow nourishing her.

Despite her hunger, Nikaya began to doze off with the pipe in her mouth, the end of it still trailing smoke. Barely moving her lips, she asked the Three Goddesses to spare her any nightmares involving the giant ants, the ones who destroyed her home. They had a habit of ruining the most peaceful dreams, leaving her a gasping, quivering mess when she awakened.

With the seats gutted, only the floor near the steering wheel provided a comfortable spot to rest. She could sit in the driver's chair, but the front window was sealed with metal plates, with only a tiny slit to see through, like a tank. The side door, where passengers had once entered, was rusted shut. Metal bars had been fused to the windows. Someone—human or animal—once used this vehicle in a time of war. She could still smell the fuel, converted from vegetable oil, but the bus would never drive again.

Like a good beaver, she had tried to make this tiny space as cozy as possible. The badgers let her carry sticks and leaves inside. Over time, she built a lodge of sorts, covering nearly every inch of cold metal and plastic with branches and mud. She imagined her granddaughter helping her. Little Nikki, the future of Lodge City, bouncing around at her feet, asking questions.

"Nana, why?"

"Nana, will you sing with us?"

"Nana—"

A terrible squealing jolted Nikaya from her half sleep. She rolled onto her side, pushed herself to her feet, wincing through the grinding in her knees. "Now what?" she said.

The noise blasted from the mouth of the cave. The sun climbed high, a time of day when the bats typically slept. But the sound grew louder. Some kind of argument, a bitter one. They shouted insults. *Fool. Traitor. Coward.* The badgers rose from their seats at the card table, alarmed but silent.

Something moved inside the cave. Nikaya could not make it out until a bat shot out of the opening. It was Gaunt again, wearing a leather aviator helmet with polarized goggles. He startled the badgers, who took cover beneath the tabletop.

The squealing inside the cave changed pitch. Instead of a screech, the bats let out a slower, mournful sound. She tried to detect what they said, but the noise coalesced into a single word: *No. No, no, no.* Bats made that noise when someone died. Or was about to die.

Nikaya thought of the beavers' song of mourning, the same one she sang for the old ones in her family who survived the Change. They lived long enough to see the promised land before joining the Three Goddesses.

For too long, Nikaya assumed that she had time to escape. But now something terrible was on its way. She needed to get out of here. The forest would protect her. The river would mask her scent. *The water flows.* If only she could get to it.

DUSK SETTLED RAPIDLY in these colder months. The low-hanging sun filtered through the barren trees. As Nikaya expected, Geller ordered her to work on the construction project near the cave. There, the badgers laid the foundation of a new garrison to replace the makeshift one in which they'd shivered all winter. On this day, Nikaya whittled a pile of logs with her teeth, sharpening every one into a pike. The bats had their caves, the beavers their lodges, but these badgers simply could not live without a human-style building. No culture for these rodents. No tradition. Just mimicry.

Nikaya kept that opinion to herself.

Two other prisoners joined her—a male and a female fox who spoke only to each other, either by whining or barking. And not a dog's bark, but a squealing little sound. *Epp epp epp!* The badgers did not like it. For all they knew, the foxes plotted to escape right in front of them. But these foxes were simple folk. Brother and sister, but also mates, Nikaya suspected. She remembered when the male cut his hand on an ax and let out a high-pitched wail until the female consoled him by licking the wound.

Nikaya, meanwhile, could not be trusted with her own kind. Two other beavers were arrested with her on the day everything changed, and she had not seen them since. Most likely, they cleaned out the guano in some other cave, far from her influence. A good call on the bats' part, she had to admit. If she even had a chance to sing a song with the other beavers, the lyrics would be all about sneaking out at night and following the stars to the water.

She wanted to sing. As she pushed the wheelbarrow, she imagined the badgers joining in, the foxes trying to hum in the background. Some melancholy tune, but a defiant one as well. She knew just the one.

*Damn the Goddesses*
*Even as they pray for me.*
*I damn the Goddesses*
*They won't take this day from me.*

The foxes glared at her as she hummed the tune and patted her tail on the ground. One of them snarled at the other. While she sat and chewed on the logs, they hauled mud. They did not like it. "All day, on your ass you sit," the female said.

Nikaya offered her the log. "Would you like to trade? Your teeth will fall out in two minutes."

Before the female could respond, Geller told them both to shut up. The foxes continued loading the wheelbarrow. The male lifted the handles and rolled it toward the growing pile in the clearing. In a few months, the soil would become a garden. The sun would arc higher in the sky, and the leaves would return. It would be beautiful.

*No, you'll never see it. You'll be gone. Remember?*

She spat a mouthful of wood and licked her teeth.

As she stretched for the next log in the pile, a terrible scream echoed from deep in the forest. Geller aimed his rifle toward the noise, resembling a real soldier for once—if not for the terror in his eyes.

Nikaya took note of everything. Where the guards stood. The distance from the bus to the barracks. The time it took the other guards to arrive.

The screeching grew closer. It came from the sky, from a bat calling for help. Everyone turned at the sound of branches rustling. As it careened through the forest, a flapping bat bounced from one of the trunks and landed hard on the roof of the bus.

Exhausted, bleeding, the bat rolled off the roof and flopped onto the dirt.

Gaunt had returned. He screeched in a broken voice. *Wind. Wind now.*

"Stay here," Geller said. He raced to the bat, who resembled a pile of leather on the ground. Three other badgers joined him, though judging from their stunned faces, none of them knew the slightest thing about treating a wounded bat. One of them, a foul-smelling badger called Nestor, was clearly drunk already. He leaned on the bus to keep steady.

*Wind,* the bat said, his chest deflating. *Wind. Wind now.*

After nearly a year, these dumbass badgers hardly knew a word of Chiropteran.

"He's telling us to run!" Nikaya said.

Geller spun around, aiming his rifle. "Stay where you are, Your Highness." Behind him, the others knelt over the bat, no doubt worrying about how this would affect their next payday.

Nikaya glanced at the foxes for help. *Epp-epp-epp,* the male said.

*Epp-epp-epp,* the female replied.

Nikaya felt it in her feet: a disturbance in the dirt. Footsteps. Some on all fours. Some in pairs.

"Leave that ratwing!" Nikaya said. "We have to get out of here!"

More of the badgers emptied from the barracks. Inside the cave, the bats must have heard Gaunt return. They cried out from the darkness. The noise pounded against Nikaya's skull.

Geller moved closer to her, his arms stiffening as he leveled the rifle.

"If I hear you say that one more time—"

His head jerked to the side. Nikaya jumped at the movement. Then she saw the shaft of an arrow lodged in Geller's neck, its sparrow-brown feathers fluttering in the breeze. The foxes panicked and took off running, side by side. Geller let go of the rifle and gripped the arrow, his eyes bulging. Blood oozed between his knuckles. He dropped to his knees. Behind him, a volley of arrows rained down on the badgers as they tried to take cover. One of the arrows caught a badger from behind. He flopped onto his stomach. The others ran, ignoring his cries for help.

Nikaya stumbled past the arrows in the dirt. More of them zipped through the air. She ran past the bat, who lay still, most likely dead. After taking cover behind the bus, she peeked into the forest. The invaders moved from tree to tree, each covered in fur. Had to be wolves. Marauders.

The remaining badgers returned fire from the barracks. Bullets tore gashes into the tree bark. An arrow hissed overhead. And for a horrible moment, the bus, the oversized tin can that served as her prison, felt like the safest place in the world.

Nikaya ducked inside the entrance. More projectiles slammed into the bus, echoing so loud she could feel it in her chest. Outside the window, Geller gripped the arrow in his neck, his body already stiffening.

From inside the cave, the bats continued to shriek, begging for mercy, while three enormous wolves cast a net over the opening. These were not the wild marauders she had heard about. They moved with a strange, mechanical purpose. Like ants.

Realizing too late they were sealed in, the bats tried to spring themselves loose. The net bulged but held firm. It was like—

*Oh, Goddesses, that was what the spider did to these people.* She'd spun her web, encasing them inside. Because that was what Nikaya wanted. The Three Goddesses would make Nikaya relive her crime before the wolves ate her.

Something tugged on Nikaya's foot. She glanced down to see the leathery wing of the bat, reaching inside the bus.

"No," Nikaya whispered, kicking him. Ignoring her, the bat tried to shimmy his way through the door, getting far enough that Nikaya could not shove him out. His thin ribs showed through his fur. One of his wings crinkled like the skin of an old human. A bloody, ragged hole punctured the other one, leaking black blood on the floor.

"Get out!" Nikaya said.

He screeched at her.

"Shut *up!*" she hissed. She pounced on top of him, trying to clamp his mouth shut.

He screeched again. This time, he lifted his wing toward the front of the bus. He made the same noise over and over until she recognized it. He was saying the word *move*.

*Move. Wagon move.*

"You can drive?" she asked. He did not understand. She gestured with both hands on an imaginary steering wheel.

*Yes*, he chirped.

"We need the keys."

*No. Wind. Wind now.*

On her brittle knees, clenching her teeth through the pain, Nikaya hauled the wounded bat toward the front of the bus. The wood chips littering the floor stuck to his fur. Outside, the screaming continued as the bats tried to break through the net. Nikaya kept moving. Nothing else mattered. If this bat was lying about the bus, she would snap her teeth around his neck while his hot blood spurted into her mouth.

Outside, the wolves marched through the camp. After spending so many months with scrawny bats and wiry badgers, the towering wolves looked like massive, unnatural beasts to Nikaya. Some of them carried bows and arrows; others sported rifles. One of them walked by Geller and yanked the arrow from his neck. The wolf popped the arrowhead into his mouth, slurped the blood, and then clipped it to his belt.

At her feet, Gaunt tore out the wiring beneath the steering wheel. For what felt like forever, the bat fiddled with the wires, baring his teeth when they failed to cooperate.

Something slammed against the rear door. Gaunt tried to crawl under the dashboard while Nikaya scrambled to the first seat. She poked her head into the aisle to see one of the wolves sniffing at the entrance. He barked, summoning the others. Then he walked along the side of the bus. He wore a hood made of animal skin. His muscular arms were shaved bare, covered in tattoos. In his thick hands, he carried an assault rifle, laced with leaves for camouflage. In a few seconds, he would reach the side door.

Nikaya reached to the floor and grasped one of the branches she had left there, for all the good it would do.

With a loud belching noise, the bus engine turned over. The wolf froze. The camp fell silent. Nikaya turned to Gaunt. With his slender, pincerlike fingers, he tapped the wires together again. The engine roared to life. A plume of smoke shot from the tailpipe. Gaunt slid into the seat. No point in hiding now.

The barking started. Voices shouted. Magazines reloaded, metal clinking against metal. Nikaya lunged for the steering wheel. She grabbed the gear shift, wrenched it into the drive position, and then stomped on the gas pedal. The wheels rolled over the logs that kept them in place. The rocking motion nearly knocked her over.

It took both of them to spin the wheel—it must have run out of steering fluid long ago. "Take that path!" she said.

Bullets and arrows pinged off the steel plating on the front, popping through the metal, each hole bursting open like a bright new star. Several wolves jumped out of the way as the bus lumbered onto the dirt road, passing the inferno engulfing the barracks.

The wolf on the side of the bus latched onto the door. For

once, Nikaya was grateful for the door being rusted shut. But then, the wolf gripped the handle and tore out the top hinge, creating an opening that was large enough to reach inside.

A bullet punctured the rear tire, making the vehicle fishtail into a tree. Pine needles showered the roof.

Gripping the tree branch, Nikaya bit into it and spit out the wood. Beside her, Gaunt struggled to maintain control of the wheel. Another tire went out. Other wolves raced alongside, aiming into the windows.

Nikaya whittled the branch into a smooth spike and lifted it like a spear. The wolf's furry head leaned inside the bus. He would squeeze his way through.

His eyes met hers. This was no wolf. It was a human. He wore the pelt of a wolf wrapped around his head so that his face appeared in its gaping mouth.

Nikaya drove the spear toward his chest. He twisted his body to avoid it, but was too late. The spike sank into his shoulder. The man grunted and fell away.

The bus jolted on the uneven road, toward the river. Gaunt turned the wheel to the right. The vehicle spun out of control. Nikaya felt her stomach go weightless as the bus lifted and then tipped over. She fell on top of the bat, who squealed under her weight.

She felt the wolves' feet slamming the dirt, getting closer.

And she smelled the water.

Shoving Gaunt away from her, Nikaya headed for the doorway. But the bat hooked its wings around her like a hideous leather vest.

"Get off me!"

*Wind*, he screeched. *Wind now.*

She did not have the time to fight him off. Instead, she climbed out the door, noting the enormous claw marks scraped into the bare metal. *Impossible*, she thought. An arrow clattered against the bus. She spilled out with the bat gripping her, screeching in her ear about wind.

Nikaya crawled to the scent of water, toward a ravine that dipped into the river valley. So close. It called to her. Here, she could fly. She was young again. No ratwings here, no politics, no humans, no wolves. Only the sound of the water, the light on the surface. *The water flows. The water flows.*

She tumbled down the hill, feeling twigs breaking against her hide. A rock poked her ribs as she landed hard on a muddy bank. The water rushed so loud she thought it was coming from inside of her skull. With the bat still clinging to her, she rolled in with a splash. A cold shock braced her. She kicked her feet, flicked her tail. She became part of the river once more.

# CHAPTER 5

## ECHO

**F**ALKIRK KNELT IN the last row of the chapel, his elbows propped on the pew in front of him. The engines hummed through the floor. Near the front of the room, a human crew member in an aquamarine jumpsuit prostrated himself before an oil painting of the Prophet Michael, surrounded by a garish gold-plated frame adorned with flowers. The image depicted the Prophet in a white robe, reaching out his arms, thin rather than frail. A dark smudge stained the Prophet's chest where all the worshippers would touch the painting on their way out. It allowed them to connect with Michael and to remind themselves that although the spirit had left his body, his soul was free. The Prophet would remain with them even here, onboard the airship *Vesuvius*, nearly ten thousand feet above the ground.

The man got to his feet, wiped his eyes. He kissed his forefingers and then pressed them to the Prophet's heart. After whispering a few words, he headed for the door. Falkirk suddenly remembered the man's name: LeClerq, a Canadian who worked in engineering. A replacement for one of the people lost in the battle. The man nodded at Falkirk on his way out. There was no saluting in the chapel, not even for the captain.

Once the door closed, the humming grew louder. Falkirk's

knees ached, so he shifted to the pew. His blue jacket crinkled over his fur. The uniform had never fit him. It was meant for a human, much like his rank.

He began his prayer as he always did, by giving thanks to God and by promising to live by the example of the Prophet. And then he spoke to his family. Amelia and Yeager, his two pups. Sierra, his mate. He would see them again someday. For now, he could only speak to them. And he could try to listen for a response.

"Sierra, Amelia, Yeager—watch over me," he whispered. "I have not forgotten you."

He immediately felt guilty for saying that. Of course he had not forgotten them. He spoke their names every day. And yet he had lived without them almost as long as he had lived with them. Their presence dimmed over time. He could not stop it. Coming here, speaking their names, merely delayed the inevitable.

"I know you needed me and I wasn't there," he said. "And now I need you." He let out a tiny whimper, like a husky pup unable to find his mother after waking from a long sleep. It sounded so pathetic he almost expected the Prophet to roll his eyes in his painting.

"I'm still here," he said. "I'm still living this life without you. I didn't ask for it. But it's happening. It's pulling me away from you. I'll be a different person when we meet again. I'm so sorry for that. There are so many things I wish I could undo. And then—"

The door to the chapel opened. Harris, the petty officer from the bridge, stepped inside. He found Falkirk and nodded. Falkirk composed himself. His tail settled into place. He perked up his ears to show that he was a happy dog, a good boy. These humans liked that. It made them feel safe.

He turned to the painting and mouthed the words, "Watch over me." Then he stood, straightened his jacket, and headed for the door.

Harris waited until Falkirk reached the hallway before saluting. A bead of sweat rolled along his freckled temple.

"We're in range, sir," Harris said.

"Ahead of schedule," Falkirk said, without hiding his disappointment.

Moments later, Falkirk entered the sliding door to the bridge, where the enormous crescent-shaped window provided a view of the countryside at dawn. The ship faced west, away from the rising sun. The evergreens below took on a grayish color in the winter, with their crowns dabbed in snow. Near the window, on the lower tier of the bridge, Ensign Unoka gripped the wheel while his copilot marked the coordinates on a tablet.

With Harris beside him, Falkirk entered at the top tier, where the crew's stations formed a half circle along the walls. Ruiz, his first officer, leaned over the communications panel, pointing to something on the screen. The orangutan Bulan read out a series of numbers to him while she fiddled with her headset. Beside her, O'Neill signed an order on a clipboard and handed it to one of the crew members, who then returned to his engineering post. There, a schematic of the airship rotated on the monitor, its two balloons resembling a giant double-barrel shotgun. O'Neill swiveled in her chair toward her own computer. The screen lit her pale face, making her appear like a ghost lingering over the console.

Harris cleared his throat to get the attention of the young enlisted man near the door. The man flinched when he saw Falkirk. "Captain on the bridge!" he said.

Upon hearing this, Ruiz swiped a binder from one of the stations and rushed over to Falkirk. A gold oak leaf on the breast of his jacket indicated his recent promotion to lieutenant commander. At the ceremony, Ruiz had shared some of his father's homemade rum, brewed before the war. He did not have any himself, choosing instead to share the last of it with his new family. For all the difficulties of this assignment, moments like that reminded Falkirk that he could belong here if he stuck with it long enough.

"Good morning, sir," Ruiz said. "How did you sleep?"

"Better," Falkirk lied.

Ruiz led him to O'Neill's console, where the screen displayed an overhead view of the area. For the first time since the tentative peace talks with the Lupine Confederacy, the *Vesuvius* was flying over wolf country. Even stranger, the wolves themselves requested it, something that must have mystified the politicians in Hosanna. The clans wanted to track a separatist group, the Mudfoot, that was trying to undermine the peace deal. In the last month alone, the separatists had overrun two wolf dens and a garrison controlled by the bats. Only an eye in the sky could do the job. Falkirk could imagine the bitter argument that must have ensued before the pack elders decided to ask Hosanna for help.

Thousands of feet below stood the border village of Cadejo, a colony of dogs founded a few years earlier. The high-powered cameras zoomed in on the hovels and shacks constructed from shaved logs and pine branches. The screen briefly switched to an infrared image.

"No heat signatures detected," O'Neill said. "The town's empty."

"All right," Falkirk said. "That's what we expected. New heading. Sixteen degrees."

"Aye, sir," Ruiz said. He relayed the command to Unoka. The engines hummed in a new pitch as the ship spun slightly north to the outpost in the hills.

"We should arrive at Camp Echo in eight minutes," O'Neill said.

On the screen, Cadejo rotated as the ship changed course. Soon, the town slid offscreen, sinking into the endless forest.

"No bodies," Ruiz whispered to Falkirk.

Falkirk stopped himself from saying, "Not yet." Ruiz had served in the failed occupation of this territory. The day before, he had briefed the senior staff about his experience in Cadejo years ago, when the occupation collapsed. To provide cover for the retreat, Ruiz was part of an interspecies unit that spent several nights there fending off the enemy. Holding Cadejo was one of the few victories in the entire campaign, but it came at a heavy cost. The villagers blamed Hosanna for not responding sooner. During the withdrawal near the end of the conflict, an old sheepdog hurled a rock at Ruiz's unit, not even caring if they turned around and shot her.

"I'm going pull up some more of the town's records on my com," Falkirk said. "Keep me informed."

"Aye, sir."

Falkirk took his seat in the middle of the bridge. A hot mug of tea waited for him in the cupholder. Ignoring it, he tapped the tablet on the arm of his chair, and the screen glowed white. He scrolled through a menu to get to the Sanctuary Union archives. A search window appeared. Falkirk made it halfway through the word Cadejo before he stopped. All around him, the bridge grew quiet, save for a few mumbled orders and the thrum of the engines. He glanced at the crew members. They went about their tasks: typing on keyboards, plotting courses, tweaking dials, and pulling levers.

No one was watching.

Falkirk exited the archive screen and tapped the icon for the network—the crude newsfeed for the Sanctuary Union military. Three bulleted items appeared, the same ones from the previous few days. They were, in order, a vague report on the peace negotiations with the wolves, a story about an ongoing food riot in one of the canine neighborhoods, and a brief sentence about the progress of the maritime expedition.

AL-RIHLA REPORTED MISSING NORTHWEST OF GOLGOTHA.

He tapped it. A new window opened, yet it repeated the same sentence, with a warning in all caps that the information was classified. When Falkirk first saw it earlier that week, he immediately tried to contact someone at Tranquility who would know something. He still had friends in the mechanic's shop at headquarters—two rat brothers who saw everything, knew everyone. According to them, the *al-Rihla* had docked at Golgotha as scheduled. It maintained contact for a day or two. Then it sent a distress call and vanished. Falkirk did the math. The *al-Rihla* disappeared during the same unseasonable storm that grounded the *Vesuvius*. He remembered watching the airship from his apartment as it swayed in its dock at Liberty One Tower, resembling a kite ready to blow away in the wind. At that very moment, the more powerful end of the storm had swallowed the *al-Rihla*.

And with it, D'Arc. And now he wondered if she would hear him if he prayed to a painting of a dead prophet.

Despite an acute case of insomnia, Falkirk had kept his cool, even as Liberty One ordered them to stake out a position at the border. As usual, he embraced routine, diving into the tedium of inventory reports and briefing notes. He focused his mind. He gave thanks for what he had. No one suspected a thing.

Falkirk hunched over the tablet and tapped the refresh button. The page reloaded with no new information. He tapped it again. Same result. It might stay that way forever. This one sentence could be the final word for these people.

"Captain, we've located the refugees," Ruiz said behind him.

Falkirk closed out of the screen and stood. "Coordinates?"

"North thirty-nine point eleven, west zero seventy-five point forty-three," O'Neill said. "Logging it into the record."

At the console, Ruiz pointed to a trail cutting through the woods. A cluster of objects moved forward on it, each casting a small shadow.

"About seventy people," Ruiz said. "They're retreating to Camp Echo."

"Finally," Falkirk said.

When the latest insurrection broke out in wolf country, Hosanna openly admitted that they could not guarantee the town's safety. The dogs of Cadejo lived too close to the border, where the wolves often made runs into Sanctuary Union territory and then blamed a rival clan. The peace process depended on all of that coming to a halt. It required the clans to unite under a single banner. But without a formal agreement, a pack like the Mudfoot could simply cause trouble on a whim, and Cadejo would get caught in the middle. Better to hide them at the Camp Echo while the diplomats finished the job.

"We detected some other movement," Ruiz said. His finger brushed along the lower corner of the screen, where the forest grew thick. Falkirk leaned closer. A blurry object moved from one tree to another, taking cover behind the trunks.

"Did you see it?" Ruiz asked.

Another blur streaked through the trees before winking out. "Yes."

"Someone's definitely stalking them," Ruiz said.

"They're getting out just in time."

"Or they're headed for an ambush," Ruiz said. "That's how these bastards do it."

Falkirk glanced at him.

"Sorry, sir," Ruiz said. "It's just . . . I've seen it before."

"It's fine. Go on."

Ruiz placed his hands over the screen in a V shape. "The wolves are trying to flush them out. This cone will get tighter and tighter." As he took his hands away, two more yellow dots blinked on either side of the refugees. "See? The Mudfoot's been waiting for this."

Falkirk exhaled through his snout, almost as loud as a horse. He pictured the gruesome images Ruiz described in his reports. Known as the most arrogant and vicious clan, the Mudfoot often tormented their prey. They ran their enemy through the forest in circles, letting them believe they could still escape. Prisoners would watch while the wolves ate their comrades. The males would paint themselves in blood while the females wore the bones as jewels.

"Sir, we have established contact with Camp Echo," Bulan said. She motioned to the microphone.

"Camp Echo, this is Captain Falkirk of the *Vesuvius*. We've been ordered to monitor your position."

"*Vesuvius*, this is Major Quince," a voice growled. An old cat. Female. He imagined her with an eyepatch, or only one ear.

"Echo, do you have visual contact with the refugees?" Falkirk asked.

"Visual contact made. We have scouts escorting them to the gates."

"There are Mudfoot in the area. Hiding in the trees."

"We know," she said wearily. Everyone in the infantry liked to show their impatience with the *Vesuvius* when it sat pretty and safe in the sky, far away from danger.

"The wolves tested our defenses yesterday," Quince added.

"How did it go?"

"The defenses work."

Ruiz leaned in closer to Falkirk. "Sir," he whispered, "we could fire a few shots into the woods. Scare off the wolves."

"Too close to the civilians," Falkirk said.

Falkirk asked O'Neill to shift the camera toward the camp. The Mudfoot had been rampaging along the border for weeks, but Camp Echo posed their first major roadblock. The cement walls cast enormous shadows. Three turrets faced the woods, each nested with snipers. More soldiers waited in the main courtyard, along with an armored personnel carrier with a mounted machine gun.

Falkirk reached over O'Neill's shoulder and shifted the camera back to the refugees. He zoomed in as far as he could. He spotted a few wheelbarrows, a stretcher with a sick old dog on it, a couple of wheelchairs. On either side of them, the trees rustled. More blurry shapes zigzagged between the branches. A simple, unavoidable question entered Falkirk's mind. How many more? How many more lives would be snuffed out today while Falkirk floated above the clouds, safe but powerless? Tomorrow, this could be another bullet point on his tablet, right under the news about the *al-Rihla*, lost at sea.

His heart quickened.

"Camp Echo, do you still copy?"

"Yes. Go head, *Vesuvius*."

"Tell your escorts to run."

"Run?"

"Drop everything and run as fast as they can. They're almost there."

"Sir, do you see something?" Ruiz asked.

"No. That's the problem. I don't see a damn thing."

Quince yelled something incomprehensible. Some shouting followed.

The dots on the trail moved faster. They left their belongings in the dirt. The dogs carrying the stretcher fell behind, and two more helped them.

"Come on," Ruiz said through clenched teeth.

"Sir, I'm picking up gunfire," O'Neill said.

"I can hear it too," Bulan said. "It's coming from the turrets."

"Camp Echo, are you under attack?" Falkirk asked.

"No," Quince said. "We're the ones attacking."

The gate opened, just a small crack. The dogs formed a line, slipping inside the gap one at a time. As the refugees entered, four soldiers created a perimeter, each one aiming their rifle into the trees.

"Get in," Ruiz said.

The overhead image appeared on multiple consoles, resembling a simple puzzle that at last came together. Smoke drifted from the turrets, where the snipers fired at will. The microphone picked out random shouting, taunting. Humans, most likely, screaming at the faceless enemy.

"Here, doggy!"

"Come get some!"

"Sit, boy!"

A few more gunshots accompanied maniacal laughter. The bitter laugh of people who had witnessed too much death.

At last, the gate closed. A simple movement from this height, like a lever pivoting on a fulcrum. And with that, it was over. The danger passed, the tension drained. Falkirk breathed again. He pulled his bobbing tongue into his mouth before anyone could notice. He figured that the hearty Cadejo dogs would have laughed at him for being so nervous on their behalf.

"*Vesuvius*, this is Camp Echo. All refugees accounted for."

Ruiz silently pumped his fist.

"Glad to hear it, Echo," Falkirk said. "Reinforcements are on their way. With medical supplies."

"Do cigarettes count as medical?"

"You have to ask nicely," Falkirk said. "We'll be monitoring your position until they arrive."

"Thank you, Captain."

Onscreen, Falkirk noticed the objects strewn about the trail. He could only imagine what they were. Clothes. Tools. Children's toys. Maybe a relic or two from before the war, for those who had lived long enough. The same things that Falkirk left behind when he ran for his life.

"Major," Falkirk said. *"You're* the border now."

"No shit," Quince said.

NIGHT FELL, AND the *Vesuvius* continued to orbit Camp Echo. For over twelve hours, the spotters detected no movement among the trees. The crew performed admirably and on schedule, showing how far they had come in the last few months. Falkirk signed the typical orders, approved the inventory status, rubber stamped the shift schedules. But as the red night lights switched on, an uneasy calm settled over the ship. For weeks, the news in Hosanna had focused on the peace talks with the wolves. Now that the border had been more or less solidified, Hosanna still needed to hammer out some of the more tedious details, such as who would control the train line, and how they would share some of the disputed water supplies. And then these attacks erupted with no explanation, only a series of denials from the pack elders. The dogs in Hosanna who complained for years about unequal treatment found common cause with the Mudfoot. They staged protests; committed acts of vandalism and arson. To them, the separatists spoke the obvious truth: that Hosanna had become corrupt, a failed project with a veneer of holiness. To make matters worse, the Archon issued a statement reminding people that the Mudfoot were not indigenous to the region and that they had invaded in the wake of the war. But, as so many of the animals pointed out, the humans no longer enjoyed the privilege of declaring an entire species to be indigenous.

Like all military officers, Falkirk banned any open speculation among the crew. No point in salting old wounds with idle gossip. Orders like that rarely worked in practice, and even then, only for a short time. Falkirk hoped that he would not need to enforce it for much longer.

To take a break from the bridge, Falkirk gave the con to Ruiz and went to the archive, a windowless cell with a mainframe and a monitor. Bullet holes dimpled the metal door, a reminder of the firefight that had taken place in these corridors. Though he could access some of the records from the bridge, the information he really wanted remained classified. Every time the *Vesuvius* passed within range of Liberty One, the signal updated the archive. He entered his password and waited for the system to load.

"Good evening, Captain," the screen read. A search window opened. Falkirk entered "MUDFOOT."

Too restless to sit, Falkirk nudged the chair aside and scrolled through the search results. There were too many reports to count, all with long, bland titles. Summaries of skirmishes along the border. Recommendations for a swift attack on Mudfoot terrorist cells. A list of steps taken to "pacify" an area, which included corralling the deer, seizing the water supply, and leaving the most aggressive wolves with no choice but to launch a futile attack. After that, the Sanctuary Union troops could take out the remaining dens and declare victory. Falkirk flipped through dozens of photos of soldiers posing in front of caves, planting the flag of Hosanna, praying to the Prophet on the wolves' sacred ground. All of it was designed to break a people who were unbreakable.

A few overhead photos showed the valley after the Mudfoot staged an attack on a chemical plant. The attack had backfired. With the plant destroyed, the chemicals poisoned the entire valley. According to the neighboring pack leaders, the Mudfoot carried a new disease as a result of the pollution, and it made them even crazier than before. An enemy with nothing to lose, disowned by their own species.

During the war, Falkirk's brother Wendigo spoke of the wolves with admiration—as most dogs did. Wendigo thought of himself as a kindred spirit. One day, while stationed at an outpost somewhere near the old Canadian border, a pack of wolves tromped through, tracking escaped humans. Wendigo and Falkirk, being the youngest in the unit, were put on guard duty. After the wolves finished their howling for the evening, Wendigo left his post, tried to speak with them. It did not go well. Their leader told him that huskies served as glorified pets, nothing more. Wendigo almost got himself killed picking a fight with them. Falkirk intervened. He pulled his brother away and apologized, saving his brother's life. Three months later, Falkirk had to identify Wendigo's body following a shootout at an abandoned farm.

He cleared the screen and started with a new search, the one that he planned to do all along: "AL-RIHLA."

He found some schematics and a crew manifest. From there, he dug up a photo of the crew taken before D'Arc came on board. When he sorted the results by the date they were saved, the same bullet point from the morning waited at the top. And yet it had a new timestamp from only a few hours earlier. A folder icon indicated that a supplemental document had been attached.

Holding his breath, Falkirk clicked on the file. It was a communiqué from the SUS *Douglass*, a supply ship that traveled from the mainland to Golgotha.

> **COMMUNIQUÉ No. 197**
> Report:
> SUS *Somerset* arrived at Golgotha with
> full inventory.
> Ground crew loaded supplies to SUS
> *Douglass*. Dr. Hunt will accompany
> Alpha specimen to Hosanna.

"Alpha?" Falkirk said.

Some of the details of the supply run followed. And then:

Transmission received from SUS *al-Rihla*. Pursuing Alphas east. Intends to warn Hosanna of potential threat. Last coordinates: 37.98, -74.15. SUS *Douglass* will relay message when it is within range.

They'd picked D'Arc because of her knowledge of Alphas. Falkirk could still smell the earthy flavor of the ants that she taught him to ride. Strange, unnatural beasts, machinelike with their hinged legs and tough shells. Falkirk knew she was special then. It was why he told her she should go on the expedition. *Don't let anyone stop you*, he had told her. *Not even me.*

As he made it to the end of the communiqué, Falkirk's walkie-talkie crackled and whined.

"Captain, this is Ruiz, come in."

Falkirk cocked his fist, ready to slam it through the computer. Slowly, he lowered his hand and switched on the speaker. "Go ahead, Ruiz."

"You're needed on the bridge, sir."

It took all his willpower to muster a simple, emotionless response. "On my way."

Falkirk passed crew members in the halls—some heading to their bunks for the night, others beginning a new shift. When he arrived at the bridge, the doors opened, and the noise of a bustling crew greeted him. Bulan held her enormous hands over the headset so she could hear. "Camp Echo, this is *Vesuvius*, do you copy?" Beside her, a bleary-eyed O'Neill called out coordinates while tracing a line on her screen with her finger. At the front of the bridge, Unoka noted the coordinates in his logbook. Outside, a sliver of blue light painted the horizon. The stars clustered in the cloudless sky, almost as bright as an emerging sunrise.

Ruiz had assembled the senior staff in the middle of the night.

"Captain on deck," the foreman shouted.

Ruiz set his coffee at his workstation and ran his hand over his parted hair. "Sir, we're tracking a distress signal north of Camp Echo."

"North?" This was in Sanctuary Union territory. "Did Echo respond?"

"We can't reach Echo."

Falkirk glanced at Bulan. Holding the microphone over her mouth, she again requested a response from the camp. Falkirk could hear the empty static in her earpiece.

"What did the signal say?"

"It's garbled," Ruiz said. "They said something about an attack. Said they were on the run. Then it cut off."

"Someone's activated a beacon," O'Neill said. Falkirk watched over her shoulder: a blinking red dot on the map, north of the camp.

"Let's get a visual on Echo," Falkirk said.

"Bringing it up now," she said. She clicked on the window, expanded it. An infrared view washed over the image, leaving a pale blue background with small yellow shapes scattered about, indicating heat signatures. *Vesuvius* carried one of the only thermal scanners that could account for varied body temperatures across different species.

"Wolves haven't moved," Falkirk said, pointing to the forest.

"Our spotters didn't see anything," O'Neill said.

"How many people are in the camp?"

"About . . . a hundred, with the refugees."

"No. Look."

"Definitely not a hundred," Ruiz said. "Roll the footage back."

O'Neill clicked on the time scale and slid it toward the beginning of the recording, when the refugees entered the gates. As she did it, the yellow shapes inside the camp zipped about in reverse, ricocheting off the walls. In the surrounding forest, the wolves lurked nearby, close enough to watch, too far for the guard towers to pick them off.

O'Neill slid the time scale forward, speeding through the refugees forming a queue near the mess hall. "They're in line for food, I think," she said.

At the two-hour mark, the dogs congregated inside one of the flimsy sheds that Major Quince erected to house them. Falkirk pictured them taking stock of what little they still carried, placing all of it onto their pallets for the night. Not long after that, they formed a giant blob in the courtyard. A single yellow dot stood apart from the group—probably Quince welcoming them, making them feel safe with a pep talk.

They assembled in the temple. Falkirk always admired these places of worship out in the field. No frills, no gold piping or ornate fountains, no giant tapestries depicting the trials of Michael and the Warrior and the Mother. Instead, this place most likely had a single image of the Prophet, along with an altar and two candles nearly melted to the nub. The dogs of Cadejo gathered here, filtering into the pews in a perfect symmetrical shape. There they remained until, at the end of the ceremony, they filed past the painting of Michael. And then, one by one, some of the dots froze in place. Falkirk's tail lowered when he saw it. Slowly, the yellow faded to green, to blue, and then vanished. A handful of the dots streamed out of the building, scattering to the edges of the camp, where the guards still watched from their towers.

"The dogs murdered them," Ruiz said, his voice breaking. He swallowed.

"The refugees?" O'Neill said.

"They're *dogs*!" he snapped. "They're practically wolves themselves. They're working together."

Cringing, Bulan stopped hailing the camp and sucked her lips into her mouth. Her eyes rolled toward Falkirk.

"I'm sorry, sir," Ruiz said, suddenly gathering himself. "I know Cadejo. These dogs—these people—they're not on our side."

"Captain!" Bulan said. "We're getting the distress call again."

"Let's hear it," Falkirk said.

Bulan pressed a few buttons. The speaker clicked on in the middle of someone shouting.

". . . heading, uh, northwest . . . to the lookout point on Collins Hill . . ."

A woman's voice. Exhausted, breathing heavily. Footsteps nearby. Branches rustling. Random people speaking at once.

"This is *Vesuvius*, we hear you," Falkirk said.

"*Vesuvius!*" the woman said. "We need evac right away!"

"Who is this?"

"Right. I'm Koster. Second Lieutenant with MEDCOM—"

"I need the security code, Lieutenant."

She mumbled something, probably a swear word. "A-61 . . . 7962."

Falkirk motioned to Parish, one of the enlisted humans. Parish immediately typed the number into his database.

"What happened, Lieutenant?" Falkirk said.

"The refugees. They turned on us. Major Quince is dead. We barely made it out."

Ruiz stamped his foot when he heard it. A bead of sweat perched on his cheek.

Koster explained that she and the other doctors had run away from the camp. Four humans, plus a dog and a cat. She gave her coordinates, which O'Neill entered into the nav system. While Koster talked, Parish waved Ruiz over to his console.

"We're heading to Collins Hill. ETA . . . nine minutes?"

The bridge was silent.

"*Vesuvius?*" Koster shouted.

"Go ahead, Lieutenant."

"They're on our tail! We're dead if you don't come get us!"

One of her comrades shushed her. Someone else told them to keep moving.

"Sir," Ruiz said, "this security code is from yesterday."

Falkirk made a throat slashing gesture. Bulan cut the audio. "It's past midnight," Falkirk said. "They never got today's codes."

"There can be no evac without a proper code."

"Can anyone hear me?" Koster pleaded.

Falkirk snapped his fingers at Bulan. She switched the audio on again.

"Dr. Koster," Falkirk said. "What's the worst menu item at the academy cafeteria?"

It was an inside joke that only a former cadet would know.

Without missing a beat, Koster said: "I'm still alive, so I wouldn't know."

Falkirk nodded. "We're headed for your position at Collins Hill. You have nine minutes."

"Sir," Ruiz said. "The wolves could be baiting us. Like they baited Camp Echo."

"I know." Falkirk faced the front of the ship. "O'Neill, send the coordinates to Unoka's station."

"Aye, Captain."

"Take us to a thousand feet."

"Sir," Ruiz said again.

Falkirk kept going. "Parish and Warner, I want infrared view on both your screens. We need as many eyes as possible."

Ruiz stepped in front of Falkirk, his jaw clenched. "Sir," he whispered through his teeth. "We cannot do this. A lot of people are already dead."

"I know that!" Falkirk snapped. For the past twenty-four hours, he watched people die as numbers on a screen, as blips, as bullet points. He wasn't going to *listen* to it happen. After gathering himself, he noticed O'Neill sitting frozen, her hand hovering over her keyboard.

"I didn't tell you to stop!" Falkirk said. O'Neill snapped to life and began typing.

The ship lurched as Unoka accelerated toward Collins Hill. The familiar weightlessness expanded from Falkirk's feet to the inside of his chest.

"Please," Ruiz said. "You know this could be a trap."

Falkirk remembered Ruiz's stories of slaughter, of bodies clogging the very river they flew over, leaving a red cloud in the water that stretched for miles. Ruiz was the expert, but Falkirk had no choice but to ignore him. So he got closer to Ruiz until his breath made the human's nose twitch.

"I've given my orders," he whispered. "Carry them out, Lieutenant Commander."

Only the animals in the room heard it. Bulan, Ignatius the cat, Hiram the raccoon. They turned briefly from their stations, then returned to their work, pretending they heard nothing.

"I've seen what these people can do, Captain."

Falkirk saw in the man's eyes a palpable terror, boiling inside of him. His voice spoke from the past, from the war that their generation would never escape.

"*Vesuvius*," Koster's voice called out. "*Vesuvius*, we're approaching the coordinates. We can't see you."

Falkirk and Ruiz remained still.

"*Vesuvius!*"

At last, Ruiz backed away. Not out of acceptance, or even obedience. Out of fear. Ruiz was afraid of him because he was a dog. Falkirk could smell it.

"We are in stealth mode, Koster," Falkirk answered. "You won't see us until we're right on top of you."

"Sir, I've found them," O'Neill said. She pointed to more dots moving across the landscape. Three of them ran out in front. The other three clustered tightly together, in the rear, staggering along, most likely carrying a wounded comrade. Falkirk tracked the fleeing soldiers while O'Neill called out the altitude. Six thousand. Five thousand. Four thousand. ETA, two minutes. Outside, the mountain expanded, spiked with dormant trees and painted white with snow. To anyone on the ground, the ship in stealth mode passed over like a mirage, a ripple in the purple sky.

"Sir, I'm detecting movement on Collins Hill," Parish said.

"Confirmed," O'Neill said.

The display showed a dozen heat signatures, arrayed in a crescent shape. Snipers taking cover as the airship arrived.

Opening fire would give away their location, rendering stealth mode useless. Someone directly below them could have been waiting for them to do that very thing.

"This is a trap," Ruiz said. "This is what they do."

But those couldn't have been wolves on the mountain. They were too far across the border. No, those were dogs, most likely. Maybe a few huskies. More defectors from Sanctuary Union, putting in their lot with the Mudfoot.

Falkirk turned to the map screen again. "All right. Are there any clearings nearby?"

"No," Ruiz said.

"Any place where we can get low enough?"

"Sir, we've lost these people. We can't—"

A bright flash burst in the sky, high above the ridge of the mountain. A second later, the thudding sound hit the window.

"That came from Camp Echo," O'Neill said. "They're using the artillery."

"Can they see us?" someone shouted.

Another explosion detonated, lighting up the smoke that lingered from the first one.

"No," Falkirk said. "They're—"

He did not need to say it. The dogs at Camp Echo intended to fire blindly until they hit something.

"*Vesuvius!*" Koster screamed. "*Vesuvius,* do you copy? We are taking fire!"

While Koster shouted, Ruiz motioned to Bulan to lower the volume. "We have to abort," he muttered to Falkirk. "I will take over this ship, sir. I will throw you in the brig. Don't make me do it."

Something slammed into the ship from behind, tilting the deck. Several of the crew tumbled from their chairs. Falkirk and Ruiz crashed into one another, landing on their knees. Sirens and klaxons blared. A string of red lights blinked. Those crew members who could reach their consoles shouted out the damage reports.

"Starboard engine number two is out!"

"The balloon is intact!"

"Sir," O'Neill said, "they can see us!"

Falkirk pictured it: a ball of fire hovering over the forest. A perfect target.

The ship rolled again, leveling out. Falkirk caught Ruiz staring at him. The man's hand stiffened into a claw over his sidearm.

"*Vesuvius!*" Koster screamed. "*Vesuvius!*"

"Pull us up, Unoka," Falkirk said.

"Aye, sir."

Falkirk stood. He refused to look at Ruiz. Instead, he pointed at Bulan. She pursed her lips, knowing full well what he needed to say.

"Dr. Koster," he said. "We have to return to our cruising altitude."

No response. Only the wind.

"Dr. Koster—"

Falkirk swore that he could hear footsteps for a moment. The audio cut off abruptly. The bridge fell silent.

"Full damage assessment, as soon as you can get it," Falkirk said.

He sat in his chair. Behind him, the crew called out the altitude and the coordinates. They relayed information from engineering. They carried on.

Falkirk slumped into the seat and stared out the window. Beside him, the tablet screen lit up with the news feed. The *al-Rihla* remained at the top of the list. Falkirk switched it off.

# PART II

# HELL

# CHAPTER 6

## A BEAUTIFUL SECRET

**T**HE WOLVES ARRIVED at the crater as dawn broke and the shadows stretched from the trees like giant fingers digging into the snow. The Cadejo dogs got there first. Dozens of them, with more on the way, so they said. On all fours—most likely for the first time since joining the Mudfoot—they swirled around the ship's engine, celebrating this latest victory in the uprising against Hosanna. Marching shoulder to shoulder, the dogs moved clockwise around the charred debris, howling their lungs out in a poor imitation of the wolves.

At the center of the whirlpool of tails and fur was the engine, resembling a granite boulder. Only one of its three blades remained attached. The metal was frayed at its base, showing where it had been sheared from its moorings.

Mercy watched from the main gate of Camp Echo. Beside her, Urna trembled at the sight. The rest of Mercy's inner circle stood in silence nearby. The siblings Mag and Quick. Carsa, the older female, scarred and gray. Creek, the orphan with the broken tail. They each placed a paw on Mercy, escorting her toward the crowd without discouraging the revelry. Creek extended a protective arm over Mercy's pregnant belly to keep the excited dogs away.

The Mudfoot had never before seen an object like this engine. Its hulking presence proved how worthless a campfire story could be. No one in her pack possessed the words to describe this massive machine that fell from the clouds.

Mercy's arrival sent the dogs into a frenzy. A strange chant began, with a word that Mercy did not recognize. "Zag-ga! Zag-ga! Zag-ga!" Several other dogs tried to quiet the loudest, to no avail.

"What this is?" Mercy asked.

"Zagga," Carsa said. "A game. To celebrate."

Though the largest dogs shouted the loudest, the ringleader was a terrier named Wicket, who did not expect to play himself, being too small. Nevertheless, he would oversee the gambling that always accompanied the game. With no money to bet, the spectators could wager the stolen booty from Camp Echo, from binoculars to clothes to helmets. After the bets were placed, the dogs ignited fire pits at the perimeter of the playing field, where they barbecued the remains of their fallen enemy. After weeks of skulking through the hills, staging secret attacks, they could at last celebrate in the open.

Everyone turned to Mercy to make a decision. They cleared a path to the engine and then dropped to their front paws in deference, their snouts on the ground. Some of them whimpered. A few others prayed. One of them, a younger mutt, stole a quick sniff of Mercy's tail. None of them smelled right to her. They carried the scent of metal and mortar, plastic and soap. What little they knew of the wolves came from human propaganda. Many of them had painted their faces red, yellow, bright green—a privilege that was typically reserved for the elite marauders of certain clans. Still, these dogs knew what the Sanctuary Union had done to the Mudfoot. They were Mercy's brothers and sisters now, even if they still thought of themselves as her children.

Walking on two legs, Mercy pictured herself as Wex,

pompously marching about his subjects, daring them to question his rituals. Slipping into that role proved so easy that it frightened her. It certainly frightened Urna, who still spoke of Wex as if he'd survived and lurked in the forest, ready to punish them all. Meanwhile, the newest members of the Mudfoot rebellion promised to keep to the "old ways" that the clan preserved—even if Mercy violated them herself when it suited her, and even if she worked with humans. Strangely, doing so made her stronger with these people. How quickly the wolves forgot the bonds of species when given a chance to finally break free of their fate. Wex understood this aspect of power, this marriage of despair, wishful thinking, and tribalism. If she wanted to survive, Mercy needed to master it herself.

"Play your game," she said.

"Mercy!" one of the older dogs yelled, his mouth filled with rotting teeth. "Mercy the Skypiercer!" A shout arose, then a long discordant howl.

"Mercy, the Champion of Camp Echo!"

"Mercy the Merciful!"

"Mercy the Merciless!"

These defectors from Hosanna had traveled so far, left behind their lives as pets. They served the Mudfoot well, sealing off the escape routes and seizing a vital enemy stronghold. Let them have a brief moment of joy before the wilderness forced them to adapt or die.

And besides, she thought, once they found out they came all this way to serve a barren matriarch, a pack without a future, none of this would matter anyway.

AS THE DOGS prepared, Carsa explained to her the history of zagga, what little she knew. A year earlier, Hosanna banned the game, declaring it too dangerous. While the former pets supported the ban, the pothounds and half-wilds regarded it as yet another attack on their ways. As a result, spontaneous games broke out in parking lots, in fields, anywhere with open space.

The fallen engine served as the central point on the playing field, known as the pivot. From there, the dogs placed markers to indicate the halos, the three concentric circles spreading outward from the center. The most important piece was the femur. Mercy asked Carsa what that meant. "It really is a femur," Carsa said. "A leg bone." With so many dead bodies at nearby Camp Echo, she did not need to ask where they got it.

The game started with the strongest dogs, maybe fifteen or so, circling the engine on all fours, howling. The femur leaned against the propeller, still pink and slick from its recent extraction. After three revolutions around the pivot, the dogs charged for the bone, their paws kicking away the dirt and snow. Briefly, the femur lifted over the scrum, then disappeared. Whoever grabbed it lay at the bottom of the pile, trampled.

Mag whispered something to the other wolves. Creek nodded. Mercy could tell that they did not approve. This game seemed like a waste of energy. And yet the dog spectators roared each time the femur changed possession.

The scrum shifted like a gibbering, shambling monster leaving drunken tracks in the snow. Until, at last, one of the dogs shot from the crowd and dashed along the widest halo. The dogs scattered. Some gave chase, while the others went in the other direction, hoping to cut off the runner's escape. The carrier, a brown shepherd with huge pointy ears, pulled away from the pack, only to find more standing in his way. Once a player had possession, the goal was to complete a full revolution around the pivot. The first player to circle the pivot ten times would win the round, and the two inner halos—the center of the violence— were worth double and triple score. This shepherd took the second halo, where he collided with his opponents. A vicious crack sent one of the defenders skidding through the snow.

The dog kept going, his teeth digging into the bone. He had so much momentum that his opponents could only nip at him as he charged by. By the time he reached a score of ten, he had a set of bloody gashes cut into his ribs. His footprints left a crimson trail behind him, and his nose glistened red.

The victor trotted over to Mercy. Carsa and Creek immediately rose to their hind legs to shield her. Ignoring them, the dog dropped the bone, a gift for the new leader. And the chanting began again.

*Mercy the Merciful.*

*No peace! No peace! No peace!*

Mercy felt Urna's warmth beside her. "Please, stop this," Urna said, her timid voice cracking. The words made sense when strung together, and yet Mercy knew she could not heed them. Not with this horde of followers preparing to kill for her.

While Wicket collected his winnings, the Cadejo dogs prepared for another round. Urna relaxed a little, but Mercy could still sense her unease. Urna hardly blinked, and her breathing would not slow down. Mercy had to accept that she could not fix her sister. She could not make Urna realize that she was no longer the omega, and never needed to act like one again.

Meanwhile, the spectators passed around their liquor and sang shanties from the war. They toasted Mercy and the battles to come. While the zagga matches continued, a few of them drifted into the woods to fuck. Some of them must have walked for miles through the cold to get here, following nothing but rumors and hope. For years, they had harbored a dread in their hearts that their former masters would turn on them now that the Colony had fallen. Even if they died tomorrow, this would all be worth it.

A great cry rose up as another troop of haggard dogs arrived at the camp, the third in as many days. The refugees from Hosanna appeared the same to Mercy: short snout, slightly floppy ears. The females showed off their swollen nipples as a badge of honor to prove how many pups they'd bred. The males often had missing eyes, broken tails, torn ears.

The wolves led the new recruits to Mercy. Only six this time, a family. But more were coming. Always more. As usual, Mercy's closest wolves closed ranks around her in case Hosanna had sent an assassin. The newly arrived dogs groveled on all fours. The lead male went first, prostrating himself, rolling over to expose his belly. His mate and cousins followed suit. Mercy sniffed them, rubbing her fur against theirs. She let the pup nip at her tail until the mother told the child to stop. No wasteful words spoken, no preening. Just the solidarity bred into their kind through years of surviving the cold, ever since the First Winter.

The male dog introduced himself as Pike, and his mate as Fiona. He said that they came to see the wolf who ruled over humans. The great queen who dared to—

"I am no queen," Mercy said.

Chastened, Pike glanced at Fiona. Before he could apologize, the zagga pit suddenly halted. A silence spread from the center of the ring. Augur and his humans had returned from their scouting mission. The other wolves gave them space as they entered. Though no one would admit it, Augur and his comrades frightened them. At first, it was for their ability to live in the wild. But now it was because they had been right about everything—about the battles, about the uprising. The wolves may have worshipped the future, but when a human handed it to them, their first instinct was to run.

Mercy cut the meeting short. "You welcome here," she told Pike. "Rest now. Hard days ahead."

She left them and headed for Augur. Behind her, she heard Carsa scolding the new dogs for the queen remark. "She is not your, your . . . your *Ar*-chon!"

When Mercy got close enough to Augur, she rose to her hind legs. The human stopped.

"I've found it," he said. "We leave in the morning."

Mercy gestured to the people surrounding them. The pack had never supported so many, and now it had become an army. "We can still stop this," she said, a line she had rehearsed many times while waiting for him to return.

"You saw what we did last night," he said. "You know I'm telling the truth. There's no going back."

"They know," she said, holding her hands over her belly. "They *must* know. I am taking my sister. We must run. No other way."

If Augur really considered himself a kind of half-wolf, then he knew the trouble she courted by taking a child and claiming it as her own. While adoption was a common practice, claiming a blood line when none existed violated both spoken codes and their own deeply ingrained instincts. Someone would find out eventually, if they did not know already.

"And then what?" Augur said. "By then we will have kept our promises. We will have saved both our peoples. And they will choose to believe rather than admit they were wrong."

Mercy noticed Creek edging closer. Mercy bared her teeth, and the young one rejoined the others.

"Tomorrow," Augur said, "when we find what we're looking for, all your questions will be answered."

A trio of dogs began pounding on a drum they had constructed out of a hollow log. A strange dance began with more howling and yipping. One of the male wolves tried to get Urna to dance with him. But she would not budge, choosing instead to stay close to her sister.

Mercy realized she could live with disappointing these people—these defectors and exiles. But when Urna discovered the truth, it would rip Mercy's heart out. That left her little choice but to follow this human further into some new Damnable, something far beyond her control.

. . .

DAWN BROKE OVER the hills. The stink of alcohol, rotting bones, and shit hung over Camp Echo. Many of the wolves woke from the spots in the camp where they passed out. Most of them formed a circle around the remnants of the bonfire, the warmth of their bodies melting a divot in the snow. One of the wolves—a loner banished from a neighboring pack—lay slumped over the latrine. A few of the groggy ones snorted as they awakened, some of them clearly unsure of how they got there. In another hour, the sun would rise over the spiked walls of the fort, waking the remaining stragglers, a bright reminder of the hard days that awaited them.

At the main gate, Mercy stood on four paws while two of the humans fitted a pack onto her shoulders. Even when not fully upright, Mercy stood almost as tall as the human. Over the last few days, she finally learned their names—or at least, the names Augur called them. They never spoke themselves, choosing to respond only with hand signs or body language. If they were merely pretending to communicate like wolves, they had not let their mask slip this entire time.

Urna paced among the sleeping bodies, watching them nervously. Mercy tried to ignore her, yet she felt her presence like a thorn lodged in her skin.

Nearby, Augur strapped on his own rucksack made of salvaged canvas and leather belts. When the woman, Preeta, tried to shift the folds of Mercy's overcoat, the wolf growled at her. She did not want her belly exposed. Preeta glanced at Augur, who waved his hand, telling her to let it go.

Mercy caught Augur's attention and nodded toward the mountains, letting out a little whine. All of it together meant, *How long will we be gone?*

Augur twirled his index finger three times to indicate the

orbit of the moon. Three days. A lifetime. If anyone in the camp had figured out her secret, they would have plenty of time to plot against her.

By snapping her fingers, Preeta signaled to Augur that the backpack was secure. Her partner, a man named Friar, crossed his arms over his chest. Mercy assumed that it meant the same thing, more or less. With that, Augur motioned to the wolves who guarded the gate. As they opened it, the sunlight poured into the courtyard. Everyone squinted. Mercy scanned the crowd for Urna and found her hiding behind a larger dog. When Mercy called her over with a quick bark, Urna nearly knocked one of the hungover wolves to the ground as she zipped across the courtyard.

Urna skidded to a halt, pawed the earth, and growled meekly. *Take me with you?*

*No*, Mercy barked.

Urna sniffed at Mercy's belly. Mercy gently batted her away.

*You stay*, Urna whined. *Pups coming soon. Stay, rest.*

Mercy wagged her tail and gave a quick bark. *Wait here.* Urna did not like it. In a show of dominance, Mercy stood close to Urna and flopped her chin on the back of her sister's neck.

"I will howl when I'm close," Mercy whispered in the human language. "If I give Dregger's call, you run."

Dregger once taught them a special howl that started with a loud whooping sound and died out in a long hiss. Urna still remembered it. "I run," she said, trembling. "Then *we* run? Together?"

Mercy barked *yes*. She pulled away quickly. Along with the three humans, she set foot on the trail leading into the woods. The gate closed behind her. A few of the guards let out a cry. It meant safe journey. Before long, the entire camp hummed with the sound. Amid the noise, she could not make out Urna's voice.

•  •  •

THEY HEADED SOUTHWEST, close to the border with the Sloat clan. Like the Mudfoot, the Sloat settled the area after the humans retreated inland. Dregger once settled a dispute with them by stringing the Sloat's leader to a pike, crucified but still breathing. It was a fate worse than death since no wolf could last long as leader after enduring that kind of humiliation. After that, the Sloat respected the border between their territories. They dared not cross it, even after the flood. The cruel fate of it always bothered Mercy. If the rivulets had curved one way instead of the other, the Damnable would have wiped out the Sloat, and the Mudfoot would have become more powerful than ever. All this talk of lopsided peace treaties and abandoning the old ways would never have started.

On a crumbling highway, the humans formed a triangle around Mercy, with two on the side and one guarding the rear. Putting Mercy at the front allowed her to notice the hint of salt in the air before the others. She had never seen the ocean before. Dregger once told her stories of fine sand, stiff grass, wind, rhythmic waves. And the best part, he said, was the endless expanse of blue wrapping around the entire world, leading to new lands that she could see only in her dreams.

Silently, the humans took note of the few lingering markers of the former world: downed light poles, faded highway signs, billboards with chipped paint. Friar held out his fist, a signal to stop. He knelt and rubbed his hand over a series of indentations in the ground, like tire tracks, only much larger and deeper. Augur extended both arms to indicate an object of massive size. Then he extended his fist and opened his hand, making a puffing sound with his mouth. A tank, he said—Mercy had picked up enough of their sign language to translate. As Augur went on, Preeta backed away to take in the width of the tracks. In a panic, she asked if there was a tank nearby. Augur replied by digging out a clump of dirt from the tracks to show her that they were years old, maybe a decade. To illustrate the point, he crumbled the dirt and let the dust drift away in the breeze.

They plodded on as the road narrowed and the grass grew high on each side, and a sound like hissing wind grew louder. Above, the moon made an early appearance, forming half a snowball amid the clouds. As they approached a hill, the hissing came with a gentle crash each time, much like the way Dregger had described it. He even mimicked the noise for her: *puch-shhhhhhh*. She almost expected him to appear on the hill to tell her she'd passed some test, that she'd proved herself worthy, that all of this had happened for a reason.

The wind rippled her fur as she reached the top, and the entire world opened before her: a bluish-gray landscape blooming with foam, the sand a blinding white. Patches of brown grass stubbornly poked through the dunes. Far in the distance, a pair of seagulls tilted in the sky, occasionally dropping toward the water before ascending once more. Mercy stepped off the road and dug her paws into the cold sand. The tiny pebbles filtered through the gaps in her toes.

Augur motioned to the others, drawing an imaginary square around the spot where they stood. Friar dropped his rucksack and pulled out a plastic tarp while Preeta got to work hammering spikes in the sand. Mercy unstrapped her bag and opened it. The smell of smoked meat drifted out. The cooks insisted that she take an extra share—one for her, one for her litter. She could not refuse.

Augur sipped water from a leather bladder, most likely extracted from a cow, or maybe a bison. As he did when she first met him, the human wore a serene expression. One of the Cadejo dogs said he resembled a sleeping human baby, even while awake. The rest referred to him as some kind of angel. And why not? Everything he predicted had come to pass, and thus he had no reason to show fear or anger. The outposts had fallen, the territory had expanded. More canines joined the cause.

"We lit the fires," he told her after they had subdued the bats. He even let some of them escape. He wanted Hosanna to know what was coming. He wanted them to hear it from desperate, panicked refugees. Let the rumor spread, like the Damnable. Let the elders point fingers. Let them drive away more canines from Hosanna and into the wilderness where they belonged.

Augur noticed Mercy panting and offered her some water. He tilted the bladder into her mouth as she drank.

"What now?" she said.

"We wait." He pointed to a spot on the beach where two waves merged and then gently crashed, the water hissing as it receded. "Right there," he said. "There, he arrives."

"You have seen this?"

"I was *there*."

"*When?*" Mercy asked.

"Tomorrow."

Friar and Preeta finished with the tent. A simple lean-to, it jutted from the sand dune and fluttered in the wind.

"Let's get warm," Augur said. He signaled to Friar. Mercy made out a few of the words, something about a "big house." Friar signed in response: *big house for a queen*. Mercy got it now: Augur referred to their meager tent as a castle. She had little experience with humor, and no patience with this talk of her as a monarch. But Friar and Preeta both put their hands out, palm down, as if resting them on the arms of a chair.

"Throne," Augur translated. Then he placed the fingers of one hand against his mouth, blew outward, and spread the fingers outward. "Warm," he said.

No matter her misgivings, this tent provided the only refuge in this desolate place. She hurried inside, carrying her bag of jerky with her mouth. The humans shuffled in beside her, sitting shoulder to shoulder to conserve the heat. She had seen them do this before. Unlike the wolves, the humans draped themselves over one another with no regard to rank and without posturing. As Augur closed the flaps of the entrance, Mercy lay on her side so that the humans could lean against her fur like her own pups used to do on the coldest days. She allowed herself a few moments to draw some pleasure from it. The consequences of her decisions would wait.

THE OTHERWISE SILENT humans did a strange thing when packed tightly like this. Eyes closed, Preeta and Friar leaned close together and hummed in unison, a song with no words that vibrated through their ribcages. Suddenly, their features softened, and Mercy saw them for the children they were, barely old enough to mate. Though a lifetime of hiding from predators taught them the value of silence, they could not resist this ritual, any more than the wolves could do without their nightly songs. It was like Augur said. They were keepers of the forest, doomed and blessed at the same time.

Augur busied himself with stitching a seam on his pants. While he worked, he swayed to their voices, occasionally bobbing his head when the song synched with the waves crashing. At one point, he raised his two fingers and pulled the flap open slightly, allowing a razor-sharp slice of wind into the tent. The sky had turned black and the sand white, and the moon glowed at half full.

It did not feel right to be relaxing here with these humans. Far away, the Damnable continued to spread, and to compensate, the Mudfoot triggered a war they could not win, recruiting mouths they could not feed. Still, Mercy's eyelids grew too heavy to lift.

She opened them wide again when, sometime later, the thick

scent of a deer mingled with the salty smell of the ocean. The animal must have relieved itself nearby. As Dregger used to say, the deer was so close you could count the ticks. Mercy's ears pointed; her blood pumped. A primal urge to peel flesh from bone overtook her. She felt so alive, and yet ready to die.

"Deer," Augur said.

"You smell it?" Mercy asked.

"No. But I knew it would be here."

Augur nudged his companions. Their eyes flickered open, and the song died out.

He gestured to them. They nodded. "It's time for you to see what we see," he said.

Preeta and Friar stared at her, their pupils enormous and black in the dark. Augur tucked his hand into his coat and pulled out a silver canteen, barely larger than his palm. As he unscrewed the top, Mercy could not help herself. She leaned closer and sniffed. Her ears curiously pointed up. *What is it?*

"The future," he said, holding it closer. With the cap off, the canister released a greasy smell, like fish. She inhaled, recalling the first time she bit into a fish, having found it flopping beside a river. Her fangs sunk into the soft gills, and the blood ran thick and cold into her mouth, oily and metallic. She could taste it again, here in this stuffy tent. And then she felt herself whisked forward several years from that moment, running along a trail in the forest with Herc and Rove chasing her, yipping and giggling, the branches and twigs snapping as she tore through them. A weightlessness lifted her. She saw her younger self and she saw through her younger eyes, both at the same time.

Time moved forward yet again to the days after Wex took command of the pack, when a murder of crows perched on Dregger's decapitated body and devoured it over the course of two days. Like a single, gangly monster, their black wings flapped while their beaks poked and pulled at the flesh, their shiny black eyes never focusing on anything in particular as they ate. She hated them even more than she hated Wex in that moment, and it churned inside of her, hardening her mind, sealing off her heart, and the taste of the fish entered her mouth again, choking her until she couldn't breathe—

She opened her eyes to find her head resting in the sand, outside of the tent.

Beside her, Augur pressed his temples with his palms. A vein inflated on his forehead. She placed a paw on his lap to show that that she sensed his pain.

"I'm all right," he said. "It's just . . . when I share this gift of sight with someone, it interferes with what I see. It creates new paths. New possibilities. My mind needs to readjust."

"We stop, then," she said.

"No," he said. "I need you to see this."

She rested her chin in the sand and crossed her paws over her snout. Above, the stars spun slowly, leaving white streaks through the blackness. Slowly, with each crash of the waves, the feeling of being pushed and pulled subsided, leaving her light and free, like a pup waking from a bad dream.

"We call it the rahvek," Augur said. "This is the last of it until we can get more. I give some to you so you can see through our eyes. Watch."

He tilted the canister until a tiny drop of greenish gel emerged at the spout. "Not too much. A single drop is all it takes." He dabbed the sticky drop onto his finger and plugged the finger in his mouth. As soon as it touched his tongue, his eyes floated shut. He lingered like that for a moment before taking a deep breath through his nostrils. He slowly pulled his finger out.

"What it do?" Mercy asked, wincing at her terrible grammar. "What *does* it *do*?"

"It makes our minds work the way they're supposed to," he said. "Before the human ways polluted us. Made us weak."

He offered it to her. Another viscous drop appeared at the end of the spout, like milk hanging from a nipple. She hesitated.

"A gift from the Queen," he said. "If you're willing to take it."

He knew how to speak to a wolf. Challenging her bravery felt like a claw raking her back. And besides, she saw what this substance could do. She saw Augur heal within hours from a horrible slash to the face. She saw him predict troop advances and retreats. He spoke of the future as if it had already happened. She wanted to go there with him.

Mercy stuck out her tongue and licked the spout. The drop hung heavy and cold, numbing her mouth. The fishy taste again. And then a ringing in her ears. A floating sensation that lifted her from the sand, into the bitter wind. The sky flickered as the sun and moon raced across it, first forward, then backward, then forward again. Somewhere far off in the water, a voice skittered across the surface.

"Stay this time," Augur said. "Focus. Focus."

She blinked, and Augur stood a full foot shorter. His hair became shinier, his face even smoother than before. A young boy, already a hunter, his muscles wiry and taut, his arms too long for his body, ready to pack on new muscle with each passing winter that he survived.

"What do you see?" the boy asked.

She could not answer.

"The past, or the future?" he said.

"Past."

The boy's face dropped. "You are not ready."

"No. I ready. Show me."

"Think of what you must do for your people to survive. Then you might have a chance."

She bit down so hard that her teeth felt like they could break. How dare he ask this of her? Had she not been thinking of this very thing every waking hour, as well as in her dreams? As the anger smoldered inside of her, a brief flash of a trail blinked in her mind. It happened again, this time more distinct: a row of tall, brittle grass on either side. She reached for the trail, trying to hold it still.

"You see it?" Augur said.

"I smell it," she said.

"Good."

And though she had never been to this place, she knew the way. She knew the way because she walked it before—no, she was *going* to walk it. She existed in two places at once now: here on the beach, and there, farther inland, where the grass grew tall enough to hide a deer.

"You see it," Augur said.

Mercy responded by bounding across the beach. The sand made a whispering sound each time her feet hit the earth. Augur trailed behind her, his footsteps getting softer as she put more distance between them.

She saw the moment that would take place in seconds: a deer, huddled against a rusted chain-link fence, limping on an injured leg. Mercy ran across the road, through the overgrown lawns of a row of abandoned houses, their roofs having collapsed long ago, the windows smashed in, the weeds creeping along the bricks. This deer thought he could hide among these ruins. He thought that he could somehow see the future and control it, bend it. Like the stag who taunted Mercy on the day her former life ended. *No more hunt. And no more Muddy Feet.* She thought she was free that day. But this was true freedom, this gift from hell.

She made it to the fence first. Here, the links had been cut so that a deer could squeeze through at the first sign of trouble. With her belly brushing the dry grass, Mercy lay flat against the bottom of the fence, a mere shadow. She felt the uneven juddering of the earth as the deer approached. A male, favoring his right front leg. No visible brands, no war paint, no sharpened horns. That made him most likely a scout from the Osken herd, separated from his partner—they always traveled in pairs. His eyes glowed with the scant light, and his nostrils flared when he picked up the scent of a predator. Unaware of her presence, he walked straight toward Mercy. When he got within striking distance, she held still.

The stag's ears twitched. The head turned, and along with it the enormous antlers. Mercy could hear clumsy human footsteps. In a panic, the deer ran toward the hole, only to find Mercy crouching, blocking the way. The deer froze. He wore the blank stare that marked his people when death found them. Eyes like dewdrops, mouth slightly open. A species meant to serve as food.

Augur arrived, out of breath, with vapor steaming from his nose and mouth. The deer could have trampled him. But his presence in the darkness, working alongside a wolf, made the stag reconsider.

"You can live," Mercy said.

The deer's head flicked toward her.

"Go," she said. "Tell your people. We are watching."

Augur must have seen this coming as well. *A generous wolf is a strong wolf.*

Silently, the deer slinked through the gap in the fence. A sharp edge cut a red line into his skin. Mercy smelled it, swallowed, resisted the urge to give chase. Once the deer pulled free, he bounced off into the darkness. The breeze carried the scent of blood away.

Mercy could still sense fear. And awe. Let them have both. Let everyone who stood in her way have both.

MERCY DID NOT remember the sun rising dull and cold over the ruined houses, shrouded in wispy clouds. Nor did she recall choosing to walk beside Augur along the beach. Her mind descended from the heights it reached the night before. The fishy taste lingered on her tongue, now dry from the salty winds. She waited for the vision of the deer to return and felt a deep void in her chest when she realized that she was trapped in the present once more.

They trudged along, leaving wet tracks in the sand, Augur's leather boots imprinting one foot at a time, Mercy's paws leaving two. Like a human and his pet, she supposed. Though she knew now that he did not see it that way. A keeper of the forest, like her. Now closer to her than Dregger or Wex. Or Urna.

Far behind them, giving space and keeping watch, Preeta and Friar stood like two dolls along the shoreline.

"I want to see more," Mercy said.

"I know," Augur said. "I said the same thing, the first time I tried it."

She recalled the vision of Augur as a child. "When you try it?"

The way he gazed out over the water, she knew that the question forced him to recall a dark time. His own Damnable.

"We were orphans, all of us," he said. "Our parents worked on an animal preserve."

"Preserve," she said.

"A place where good humans kept the animals safe. From bad humans."

Her ears sagged, a sign that she could hardly believe that such a place existed. Augur had already told her that his people had a deep connection with wolves, that they lived alongside them, but had never gone into much detail. Now he told her everything, as much as she could understand. When he explained that his parents studied the wolves, she assumed he meant that they probed the wolves for a weakness, so they could attack. But no, his parents were part of a team of scientists trying to repopulate the area with new wolves nearly a century after humans had hunted the last one to extinction. The scientists even named the wolves the Toqwa pack, a word meaning rebirth.

And one day, like everywhere else, the animals changed.

"But the wolves refused to follow the Queen's orders," Augur said. "So the Alphas came to kill us all. Quarantine, they called it. I was nine years old."

Most of the adult humans died in the raid. The Toqwa took the children into the forest. They raised them. Taught them to survive. "This is the way it was meant to be," Augur said. "It was only after humans were corrupted that they viewed wolves as the enemy."

Whenever the Toqwa wolves died, a human would take their pelt. It served as a disguise and a shield against the elements. But really, the pelts symbolized the bond between the species. They represented the only way forward. Something the humans and their pets in Hosanna would never understand.

"What happened?" she asked.

"Special Operations," he said. "Hosanna's secret police. They raided our den. Hired mercenaries to do it. Bears. Only a few of us escaped."

For the first time, he told Mercy that he once had a mate, a woman named Yora who grew up on the preserve with him. She carried their daughter, Sherin, in her belly. A bullet meant for Augur struck Yora in the chest, filling her insides with blood.

His voice trailed off. She brushed her cheek against his hand to let him know that he was not alone. Though he was no wolf, he had suffered, as she had. He had shivered in the cold, he huddled with his people for warmth, he hardened his heart into a block of ice in order to survive.

"Soon after that . . . we found something," he said.

Earlier that year, the remaining Toqwa came across the wreckage of the humans' airship, the *Upheaval*. It was a smoking mass of twisted metal. The charred balloon lay crumpled like a collapsed lung, its reflective surface still shiny. They found one of the crew still alive, trying desperately to carry as many of the rahvek canisters as he could. He begged for his life. He promised that the canisters would bestow immense power upon whoever possessed them. The rahvek was a dirty secret Hosanna kept, harvested from the Colony. For all the contempt the humans held for the ants, they wanted the Queen's knowledge at any cost. The human demonstrated the rahvek's power by giving some to Yora. It revived her. Then Augur himself tried it.

"What I saw, that first time," he said. "It was beautiful. The land at peace. Hosanna fallen silent. And a mighty wolf pack, roaming the hills, taking their rightful place as rulers of this world."

That gaze over the water again. His vision still remained too far in the future.

"Your mate?" she asked.

"We gave her a stronger dose. Hoped it would heal her. It failed. We knew then that the chemical can be harmful if taken too quickly. There will come a day when I will no longer be able to use the rahvek. You saw last night how dangerous it can be."

"Yes."

"Still, we managed to save Sherin. For now."

"For now?"

"Sherin will not survive the winter," he said. "Seeing her die is the price I paid for using the rahvek."

Mercy lowered her tail.

"It's all right," Augur said. "She is in pain. Her suffering will end. As for Yora: she saw the day promised to us. To all keepers of the forest. You will too."

They approached a hill. The waves crashed against it, sending rivulets of foamy water through the cracks in the rock. As the water receded with a great hissing sound, Mercy heard a high-pitched sound. A squeal. She raced to the hill, clambering up the soaked boulders. On the other side, a fresh set of tracks had shifted the white sand. The tracks led to a ball of white-and-black fur, crawling along, shivering. No ears, no eyes, barely larger than Mercy's front paw. A mouth opened, filled with bright white fangs, and let out a sad little yelp.

Mercy scrabbled down the side of the hill and ran toward the animal. It was a pup, a male. She smelled blood and amniotic fluid caked into the dog's coat. When she arrived, the pup blindly stuck out its tongue, his eyes still sealed. Mercy lay in the sand and curled her body around him. The pup clamped his lips around one of her nipples and sucked desperately, the way pups do. It hurt, and the pain made her remember how her own pups would gnaw at her. She tilted the little one's mouth so that he could get a tighter grip. The milk flowed, releasing in a painful burst.

Somewhere off in the distance, Augur's feet crunched in the sand. He would come no closer.

Mercy licked the pup as he drank. She coiled her tail around him, sealing in their warmth. A pack unto themselves. There was no Damnable anymore. No war, no phony peace treaty. No coup by Wex, no illness for Urna. For this moment, everything was made whole again.

# CHAPTER 7

## THE PILGRIM

(UNOFFICIAL) LOGBOOK OF THE SUS AL-RIHLA
JANUARY ~~1819~~
_WEATHER_: WINDY.
_PERSONAL HEALTH_: CONTRACTIONS STARTED.

'ARC'S HAND SHIVERED as a clenching pain swept from her stomach to the ball-and-socket joints of her shoulders. The pencil fell from one hand, the logbook from the other. They clattered on the deck of the lifeboat. A bitter wind rustled the pages. She could no longer hear it over the siren screaming in her ears. It took a few seconds to realize that it was her own voice screaming.

She squeezed her St. Jude medal until it grew warm in her palm. A cloud bank rolled above, puffy and gray and impenetrable, the sunlight behind it so dull it cast no shadow. She could hear the Old Man's voice in her head, though she could not make out the words. It was like the day she changed, the day she awakened and found herself on a boat like this one, adrift under the same milky sky.

The burning sensation rippled through her again. She gripped the sides of the boat and dug her nails into the wood. Something shifted inside her, like bones rearranging themselves, and again she wondered if this was the past or the present. On the day she changed, her spine extended with series of pops and cracks. Her paws stretched into hands, like some deformed flower, all before her primitive brain could grasp what was happening. In those brief flashes of terror, she wanted to bite her own arm and whip her head from side to side until she tore it off.

"No," she sputtered. As if she had a say in what was happening.

A salty puddle sloshed in the boat. As the bow tipped forward, the water rushed around her, sweeping away the logbook. Between her legs, a steady drip of blood oozed out, sticking to her fur and turning the water pink. Everything below her waist became dead weight, a parasite hooked onto her body somehow, making her weak and dizzy.

Another shifting inside of her. She pictured a fist spinning in her gut. The fist slid toward her thighs and released. Something small and wet flopped into the pink water and then lay still.

*Life is the mission*, she thought. *This* is *the mission*.

She leaned forward to find a soaked pile of fur. Black and formless, still tethered to something inside of her by a slimy wire. She licked it furiously, and her tongue prickled with the taste of iron. The pup rolled to its side, its tiny paw stiffly curled into its belly. She exhaled on it to provide some warmth. A cloud of vapor covered the baby. When she tilted the pup, the head flopped from one shoulder to the other. The dog must have died when the wave hit.

Another tightening sensation forced out a blob of flesh, covered in dark, sticky blood. The placenta. With the dead pup nuzzled between her legs, she devoured this alien organ, something that could not possibly have come from her. The flesh proved stubborn—she needed to bite hard and then rip each piece away. The taste reminded her of Alpha meat, gamey but rich.

She was alive. Her child was not. For the first time in so

long—perhaps the first time ever—she could clearly remember when her first litter was born, before the Change. She survived then because she ran away. And they didn't. They did not even have names, thanks to her.

Unable to cry, she felt a void open in her heart. A dead space where she could drop these memories—for now at least. *No*, she thought. *I am a beacon of light, guiding the other ships home.* Her pain would make her kinder, not harder. She would feel more, not less. All of that still made sense somehow.

She stuffed the last of the flesh into her mouth and chewed. It squished between her teeth until she swallowed it in a heavy gulp.

"HEY THERE, MOUNTAIN Girl."

D'Arc lay in the raft with the weight of her dead child on her chest. Somehow, the raft had expanded so that it was wider than the *al-Rihla*. The entire crew stood on the deck. Moab the bear. Captain Vittal. Kang the cook. The Navy woman and her cat friend, each with hand-rolled cigarettes between their lips. Wilson with his arms folded, hiding behind Harlan.

"You still seasick, Mountain Girl?" Harlan said. His mouth did not move. Neither did the ocean, which resembled the surface of a pond.

D'Arc sat up, still cradling her son.

"Whatcha got there?" Harlan asked.

"Tristan," she said. "His name is Tristan." After her former master.

"Tristan, huh?"

She glanced at her child and found instead a massive ant larva in her arms, bright white and wriggling, its prehensile limbs forming little nubs under the surface of its skin. She held her child closer. She did not want anyone to get near.

A searing pain in her gut made her wince. When she opened

her eyes, she was back in the lifeboat, bobbing in the waves. The sun poked under the clouds near the horizon, on its way down. Beside her, facing away, Tristan's body swayed along with the boat. She rested her hand on his cold fur. And then, before she could give it any further thought, she lifted him over the gunwale. He was so impossibly light, an empty sack. She set him gently in the water and pressed him under until a few bubbles rose to the surface. When she let go, the pup sank and disappeared. She leaned on the rail as another burning contraction forced her to lie on her side and tighten her fists. The film of icy water on the deck felt cool as it sloshed over her.

JANUARY 20
WEATHER: CLEAR SKY. COLD.

0133 FEMALE BORN. NUTICAL. NAUTICA.

LIFE IS THE MISSION.
LIFE IS TE THE MISSON.
LIFE IS THE

PRSONAL HLTH: BLOOD LOSS. TIRED.

THE SECOND PUP would not nurse. D'Arc coaxed her, cradled her, nudged her, breathed on her, licked her. Still, the baby would not latch on. The little mouth would fall away from the nipple each time, dribbling the milk onto D'Arc's belly, her tiny heartbeat racing. In the moonlight, Nautica looked no different from the larva in D'Arc's dream. With her white fur and her eyes sealed shut, her ears barely poking from her skull, only her stubby snout and yawning mouth gave her any form. Her cries came out in weak little squeals, barely audible over the waves.

D'Arc had managed to bail out most of the water in the boat before Nautica arrived, though the last stubborn puddle would always remain. Once again, she glanced at the hooks on either side, where the oars should have been. When she found the boat capsized, the oars had already floated away. Without them, she would drift forever on this steel-colored sea. She still had her sword, but it was too thin to use as an oar. In frustration, she tried paddling with her hands until they went numb. A waste of energy. The Atlantic would decide if she ever made landfall again.

The sky brightened. The iron taste of another placenta still tingled in her mouth. In the growing light, she could make out the filmy slits of Nautica's eyes, her sharp teeth. Her tail, the pads of her paws. A dark snout like her father. It seemed so wrong to think of her time with Falkirk now, yet it made sense, since she conceived her pups in a similar space: hemmed in, standing in water, wondering if she would see another day. The end of the world had come, not as a fiery judgment, but with the gentle lapping of waves, smoothing all the sharp edges to sand. Falkirk felt so warm when everything else had gone cold. Being with him became a defiant act of living after the world had drowned.

And now this. When the sun poked its yellow scalp over the horizon, D'Arc could finally see Nautica. So beautiful. A tiny warrior of a new generation. Another beacon of light. Life would be her mission.

But Nautica was dead.

Again, D'Arc placed her child into the water. This time, when the ocean accepted her sacrifice, D'Arc imagined herself stepping off the side and sliding into the darkness. The sea muffling the wind at last, until she could hear nothing else.

Another movement in her belly, so excruciating that she wanted to bite the gunwale.

"No," she begged. "Please, no more."

Something inside her was searching for the light, not caring about the flesh that it stretched to the limit. *We are not finished here*, it said.

D'Arc flopped onto her side. Her medallion pinged onto the deck with St. Jude facing down.

JANRY 32
<u>WEATHER</u>: SUNNY. SUMMER?
COLD AGAIN. COLD FOREVER.

THE THIRD PUP spilled out still partially wrapped in its amniotic sac. D'Arc barely had the energy lick the membrane away. She did not have to. This dog, a male, wriggled free of it and cried out. He had dark fur and a pointy snout. So much like a husky. Without thinking, she pressed him against her until her nipple stifled his cries. He sucked the milk with a squeaking sound. D'Arc rolled over, reached for the remnants of the sac, and jammed it into her mouth. She was so thirsty that the blood went down as easy as spring water. *I help you, you help me*, she thought. This one must have hidden behind his siblings, who bore the brunt of the wave and the impact of the water. And who knew how long she had with this one, whose name she did not yet know? The dog with no name. From the war with no name.

*Whatcha got there, Mountain Girl?*

"Go away," she said.

She wondered if she and this pup were the only survivors of the *al-Rihla*. She remembered those last few seconds on the ship when the ocean punished them all for their arrogance. Maybe the ocean reclaimed everyone, everywhere. That's what it wanted, right? She had seen it before. The humans still worried about it. One day, there would be nowhere to go, and everything that people like her had built would be reduced to floating debris bobbing on the waves.

No, no. That couldn't be true. She gripped the St. Jude medal again. It brushed against the pup's head. The tiny dog lifted his mouth away and licked the medal a few times before deciding it did not have what he wanted. He returned to his suckling. She watched him, this new life sprung from her body. An extension of her and all the things she endured.

*Wait till you hear about this day,* she thought. *Wait till I tell you all about this.*

A COLD RAIN swept over the boat, troubling the surface of the water. D'Arc wrapped her rain slicker around her body to keep the infant dry. As he nursed, D'Arc tilted her head and caught the raindrops in her open jaw, closing it every minute or so to swallow. Every sip made her feel stronger, lighter. The fog clouding her brain lifted. She occasionally peeked underneath the coat to see her son still clamped to her chest. As far as he knew, this is what shelter looked like.

Before long, the rainwater collected in the bottom of the boat again. Soon, the water submerged her legs, and she remembered the first time the Old Man took her to a pond near the ranch so she could swim. It was summer then, a season that seemed impossible now. Mort(e) watched from the edge while she paddled across, unable to believe the buoyancy. Every time she splashed, she tried to catch the columns of water in her mouth as they rose and fell. She asked him to join her. When he said no, she clapped her hands on the surface and soaked him. He spent the next few minutes rubbing the fur on his head until it dried.

The rain lightened, and D'Arc leaned forward to cup the water in her hands and toss it over the side. It was the best she could do without a bucket. Her coat opened slightly, allowing some of the rain in. The pup slipped away from the nipple and cried out. She saw his tiny face, a beautiful little angel who screamed in terror.

"I know," she said.

She kept bailing until she could no longer lift her arms. The pup bawled the entire time, his tinny voice like a child's toy with a low battery. Once the puddle reached an acceptable depth, D'Arc huddled at the bow and tried to coax the pup to take another nipple. He refused, choosing instead to scream at her some more. In a panic, she jammed his face into her chest. The pup bit her and screamed some more.

A song. That's right—parents sang songs to their children.

She didn't know any.

Wait—she did! She did! But the lyrics . . . what did those beavers sing?

> We will meet again
> In the darkness,
> Where you and I
> Will be the only light.

The pup stopped crying for a moment, then started again as she searched for the lyrics. "Right, right."

> And by our light
> We . . . call everyone home,
> Where in the darkness,
> We are the light.

"A mean old beaver taught me this song," she said. The pup murmured. D'Arc started over. Around the third or fourth time she said that they would meet again in the darkness, she stopped. Part of her didn't like it. The pup halted his feeding and whined at her again, so she kept going until the rain clouds at last drifted farther out to sea.

•  •  •

THE SHORELINE APPEARED as a looming blackness, a slit in the horizon that her tiny boat would pass through on her way to the land of the dead. D'Arc nearly screamed when she first spotted it. The sleeping pup on her chest reminded her to keep quiet. By then, the beavers' song played in her head on an endless loop. She absently hummed parts of it, her dry tongue sealed to the roof of her mouth. Her empty stomach gurgled. Her limbs shook.

To the east, the clouds lifted, unveiling more of the shoreline. It may have waited there for days without her noticing it. She removed her coat and gently wrapped it around the baby. The pup stirred, its little tongue poking out and then retracting. She set the bundle on the deck and crept to the front of the boat. With her chest resting on the bow, she paddled the water along each side until she felt the small craft moving forward. Delirious, she mumbled the words to the song, sometimes adding her own. "Where you and I . . . will be a beacon of light."

Behind her, the pup awakened and cried out, his voice piercing her ears. She could not comfort him. D'Arc giggled maniacally as she imagined herself dropping dead in the seconds before the boat made landfall. Her son would climb over her corpse and be on his way to his destiny. Sure, that made sense. That was what her life amounted to. What all life amounted to: a stepping-stone for the next generation by any means necessary. This is what should have happened the last time, when she survived and her children died. There would be no passing of the torch, no ritual, no sentimentality. The living would discard the dead, over and over, while pretending to find meaning in it somehow.

Her hands grew numb while her shoulders burned with a fire that crept all the way to her tail. The medallion swayed, sometimes bopping her nose. The baby's squeals began to sound like fully formed sentences. When the pup screamed so loud that he lost his voice, D'Arc could have sworn that he asked about his brothers and sisters.

"Gone," she replied, gasping. "They're gone."

The pup cried louder. It meant, *Where?*

"They're nowhere," D'Arc answered. "And everywhere. They're all around us. All the time. Can't get away."

*Come back here with me*, the pup said. *Keep me warm.*

"I can't, sweetie."

A gap opened in the land mass, revealing a bay of some kind.

*Come back here with me*, the pup insisted.

"We're almost there," D'Arc said.

*Why are you leaving me?* the pup said.

"I'm right here!"

*Sing me the beaver song again.*

D'Arc tried, but the song came out in gasps and wheezes. Every time she flubbed a line, the pup ordered her to start over.

The land rose higher in the sky. The beach became textured, sprinkled with dormant brown grass. They passed an ancient metal buoy, its once-red paint bleached pink from the sun. She continued to make progress until, frustrated with the paddling, she gripped the docking rope in her teeth and jumped into the water.

*No!* the pup screamed. But this was the best way a dog could do it. At last she felt her foot touch sand. The sudden gravity of it made her dizzy. She hauled the boat onto the beach, pulling it as far as she could. Once the boat was secure, she crawled back in and cuddled with the baby. The pup went quiet and scrunched his body against his mother. He squeaked a few times. And she heard another question.

*Who am I? What's my name?*

"I don't know yet." she yawned.

THE SUNLIGHT BURNED through her pink eyelids. She tried to sleep, but her empty stomach would not let her. She opened her eyes to the cold blue overhead. The tide came in, digging a channel in the sand that allowed the boat to sway in either direction. The pup still slept on her chest. He must have been grateful for the stillness of land. The predictability of it.

D'Arc heard movement outside of the boat. Grains of sand crunched. There was a whisper, then a conspicuous silence. She pulled the pup in tighter and tugged the coat over his body to hide him. Then she searched for her sword, which rested at the stern of the boat.

Cradling the pup, she peeked over the side. She saw the tracks first, stretching over the nearest sand dune. They led to a pair of deer—two bucks—standing on all fours. She had seen their kind before, once while living on the ranch, again while living in Hosanna. Their eyes carried an innocence, like two marbles on the sides of their heads. But the eyes hid a brutal nature. These bucks could kill without changing the expression on their faces.

They were scouting her.

When D'Arc sat up quickly to reach for the sword, she saw a third buck, waiting right beside the boat, his antlers twisting and curling in every direction like petrified snakes.

"You're a pilgrim," the buck said.

She could not answer yes or no.

"You seek the Mudfoot," the buck added, his voice so nasal she wondered if he could breathe through his nose at all. "No Mudfoot here."

She sensed the other deer getting closer, ready to surround her with a forest of pointy antlers. About two hundred feet out in the water, the old buoy tilted back and forth like a toy.

"I'm from Hosanna," she said, her voice shaking.

"All pilgrims're from Hosanna."

"I was on board the SUS *al-Rihla*."

"And now you're here. You seek the Mudfoot. No Mudfoot here."

"No Mudfoot here, right," she sighed. She had no idea what a Mudfoot was.

When she saw for the first time their chiseled teeth, she recoiled. The bucks got closer. She smelled their breath, which carried a tinge of rotten meat. Her pup must have smelled it as well, confusing it for food. When he wriggled against her, the deer noticed the squirming lump under her coat. Their elaborate antlers rotated as they glanced at one another. One of them placed his hooves on the side of the boat, rocking it toward him.

"Give," the buck said.

D'Arc could not get to the sword, nor could she fight the deer with one hand holding the baby. She would have to settle for distraction. So she let the pup's head poke out of the opening in her coat. On this day, of all days, the dog's eyes finally opened, just in time to meet the creatures who would kill him. And somehow this made him luckier than his siblings.

The deer backed away. The boat rocked in its divot when the buck removed his hoof. "Wolf," one of them said. The other two repeated it. *Yes, this pup is a wolf,* D'Arc wanted to say. *Almost a wolf, like his father. Oh, you should have seen him. So beautiful. So noble. He would have killed you all.*

"The Mudfoot have no young," the first deer sputtered. "Where you find it?"

They did not realize she was the mother. Could they not smell this pup? Could they not see the terrible ordeal at sea had carved into their faces?

"Damnable take the young," the other deer said. "Mudfoot are cursed."

"They find a way!" the other said. "They survive."

"Not this one," the first deer said.

D'Arc realized that she could stall them no longer. The two deer lowered their heads, aiming their antlers at her. The one behind her did the same.

"If you want this little one so bad, you can have him," she said. "I can show you where I found him."

It was enough to make the lead deer raise his snout and wait for her to continue. She took the opportunity to shift her weight and rock the boat toward him. Then, as hard as she could, she rocked it the other way, capsizing it. The deer hopped out of the way as the side of the boat slammed into the ground. D'Arc landed hard in the sand. The baby cried out. Clutching the child, she crawled toward the sword while the bucks slammed their hooves against the hull, each strike as loud as a gunshot. D'Arc gripped the handle as the deer lifted the boat away. She swung wildly, and the blade connected at the buck's ankle, severing it. The deer dropped to the ground, its eye unblinking, its jaw hanging open in shock.

D'Arc rolled to her feet. One of the deer mounted the hull, ready to pounce on her. The other stalked around the side of the boat. She held them at bay with the tip of the sword while the pup squealed. And again, she heard the question: *Why?*

"Because the world isn't fair," D'Arc said.

The deer on the boat leapt at her. In her weakened state, she dodged too slowly. Her blade hit flesh, but the antlers cracked against her ribs. Her arm went dead. Her hand became like a claw around the pup, who shouted in protest. The deer limped as a red gash opened on his side, weeping blood on the fur. The buck stared at her stupidly, as if awaiting instructions.

The blade shot sparks as it connected with the antlers, sheering off some of the points. The wounded one limped around her. They meant to attack from both sides. As D'Arc got closer to the water, her foot sank into the wet sand. A few feet later, the first wave flowed past her shins.

The baby told her not to do it. But then two more deer crested the nearest dune, driven by the scent of dog. They were so ignorant of what she had seen. When the Alphas returned, none of this would matter.

The deer on the hill let out a low squawking sound. The bucks stopped and turned to the noise. Even the deer on the ground lifted his head to listen, ignoring his severed hoof. It was some kind of warning. Something was coming. Ignoring D'Arc, the deer tried to help their comrade walk. One of them stood on his hind legs to lift his friend.

D'Arc ran from the boat until her legs became like wood, and her heart flared like a torch inside her chest. As the adrenaline wore off, the cuts in her ribs pulsed in rhythm with her heartbeat. She lifted the pup away from her chest to find blood on his fur. The little one licked it as he cried. It was somehow the sweetest thing she had seen in a long time. It was her blood. When she probed her wound with her hand, her fingertips brushed against something hard and sharp and sticky. Her stomach turned. She lifted her arm to find a broken antler lodged in her side. She tried to pull it loose, and a lightning bolt shot from the wound, nearly making her faint. She dropped to her knees, taking care to cradle the baby to the ground. The pup dug his claws into the cold sand.

D'Arc was so tired. She wanted to sleep more than anything. The pup tried to keep her awake by biting her ear. She could hardly feel it. *Drop me in the sea*, she thought. *Let me join the others.*

She could hear more words in the pup's squealing. *No! Don't leave me!*

"I'm right here," she whispered.

A thick blanket slid over her. The world went black and silent.

D'ARC WOKE TO the sound of a crackling fire and immediately thought that she must have died. The scent of it carried her to the ranch, where she and Mort(e) would spend every fifth night relaxing by the fire, reading. She would annoy him with questions. She never ran out of them.

No, that was all gone. She opened her eyes. A campfire burned on the sand. Above, the Milky Way spilled from one end of the horizon to the other. She tried to sit straight, and something stabbed her rib, a pain so intense it made her gag.

She lay on her coat. Footsteps shifted the sand around her. Walking on all fours, a pack of dogs circled the fire, their faces painted blue and green and gold and red. They sniffed her. One of them, with a long snout painted yellow, smelled her chest, noting the scent of milk. D'Arc covered herself but did not make a sound. These were wolves, she realized, not dogs. She knew then that her pup was dead.

But no—someone had placed a bandage on her wound after extracting the antler. Her ribs felt tender, but she would live, if she avoided infection. Gently, she sat straight and let the wolves continue to sniff at her. The yellow-faced one grunted at her and flicked his snout. D'Arc tilted her head, unsure of what he was doing, but driven by instinct nonetheless. The wolf made a coughing sound, and a steaming hunk of soft meat fell out of his mouth and into D'Arc's. It happened so fast she could not react other than to swallow it. The regurgitated food had no taste—instead, she felt only the warmth of it landing in her empty stomach. She opened her mouth and begged for more. Another wolf obliged. As she swallowed the meat, she wondered if it came from the same deer who attacked her.

"Where's my baby?" she asked.

They heard her, though none of them answered. She realized then how young they were. And they had no leader, it seemed. Finally, one of them elbowed through the crowd—a female with red paint on her face, shaped like a skull. In a bizarre gesture, she rested her chin on the crown of D'Arc's head. D'Arc wondered if she meant to show dominance. But it was some kind of cuddling, an act of sympathy.

"We found you alone," the wolf said. "I smelled another. But the scent trail . . ." She flared her nostrils, then shook her head. D'Arc tried to stand, and a searing pain put her in place. The wolf huddled closer to protect D'Arc from her own body.

"I have lost pups too," the wolf said. "Your milk is fresh. You will have more."

D'Arc could feel nothing because she had nothing left. She had become an empty husk, scraped clean, disintegrating into particles. Soon, she would be spread over the beach, indistinguishable from the rest of the sand.

"You are pilgrims?" she asked robotically, still unsure what that meant.

"Exiles," the wolf said. "In search of a new pack."

"The . . . Mudfoot?"

"Yes. You seek them as well?"

D'Arc could not answer. She snuck a glance at the pocket of her coat, where the logbook stuck out. The wolves had not read it—maybe because they couldn't—which may have saved her life.

The wolf introduced herself as Quay of the Opa clan. "You are from Hosanna," she said. "This I know." She nodded toward D'Arc's sword, which someone had wrapped in cloth.

"Do you know where the Mudfoot are?" D'Arc asked.

"A day's march. They need soldiers. But they need you most of all."

"Me?"

"Fertile ones. The Mudfoot nearly died out. Now they have life again."

"Have you heard?" another wolf asked. This one wore green paint in a long streak that started at his eyebrows and traveled along his spine.

"Heard what?"

"The leader of the Mudfoot bore a son yesterday," he said. Another wolf howled in response. Soon the others joined, but the skull-faced female shushed them with a bark.

"The packs will unite behind her now," Quay said. "The humans are doomed. Hosanna will fall."

A terrible calm settled over D'Arc. These wolves had her child. She was sure of it. And the world had already killed her, more or less. She could do whatever she wanted. She was a beacon of light, after all. Isn't that what it meant? To burn so brightly that it scorched everything in its path?

"How soon do we leave?" D'Arc said.

# CHAPTER 8

## QUITE THE STICKUP

**M**ORT(E) WAITED IN the wooden elevator that hung off the side of the dam. A tarp sealed him in, shielding against the early morning wind. The floor of the contraption was made of polished tree branches, stacked and glued neatly together, and suspended by a thick hemp cable. With no one to operate the hand crank, the elevator swayed in the breeze, the pulley squeaking a bit.

Mort(e) and the beavers had slipped inside before the sun rose, confident that no one saw them. Ten armed robbers in all, lying in wait. Sunday was a day off for the beavers, when they usually joined others at the temple to sing songs in praise of the Prophet. Any minute now, Mort(e) would hear the chimes and the droning voices. The city would stop moving for a brief time. That was when they would strike.

Beside him, Castor adjusted his armor, which consisted of two wooden boards hung with leather straps on his shoulders, covering his torso. It was completely useless and cumbersome, yet it represented some tradition for his people. A tradition less than a decade old, of course—though try telling that to the beavers. Castor had worn the same armor when they broke the siege at Lodge City. Though he'd never served in any military, the beaver enjoyed the trappings and costumes associated with it.

Mort(e) decided to keep his jokes to himself. Castor had agreed to help, as did most of his friends. Let him wear his silly armor.

The church music began exactly at nine, precise enough to set a watch to it. For perhaps the hundredth time that morning, Mort(e) ran his palms over his flak jacket, checking the pockets for ammunition, his field knife, a map. He lifted the rifle, a Russian-made Nikonov with the wooden stock painted black.

A whistle sounded, changing to a higher pitch before lowering. It came from his spotter, a beaver named Blythe, Castor's niece, who was camped out in the hotel. Mort(e) parted the tarp with his telescope and peered outside. Blythe's signal meant that the convoy had left the hideout building and would turn the corner any second now, on their way to the checkpoint. After that, they would proceed along the highway ramp and onto the bridge, making them the first vehicles to cross since the beavers reinforced the structure—on schedule, Castor would always point out.

The first vehicle appeared: a motorcycle with a human rider, wearing a black leather jacket and a helmet with a tinted face shield. No weapons were visible, though his coat could easily conceal them. Next came two heavy trash trucks, each painted a bright green, like giant metal turtles. Taking the rear was a maroon SUV with a driver and a passenger in the front seat.

*Oh, you figured this'd be easy*, Mort(e) thought. *A nice bright Sunday for you to slip through.*

Mort(e) imagined these people sitting around in some bar or basement or restaurant, the way humans often did, slouching, their feet resting on the tabletop, expecting the world to hand itself over to them. Every human Mort(e) killed must have felt this way before running into him. Every one wore the same terrified expression when they realized their time had run out. For all their maneuvering, all their confidence, their entire plan depended on transporting their stolen goods across a narrow bridge where anything could happen. All their skills and talents, reduced to simple, unavoidable laws of physics and geometry.

Mort(e) could not keep from tilting the telescope upward, toward Liberty One Tower, where the *Vesuvius* had been docked for the last few days. From here, he could see the damage to the engine. Rumors had flown around Hosanna all week about what happened. Another fish-head attack. More sabotage from the Sons of Adam. A mutiny. Everything was on the table. The gossip that interested him the most involved the *Vesuvius* taking damage in a rescue mission to save the *al-Rihla*, somewhere out at sea.

If there had been such a mission, it had clearly failed. The *al-Rihla* was lost. When the news reached the pub, a few beavers raised their glasses to the ship. Castor told them to shut up. After that, Mort(e) became more focused than ever on the task at hand. Everything depended on stopping the convoy. The certainty of it, the finality, felt clean to him somehow, like a sharp knife withdrawn from a wound before it could bleed.

His mouth watered, and the taste of salt and brine returned. This always happened when he dwelt too much on the *al-Rihla*. Another vision began, like a flip-book starting at the beginning. Mort(e) lowered the telescope and allowed the hallucination to wash over him. He floated in water. He breathed through gills. He sensed movement, currents, the songs of the fish that rattled his skull. It was his third vision that morning alone. They had become more frequent in the last few days as he prepared for this confrontation, this revelation. For all he knew, the Sarcops chose this method to communicate with him. And they wanted him to complete this mission. They made that point clear. If he failed, they would haunt him until he died screaming on Marquez's operating table.

The hallucination ended. He swigged some water from his canteen and sloshed it around in his mouth before spitting it out. Mort(e) took the goddamn pills this morning, so these daydreams should have stopped for now. He remembered Marquez telling him to set an alarm, or to have the beavers remind him, anything to stay on the regimen. "The pills will keep the visions at bay," Marquez told him. *At bay. Nice, Doc. Real funny.*

"Mort(e)," Castor said. "You're mumbling again."

Mort(e) raised the telescope to find the convoy at the checkpoint. Three human soldiers exited their cinderblock pillbox, holding out their hands to get the convoy to stop. While one of the soldiers pulled a spiked chain across the road, another spoke to the driver, and the third inspected the underside of the vehicles with a mirror attached to a pole. Mort(e) knew these men. Every morning, they waved to the beavers as they entered the construction site, though they always gave Mort(e) a funny look.

For all their smiling and promises to do their jobs, the soldiers at the checkpoint let the trucks through without checking what was inside. Their papers were in order, Mort(e) supposed. How nice. The soldiers hurried to remove the chains and barbed wire. The lead officer tipped his cap as the convoy rolled past.

Castor gave the next signal by slapping his tail on the floor three times. Mort(e) stepped off the elevator and onto a platform that jutted out from the dam. Below him, the corkscrew turbines churned the river into white foam. When he poked his head over the top, he saw two more pairs of eyes across the way: Kerdigan and Von, both Castor's nephews. Kerdigan had already named his kid after Castor, and Von promised to do the same. Together, they climbed behind a stack of logs which concealed them from the road.

As Mort(e) expected, the convoy stopped at the edge. Though the city had assured them that the bridge would hold their weight, few humans seemed capable of trusting a rickety structure made of logs, built by animals they once hunted. Animals they almost drove to extinction by turning them into hats. Fucking *hats*.

The motorcycle went first. The truck followed until its wheel rolled over a seam in the wooden planks, sending a creaking noise through the entire bridge. The driver shouted to his comrades. They argued for a bit, with one of them asking if they should proceed. The bridge was *designed* to make noise, Castor often said. When it stops creaking, *that's* when you run.

Satisfied for the time being, the drivers continued. *Finally*, Mort(e) thought. A phantom cloud of water bubbles gurgled near his ear. He twitched his head, and the noise stopped. To be safe, he sipped from his canteen again and rinsed out the salt water that wasn't there.

The trucks ambled along between the lampposts lining the sides of the dam. As soon as the last truck passed the fourth post near the center, the music started. A loudspeaker attached to the side of the dam blasted a recording of the beavers' most obnoxious song—even Castor admitted he hated it. An old female beaver sang it, sounding much like that ornery hag Nikaya. The drivers, alarmed at the distraction, slowed their vehicles once again. And when they did, the fifth lamppost tipped over and crashed right in front of the lead motorcycle, barely missing it. In a panic, the driver tried to reverse it with his feet. Before the rear truck could back away, the lamppost behind it tumbled over, sealing in the convoy. As if to drive the point home, the post had cracked in the middle, with a long shard pointing right at the humans.

There was no need for a signal at that point. Once the crashing stopped, Mort(e) and the beavers emerged from their hiding spot, rifles raised, screaming over the music. Mort(e) grabbed the cyclist by his leather collar and yanked him off the bike. The man landed hard on his ass, and the visor on his helmet snapped open. A beaver pinned him there by pointing a rifle in his face.

Mort(e) positioned himself at the driver's side of the first truck. "Get out! Put your palms on the window! Palms on the glass, *now!*" The beavers surrounding the second truck did the same. Mort(e) made sure to pick the younger ones for this job, the ones with something to prove in the big city.

The humans obeyed and stepped out—willingly, it seemed. Mort(e) recognized them and rattled off their nicknames as they emerged. Slinky drove the lead truck, with the Jerk next to him. In the early morning light, Slinky had a pallid complexion, though his skinny frame was all muscle. The Jerk's bald head glistened. He spat the unlit cigarette out of his mouth as the beavers forced him to put his hands on the side of the truck and spread his legs out. In the second truck, the Waddler and Bozo stepped out, followed by Meat. By process of elimination, that left Dum-Dum as the cyclist. The humans wore bluish-gray sanitation uniforms, crisp and clean, still creased with folds. They hadn't even tried to make their disguises authentic.

With the humans neutralized, a beaver entered each truck and tried to open the compactor. Kerdigan took the front vehicle, Von the rear. Whatever was inside, the beavers would extract it and slide it down the ramp and into the water, where two rafts awaited to ferry the cargo away from the city. The humans could go to Tranquility if they wanted, but Mort(e) suspected they would simply walk away. The few honest Tranquility agents would ask too many questions. The crooked agents would probably kill these poor bastards to cover their tracks.

"This is quite the stickup," the Jerk said.

Mort(e) slammed the butt of his rifle into the back of the man's knee. He crumpled to the ground. Mort(e) figured that he might have to make an example of one of these men. Might as well be the Jerk.

The man staggered to his feet again. His knuckles whitened as he kept his hands flat on the side of the truck. In the cab, Kerdigan fiddled with the levers. None of them seemed to work. The Jerk watched him. Von did not seem to fare any better in the second truck. Mort(e) decided to give them a few more seconds before demanding that the humans do it. To convince them, he might have to break the Jerk's nose.

"You can still walk away," the Jerk said. With that, he turned to Mort(e)—and his entire head had become that of a fish. A Sarcops. A bulbous skull, enormous eyes with no pupils, a wide mouth, gills gaping at his neck, brushing his collar.

Mort(e) had come too far to let another hallucination stop him. He could fight through it if he concentrated hard enough. He felt the others watching. He had told them to punish anyone who spoke, and they must have been waiting for him to follow his own rule.

Mort(e) flipped his rifle around and prepared to drive the butt into the fish-head's face. And at that moment, an explosion at the western end of the dam clapped in his eardrum. The lampposts swayed. The blast took out the checkpoint, now a smoking ruin. Amid the rubble, Mort(e) could make out only the rings of barbed wire, bent into strange angles.

Those soldiers were paid off, Mort(e) realized. And now they would never talk.

The fish-head man turned from the truck and faced Mort(e). "There are more bombs," he said, his voice gurgling as if underwater. "In case something like this happened."

"Kerdigan, get out of the truck," Mort(e) said. "Von, you too." The beavers were happy to obey.

Mort(e) poked the Jerk with the barrel of his rifle. "Open it."

"Did you hear what I said? There are more bombs. Right under your precious dam."

"Bullshit. We inspect it every day."

"I know you do. Now tell me: how many die this time if the dam goes?"

"What's in the truck?"

"The future."

"Show me, and you live."

"Let me go, and *you* live."

"We can't let you go now," Castor said.

"Then you die. All because you couldn't say no to this cat."

"Don't listen to him," Mort(e) said. "He's lying."

"I'm the one who can promise you'll survive this day, beaver," the Jerk said. "This cat is willing to sacrifice all of you. He has nothing to live for. But I'll wager you do."

A nervous energy rippled through the beavers. The humans remained eerily still, awaiting instructions.

"I can smell it," the Jerk said. "I can smell the confidence draining away."

"Shut up," Mort(e) said. "I beat you once. I can do it again. You think I can't?"

"Arthur," Castor said. It was Mort(e)'s code name for this operation. The beaver kept his rifle on the cyclist, who lay flat on his stomach, arms out.

"Let's at least keep them here," Mort(e) said. "Wait for Tranquility."

"If one Tranquility agent steps on this dam, it goes," the Jerk said. To his right, the other human turned around. Mort(e) growled and aimed at him, but the human remained unmoved. His head resembled that of a catfish, with slimy whiskers dripping onto his coat.

"We're willing to die for this," the Jerk said. "Are you?"

That did it. It broke Castor. Mort(e) could sense the others deflating, shrinking away.

"Let them go," Castor said.

"They're bluffing!" Mort(e) said.

"Stand down," Castor told his friends. The blaring music stopped. Two of the beavers moved the fallen lamppost out of the way. The rest of them retreated to the edges of the dam to make room for the trucks.

The humans got into their vehicles. The vegetable oil exhaust fumes belched in Mort(e)'s face as the trucks passed him. Taking up the rear, the cyclist hopped onto his bike and restarted it.

*Fucking beavers*, Mort(e) thought. Civilians. Farmers. He saved their asses, and they didn't have the guts to fight beside him. Mort(e) realized he may have been speaking out loud, but he didn't care. They needed to hear it.

The motorcycle rider got his bike started on the third kick. The tire burned on the ground.

Mort(e) bolted for it.

"No!" Castor shouted.

The cyclist saw Mort(e) coming in his rearview mirror and tried to accelerate. Mort(e) swung the stock of the rifle and clocked the rider in the side of the helmet, knocking him off the saddle. With the engine still running, Mort(e) got on the bike and cranked the handle. The engine growled, jerking the motorcycle forward. He sliced through a cloud of exhaust fumes. The trucks gathered speed, with the rear vehicle surging ahead, riding alongside the other. Mort(e) swerved toward the side of the dam, where the crane jutted out over the water. The hemp cable lay coiled beside it, with its hook sticking out like the head of a snake. Slowing the bike, Mort(e) leaned over and snatched the hook. The weight of it nearly tipped the motorcycle, but he kept it steady. The cable zipped along the ground. In his rearview mirror, the stacked coil unraveled one level at a time.

Mort(e) hooked the cable to his handlebars and cranked the accelerator again, lifting the front wheel slightly. Like two giant beetles, the trash trucks barreled down the sloped ramp of the dam. The tires bounced at each seam. The bridge wobbled, but remained intact. *Son of a bitch* can *hold 'em*, Mort(e) thought.

Keeping one hand on the accelerator, Mort(e) lifted the hook, held it out to his side. He could take one of these trucks. Only one. No time to think. Just choose.

The left one.

He clamped the hook on a handle on the side of the trash compactor. The same one that garbage men would hold on to while making the rounds through some suburban neighborhood. A memory filled Mort(e)'s mind of his days as a pet, standing on his hind legs, watching the green beasts as they passed in front of his master's house.

The cable lifted as it tightened. Mort(e) swerved to avoid it. Behind him, an awful wrenching sound began, full of cracks and splinters. The crane tore away from its base. Wood as thick as tree trunks shot out over the water like twigs. What was left of the crane scraped along the dam before snapping in half. The truck spun out of control and tipped over, slamming onto its side and skidding to a halt.

The humans exited from the door, resembling sailors coming out of a submarine hatch. The other truck braked. When Mort(e) tried to drive around the wreck, a hail of gunfire forced him to spin out and take cover behind the truck.

Mort(e) waved to the beavers. "Get down!" They already had, of course.

A pair of boots came running toward him. Mort(e) turned in time to see the cyclist sprinting, hoping to rejoin his comrades. With a speed Mort(e) had never seen in a human, the man vaulted on top of the truck and jumped off on the other side, landing with a crack on the planks. Mort(e) peeked around the side, and a volley of bullets sparked against the hood. He pulled back. With the last of its passengers on board, the other truck sped off.

Mort(e) surveyed the damage. A smoke trail drifted from the pile of rubble at the checkpoint. A small island of debris floated downriver. The remnants of the crane fell into the water, pulling the cable with it.

Once again, a trickle of imaginary bubbles drifted by Mort(e)'s ear. He was too tired to wave them off.

THAT AFTERNOON, MORT(E) sipped his last drink ever at the Grumpy Beaver. He simply had nowhere else to go. He never came here on a Sunday and didn't know it could be so quiet. The few patrons left him alone in his corner, their voices conspicuously low. He could hear them slurping their Lodge City Specials through their buck teeth. The bartender slid an Archer toward him, then walked away, pretending to clean a spot at the other end of the bar. All day, sirens whirred and voices shouted as the stubborn forces of civilization sought to bandage the open wound near the river. A crew of firefighters put out the blaze at the checkpoint. Tranquility agents blocked off the crime scene and rounded up the few beavers they could find. The beavers told them nothing, insisting that they were at the temple mourning the Prophet along with everyone else.

The Archer went down smooth. It was good for warding off the sounds of the ocean and the taste of salt. The side effect: bad memories, especially of his life before Hosanna. Today, the tradeoff felt worth it.

A more recent memory landed in his mind. In the moments after the truck had tipped over, Mort(e) had retreated to the beavers to find Castor cradling his nephew Kerdigan. A stray bullet had punctured the young beaver's lung. His mouth gasped for air. Mort(e) could do nothing, and the beavers had little interest in making him feel better about it. They hustled Kerdigan to the slide at the edge of the dam and took their wounded friend to the water, where they would ferry him to a safe place. But before they left, Castor glared at Mort(e) with a searing anger. In that moment, it seemed as if the patient beaver had finally quit the hopeless project of fixing his friend. Mort(e) knew then that he would never last here. He burned everything he touched. He drove people away. He deserved to lose the only friends he had left.

In the morning, he would pack his things and begin the long march to his beloved ranch. There, he would find dust, rotting crops, a few remnants of the Alphas that he had raised with D'Arc. Mort(e) would go there and wait to die. Maybe he would survive long enough to see the first wolves sweeping across the land on their way to Hosanna. He would wave to them from his rocking chair. If they had any mercy, any compassion at all, they would shoot him before moving along.

He heard unfamiliar voices at the door. More Tranquility agents, no doubt. An oversized beaver named Shiloh guarded the entrance. Too young and cocky to know any better, Shiloh demanded to know why Tranquility targeted the beavers in their investigation. "After all we did for this city!" he said.

Mort(e) listened from his stool. He had no identification on him, no papers. He was another old stray. The only people who could verify his identity were dead or long gone. He considered waiting here for the agents to arrest him. He would follow their orders without resisting. Just a smile and a nod. It would be like living as a pet again.

The arguing outside quieted to a whisper. Another beaver intervened, scolding Shiloh for his lack of respect. "Don't you know who this is?" he asked.

More crosstalk followed. "Please come in," another beaver said. "You are welcome here."

The group entered, with a tall figure following close behind. The beavers shuffled and bowed like the pathetic court of some exiled king. Mort(e) spun on his stool. The figure came straight for him. It was a dog with bright blue eyes, grayish-white fur, and an airman's vest, blue with gold piping.

Falkirk. *So this is the bastard they sent to arrest me.*

"This day keeps getting better and better," Mort(e) said.

The bartender hustled together a drink—a terrible draft beer that would make a drunk human recoil.

"Oh, sure, get him a free one," Mort(e) said. "He only spent the Battle of Lodge City wrapped in a spiderweb."

Falkirk would not take the bait. He waved off the drink. "We need to talk."

"I was mourning the death of the Prophet," Mort(e) said robotically. "I don't know anything about an incident at the dam."

"Not about that." Falkirk glared at the bartender, who sequestered himself at the other end of the bar. A quick glance got the table full of beavers to look away.

Falkirk took the stool next Mort(e). The detergent from his officer's uniform nearly overpowered the scent of his dog hair. Mort(e) blocked it out with another sip of his drink.

"I don't care what happened at the dam," the husky said. "Though I know a lot of people who do."

"What do you want, then?" This dog, acting so important. His authority came from humans. They could take it from him whenever they wanted. He either didn't know that, or didn't care.

"You heard the news about the *al-Rihla*," Falkirk said.

"Yes. But I guess it doesn't really matter. Your people will be at the city gates any day now. You'll have to pick a side."

Falkirk turned away. "I'll take that drink after all," he said. The bartender slid a mug toward him, leaving a wet trail in its wake.

"That's why I'm here," Falkirk said. "My *people*, if you want to call them that."

Mort(e) wondered how much his crew trusted him, what with so many canines leaving Hosanna. So many had been arrested for waving a flag with an image of a wolf's paw covered in mud, a symbol of the rebels. Tranquility had begun arresting dogs by the dozen, quartering them in cells like strays in an animal shelter. The canine representative on the council went silent on all of this, issuing a bland statement about the need for law and order. Every day, his office used a column of bodyguards to repel scores of protesters, many of whom probably joined the Mudfoot shortly after. All it took was one rogue wolf clan to drive both the dogs and the humans crazy.

Hosanna would burn. Mort(e) knew that now. And loyal pets like Falkirk would probably be impaled on the last flagpoles standing.

"Hosanna is keeping a closer eye on things than people realize," Falkirk said. "Most of the wolf clans want peace. They've been sending us information on the separatists."

"Is that what they're called now? Separatists? If you ask me, it looks like they're trying to unite everyone."

"They can't. Not without the support of the clan elders. The real leaders are committed to peace. It might stick this time. That's why these Mudfoot are so scared."

"So scared they're overrunning every outpost, every base—"

"So scared they have to rely on refugees and strays to build an army," Falkirk said. "They can't go any farther. They need the other clans."

"I find myself saying this a lot," Mort(e) said, "but what does this have to do with me?"

"It has to do with both of us, actually."

Falkirk pulled a folded piece of paper from his inside pocket and flattened it on the bar. The corner of the page curled as it encountered a wet spot. The paper showed an image of wolf and dog soldiers marching along a dirt road. A few of them knew they were being photographed, and they gestured to the camera. Others walked on all fours, a pretentious way of showing that they stuck to the old ways—despite the fact that many of these warriors had been born *after* the Change. In every species, the young could not resist mimicking the old until they became old themselves.

It was the same kind of photo Mort(e) had seen many times since the Mudfoot uprising began. Every day, more dogs joined, some brazen enough to take pictures of themselves in war paint, armed with anything from spears to rifles. Someone had printed numbers over the heads of each person in the photo. In the corner of the page, a key gave the names of every person identified. At the top of the list, in bold letters, hung an ominous word: MALEFACTORS.

"We lost contact with the *al-Rihla* near the coast," Falkirk explained. "They were investigating something. Reports of flying ants."

Mort(e) snickered. *Might as well bring in the ants too*, he thought.

"This photo was taken near the beach," Falkirk said. "If there were any survivors of a crash, this is where they would have landed."

Mort(e) pressed his stubby fingers on the photo and spun it toward him.

"Right side," Falkirk said. "Number 28."

Among the dogs walking upright, a single figure stood out. A tall canine, female, long snout, a patch of dark fur extended over her white face. A silver medallion glinting in the center of her neck. Slung over her shoulder, a strap held a makeshift scabbard fashioned from cloth. In the scabbard was the handle of a samurai sword. Mort(e)'s eyes zipped to the key, which listed number 28 as UNIDENTIFIED.

"Don't waste time thinking it can't be," Falkirk said. "I already did that. It's her. You know it."

Mort(e) heard something like distant shouting. It was blood rushing to his ears, burning them.

"We need to go get her," Falkirk said.

"Do we? She defected. Like a lot of other dogs. You can still join her."

Falkirk leaned in and whispered. "She won't survive. None of them will."

"You overestimate your chances."

"See, that's the thing. We know the Mudfoot are getting stronger. Which is why we're going to fix it."

Mort(e) didn't like the sound of that.

"The *Vesuvius* has been ordered back to wolf country," Falkirk said. "We're bringing heavy ordnance. Incendiary bombs. Thermite. Everything will burn. The other clans gave us their blessing. They say the Mudfoot are diseased anyway, so we should cleanse the entire countryside with fire."

The husky stopped. Most likely, he had never received such an order before. And it had already changed him. Maybe it broke him.

"My ship leaves soon," Falkirk said. "We can get there in—"

Mort(e) raised his hand. "I can't."

"What?"

Mort(e) tapped his temple with his finger. "I'm no good to you. I'm damaged. Ask the beavers. I'm going crazy, and it's only getting worse."

"You weren't crazy before?" Falkirk said. "I *need* you. Trust me, I wish I didn't. But you've been to wolf country."

"So have your comrades. You must know someone who was part of the occupation."

"You're not listening. I need someone with your connections. The wolves have a nickname for you, don't they?"

Mort(e) waited for him to say it.

"Tekni, I believe they called you," Falkirk said. "What does that even mean?"

Mort(e) had not heard the name in so long, and it sounded like a joke coming from Falkirk. "It doesn't mean anything," Mort(e) said. "And besides, none of that matters. Not after today."

"All right, fine. Tell me what happened."

To stall, Mort(e) licked his paw, rubbed it over his face. "It was a convoy. Some humans shipping something out of the city. Something big. Something they needed to hide."

"And you stopped them."

"We got one of the trucks. The other got away."

"What did you find?"

Mort(e) laughed so bitterly that he hardly recognized the sound of it. "It was empty. A decoy."

He described the hydraulic door of the truck opening, revealing a void that seemed to stretch on forever. And then a tense silence from the beavers as the bleakness of it all sunk in. All that effort—one beaver dead, another dying, the dam torn apart—and they came away with nothing.

"They toyed with me somehow," Mort(e) said. "They *knew* I'd pick the wrong one. It was like—" He stopped there. Had it not been too crazy to say out loud, he would have told Falkirk that he felt an invisible force compelling him to choose the wrong truck. He drowned the thought with a thick gulp of his drink. "Still want me?" he asked.

"The Mudfoot are at the edge of Mournful territory," Falkirk said. "If I go there, it's an act of war. But the Mournfuls know you. All I need you to do is get me safe passage."

Mort(e) drummed his fingers on the bar. "You could pretend you're another deserter."

"Do you know what they do to spies? Do you know what they'd do if they found out I'm an officer?"

"Then tell your masters to send a human."

Falkirk growled. "My masters don't know about this."

Mort(e) waited for him to elaborate. But he didn't need to. Falkirk the Good Boy was going rogue.

"You heard what's happening," Falkirk continued. "The leader of the Mudfoot gave birth to a son. The first child born in a year. They're getting stronger, and D'Arc's caught up in it . . ."

He trailed off. His ears twitched. There were voices outside. Falkirk gripped Mort(e)'s shoulder. "Is there another way out of here?"

Mort(e) heard Shiloh at the door again, interrogating another group of unwelcome guests. Tranquility agents. Had to be. They had pieced it all together and realized that the main culprit had the audacity to hide in plain sight. *Hey, good for them*, he thought.

"The kitchen," Mort(e) said.

The urgency overrode his despair from a few minutes before. He felt himself propelled from the seat and into the kitchen, where the chef had left a fresh pot boiling on the stove. In the bar, heavy boots clopped on the wooden floor. There must have been three officers, most likely armed.

With his hand still on Mort(e)'s shoulder, Falkirk pushed him toward the rear exit. "I'll hold them off. You stay out of sight. Meet me at Liberty One Tower tomorrow at noon."

"I didn't say I'm going with you."

"You're going, choker. For the same reason I am."

Falkirk gave him one last shove and then turned back to the bar. Mort(e) opened the door, hesitated. Did Falkirk know all his reasons? Finding D'Arc, perhaps. But he also had nowhere else to go, nothing else to do. No one else who cared.

Mort(e) listened as Falkirk spoke to the officers. The husky put on his best commander voice, telling them that there was no cat here. "Got the call on the radio," he said. "I was in the area, so I checked it out. It's clean." They meekly apologized, making sure to finish every sentence with *sir*. Falkirk apologized to the staff, and then they were gone.

The taste of brine filled Mort(e)'s mouth again. He let it pass, though he would never get used to it. Swallowing, he stepped through the door and into the sunlight.

# CHAPTER 9

## THE MATRIARCH AND THE RATWING

IKAYA WADDLED AS fast as she could along the trail, heading deeper into the forest, where the canopy blotted out the overcast sky. She weaved through thick trees, scraping her fur as she hurried past. Her stumpy legs brushed the weeds and ferns, creating too much noise. The ratwing Gaunt clung to her like a tumor, his wings girdled around her torso. He squeaked something in her ear.

"Shut up," she whispered.

He squeaked again. It meant run—"feet fast"—the same thing he had been saying for days. Another squeak and a chirp meant that he smelled something. She did too, a thick, rotten smell, wafting through the trees.

Somewhere far behind her but closer than before, a heavy footfall snapped a twig. A wolf was tracking them.

Nikaya counted the ways in which she wanted to murder Gaunt.

She could have drowned him. On that first day, after the prison break, he made it easy for her by wrapping his wings around her as she swam. With a big lungful of air, she could have dived to the riverbed while holding on to the thin bone in his wing so he could not flap away.

Later, after they came to rest on a riverbank, she could have smashed his head in with a rock while he was passed out. Despite her renewed strength from working in the caves, she did not trust herself to do it in one strike. Who knew what a bat could do when injured and flailing for its life?

Still later—after he convinced her in his stilted English that he knew the safest route to Thicktree—she could have punctured his jugular with a sharp stick or poisoned his food with some bad berries. Or she could have shoved him off the side of a steep rock face. That was her favorite. The irony of a bat falling to his death. He whined every day about his injury while she carried his ratwing ass, despite her arthritic knees. What better way to find out if he told the truth?

His screeching interrupted her fantasy. He pointed the long finger bone on his right wing toward an opening in the trees. *There!* his screeching announced. *There! There!*

"What?" she asked. "What is it?"

*There! There!*

She needed to keep him alive. If she could bring him back in one piece, the bats would have to pardon her. Oh, they would do more than that. They would apologize. They would take the blame for everything that went wrong in Lodge City. *They* were the aggressors. *They* betrayed the beavers' trust, those ingrates. With any luck, Gaunt would drop dead just a few seconds after she laid him in front of his people.

Another set of feet troubled the leaves and sticks on the forest floor. Then another. Beasts advanced on all fours as if the Change had never happened, not bothering to hide anymore. They must have thought her a fat morsel bobbing along with an appetizer attached. Gaunt swore he knew how to get around them, but unless they could find a place to hide in this clearing, there would be nothing left of them except a patch of dried blood, which would wash away when the rains returned in the spring.

She could still kill him right now before all that happened. Might be worth it.

They emerged from the trees atop a sloping ravine, lightly dusted with snow. Descending the hill would take too long and would surely result in a bad slip, though Nikaya supposed the bat would break her fall. But there was something else. Gaunt chirped in her ear again, a word she could not translate. He pointed to a pile of boulders near the center of the ravine, where the elements had torn open the earth and exposed its bones.

She stopped. They were not boulders. Too round, all the same shape. "No," she whispered. "No, no, no . . ."

Despite the snow covering them, she could tell that these objects were the husks of dead Alpha soldiers. Some were freshly deceased; others, rotting for days or more, their carapaces cracked open by the weather. Well over twenty, she guessed, piled haphazardly like the debris of a collapsed building, with beams and broken walls jutting out in unnatural directions. An ant graveyard. Gaunt must have seen it on one of his recon missions.

Nikaya picked one at random and rubbed away the snow from the thorax. The carapace was clean. No branding. These were not the ants that destroyed Lodge City, the ones who so often hunted her in her dreams.

A tree shivered, losing its snow into the wind. The wolves would arrive any second. Nikaya hauled the bat into the circle of the dead. She got to her knees and wedged herself between the abdomens of two petrified Alphas. One of them must have been there for a while, for its exoskeleton let out a hollow sound when she bumped it with her elbow. Cringing, she rolled the husk so that it lay partially on top of her, shielding her from view. For once, Gaunt did not complain. Nikaya hoped that the rottenness of the corpses would mask their scent.

When the wolves got close, their breath heavy and wet,

Nikaya tried to think of the first time she showed a live Alpha to her granddaughter. The ant had gone astray, like so many did after the Colony fell. Confused, unable to fend for itself, the insect wandered into an area that the beavers had cleared out for a new lodge. The adults formed a perimeter around the Alpha as it doddered about, inspecting the tree stumps, each perfectly carved into a cone.

When Nikaya heard about the Alpha, she wanted to see for herself. Little Nikki begged to come along. She brought a million questions with her.

"What are those things on its head, Nana?" the young kit asked.

"Antennae. She smells with them. And hears. And sees, I guess."

"It's a she?"

"They're all she's."

"Is *she* here to eat someone?"

"She's scared," Nikaya remembered saying. "She's searching for her ant friends."

Sweet little Nikki began to cry.

"Come on," Nikaya said to her granddaughter. "Don't let them see you cry."

"But it's so sad," Nikki kept saying. "She's all alone."

"Would you rather she eat someone?"

"No."

"What about that brat at school who picks on you?"

Nikki giggled a little, though her sobbing stifled it. "Jenner," she said. Nikaya remembered the name.

"Want me to go get Jenner, feed him to her?" Nikaya asked.

She laughed, wiping away her tears.

Gaunt interrupted the memory by squeezing Nikaya tight in his wings and hissing. The sound meant *Be still*. The wolves were close. Nikaya had been so distracted that she didn't realize, until that very moment, that her tracks in the snow led right to her position. She couldn't do anything about it now.

Somewhere beyond the graveyard, she heard the panting of a dog. Then whining, like a pup begging its master to stay close. She realized that the dead Alphas terrified this small pack. No one this far out into wolf country had seen the ants in years, and these young dogs must have merely heard stories. Pride swelled in Nikaya's chest, something she had not felt since she went to prison. Her own granddaughter saw no reason to fear these creatures, yet these hunters could come no closer. *Good, now* you *can have nightmares about them*, she thought.

The wolves argued with one another in barks and grunts until at last they trotted deeper into the ravine. Nikaya held her breath as they passed. They must have told themselves that the beaver and the bat had continued to the bottom of the hill, the easiest route to safety. The farther they got from this hellish pile of corpses, the more the story would make sense. With Gaunt propping his cheek against hers, Nikaya lifted her head to see three white tails vanish into the trees.

"You said we'd be safe," she hissed. "You said we were going around the packs."

He chirped something, but she pushed him away. He let go of her and collapsed in a pile of leather and fur.

Ever since escaping, they had gone in a giant circle. She agreed to carry Gaunt not only for the pardon, but because he swore—insofar as she could understand—that he had seen the packs moving east, to Hosanna. A growing army. Their best bet, he told her, was to head southwest, along the rise of the mountains. From there, they would make their way through a mountain pass, hoping to reach the forest and a new chain of rivers that would mask their scent. This grueling trek must have looked so easy while flying over it. But perhaps he was leading her to another bat cave where he would tell his comrades that she tricked him, broke his wing, held him hostage. She couldn't put anything past these bastards.

Among his screeches, she could detect a single phrase, repeated again and again. *Too many. Too many.*

"Too many what?" she asked.

He said the Chiropteran word for *wolf.* It literally meant puffy tail, which made them sound like cartoon characters. This annoyed her. "Yes, I noticed that there are too many."

*No, no,* he told her. Wolves from all over joined them now. From far beyond the frontier. More than anyone could have anticipated.

"So we're walking right into a wave of them," she said.

He said yes.

"And the mountain pass?"

He repeated the word *no* several times. More wolves from the west would use that same route.

Nikaya glanced at the rotting face of the Alpha ant. Maybe she should drag this thing along, operate it like a puppet to scare the wolves away.

"So, we have to *climb* the mountains," she said. The nearest peak spiked into the horizon, a sharp block of stone and ice. She could die there of exposure and starvation, or she could wait to get eaten here.

To his credit, Gaunt kept his mouth shut.

ANOTHER HILL, ANOTHER long day dragging her feet as the dirt gave way to rock, cold and hard. It would be difficult for the wolves to track them on the dry granite. They stopped when they came across another circle of dead Alphas. There were four this time, all facing one another, their bodies like points on a compass. While Gaunt let out a sustained hiss, Nikaya was too tired to get anxious. The last ants on Earth were building weird art installations. So what? She needed to eat.

Every day at dusk, as Nikaya dropped Gaunt from her shoulders, the bat seemed the most vulnerable, like a sick newborn. He slid the goggles from his eyes, which left painful rings around the sockets. With his long finger bones, he probed the hole in his wing. It was too wide to heal any time soon. When he noticed Nikaya watching him, he stopped and looked away, toward the mountain range that blocked their path.

Nikaya left him to forage for food. She started by nibbling off a few branches. By not chewing on anything for nearly two days, her teeth had grown long enough for her to notice a difference. She needed to wear them down a bit. More importantly, she needed to let her mind drift after so many hours in a panic state, sniffing for dog fur and trying to decipher the bat's stupid language.

The sugary layer beneath the tree bark did not taste right. The northern hardwoods that grew here were too high in the mountains, too far from a body of water. She longed for a birch with roots that stretched into a muddy riverbank. While she imagined it, she held the branch in her hands like a pipe and pretended to smoke it, a simple pleasure she might never experience again.

She moved on to searching for fruit and berries for the bat. This far into the hills, she could find only a few shrubs with shriveled berries from the summer, still frozen to the stalks. She plucked them until her fingertips went raw, and then carried a pile of them pressed against her belly. The bat would complain again. She would tune it out.

When she returned to the ant graveyard, she found Gaunt facing the downward slope of the hill. Like a crab, he scuttled toward the body of an Alpha, his hind legs pumping while his wings slapped against the earth. He used the Alpha's body as a ramp, launching himself from it, flapping madly. In that instant, the hole in his left wing showed prominently, a gaping void in the flesh. Gaunt floated for a moment, then crashed, carving out a muddy groove in the thin layer of snow.

*No one gets to fly away*, Nikaya thought. *We're both stuck here.*

His head lifted first, the goggles askew. His ribs rose and fell with each frustrated breath. Judging from his reaction, this was not his first attempt. Gaunt was one of the few bats who could fly from a sitting position. Most of his people needed to free fall from a high place in order to gather enough speed. Neither option would help him now.

Nikaya walked closer, and the bat's ears twitched. Embarrassed, Gaunt tried to prop himself on his front limbs as if nothing happened. He sniffed the berries, and his tongue flicked. She could see the anger in his face. A flightless bat who needed to beg for food. Without his usual chirping, he planted his snout in the pile of berries and began nibbling. Nikaya tried to back away, but Gaunt leaned into her and snatched every last bite, his mouth slurping as the berries burst open. His tongue shot out and picked off the last one. It left a wet mark on her hand. She groaned in disgust. He turned and hobbled away.

"You're welcome," Nikaya said.

The bat sat upright like a human and wrapped his wings around himself. Nikaya plopped onto the dirt a few feet away, and they faced the mountain together, the place where they would both die, if they were lucky enough to get that far. Nikaya dreamed of starting a fire, building a lodge, smoking her pipe, singing her songs. Any one of those things could get them killed out here. She steeled herself to sleep another night in the cold like some stray, only this time she would do it lodged between the rotting husks of mutant insects.

They could not stay here. Sooner or later, a pack of wolves that did not fear the Alphas would arrive. In the early days of Lodge City, she had worked out an arrangement with the nearby wolf packs, offering goods from Hosanna in exchange for observing the border. Castor called it a tribute, a word he must have learned from a human. Whatever the name, it worked. Greedy people were at least willing to negotiate. But these Mudfoot wolves, out on some crusade for a mad queen—they would not have the courtesy to kill her before tearing her apart. When that happened, this lazy ratwing would suddenly find the strength to fly again, of that she had no doubt.

Nikaya hummed absently. The vibration in her throat gave the illusion of warmth. That's how it often worked among the beavers. Someone would take the lead, letting their mind wander, and the others would follow along. She mumbled the words. Out of the corner of her eye, the bat turned to face her, both annoyed and curious. It was a tune she had taught to her grandchildren.

> *I know I'm a beaver*
> *'Cause of my great buck tooth.*
> *I'll always be a beaver*
> *There is no other truth.*

The next lines were about the parts of the beaver: the ears, the fur, the tail, the hands. The young ones would point to themselves as they sang. Then they got to the part that always made them laugh:

> *My tail is for swimming,*
> *And I'll tell you what—*
> *It follows me all over;*
> *'Cause it's stuck to my big butt.*

And with that, the children would turn and wiggle their behinds. The adults would laugh while shaking their heads in mock-disapproval.

Delirious, exhausted, Nikaya doubled over with laughter at the memory. She asked the Three Goddesses to either get her over that mountain or to let her die now, with this silly image rattling around in her tired mind. As she whispered a brief prayer, Gaunt slipped closer and wrapped his wings around her. The bat must have been freezing. Had she the strength, she would have elbowed him away. But he was warm. No point in wasting energy.

He squeaked at her. He wanted her to keep singing. Anything to pass the time.

So she did, going through all the childish lyrics. The bat may have understood every other word, if that. She at last got to the part about the other animals in the forest, and how they could not do the amazing things that beavers could do. Wolves could hunt, but could not swim. Bears were strong, but could not build. *Humans think they're so smart*, the song continued. *They taught the dogs to sit.*

She stopped, suddenly recalling the next two lines. She remembered little Nikki singing them, giggling, completely unaware, because that was expected of children.

Gaunt jostled Nikaya, demanding that she continue. When she remained quiet, he squawked in her ear so loud it made her teeth grind.

"And no one's got it worse than bats," she sang. "Because they smell like shit."

Gaunt remained still.

"Sorry, that's the line."

The bat withdrew his wings, screeched a few Chiropteran swear words at her, and returned to his original spot.

"There are two more verses about the bats after that," she said. It was true. The verses described how the bats could not be trusted, how they lied and stole and betrayed. How the Three Goddesses cursed them. Gaunt let out a string of words that Nikaya could not translate.

"Oh, come on," Nikaya said. "Quit the self-righteous routine. It's just the two of us out here. We're not performing for anyone."

Gaunt hissed the word for rotten at her.

"You have songs about *us*, don't you?"

*No*, the bat screeched in his language. He pointed to the mountains and said the words for *climb* and *tomorrow*. Then he covered his mouth with his wing—much like the bats did to Nikaya when they arrested her—meaning that she should keep quiet for the rest of the evening.

That was fine with Nikaya. She returned to her humming— lighter this time, with occasional pats on the earth with her tail. The bat remained perfectly still, another boulder on this hill.

Night fell.

She had to admit it. She *was* cold again without Gaunt's wings wrapped around her.

NIKAYA WOKE LONG before morning. Sleeping among the Alpha carcasses proved even more of a problem than the cold. Too many bad memories. She recalled the early days of the war when she'd emerged from the riverbank a changed creature, uplifted. And she saw the Alphas, marching in formation ten wide, five deep, their hides gleaming in the sun. While the other beavers cowered in their lodges, she watched a helicopter buzzing over the ants. The chopper dropped low, and a human wearing a white helmet tossed a device from the side door. Before it hit the ground, the ant formation changed from a rectangle to a triangle to avoid it. The device exploded. Though Nikaya could feel the sound of it, the ants did not seem to notice. And then, something happened that few people believed whenever she told the story: the ants quickly piled on top of one another into a wriggling mass. It grew higher and higher until the peak reached the chopper's landing skids. By then, the pilot must have realized the mistake he had made. The ant at the top of the pile latched on to the left skid. When the chopper tried to lift away, the other ants held tight to one another, forming a chain that rooted itself in the ground. The helicopter wobbled. The man with the white helmet fell from the door, vanishing in the writhing mass of bodies. The helicopter spun, twisting the pile of ants until it, too, plummeted to the earth, lost in a bright orange fireball and a cloud of smoke.

All of that had happened on her first day in this new world. The pets who changed may have read a book, and the farm animals may have jumped their fences, and the predators may have made peace with their prey. But she witnessed the war to come.

These ants who died here, in this formation, did so on purpose. With or without orders from their Queen, they never did things like this by accident. Nikaya wondered if they completed some mission and then waited to die. Perhaps these mausoleums appeared all over the globe, forming patterns that only they could read. If Nikaya met her end in those mountains, carrying a ratwing, there would be no one to bury her or erect a monument to what she had accomplished. If anyone remembered her, they would tell stories about her ghost haunting the hills, snatching children. "Write a song about that," she mumbled.

Nikaya got to her feet and sniffed around. No wolves. No sign of the bat either. She scuttled to the other side of the Alpha, where Gaunt slept the night before. He was gone.

"No you didn't," she said.

Something else was missing. The Alpha—the northern point on the compass they formed—had crawled off in the night. Nikaya's hand drifted to her chest as her heart pounded.

There was no way Gaunt could have flown away. Not yet. Maybe not ever again. So she dropped to her knees and dug her snout into the dirt and immediately found the scent, still fresh, a mingling of bat leather and ant hide. It wove through the corpses before breaking free and trickling into the ravine.

She continued on her hands and knees into the forest. Whenever she lost the scent, she searched for clues. A footprint in the mud put her on track again. After that, a trampled patch of weeds. At last, she spotted the Alpha propped against an evergreen, its jaw yawning open like a baby bird waiting to be fed. It remained perfectly still. Perhaps it had died for real this time.

Nikaya tilted her gaze upward and saw Gaunt hanging from the first thick branch he could find. In his flying days, he would have held on by his feet. But in his panicked, wounded state, he wrapped his wings around the bark. The Alpha waited for him to fall.

Nikaya once again reminded herself that she needed this ratwing. She plucked a rock from her feet and tossed it at the Alpha. No reaction. She threw a few more. The ant did not budge.

One last test. Nikaya picked up a long branch, held it like a spear, and approached cautiously. When she got within range, she poked the Alpha's thorax. She jumped when the middle legs curled inward, but realized that she had merely triggered some reflex. She poked again, harder this time, and the beast slumped over. One of its brittle antennae broke off on impact.

Shaking, Gaunt shimmied down the tree and immediately got behind Nikaya. If the Alpha woke again, it would snap at her instead of him.

"I'm not your bodyguard," Nikaya said.

The bat seemed so young, a frightened child who failed to grow up while the world crept in around him. She'd heard stories about his kind leaving behind the youth who could not fly. He must have felt like that, stuck in a place bent on killing the unworthy.

"What happened?" she said.

Through a series of gestures, screeches, and pantomiming, Gaunt explained that he spotted some birds flying overhead, and ventured to a lookout point to see where they were going. The

Alpha awakened and followed him. Gaunt mimicked the beast waddling about.

"Why did it go after *you?*" Nikaya said. "Why not me? I was sleeping right there."

Gaunt tapped his temple and uttered the word for empty. The bats used that word to describe their old ones when they went senile. This ant's brain had been empty for years, judging from the spreading cracks in its exoskeleton and the fluids seeping out. Gaunt poked Nikaya's arm with his wing and said, *Like you.* And then he laughed nervously, still shaken from his brush with death.

"That's enough," Nikaya said. "Take me to this lookout point."

If birds had roosted nearby, they could send for help. But the wrong species could get them killed. Who knew which birds sided with the wolves these days? She tried to remember which nesting birds she may have angered when clearing the forests to make way for Lodge City. Even the ones she bribed took the payment reluctantly. They would love a chance to pick her apart with their hooked beaks. And if any birds had fallen prey to the spider that she unleashed on the bats, then no bribe would get her out of trouble.

After a brief ascent through the forest, Nikaya and Gaunt came to an opening in the trees, leading to a steep drop into another ravine spiked with sharp granite. Though a stream may have trickled through during the warmer months, it had since run dry, leaving behind bare stone. Far in the distance, the real mountains awaited.

Gaunt pointed to his ears. He could hear something. After a few seconds, Nikaya could hear the noise as well, like a tiny room full of people. An uneven series of honks, shouted in every direction.

"Oh, don't tell me," Nikaya said. She walked out to the edge of the promontory. Gaunt asked her what she saw. He could hear it, but only she could see it.

Alongside a frozen pond about a mile away gathered a colony of geese, forming a great circle. Hundreds of them chipped away at the ice with their beaks to get to the water. Despite the distance, Nikaya could tell that they were famished, dehydrated, leaner from their long trip from the south. Even worse, they were at least six weeks earlier than usual, which meant that something had driven them north before they wanted to go.

Gaunt asked what was wrong.

"I was hoping we could find someone to help," Nikaya said. "But it's no use with these people."

Gaunt asked why the birds had stopped at the pond.

"They're waiting for the winds to pick up," she said. "I've seen this before. They're too tired to go over the mountains today. So they'll regroup, count their dead, then use the air current to carry them over the top."

Gaunt motioned in the direction of the birds. It meant, *Let's go!*

"No," Nikaya said. "They hate us. We have to find another way."

The geese would never help. They sat out the war, refusing to serve as scouts as most of the other birds had done. After the war, they refused to trade with anyone. During migration season, they acted as if they owned the skies and left their green shit everywhere. With no real leader, and still living as they had before the Change, they felt little need to interact with their neighbors. For all she knew, they'd made their peace with the wolves months ago.

Nikaya started to walk away. Gaunt wrapped the tip of his wing around her arm and put his hideous fangs in her face. A stream of Chiropteran curse words flowed out, carried on the bat's putrid breath. She could make out only a few lines. *You will do*, he kept saying. *You will do!*

"I can't *do*," Nikaya said.

*Speak to them*, the bat pleaded.

"Listen, ratwing. Our best bet is to wait for them to leave. Then we climb."

*No!* the bat squeaked. Then he said the word for wolves. And ants. Wolves and ants, wolves and ants, on their way here.

"I know," Nikaya said.

*Birds, only chance*, Gaunt said. *Or we die here.*

Nikaya almost said yes, they *would* die here, as a matter of fact.

*You good at words*, the bat said. *You will do!*

The bat had never complimented her before. Not that she ever gave him a reason.

*You talk good*, Gaunt said. *Birds listen. Everyone listens.*

She watched him. She waited for his eyes to wander, his tongue to flick out of his mouth. Anything to give away what he was really planning.

"Oh, I get it," she said. "You think you can hand me over."

Gaunt covered his face with his wings and screamed.

"That's why you're in such a hurry, isn't it?" Nikaya said.

Gaunt pounded his chest with his wings. He said the same thing again and again. *My fault. My fault.*

"What are you talking about? What's your fault?"

*Wolves angry*, he said in Chiropteran. *Because me. Because me!* Gaunt gestured to the mountains again and started shouting. Nikaya could not translate all of it, but she didn't have to. Gaunt blamed himself for the attack on the garrison. She remembered it well enough. The other bats did not want him to scout the wolves. He did it anyway, and it got them all killed. And now he needed to warn the others. As quickly as possible, no matter the cost. Dying in the process would probably be a blessing.

Gaunt stomped toward her. He poked her shoulder, hard enough to knock her off balance. *Thought* you *would understand*, he sneered.

*Well played*, she thought. He'd found her weakness. Probed

it. Rubbed in the salt. He would make a good politician someday if he lived through this.

"The birds might be hungry enough to eat us, you know," she said.

*No*, he squeaked. *They listen. You see.*

Nikaya went to the lookout once more. From here, the geese seemed friendly. They groomed one another and brought food to the weak ones. A few of them floated in the pond, perhaps knowing that this could be their last chance to do so. When the time came to fly over the mountain, many of their number would fall. Even after the Change, a long winter would humble anyone. This made the birds dangerous. It also made them vulnerable.

"All right," Nikaya said. "We will try."

The bat flapped his wings. He said something about water. She asked him to repeat it.

*Water moves*, he said in his language.

She laughed. "*The water flows*, you mean."

*Water moves*, he repeated. *We are water.*

"Sure," she said. "We are water."

# CHAPTER 10

## GONNEY

*(UNOFFICIAL) LOGBOOK OF THE SUS AL-RIHLA*
*DATE UNKNOWN*
*(MY NEW COMPANIONS FROM THE OPA PACK DO NOT KEEP*
*TRACK OF DAYS AND MONTHS.) QUAY SAYS ONE AND A HALF*
*FULL MOONS BEFORE THE WEATHER BREAKS.*

*WALKED ABOUT EIGHT MILES TODAY. QUAY SAYS SHE CAN*
*SMELL THE PACK.*

*AT NIGHT, MADE A NEW SCABBARD FOR THE SWORD OUT OF*
*SOME CANVAS MATERIAL.*

*<u>PERSONAL HEALTH</u>: INJURY IS HEALING WELL. PUNCTURE*
*WOUND IS SORE, BUT SCABBED OVER.*

*DATE UNKNOWN.*
*ARRIVED AT MUDFOOT CAMP LATE IN THE DAY. THOUSANDS OF*
*CANINES HERE. MORE ON THE WAY. ALL DOGS AND WOLVES AND*
*THOSE IN BETWEEN.*

*MOST SLEEP OUT IN THE OPEN. THE LEADERS STAY IN A CAVE.*

THE NEW PEOPLE WHO ARRIVE ARE GIVEN SPACE AT THE EDGE
OF CAMP. THEY ARE EXPECTED TO KEEP WATCH.

FIRES BURN AT NIGHT. THE STRONGER WOLVES PASS FOOD
AROUND. ENOUGH FOR EVERYONE. ALL MEAT. "A GENEROUS
WOLF IS A STRONG WOLF," THEY SAY.

WORD SPREADS THAT WE ARE WAITING HERE WHILE THE WOLF
MATRIARCH RESTS. SHE IS TIRED FROM GIVING BIRTH, THEY SAY.

THE WOLVES HOWL ALL NIGHT. I AM TOLD THEY HAVE HOWLED
NONSTOP SINCE THE WOLF MATRIARCH ANNOUNCED THAT SHE
HAD A SON.

<u>**PERSONAL HEALTH**</u>: STOMACH IS GROWLING. HAVE NOT EATEN
MAMMAL MEAT BEFORE. NIPPLES LEAKING. SEVERAL PEOPLE
HAVE NOTICED, EVEN WHEN I COVER. SMELL IS TOO STRONG.


**FEBRUARY 3**
(A REFUGEE FROM HOSANNA TOLD ME THE DATE.)

AT DAYBREAK, THE WOLF MATRIARCH CAME OUT OF HER CAVE
AND SHOWED EVERYONE HER SON. THE HUMANS STOOD AT HER
SIDE. ON ALL FOURS. THE ENTIRE THING LASTED MAYBE THREE
MINUTES.

EVERYONE IS STILL HOWLING IN CELEBRATION.

SOMEONE HAS STREAKED MY SON'S FUR WITH CHARCOAL, SO
HE LOOKS MORE LIKE A WOLF. I CAN TELL HE DOES NOT LIKE
IT. HE TRIES TO LICK IT AWAY FROM HIS PAWS. I CAN HEAR
HIM GRUMBLING ABOUT IT IN MY MIND.

*I SLIPPED AWAY TO WATCH THE DOGS PLAY ZAGGA FOR HOURS. ONE OF THE DOGS SHATTERED HIS LEG SO BADLY THE BONE BROKE THROUGH THE SKIN. I LAUGHED WHEN I SAW IT.*

ON HER THIRD day at the camp, D'Arc passed the time by offering to dig a latrine ditch. Quay insisted on helping. Everyone agreed that if the growing pack planned to stay here, they needed a bathroom. No amount of swagger about living in the wild could change that simple fact.

Most of the wolves were still asleep when the work began. They snorted and shifted at the sound of the shovels piercing the frozen dirt. Their bodies created a furry landscape throughout the clearing in the forest, with more of them nestled among the trees. Only the vapor flowing from their nostrils distinguished them from rocks or fallen logs. While the wolves' coats blended with the environment, the occasional dog would stick out, having more brightly colored fur, bred to please their human masters. A few patches of burnt orange indicated the foxes who had rejected the peace talks and joined the rebellion.

During her breaks from shoveling, D'Arc would lean on the handle and watch these people. By now, she could spot the various packs that banded together at night. The Opa, who brought her here, wore a light gray fur. Beside them, the Hachi, had darker coats meant for sneaking through the granite mountain passes. Beyond that were the brownish white coats of the rival Junpaw and Pabka clans—once related, now competing for a river delta far to the south.

D'Arc recalled her brief time at the academy, where her bunkmate, Razz—a pug who made moonshine—showed her a map of wolf country, color-coded by clan. "This map'll be out of date by next month," the pug said, slurring her words while she sipped her liquor. "Borders're always moving. Wolves're always cutting each other's tails off."

Whatever violent history they all shared, here the canines rested together, as docile as the pets who camped with them, in a community that Hosanna promised but had never delivered. And yet D'Arc had never felt so alone. Staring at the cave where her child was held captive, she wondered if anyone here could help her get him back.

"You need to rest?" Quay said beside her. The wolf wedged her shovel under a rock and pried it loose from the earth.

"I'm fine," D'Arc said, fighting the urge to cover the wounds on her ribs. The scabs had hardened into rough, purplish blotches that grew itchier each day.

D'Arc stuck the spade into the earth and jammed it deeper with her foot. She considered telling Quay everything and asking for her help to find her son. But it couldn't work like that. D'Arc could not even reveal her name to these wolves, choosing instead to call herself Madre, the name she'd used in her interactions with the beavers, back when the ranch was her entire universe. Quay believed in the cause, as far as she understood it. She said that the wolves, at long last, had a true leader who could fight the humans—not some tribal warlord hoping to bestow territory on his sons. Whenever D'Arc asked her what specifically the humans had done to the wolves, Quay would tell her of the many calamities that befell her family, from illness to natural disaster to famine. Sometimes, she blamed the humans directly, mainly for their interference in the natural order of things. Other times, she faulted them for not helping more. That her newfound leader allied herself with humans did not strike Quay or the others as a contradiction. If anything, it only reinforced their belief that Mercy the Great was special, rising from the ashes of the

War with No Name. She would lead them to Hosanna, where she would separate the traitors from the people who saw the light.

Again and again, the canines gave D'Arc a variation of Quay's story. To hear them tell it, they suffered and toiled for years while the humans plotted against them. Oddly, the dogs from Hosanna often sounded angrier about the occupation than the wolves, who themselves never knew the softness of a bed, or the warmth of a stove in wintertime. During the endless zagga games, many of the chants from the crowd mocked the losers by comparing them with pets. They called the defeated ones gonneys. Fake wolves. The dirtiest word in the camp. And when one of the dogs drew a penalty—D'Arc could not figure out which arbitrary rule had been broken—they chanted the word "choker" as the disqualified player limped off the playing field, humiliated. D'Arc remembered the word from the stories Mort(e) told her about the early days of the war.

"Who cut your balls off?" someone screamed.

The ejected player silenced the hecklers by grabbing his crotch and shouting, "Pray you grow a pair this big some day!"

Quay was no gonney. She knew how to survive out here, what to eat, where to find good water. She knew as well that they needed to slope the latrine so that the spill directed away from the camp. Though D'Arc knew the basics, she let Quay take the lead. No need to give away her past. Better to let everyone think that she left Hosanna like so many other dogs, searching for adventure, convinced she would never get ahead in a human city.

Over the last few days, Quay often asked her about how bad things had become in Hosanna. The Opa wolves heard only the worst rumors, and D'Arc quickly realized that she would have to toss them some red meat. So she embellished stories of the terrible food at the academy mess hall. She described the squalor of some of the canine neighborhoods—disparagingly called the Kennels—though she borrowed many of the details from the flood, which had destroyed most of the districts, canine or otherwise. And she never mentioned that some of the dog communities insisted on having their own sections of the city. It was all too complicated to explain. D'Arc lied through omission, and by conjuring tales until it felt like someone else was speaking in her voice. The Opa believed all of it because they wanted to.

When they finished digging, Quay and D'Arc lined the pit with rocks. By then, the camp was awake. Hunting parties formed at the perimeter, hoping to catch some deer who had strayed too close to the pack. More people joined in the small construction project, enough to form a line to pass the stones from hand to hand. The workers bantered. One of them asked if they would build a hotel next. Someone demanded maid service, another a hot tub. Someone else asked if anyone had heard about when the pack would move again. Quay laughed. "Now that we dig this pit, I bet we leave today."

"We can take it with us, right?" someone asked.

Their laughter quieted when they noticed one of the humans making his way through the crowd with one of the Mudfoot wolves at his side. Both walked on all fours. The human wore a wolf pelt over his shoulders, the color of smoke, and his movements came so close to mimicking an animal that only his missing tail gave him away.

Whenever the humans emerged from their cave, the wolves watched with a mixture of awe and dismay. Many had simply never seen one before. The canines stepped aside as the pair headed for a Junpaw wolf resting on her back, nursing her two cubs.

D'Arc watched the exchange while handing over the rocks. The human and the wolf had done the same exact thing the day before, at the same time and with the same mother wolf. This human often stood beside the leader, Augur, while the Mudfoot wolf was part of Mercy's inner circle. D'Arc wished she could record all their names and routines in her logbook, but she worried that someone who could actually read would find it. For now, she kept it all in her mind.

After a few minutes, the human nodded toward the cave. The Junpaw rose to her feet while her young ones tried to hang on to her. Her stomach was still bloated from carrying the litter, which gave her a wobbly gait. She followed the human and the Mudfoot to the cave. As she disappeared inside, a wave of intense jealousy spread outward from D'Arc's chest.

"I told you," Quay whispered to her. "The females are important. They need breeders."

She went on about the Junpaw clan, how they survived a terrible winter in recent years. "Good blood," Quay said. "Strong hunters."

"Good milk," D'Arc blurted out. She almost dropped the stone she held when she realized what she had said. The thoughts came rushing into her head, the entire scenario unfolding. She knew how she could get close to her son again. These wolves needed her. They had no choice but to trust her. And from there, it would only be a matter of time before she could find a way to pry him loose.

It was like the Old Man said in all those years of training: know the terrain, know the enemy, know how to get in and out. She could do this. She imagined every single wolf in the camp chasing her as she carried away her son. As she carried away their future. It did not make her afraid. Instead, she felt so giddy she almost laughed out loud.

"You're holding us up," Quay said. D'Arc gave her the next stone.

FEBRUARY 4
WEATHER: BRIGHT, SUNNY WEATHER.

ALL WORK CAME TO A STOP TODAY FOR A FUNERAL. THE TOQWA
CHILD SHERIN DIED IN THE NIGHT. THEY BURNED THE BODY
ON THE HILL OVERLOOKING THE CAMP, WHILE THE HUMANS LET
OUT THEIR SAD HOWLS.

QUAY TELLS ME THAT AUGUR WAS THE CHILD'S FATHER. HE
PULLED HER FROM THE MOTHER'S CORPSE AND BIT OFF THE
UMBILICAL CORD.

WHILE THE FIRES BURNED, MERCY SAT BESIDE THE HUMAN,
LEANING INTO HIM. HE BURIED HIS FACE IN THE WOLF'S HIDE
AND WEPT. HE KEPT HOWLING, AND THE SOUND GOT MORE
RAGGED EACH TIME.

"NOW THEY HAVE BOTH LOST CHILDREN," QUAY SAYS.

THE STORIES OF WHAT MERCY HAS ENDURED HAVE BEEN GOING
AROUND THE CAMP FOR DAYS. NO ONE CAN COMPLAIN WITHOUT
SOMEONE ELSE REMINDING THEM ABOUT WHAT MERCY WENT
THROUGH.

I AM GOING TO BED NOW. THE FIRES HAVE BURNED OUT. THE
HUMAN AND THE WOLF ARE STILL HOLDING THEIR EMBRACE.


FEBRUARY 5
WEATHER: BRIGHT AND SUNNY AGAIN. TWO DAYS IN A ROW.
CAN'T REMEMBER THE LAST TIME THAT HAPPENED.

COMPLETED THE LATRINE WITH QUAY. ALREADY SOMEONE

*WANTS US TO HELP BUILD ANOTHER ONE. TOMORROW, I TELL THEM.*

*AT NIGHT, QUAY ASKS IF I CAN TEACH HER TO READ. I TRY MY BEST. SHE QUITS IN FRUSTRATION AFTER 20 MINUTES.*

*WORD SPREADS THAT THE PACK WILL MOVE SOON. SOME SAY WE ARE RUNNING AWAY FROM THE OTHER WOLVES. BUT QUAY THINKS WE ARE GOING TO THE WOLVES. THEY HAVE A WINTER SUMMIT THIS TIME EVERY YEAR. THEY CALL IT A KEN-RA. MERCY WANTS TO GO. NOT SURE IF SHE IS INVITED.*

*PERSONAL HEALTH: TIRED. BUT STILL AWAKE.*

WHEN THE GUARD noticed D'Arc striding toward him, he dropped to his front paws and straightened his tail. It was morning again, and the few wolves who were awake stopped in place and watched D'Arc as she approached the mouth of the cave, where Mercy and her human allies slept. D'Arc knew this guard's name by now. On the rare occasions when he spoke, he called himself Quick. He and his brother, Mag, took turns patrolling the area between the cave and the rest of the camp. By then, thousands of footsteps had trampled the earth and torn out most of the grass. And yet the few feet in front of the cave remained pristine, a testament to the awe that these wolves inspired.

Quick was not about to let anyone disturb the grass without a good reason. D'Arc stopped right at the edge. She wore her sword on a canvas strap, which crisscrossed a shawl fashioned from wool.

Instead of asking what she wanted, Quick arched his spine, bared his teeth, and lifted his tail. Wolf language was like reading a badly written comic book, the Old Man had once told her.

Words, images, expressions and movement all worked together. She knew enough to understand that this wolf wanted her to get to the point.

"I was told I could help," D'Arc said. When Quick refused to acknowledge this, she placed her hand on her chest and added, "For the wolf prince."

He must have smelled her milk. All the wolves wrinkled their noses when she came close.

Quick scraped his paw on the earth three times, quickly. An older wolf emerged from the darkness of the cave. Carsa, they called her. Patches of bare skin pocked her gray coat. Her gums were the same color as her fur. When her eyes met Quick's, the younger wolf tipped his head forward twice, puckered his lips, and flicked his ears. Carsa disappeared inside.

They waited. More onlookers from the camp slowed their gait as they passed.

From deep inside the cave, Carsa barked at Quick, the sound echoing. He led D'Arc to the entrance. Before she could go inside, Quick told her to remove her sword. "Weapon safe with me," he said.

A reasonable request. She released the sword from her shoulder, which suddenly felt cold without it. Then she stepped through the threshold into the warmth and darkness, like sliding inside of a lung. Carsa gave her room to squeeze by. D'Arc's eyes adjusted, allowing her to make out a rug made of woven hemp covering the stony floor. In the middle of it, the wolf they called Mercy lay propped on her elbow, with her back to the entrance. Her massive tail rose and fell.

Her head rested in Augur's lap. The human sat with his legs crossed, his hand brushing her head, grooming her. Much like Tristan used to do to D'Arc at the end of a long day, when they would fall asleep watching game shows and baseball.

While Mercy remained still, Augur gave D'Arc a side-eyed

glance. His tattoo formed a mask around his face, with the fangs painted around his lips. His leather tunic and pants made him resemble an animal himself, a beast stitched together from other creatures.

The man's silence encouraged her to get closer. And when she did, she saw on the other side of Mercy's body a tiny ball of fur, silver and shiny. A rush of blood made D'Arc wobble a bit. She steadied herself and tried to focus on what Quay had told her to do when she arrived. She dropped to her knees, then slid her paws forward and lowered her chin to the floor. A sign of submission to a higher wolf. To greet her, the man leaned over and brushed his cheek on her forehead.

D'Arc edged closer. The pup's eyes remained closed. His mouth and tongue lapped at Mercy, but she had gone dry. He whimpered, and the tinny sound of it carried words that only D'Arc could hear. He asked her, *Why? Why is this happening?*

*I don't know*, she thought.

Mercy stretched her paw over his tiny body and pulled him closer. Mercy's brow shifted as her wet eyes rolled toward this strange visitor. Here, she did not resemble the proud warrior queen that all the dogs from Hosanna had come to praise. Instead, she was one of them, an overgrown pup who wanted someone to comfort her.

A low-pitched noise rumbled in Mercy's throat.

"Do you speak their language?" the man asked.

"Only a little," D'Arc said.

"She thanks you."

Mercy looked away.

D'Arc reached out her paws, making sure to do it slowly. Mercy got to her feet, leaving the pup squirming beneath her. The wolf leaned toward the child, licked him a few times, then nudged him toward D'Arc. A chill passed between mother and son, and the pup shivered and cried out.

*I want to go back to the boat,* D'Arc heard him say. She scooped him from the floor and lifted him to her chest. He would not suckle and instead twisted his mouth away from her, screaming. *No!* he said in her mind. *Not until you promise to take me to the boat.*

*The boat is not home,* she thought. *There is more to the world.* So much more, she remembered. The Old Man was right. So many other things that could hurt you, things you could never imagine until they're sticking out of a wound in your side.

*Who's the Old Man?* the pup asked.

The question opened too many doors. D'Arc could not begin to answer, so the pup repeated himself in a series of annoyed barks. The human and the wolf tilted their heads at the same time.

"He's feisty," D'Arc assured them.

*Go away if you're not taking me to the boat,* the little one said.

"Here," D'Arc said, finally connecting with the pup's mouth. He began to suckle, but also bit hard. She yanked him away for a second to show him he could not do that and then reattached him before he could say anything else. His muscles softened. He relaxed in her arms. She lowered to the ground and sprawled out, allowing him to nestle into her warmth.

*Can we leave now?* she heard the baby say. D'Arc responded with a gentle "Shhhh," and then nudged him along to the next nipple.

"He likes you," the man said.

"Can't tell yet," D'Arc replied.

Mercy leaned over and gave the pup two long licks on his back. D'Arc resisted the urge to swat her away. She had long since accepted that this moment would be tainted. Might as well let the wolf who stole her child show some affection. Besides, D'Arc had already studied the layout of the camp. Even if she managed to snatch the pup away, she would never reach the nearest river to wash away her scent. The old human towns, long since reclaimed by the forest, would hide her for only so long. And fleeing inland would lead her into the Mudfoot's former territory, the Damnable. "The young ones die there," Quay had told her. "Nothing comes out the same."

The hopelessness of it all sunk into her heart. Maybe there was nothing she could do except say goodbye.

*No!* the baby squealed in her mind. *You can't!*

With the pup still barking at her, D'Arc asked, "What will you name him?"

"We cannot say yet," the man said. "A season must pass."

A long stare from Mercy explained everything. Only after nursing would the wolves have the audacity to give this child a name. Anything before that would invite the Damnable to take him away, as it did all the others.

An argument began outside the cave. It quickly escalated to barking and growling. Another wolf barged in, a female, shoving her way past Carsa. D'Arc recognized her as Urna, the omega of the Mudfoot. With a scrawny frame and thinning fur that fell out in patches, this wolf was no match for Carsa. The old warrior let her go anyway, no doubt as a courtesy to Mercy. Urna, for her part, did not seem smart enough to realize that. She leaned into her hind legs, lowered her snout, and gritted her teeth.

Mercy gave her a quick bark. *No*, it meant. *Friend.*

*Tell that ugly dog to be quiet*, the pup said.

Urna would not listen. She gave several warning barks while batting her paws on the ground. The human must have noticed what bothered her. He pinched the edge of D'Arc's shawl. D'Arc could not resist him without disturbing the pup. The human lifted the cloth, revealing the wounds on her side. Mercy yipped when she saw it.

"It's not the disease," D'Arc said. "It's not the Damnable."

The man nodded to Carsa, who appeared alongside D'Arc faster than she could blink.

"Thank you for your help," the man said coldly.

Again, Mercy did not need to say anything. An icy stare got her point across. D'Arc forced herself to pluck the baby from her chest. The pup screamed. Mercy scooped the pup into her arms and returned to the same position in which D'Arc had found her.

Another wolf arrived at the mouth of the cave. D'Arc was outnumbered. She needed to retreat. Because her son needed her to live.

Remembering her manners, D'Arc lowered her head in submission. The human leaned over her and pressed his chin onto her forehead to remind her of her place here. D'Arc walked out with Carsa at her side. When she passed Urna, the omega sneezed. D'Arc could not tell if she did it on purpose. On her way to the entrance of the cave, she came face to face with the Junpaw, the female wolf who entered the cave the day before. She must have seen D'Arc enter and immediately ran to the cave to ask what was going on. Her two pups cowered behind her, scared but still feigning anger. D'Arc hurried past them.

From inside the cave, the pup continued to call for her. *Where are you going? Where are you?*

FEBRUARY 6
WEATHER: OVERCAST.

ENTERED THE CAVE TODAY TO HELP NURSE THE NEWBORN MALE. MERCY AND AUGUR THANKED ME FOR MY SERVICE.

QUAY WILL NOT SHUT UP ABOUT HOW HONORED I SHOULD FEEL TO HAVE BEEN SO CLOSE TO THE WOLF PRINCE.
IN THE AFTERNOON, THE WORD WENT OUT FROM THE MUD-FOOT: THE CONFEDERACY OF WOLVES IS HOLDING A KEN-RA, AND MERCY WILL LEAVE FOR IT TOMORROW. SHE IS BRINGING

*THE CHILD, ALONG WITH HER CLOSEST ADVISORS. EVERYONE THINKS THAT SHE IS PLANNING TO WORK OUT A PEACE AGREEMENT. QUAY THINKS THAT MERCY WILL ASK THE OTHER PACKS TO SURRENDER. OR TO JOIN HER.*

*THEY LEAVE AT FIRST LIGHT.*

<u>PERSONAL HEALTH</u>: *NO SLEEP TONIGHT.*

D'ARC WAITED FOR a thick bank of clouds to seal in the moon before making her move. With her sword strapped on, unsheathed, she slinked through the camp, past the snoring wolves, each pack forming a low pyramid as they huddled around their leaders and dozed off for the night. A few of them stirred and yawned. At least two—the most hardened hunters, she imagined—awakened after their nostrils detected a disturbance in the air. But because D'Arc headed for the latrine, they paid her no attention, grateful that she did not relieve herself in front of everyone, as so many of the wild animals did here.

The Junpaw clan slept at the edge of the camp, circling a dead tree stump. Their leader—a male—was old and weak, barely hanging on to power. Many of the wolves still clung to the ones who led them through the early years of the war. She could imagine this old Junpaw concocting a plan to resurrect his pack through the Mudfoot. If they could only prove themselves worthy—or at least useful—then whatever mistakes he had made over the last few years would be forgotten.

The mother wolf slept with her two pups still clamped to her chest. They must have fallen asleep trying to salvage whatever remained from her session with the wolf prince. D'Arc tried not to dwell on the possibility that the pack coerced this female to serve the Mudfoot. Maybe the Junpaw had offered her as a gift. In the seconds that followed, D'Arc would have to flush out all pity, all remorse. Everything depended on it.

On all four limbs, she pressed the blade of the sword to the wolf's neck so that the coldness of it could seep into the skin. As the wolf's eyes opened, D'Arc clamped the muzzle shut with her hand.

"Shhhhh," she said. A gust of wind covered the noise. One of the pups squirmed.

The Junpaw snorted in disbelief. Then she blinked a few times, more slowly, as the awful truth of her predicament became clear.

"Tomorrow, Mercy and her circle go to meet the council," D'Arc said. "They are bringing a wet nurse. That's you."

The Junpaw nodded.

"Not anymore," D'Arc said. "You're sick. Don't want to infect the wolf prince. Got it?"

"Who are you?" the Junpaw asked, teeth clenched.

"I don't know." It slipped from D'Arc's mouth. She couldn't help it.

"You are the Opa's pet dog," the Junpaw said. "You think you can—"

D'Arc silenced her by pressing the blade harder into the skin. The Junpaw whimpered.

"If one of your children wakes up," D'Arc said, "the last thing they'll see is my sword."

The Junpaw's eye rolled in its socket, searching for anyone who could help. But they were all dreaming. A male sleeping right next to her twitched a little before nestling into a more comfortable position.

"If you go to the ken-ra, your children won't be here when you return," D'Arc added. "Stay here with them, and you all get to live."

She decided to sneak away before this mask she wore fell off.

She let go of the wolf's muzzle. The mouth opened, ready to speak, but then shut again.

D'Arc slipped behind the wolves of the Hachi pack. As the Junpaw disappeared from view, the mother wolf pulled her two pups closer.

FEBRUARY 7
WEATHER: FREEZING RAIN. MISERABLE.

THE JUNPAW CLAN ISSUED A SERIES OF HOWLS FIRST THING IN THE MORNING. THREE OF THEIR OWN WENT MISSING IN THE NIGHT. A FEMALE AND HER TWO PUPS. THE JUNPAWS SENT THEIR BEST TRACKERS TO FOLLOW HER SCENT, BUT IT LOOKS LIKE SHE SIMPLY ABANDONED THE CAMP, THE FIRST TO DO SO, AS FAR AS ANYONE KNOWS.

THE HUMAN AUGUR APPROACHED ME AT MIDDAY. HE INSPECTED MY WOUNDS TO MAKE SURE I'M NOT SICK. THEN HE ASKED ME TO JOIN MERCY AND HER INNER CIRCLE AS WET NURSE AS THEY MARCH TO THE KEN-RA. I ACCEPTED. AUGUR TOLD ME TO BE AT THE CAVE AT FIRST LIGHT TOMORROW. LONG JOURNEY AHEAD.

QUAY BURST INTO TEARS AS SOON AS AUGUR WALKED AWAY. SHE TOLD ME THAT SHE KNEW I WAS SPECIAL. SHE WISHED SHE COULD COME WITH ME.

THE ENTIRE CAMP SINGS WELL INTO THE NIGHT. THEY MAKE UP NEW LYRICS AS THEY GO, ALL ABOUT MERCY THE MERCIFUL AND THE PEACE SHE PROMISES. TRUE, LASTING PEACE.

PERSONAL HEALTH: I FEEL STRONG. RESTED. READY.

I AM A BEACON OF LIGHT. GUIDING THE OTHER SHIPS HOME.

# CHAPTER 11

## ABSOLUTE BEARING

**T**HE SENIOR STAFF filed into the narrow wardroom of the *Vesuvius*. It was one of the few chambers on the ship that one could describe as cozy, with wood panels on the walls, a bookshelf of maritime volumes, and a painting of the airship flying toward the sunrise. The chef had prepared a bean soup with an insect puree, flavored and spiced so that the humans would mistake it for crab meat. Falkirk rose to greet the officers as they arrived, each wearing freshly pressed aquamarine jumpsuits. They took their assigned places in order of seniority. Ruiz pulled out the chair to the right of the captain; O'Neill was to the left. Bulan and Unoka filled the remaining seats. An empty spot remained for the lead security officer— a cat named Limbo—who had excused himself to oversee a training session with the new marines on board.

With everyone seated, Falkirk asked Unoka to give the invocation. The pilot interlaced his long fingers at his chin and cleared his throat, making his Adam's apple bob. He thanked God for the food and for bringing them together. "May the Prophet Michael watch over us," he concluded. As soon as he finished, Bulan's hairy arm shot out and grabbed her spoon. While she slurped the soup, the others unfolded their napkins.

An oppressive silence took hold, interrupted only by the sound of the utensils scraping the porcelain. Falkirk let it go. He figured that any attempt to make small talk would only add to the tension. At dinner the night before—soon after setting out from Liberty One Tower—they had a lively discussion about everything from the expedited repair schedule to the rumors of wolf attacks at the edge of the city. When Unoka claimed the controls handled differently after losing an engine, O'Neill groaned. "Oh no, are we gonna hear another story about piloting during the war?" she asked.

"Don't tempt me," Unoka said.

Ruiz piled on by impersonating Unoka's Nigerian accent: "I flew a Soviet-made cargo plane with only one engine . . ."

"Through a hurricane!" Bulan added.

"Through *two* hurricanes!" Ruiz continued. "I had to get out and push!"

"It's all true," Unoka said. "Let me tell you the story again."

"No," they had said in unison.

No such banter this time. Amid the awkward silence, Bulan abandoned her spoon and lifted the bowl to her lips to drink the last few drops. When she finished, she wiped her mouth with her wrist and moved on to the insect dip. Her long arm hair absently brushed against Unoka, but he ignored it.

Falkirk did not want this dinner to end on a bad note, so he asked O'Neill to open the liquor cabinet. She pulled out a bottle of whiskey, along with five glasses that she slid in front of her colleagues. "I figured we should, while we still could," Falkirk said. He pulled the stopper out of the bottle.

"Sir," Ruiz said. "Before we do that, I wanted to ask you about the course correction you made today."

Falkirk did not react. He continued filling the glasses until only Ruiz's remained empty. The first officer held on to his as he awaited a response.

"What would you like to know?" Falkirk asked. "Besides what I have already told you?"

"We expected to track the Mudfoot on this mission. Instead we're flying over Mournful territory. There haven't been any reports of trouble there since the peace talks began."

Again, Falkirk tried not to react. Ruiz played a tricky game here. As first officer, his primary assignment was to execute the captain's commands, and never to criticize them in front of the others. With these innocuous questions, he toed that line, though barely. Falkirk would have to play along.

"We have an operative on the ground," Falkirk said. "He has a small window to make contact with us. Then we'll be on our way."

He had rehearsed the line many times, and still it came out hollow. The Mournfuls had pushed the hardest for peace. They stood to gain the most from it. For the first time since implementing this plan, Falkirk needed to embellish.

"Tranquility went to great lengths to put this operative in place," he said. "They regard his intelligence as essential. As you can see by our new heading."

Each of the officers glanced at Ruiz, and Falkirk knew then that they had discussed it among themselves already. The tightened muscles in their jaws gave it away. At some point earlier that day, they must have devised a plan to confront him. When he reached for Ruiz's glass, the lieutenant commander covered it with his hand. "I'm okay."

Falkirk had considered offering a toast to the end of the conflict with the wolves. No one seemed interested, so he allowed them to sip their whiskey in peace.

"I don't always agree with the orders we get," Falkirk said. "But, like it or not, Tranquility sees a bigger picture than we do. And this ship is a tool for them. Do you have something specific to raise, Lieutenant Commander?"

Ruiz twirled the glass on the table with his fingertips. Falkirk had called his bluff. He invited criticism, but knew that the first officer could not give voice to it.

"Sir, if I may," O'Neill said. "We've been working to improve some of the long-range radars. If we fly at a slightly higher altitude, we can use them to scan a wider area without going too deep into Mournful territory. That way we can get to the Mudfoot more quickly."

"Thank you, but no," Falkirk said. "Tranquility wants the Mournfuls to see the ship. A reminder of the deal they struck with us."

"There's something else to consider," she said. "Three of our crew members failed to report for duty when we disembarked. All of them canine."

"I read the report," Falkirk said. "There will be more deserters before this fever breaks. That's why what we do in the next few days is so crucial."

*Go ahead, say it*, Falkirk thought. *Say you don't trust me.* He glanced at Bulan and Unoka. The orangutan busied herself with her food. Unoka lowered his eyes. O'Neill and Ruiz must have tried to bully them into confronting the captain. If there was a plan, they were not on board. Not yet, anyway.

"Sir," Ruiz said, rubbing his chin, "I want to take full responsibility for what I'm about to suggest. The other officers don't know about it."

"Go ahead."

"We have a full complement of marines on board. I'd like to extend their shifts. Put three of them in engineering. Three more on the bridge."

"The *bridge*?"

"We have six dogs on board—"

"Plus me," Falkirk said.

"I'm not counting you, sir, you know that. But we have six."

Falkirk waited for him to finish his point.

"After what happened at Cadejo," he stammered, "and after the attacks in Hosanna, I think it's for the best." Ruiz looked around the room as if asking for support. Only O'Neill met his gaze.

"And the course correction prompted this?" Falkirk said.

"Many things prompted it."

The questions would continue to mount in the coming hours. Falkirk knew that. He needed to give Ruiz something, if only to buy some time.

"I don't mean to offend, sir," Ruiz added. "I know we're supposed to be past this. I know what it says in the Hosanna Charter about all the species coming together. No one above the other. I still believe it. But we're on our own out here. And people have tried to take this ship from us before—"

"You're right," Falkirk said. "You have a responsibility to the crew. I understand."

Ruiz exhaled.

"A team in engineering, and a team at the armory," Falkirk said. "But not on the bridge. People are already on edge. We don't need to shove them over."

Ruiz nodded. O'Neill's shoulders went slack.

Bulan rapped her knuckles on the table. "Can we move on to dessert now?"

"Yes, for Christ's sake!" Unoka said.

The tension drained from the room. Falkirk pressed a button on the table that summoned the chef. For a few blissful minutes, the banter returned. Bulan made fun of the beads of sweat on Ruiz's lip. The first officer wiped it away. Falkirk sat and listened, chuckling mechanically at the right moments.

He would miss these people. They deserved better from him.

IN THE DEAD of night, Falkirk curled on the deck beside his bed. After years of sleeping on the floor of a pen, he could never get comfortable on a mattress. The ship's engines purred through the deck plates, though at a different pitch with one of the turbines missing. A dull nightlight glowed in the corner, shielded by a stack of books Falkirk had moved while rummaging through his things. Beside him, the few items that he would bring with him for his journey lay in a neat row: a hunting knife taken from the armory, a poncho that could double as a tent, a sidearm, and a belt. All of it would have to fit inside of his uniform. He figured the gun would not arouse suspicion, given that Ruiz asked for more armed guards on the bridge. If the first officer asked, Falkirk would say, "This is what you wanted, remember?"

In the morning, he would steal some protein rations from the mess hall. As he pondered how many he could reasonably take, he realized that he had nothing sentimental to carry with him. No good luck charms or jewelry. He was truly his mother's son. In their days at the shelter, surrounded by snow in every direction, she whittled him down until he became as sharp and true as an arrowhead. It kept him alive and focused, and left little room for anything else. She would have been proud.

Though he needed sleep, Falkirk dragged himself to his desk. One more chore to complete. From the top drawer, he removed a folder, now worn and creased from weeks of flipping through it. Inside were all the printouts relating to the *al-Rihla*. Maps, reports, itineraries, manifests. One by one, he tore them into pieces and dumped the bits of paper into the waste bin.

The last set of documents consisted of Captain Vittal's reports to Hosanna. He skimmed to the last page, where the final message cut off and the *al-Rihla* vanished. With an icy professionalism, Vittal described her situation. "Adrift," she wrote. "Engine room flooded. Propulsion and navigation disabled." She gave her last known coordinates after sighting an Alpha. And then, a list of the missing, by name, species, rank, and assignment. Eleven people. The eighth person was listed as D'Arc:

canine, midshipman, zoology. At the end of the line, a pair of parentheses housed a single word: pregnant.

It was the reason why he was doing all this, and he still could hardly believe it. Life—a future—had taken root in this barren soil.

He couldn't tell Mort(e). There was no telling how the cat would react. How could a choker like him understand any of this? Mort(e) had no memories of children being born, growing, spiraling away from their families, and becoming little galaxies unto themselves. Falkirk's first pups, Amelia and Yeager, would have been almost old enough to enlist in Tranquility, had they survived. They should have been here, helping to protect this fragile peace. They would have been so much more patient than Falkirk and the others of his generation. They would have listened to the people who wanted to defect to the wolves, rather than writing them off. They would have shown all those lost souls a different path. A way to hope again.

Falkirk's walkie-talkie beeped, startling him. "Captain, this is the bridge," Ruiz said, sounding tired yet determined at the end of his shift.

Falkirk unrolled the jacket to retrieve the device. "Captain here. Go ahead."

"Sir, you told us to inform you when we crossed the border."

"Thank you. Do we still have contact with Tranquility?"

"No. The signal cut out about an hour ago. As we expected."

The communications range had expanded in the last few months, with more wolf packs allowing the Sanctuary Union to build radio towers. But they had flown far beyond the last one, and now the *Vesuvius* was on its own.

"Sir."

"Yes, Ruiz."

"I'm calling you from your office. I didn't want anyone to hear."

Falkirk knew what was coming. "Go ahead."

"Are you going to tell me what's going on with this mission?"

"We've been over this, Lieutenant. You know what I know."

"I'm just saying . . . you *could* tell me. If you needed to."

Falkirk lowered his head. Through all of this, no one had offered to simply help him, or even to listen to him. The man whom he would betray now extended his hand, perhaps the most hopeful thing between their two species since the uprising began. Falkirk could do nothing with it.

"Ruiz, I can promise you that this will be resolved tomorrow," Falkirk said. "All of it. And then we'll be on our way. You have my word."

Silence on the other end. "We'll arrive at our destination at 0730," Ruiz said coldly.

"Good. Thank you."

"Bridge out." The device beeped and went dead.

The piece of paper had crumpled in Falkirk's fist. He hardly noticed. Falkirk tore it apart and dropped the debris into the trash. He curled into a ball and listened to the engines, the heartbeat of the ship that he would never hear again.

THE DOUBLE DOORS slid open, releasing a whoosh of cool air.

"Captain on the bridge," Harris called out.

Falkirk stepped through the threshold and immediately took stock of the room. O'Neill tapped on her keyboard. Bulan pinched the mouthpiece on her headset. Unoka steered the ship southwest, away from the sunrise and into a rapidly brightening horizon. Parish pointed at Warner's screen and whispered something. Ruiz approached from the captain's chair, holding a tablet with the latest commands and other reports.

Everything was in order except for one thing: Falkirk's pistol hung from his belt, tilting it at a slight angle and pressing against his thigh. It caught Ruiz's attention right away. The lieutenant

commander slowed his gait and glanced at O'Neill, who acknowledged him with a light flick of her chin. *Yes, take a good look,*
Falkirk thought.

"Five minutes until we reach the coordinates, sir," Ruiz said.

Falkirk took the tablet from him. "Any activity on the ground?"

"Minimal. Another pack moved toward the border during the
night."

Falkirk tapped the screen and scrolled through a series of
timestamped maps of the area, displayed in silvery night vision.
Red arrows indicated the Mournful packs moving to the south,
toward the edge of their territory. Circles showed suspected
Mudfoot marauders—though at this point, Tranquility regarded
any refugees, deserters, and merchants straying into the valley as
potential insurgents. Falkirk placed his fingers on the screen and
expanded one of the circles. Instead of showing him something
useful, the screen metastasized into a pixelated jumble.

He turned to Bulan. "Any contact with the Mournfuls?"

She covered her mouthpiece. "No, sir."

The room brightened as the sun emerged from a cloud bank.
On the ground, the dormant trees cast long shadows on the
snowy forest floor.

"The operative has one hour, thirty minutes to make contact,"
Falkirk said.

"Hour, twenty-six," Ruiz corrected.

"Do you already have a course plotted for the Mudfoot territory?"

"Of course," Ruiz said with a smile, his first in some time.

A red light blinked over the operations panel, where Ensign
Warner sat. Falkirk tried not to react.

"Sir," Warner called out, "we have a fire alarm on deck one."

It was beginning. His plan, his stupid, foolish plan that
would mean the end of the life he had built from nothing. All
the instincts he tried to hide while serving as captain suddenly

revealed themselves. His tail jumped. His tongue forced its way out of its mouth, grasping for cooler air. His senses heightened. He could still turn away.

"Have you alerted any crew in the area?" Falkirk asked.

Warner pressed his earpiece with his finger. "Yes, but . . . they're saying they detected some smoke. No fire."

Ruiz tensed next to him. More heads turned to Warner's post.

"Patch the crew in," Falkirk said. Warner pressed a few buttons on his console, then pointed to him. "This is the captain," Falkirk said. "What are you seeing down there?"

Someone yelled in the background, while another crew member spoke into his walkie-talkie. "Some kind of malfunction in the torpedo room," a woman's voice said. "Might be in the wiring."

Falkirk nodded to Ruiz. He needed to really sell this next part, to throw off any suspicion. "You ordered an inspection the other day, right?"

"Yes, sir. All that circuitry is supposed to be switched off until we can get a full refit."

Falkirk pretended to be annoyed at his answer. "I'm going down there. You keep the bridge. If it's a short circuit, this won't take long."

"Wait, sir," Ruiz said. He pursed his lips to keep them from quivering. "Are you sure? I could do it."

"My first assignment was in the lower decks," Falkirk said. "Let me do it."

"Yes, sir."

Falkirk headed for the door. "Bulan, if we hear from this operative, patch him directly to my com."

"Aye, sir."

The doors whooshed open. Falkirk winced when they closed behind him with a gentle *kshh*. He realized that he did not do what he had planned to do since this began: take one last look at the bridge, his bridge, his greatest accomplishment. It was too late now.

He took a flight of stairs to the bottom deck, where the engines vibrated through the floor. There, he passed a pair of marines in the corridor, rifles strapped to their shoulders. Both were humans, with freshly shaved scalps that reflected the track lighting overhead. They straightened when they saw him. At the end of the bulkhead, another pair of guards waited. Two more humans with guns to make him more nervous. Just beyond them stood the door to the torpedo room.

The two marines stepped away from the wall and blocked Falkirk's path. One of them, a boy of nineteen, scrunched his nose and mouth, as if flexing a muscle he could not hold. Behind Falkirk, the two other marines closed the gap.

"Captain!" Ruiz shouted from the other end of the corridor.

"What's going on?" Falkirk said. But he already knew. It made sense that Ruiz would do it here, in a confined space, away from the senior staff. Falkirk was almost proud of his first officer.

Ruiz arrived at the phalanx of guards, out of breath. "I'm placing you under arrest. As of this moment, I am taking command of this ship."

One of the braver marines reached out and gripped his arm. Falkirk wrenched it free in one quick movement.

"That fire alarm was your signal, wasn't it?" Ruiz said. "Once you decided to respond to it, you left me no choice."

Falkirk snorted. "Think about what you're doing here, Ruiz. What are you going to say at your court martial? That you arrested me while I was doing my job?"

"I'm going to tell them that there were no orders to go to Mournful territory. You made it all up."

Ruiz had been monitoring him this entire time, ever since he first set foot on the *Vesuvius*. Not because he wanted to, but because he had lived through the war, like all these other humans, and could never let go of it. Falkirk pictured this man rummaging through his things, tracking his keystrokes on a computer. Collecting data. All to make sure that this animal, this thing that had once been a pet, could be trusted.

In the second it took Falkirk to glance at his sidearm, a gloved hand swiped it from its holster.

"I gave you the chance to talk to me," Ruiz said, his voice breaking. He turned to the marines. "Put him in the brig. Keep him away from the others."

The men tried to frog-march Falkirk along the corridor, but he held his ground. "What others?"

"Bulan and Unoka," Ruiz said. "And the six dogs."

"Ruiz, listen to me—"

"No," Ruiz snapped. "Take him."

As the marines pushed and pulled him, Falkirk glanced at the torpedo room door. So close. An escape hatch. He could have simply dropped out of the ship with a parachute and no one would have realized. His backpack waited for him there, hidden beneath a loose deck plate. Someone might find it long after his court martial.

The phalanx of humans marched him past the room, and he felt his entire life dropping away into an abyss. His sight went hazy, as it often did out in the snow. He imagined everything covered in white, in every direction, the way the world looked on the day he changed. And he could hear his mother's voice, carried in the wind. *The white takes you*, she had said, the last words she ever spoke to him. He thought he could run from it, but the blankness of it all had no end.

Ruiz's walkie-talkie clicked on. "Bridge to the captain, come in!"

"Captain speaking. Go ahead."

The panicky voice from the bridge said something that Falkirk could not make out. Ruiz's face dropped. The man pressed the walkie-talkie close to his mouth.

"Can you shut it down?" Ruiz asked.

Falkirk did not hear the answer, as the marines shoved him forward with a grunt.

"Wait!" Ruiz called. He ran toward Falkirk. The marines waited for him. "What did you do?" he said.

"Nothing," Falkirk replied.

Ruiz drew his pistol but kept it pointed at the deck. "One of the torpedoes just armed itself. And the hatch is sealed. Now you better tell me what the fuck is going on."

"I don't know. I didn't do it."

Ruiz gritted his teeth and aimed the gun. The marines flinched. "Who else is in on it? Tell me!"

"I don't know!" He meant it. If the torpedo exploded, they would all float to the earth as burning confetti. Hosanna would track their debris for miles.

The walkie-talkie crackled. "Sir!"

With his free hand, Ruiz tapped the button. "Go ahead."

"The launch sequence has started! We cannot abort from the bridge! Someone has to do it manually!"

"Fuck this."

Ruiz lowered the gun and darted toward the torpedo chamber. "Keep him here," he said. As soon as he entered the room, his footsteps stopped, as if he'd run straight into a wall. The marines stiffened.

"Sir?" one of them said.

The lieutenant commander emerged at the threshold, walking backward, his hands behind his head. The walkie-talkie continued babbling, but Ruiz did not answer. "Come in, sir! Bridge to Ruiz, come in!"

The silencer of a pistol was plugged in Ruiz's open mouth. He made a stifled choking sound as he backed up another step.

Fuck. This was not part of the plan.

Mort(e) the Warrior stepped into the hall, using the pistol to lead poor Ruiz by the lips. "Drop your guns on the deck." Mort(e) said.

The marines placed their rifles on the floor. "Flat on your stomach," Mort(e) said. "You can relax. The torpedo's fine. Just a false alarm."

While the marines splayed themselves on the deck, Mort(e) tore the walkie-talkie from Ruiz's jacket and tapped the button. "Maintenance crew here. Situation is under control."

"Who is this?" came the response. Mort(e) slammed walkie-talkie on the floor and smashed it under his boot.

"You said there was another way out," Mort(e) said.

"There is," Falkirk said. "Come on."

Mort(e) gripped Ruiz by the collar. "You come with us. Hope you brought a parachute."

Ruiz gasped. His teeth clicked against the silencer.

Falkirk rushed into the torpedo room and dislodged the deck plate right by the door. Underneath, two packs waited. As Falkirk handed one of them to Mort(e), the cat yanked the gun from Ruiz's mouth and pointed it just past his shoulder. Falkirk turned in time to see one of the marines reaching for his rifle. Mort(e) fired. The silencer coughed in Falkirk's ear, the shockwave so close it felt like a punch to the face. The marine returned fire. Bullets sparked off the ceiling. Mort(e) dragged Ruiz while shooting wildly, hitting nothing. Falkirk followed, staying low as another round shattered a light above his head. The three of them met at an intersection, where they took cover at the corner. The fire alarms blared, with the track lights blinking red.

Ruiz went limp. Only Mort(e)'s knobby hand on his collar held him up. The color drained from the human's face. Falkirk saw a glistening red patch on the Ruiz's shirt. He immediately clamped his hand over it.

"Ruiz! Ruiz, I'm sorry!"

The human coughed. His face twisted with rage. "We trusted you . . . you betrayed us."

"We have to go!" Mort(e) said. He dragged Ruiz along, leaving a trail of blood. Ruiz groaned, his voice squeaking as the pain grew unbearable. Falkirk walked at his side, his hand stopping the blood. It felt so hot that he thought it would burn his palm.

"So sorry," he kept saying. "I'm so sorry."

"Where is it?" Mort(e) said.

"Two more doors. Keep going, I'll catch up."

At a bulkhead, Falkirk found a control panel and tapped in the code 0105—a panic code when the hull was compromised. A door sealed off the corridor, buying them some time in case the marines followed. When Falkirk was finished, he gazed at his bloody fingerprints on the panel.

Mort(e) waited at the end of the hall, Ruiz lying at his feet as if dropped from above. On the door behind them, yellow tape stretched across the threshold, warning people to stay away. Falkirk pushed Mort(e) aside and entered an override code into the keypad.

"You were supposed to drop out of the torpedo hatch if I didn't make it," Falkirk said. "That was the deal."

"You need me," Mort(e) said. "But I need you too." He tapped the side of his head with his finger. Falkirk understood. The old cat really was going crazy—crazier than before, crazy for real this time. And he could not see this through by himself.

When Falkirk finished the code, a green light blinked over the keypad. The double doors creaked open, tearing the yellow tape in half. A howling wind sucked through the hallway, flattening Falkirk's fur against his body. The whistling sound grew louder and louder.

"You sure about this?" Mort(e) said.

"Don't worry!" Falkirk shouted. "We'll fit!"

The doors opened to reveal what was left of a supply room. In the middle of the floor, a giant gash bisected the room—courtesy of the anti-aircraft guns at Camp Echo. Though narrow, with jagged metal pointing toward the ceiling, the hole could fit a grown husky and a house cat.

Ruiz remained on the ground, squinting against the wind tunnel they had created. Another siren went off, this time alerting the crew to a breach in the hull, a drop in pressure.

Mort(e) checked the buckles on his parachute. Falkirk pulled a roll of gauze from his backpack. He knelt before Ruiz and unspooled the fabric. He stuffed the wound with it, and the blood changed the white cotton to bright red on contact.

"Get away from me," Ruiz groaned.

"Time to go, Captain," Mort(e) shouted.

"We're going to level everything," Ruiz said. "We're not taking any chances with you people this time."

A despair washed over Falkirk that almost felt blissful in its completeness. He wanted to leap from the ship and let the wind carry him to the snow. *The white takes you. The white takes you.*

He forced himself to his feet. Mort(e) grabbed his bicep and pulled him along. In a daze, he stood there while the cat inspected his buckle. Mort(e) showed his approval with a pat on Falkirk's shoulder. "Don't worry, Captain. He might survive. Now let's finish what you started."

The cat leapt through the gash in the floor, vanishing.

Falkirk stood over the opening. He turned toward Ruiz, then stopped. No. No need to look at the human again. It was over. That bridge had burned. He could only move forward now.

He took a deep breath, held it until his lungs felt ready to burst. He let himself fall through the opening. The ship lifted away as it released him. A terrible wind screamed in the voice of every person he had ever known.

# PART III

# REUNION

# CHAPTER 12

## KEN-RA

**T**HE LEAD SCOUT barked, a signal for the others to stop. Mercy stood at the center of the single file line they had formed, where she would be safest. From there, she worked her way to the front. Her pup, the heir to the Mudfoot, rested in a canvas pouch strapped to her shoulders, where his sleeping body warmed her fur and his milky breath blew in her ear.

At the front of the line, Augur knelt by a rusted piece of metal protruding from the dirt. The lead scout, Creek, pawed at it, revealing it to be a train track. Though the overgrown grass covered the rails, the human engineers had built them to last decades. The bed of rocks and the sturdy wooden ties kept the railway intact.

Soon the entire party arrived: her bodyguards, Carsa, Mag, and Quick; the humans Friar and Preeta; and a wet nurse, the stray dog from Hosanna. The little one had quickly developed a big voice and could give away their position if they did not satisfy his thirst.

Urna arrived at the gathering last, carrying something in her mouth. Mercy bared her teeth while lowering her tail, which told Urna to keep still. Instead, Urna dropped a clutch of yellow flowers at her feet. They were the ones after which she was named. Her expression said, *Look!*

They had not seen these flowers since the Damnable turned them all to dust. Mercy acknowledged Urna by exhaling loudly from her nose. They had more important things to worry about.

Every year, the Lupine Confederacy held the ken-ra in a different place, with the location announced at the last minute to throw off spies from Hosanna. This year, the directions they sent to the packs were simple: find the old train tracks and follow them north. How far exactly? *You'll know*, came the response.

For as long as she could remember, Mercy had heard stories of the ken-ra. Dregger had attended every year since the Change. On his return, he would regale the pack with descriptions so detailed that the children listened with their paws half-covering their faces. Dregger told them of the marauders decorated in their finest war paint, the elders and their horrific scars, from missing eyes and ears to entire limbs sheared at the joint. The powerful cavalry riding on enslaved horses, the stallions so loyal that they would take a bullet for their master. For days afterward, Mercy's sons would pretend to be the great warriors from their father's stories. She would have to separate them when they fought over who got to be a Mournful, who got to wear red paint, who carried a scimitar.

Upon finding the train tracks, Augur ordered them to stop gawking and to march in their original order. For all they knew, a rival clan hoped to ambush them at this very spot. With the extra weight she carried, Mercy was grateful that her human companion took charge of the situation without waiting for instructions. He simply knew, like he knew everything. The scouts took their positions at the lead, the stronger but slower warriors at the rear, with Mercy and her inner circle of Urna and the wet nurse tightly packed at the center. Not an ideal formation, especially so far outside of Mudfoot territory. But after today, they would not need to worry about any of that.

Mercy wanted her sister to walk closer, but Urna maintained

her distance. She was slow to accept the pup as her nephew. Upon first meeting him, she sniffed the pup and then stared at Mercy, waiting for an explanation. Mercy would not offer one. The Mudfoot had a future again, and Urna, of all people, would not be the one to question it. After the ken-ra, the baby would grow stronger by chasing Urna, wrestling with her, nibbling on her ears. Urna would serve the pack by making the child feel safe.

After a few miles, Augur allowed Mag and Quick to take the lead. Though he walked on two feet, Augur maintained a crouching stance with his fingertips touching the earth, so as to stay under the grass that rose on either side of the tracks. When Mercy reached him, he walked alongside her. He reached inside the pouch and stroked the pup's head. Mercy could not picture Wex ever doing such a thing. The Damnable, and his lust for power, left him devoid of any affection. Even the act of mating seemed a nuisance to him, a task no different from patrolling the perimeter at nightfall.

As Augur leaned in to let the pup sniff his nose, Urna whined a little. She clawed at the dirt and wheezed. It meant, *Are you scared?*

Mercy huffed a quick no. But it really meant, *Don't ask.*

"There's no need to be scared," Augur said.

Urna rolled her shoulders forward, bared her teeth, pointed her ears. All of those things together meant *bad wolves.*

"We liberate the wolves today," Augur said. "The *true* wolves."

"Did the Toqwa ever go to the ken-ra?"

"At first. But they saw where things were headed. Like your clan did. Only a matter of time before the Confederacy surrenders to Hosanna. In one way or another."

Augur had spoken of the various pack leaders who secretly worked for the humans. Were it not for the Damnable cutting off their territory, Wex and his band of traitors would have surely sought their help as well, all while claiming to uphold the traditions of the Mudfoot. In many ways, the humans encouraged the hatred for Hosanna, so long as it allowed their clandestine wolf allies to maintain control.

"Dregger, no," Mercy said. "Dregger never would have."

"And now he is dead," Augur said. "Quite the coincidence."

Dregger so rarely spoke of his difficulties as leader. He believed that this protected Mercy when it actually controlled her. If only he had trusted her, perhaps they could have stopped Wex, saved her children. But then—

The thought forced her to slow her pace as she contemplated it.

—but then she would not be here, with this human who *did* trust her.

"I want to see horses," Urna blurted out.

Mercy realized that her sister had never seen one before.

"Want to ride a horse," Urna added.

Augur laughed. "You might, actually."

At the front of the line, the scouts patted their feet on the ground—a warning. And this time, whatever they saw was so close they didn't dare bark. Augur dropped to his knees and raised a fist, signaling the party to stop. Mercy's tongue went dry while her tail danced about in a panic.

The pup's cries began as a breathy whimper that drummed against Mercy's spine. She heard something behind her. Turning, Mercy spotted the wet nurse approaching. This dog from Hosanna had become too clingy for Mercy's taste, and her footsteps made too much noise. To make her stop, Mercy peeled her lips back to reveal her fangs. While the dog obeyed, the pup continued to cry out for his milk. Mercy tried to wriggle the pouch free. Augur's warm hand on her side steadied her. With a tenderness she had never witnessed before—and could never imagine in a human—he lifted the pup, held him under his chin. He nodded to Urna, who leaned in and licked the pup. Mercy joined them, and the three formed a cocoon, shielding the young one from the dangers that awaited. They allowed the wet nurse to enter the circle so she could do her job.

In the vapor of their collective breath, Mercy felt the last barriers between her and these humans falling away. It was like Augur said: they were one people, with the same hearts pumping the same blood, the same story on the same land. The pup fell silent again, his head lolling to one side.

Some time passed—Mercy could not know how long. The scouts barked again, this time signaling that the danger had passed. The pack began to move at the moment that the pup fell asleep. Augur returned him to the pouch on Mercy's back and gently ran his thumb along his forehead. No more words were needed. They continued along the dead railway, their footsteps so soft that the wind carried them off. Within minutes, the pup began to snore.

THE DISTANT HOWLS began when the scouts came upon the remains of a collapsed bridge. An intricate web of vines had choked the concrete pillars of the structure until the middle gave out, leaving a pile of twisted rubble on the tracks. On top of the pile, two wolves stood guard, holding shotguns. Their howls summoned more wolves behind them, who answered with calls of their own. Judging from their yellow and red face paint, their bone necklaces, and the scimitars strapped to their belts, the guards came from the Mournful pack. As Mercy expected.

There was no point in approaching cautiously. The wolves at the summit already knew of their arrival. The howls invited them in, daring Mercy and her people to trust them.

The calls got louder when the guards saw the humans among the Mudfoot. To show they meant no harm, Augur and his comrades walked upright, arms outstretched. This small pack must have resembled the humans from thousands of years ago that Augur described, a pack with no hierarchy, only allies and friends, protecting one another through the long winters.

These guards would never understand any of that. Aiming from the hip, they pointed their rifles at the approaching party, something they never would have done to Dregger. The wolves had banned violence from the ken-ra. This one time a year, enemies would face each other as equals, as cousins. Or so she hoped.

The guard who seemed to be in charge pointed to Augur. "Not you. Wolves only."

Mercy's inner circle gathered around her. The wet nurse hid behind Carsa. Mag and Quick formed a wall in front of their leader. Urna pressed close to her, shaking, but still holding herself together. All at once, they rose to their hind legs. Mercy decided to do it this way in case they needed to reach for their weapons. Besides, they already stuck out too much. Might as well do this one thing to show they meant no harm.

Augur removed his backpack and gave it to Mag. This startled the guard, who raised his shotgun. As Augur stepped away, the guards whispered to one another nervously. One of them said something about the Damnable. All these wolves believed the Mudfoot carried a disease of some sort. Mercy took some pleasure in their fear.

"I hope they like the gift you've brought them," Augur said.

Before Mercy could respond, the pup squirmed in his pouch. The guards craned their necks to see. Augur reached for the baby and stroked the space between his ears. "You'll know what to do," Augur said.

"Yes," Mercy replied.

He cupped his hand under her chin. She licked his cheek.

Mercy climbed the wall of rubble. The first guard waved her through, along with the rest of the wolves. As they made their way along the tracks, more marauders emerged from the trees. They quickly formed a gauntlet, barking and sneering. Some of them dropped to their front paws and growled so viciously that puddles of spit formed beneath their mouths. The pup awakened and immediately cried out for milk. The wet nurse reached for him. Mercy's hand shot out and grabbed the dog's wrist.

"No time for that. He will cry if he must."

The Mudfoot tightened their small formation. The twins appeared the most nervous, with their eyes darting about, assessing all the threats around them.

"They're children," Carsa said. "Little brats trying to scare us." She shook her fist at them. "You were sucking from your mother's teats last spring!"

The tracks curved around a bend and ran along a rusted chain-link fence. The clearing in the trees spread out to reveal a dilapidated train station made of brick, with a partially collapsed roof, blown-out windows, and a dust-coated interior strewn with debris.

*So that's why they met here*, Mercy thought. One of the clauses in the peace treaty called for the wolf clans to return a train that they had seized after the occupation failed. It would most likely run through here. Besides, the wolves preferred to host their meetings in these monuments to the human age. At least one of the ken-ras had taken place at the remains of a mall, another on an airport runway. Dregger always said that the wolves with too much time on their hands enjoyed the symbolism of it all, the conquest and the destruction. Like dragging an enemy's carcass through the grass.

Towering over everyone else, three pack leaders on horseback awaited the intruders. Only the most powerful clans could afford to keep these slaves. The clans that complained the loudest about the practice always ended up adopting it themselves when given the chance. The Mournfuls, represented by their leader, Grieve, wore the most elaborate face paint and trinkets. Red, blue, green, and gold paint coated Grieve's snout and eyes, while bones and skulls—including the barely knitted scalp of a human child—dangled from his chest. To his left, Harrek the White of the Earthblood pack yanked on his horse's bridle, his face covered in powdered chalk. To Grieve's right, a young wolf named Streak represented the Bounty clan. He had recently taken over for his father and wore green paint, with red lines that streamed down his cheekbones like bloody tears.

More marauders on horseback lined the wall of the station. On the roof, soldiers dangled their feet off the gutter like spectators at a zagga match. And off to the side, yet another abomination awaited: a pair of deer, two powerful stags. The larger one smiled at Mercy, baring sharpened teeth with a hint of red to them. So that's how it was. No outsiders allowed ever, save for these diplomats sent to broker a treaty with the most powerful wolves at the expense of everyone else. The deer were always expelling their weakest and their oldest, as well as those who disobeyed—all of whom could be banished to wolf country as a peace offering. Mercy could not know for sure if these were the same deer who killed Wex. They all looked the same, and their blank eyes gave away nothing. Regardless, Grieve and his allies needed the deer's blessing to work out a ceasefire with Hosanna. And no pack would benefit more from this power grab than the Mournfuls.

The crowd urged Mercy and her comrades to stand before the three mounted wolves. On the way, Urna nearly tripped over a loose rock. Mercy grabbed her sister by the shoulders and straightened her. Mercy made sure to dig her nails into Urna's skin. An unmistakable message: *Know who you are.* Or, for Urna, *know who you once were. Do it for me, and I won't ask anything of you again.*

A few of the onlookers sneered at Urna, knowing that she had been infected with the rot that destroyed the Mudfoot. Mercy felt their hatred like a mist surrounding her. For so long, it had made her feel weak, but here, she drew strength from it. Every one of these people would pay for what they had done. On this day, she would explain it to them and watch their faces fall when the cold reality flooded their hearts.

Grieve raised his hand, and the shouting stopped.

"The Damnables have arrived," he said, in his smooth, human-like way.

"No Damnable," Mercy said, cursing her inability to speak more clearly. "You talk at me with respect."

Grieve feigned surprise, which only amused his sycophants more. Harrek laughed so hard that his horse needed to readjust his stance.

"Pack leaders are equals at ken-ra," Mercy said, quoting something Dregger told her one night. She had rehearsed it in her head hundreds of times on the way here.

"You are no pack leader," Grieve said.

"I am Mercy of the Mudfoot." The wolves erupted in laughter again. For a female to proudly call herself a mercy dog was unthinkable. Still, she pressed on. "You have wronged us. I demand to be heard."

"You demand nothing, you dried up breeder. You stand for nothing. You lead nothing. The ken-ra is for pack elders. You are merely a survivor."

"Merely," she said. The pup, fully awake, crawled from his pouch and mounted his front paws on her shoulder.

"And this," Grieve said, pointing to the child. "The Damnable left you all sterile. But out of nowhere, you produce a male heir at the very moment your patriarch dies. How convenient."

"This is patriarch now. This is the future."

"He barely even looks like a wolf. Did you breed him with that human lover of yours?"

"This Dregger's son."

"Saying it does not make it so."

"No," she said. "But *you* are the talker. *We* act."

"Yes, you act. By inciting a war with your army of misfits. Look at you. Diseased wolves. Outcast humans. Refugee dogs, like this . . ." He gestured toward the wet nurse. And when he did, his hand hung in the air for a moment, his eyes narrowed. He recognized this dog.

Mercy would have to deal with it later. She pointed at the stags, who both blinked at the same time. "What kind of wolf brings deer to ken-ra?"

"A wolf who sees the *real* future," Grieve said. "We cannot survive hunting other people as food. Those days are over for all of us."

"And who tells you to give up the old ways?" she said.

"We did! We decided it together at the last ken-ra. The one Dregger was too good to attend."

"Did you agree—*together*—to destroy our land?"

"What are you talking about?"

"The Damnable. Humans did it. With your help."

Grieve waved it off. "The attack on Hosanna triggered the flood. If you have a problem with what happened, swim out to sea about fifty miles and take it up with the Sarcops."

"We ask you for help," Mercy said. "And you leave us to die."

"You wanted to be left alone," Grieve said. "Dregger himself said that if a Mournful ever set foot on his territory, he'd be treated as food. Your people were proud of that stance once. You called us gonneys. Fake wolves. And now you're sad about the consequences."

"Consequences were good . . . for you."

"Because we adapted. You didn't."

This was going nowhere. Mercy needed to appeal to those in the audience who had no choice but to go along with the Mournfuls' plan.

"All of us can be one pack." She interlaced her fingers to illustrate. "A pack that works with humans who are worthy. This

Mournful wants you to take orders from bad humans. The ones who hate us."

They were not ready to hear the next part. She decided to say it anyway.

"I forgive what you have done to Mudfoot. If you join us."

This elicited the loudest laughter so far. Amid the jeers and shouting, Grieve jerked the bridle and stepped closer. Urna made a move to run. Mercy steadied her with a pinch to her ribs.

"I don't expect you to forgive us," Grieve said. "But I don't care, either. Your rebellion won't survive the winter. We are making peace with Hosanna on our terms. By the fall, no one will remember your name."

"You still think bears will help you," Mercy said. "They will not. Not this time."

This killed the last bits of laughter.

"I have never worked with the bears," Grieve said. "You come here, a traitor, and you accuse *me* of treason?"

Mercy opened the backpack that Augur gave her. She upended it, and a hunk of flesh dropped out. As soon as it landed, she kicked it toward Grieve. The object came to rest at the horse's hooves. The gift that Augur promised was a severed bear's claw, cut off at the forearm so that the two bones protruded from the wound. A ring made of steel glinted on one of the digits, indicating that this bear enjoyed wealth and power, much like the Mournfuls. Hence their secret alliance. For as long as it lasted.

"Those outcast humans," Mercy said. "You will call them the Toqwa. They are a pack. Like us."

A light murmuring from the audience. Grieve remained perfectly still, though his horse lowered his head and sniffed at the claw.

"They find where the bears sleep," Mercy said. "They wake them. Females and cubs they let go. But the males . . ." She nodded toward the severed limb. Earlier that day, Augur described it for her, how the bears emerged dazed from hibernation, like drunkards stumbling about. They slept with their backs facing the entrance, where their thick hides would protect them from the elements. When the slaughter began, a few of them asked why. A few of them asked how—how could the humans have known where the bears hid for the winter when no one else did? The Toqwa would not tell them. They merely went about the quiet, brutal work of avenging their kin.

Mercy raised her voice for all to hear. "You can sign phony peace treaty with Hosanna. Or you can join us. All of you." She fixed her gaze on Grieve's horse, a brown beast with a giant white stripe bisecting his long face. The horse blinked.

"Join what?" Grieve said. "An army of thieves and half-breeds? You think you can—"

The horse reared onto his hind legs, going nearly vertical, while his brown eyes remained glassy and dead. With his hooves raised, he must have rose to fifteen feet in the air. Veins puffed out from his muscular neck. Grieve tumbled from the saddle and landed hard. The horse spun around, ready to bring the full weight of his hooves on his master, who lay cowering on the ground.

Gunshots echoed off the ancient walls of the station. Mercy and her party crouched, putting their hands over their heads. Urna hugged her from the front. Behind her, pressing against the pup, the wet nurse shielded the young one with her body. She cooed in the child's ear. "It's okay, shhhhh."

The horse lay dead. A final breath lifted his ribs, then exited in a sad groan. Most likely, the wolves captured him as a colt and trained him for years. The dull claw marks on his hide told his story.

The rest of the horses remained still, their expressions blank as usual. Their riders, on the other hand, appeared ready to leap from their saddles at the first sign of trouble. Every one of them placed his hand near a blade or a gun.

A team of bodyguards rushed to Grieve and helped him to his feet. "Get off me," he said, shoving them away. He glanced at the dead horse and shook his head. A cloud of gun smoke ascended behind him.

Mercy willed herself to stand again. Her companions joined her.

"You did this," Grieve said.

"No," Mercy said. "*You* did."

She stepped away from the protection of her friends so that they could all get a good look at her. And her son.

"We return tomorrow. Make your choice. Join us, or live as slaves to these gonneys."

Grieve tried to stare her down. But it was no use. She saw the fear in his eyes. Smelled it in his breath. He would not sleep well again for the rest of his life, knowing that at any minute even the lowliest of his subjects could turn against him.

She turned to her friends. "We go now," she whispered.

"That's it?" Carsa asked.

"Yes. Let them argue."

They stayed within the narrow train tracks as they made their way out of the station. The crowd split to make room. And as they did, the wolves descended into mad barking, sounding much like a zagga game. The noise startled the horses while Grieve and his fellow nobles tried to maintain order. When Mag tried to steal a glance at the mayhem, Mercy told him to keep moving. The ken-ra would sort things out, separating the strong from the weak as it always did.

THE GUARDS WERE more agreeable on the way out. They placed their rifle butts on the ground and lowered their heads as the Mudfoot passed. The pup cooed at them, and then let out a little sneeze.

Augur waited for them on the other side of the wall of rubble. The guards mumbled something about humans and their stink. He ignored it.

"Preeta has a camp ready for us," he said. "Follow me."

Walking on all fours again came as a relief for Mercy. The pup agreed. He fell asleep as soon as he went horizontal. His fist gripped a handful of her fur and would not let go.

"Grieve is afraid," Mercy said.

"Good. And you?"

"Not afraid."

They veered away from the tracks, into the woods. While the wolves that attended the ken-ra typically stayed close by, Mercy had decided against it. Too risky with the child. Besides, staying in the hills distinguished them as true wolves, another slap in the face for Grieve and his allies.

The path ahead grew steeper. With the short day coming to a rapid close, Mercy wanted nothing more than to curl beside Augur and the pup and drift off to sleep. Ever since the child arrived, her dreams carried her far away from the Damnable and the horrors it created. Sometimes, if she slept in the right position, or ate the right amount of food, she would smell the river before it became cursed, along with the scent of all the wolves who were lost.

As she imagined laying her head on the soft earth, she heard Urna whining behind her.

Mercy tilted her head and sighed. *What is it?*

"We can go home," Urna said. "Before it's too late."

Mercy stopped. The wet nurse, trailing behind them, nearly bumped into her. Mercy gave her a stern growl, and the dog understood to continue without them.

"Before what's too late?" Mercy said.

Urna nodded toward the sleeping pup. "They know."

"Know what?"

"They know."

Mercy growled: *Say it!*

Urna barked at the pup—a warning shout normally saved for an outright attack. "He is . . . no Mudfoot—"

Mercy rose to her hind legs, grabbed her sister by the scruff of the neck, and pinned her against the trunk of a fallen tree. Urna yelped but did not resist. When the pup awakened and began to cry out, the wet nurse turned and looked.

"Wex killed my children," Mercy said into Urna's ear. "Remember? Killed our blood. The forest gives it back."

"Please," Urna said. "We can go home."

"This child is our home! This is our future."

"The human lied—"

Mercy squeezed on her sister's neck.

"Go ahead and beat me," Urna said. "Like Wex did."

Mercy let go. Urna grabbed her hand and pressed it to her neck again. "Do it. You are leader. I am omega."

Mercy yanked her hand away. "Tomorrow, you will understand."

"What about day after?" Urna said. "And day after that?"

"We do this. Or there will be no days to come."

She gave Urna one last shove and walked away. The wet nurse remained on the trail, frozen in place. Mercy trudged past her without a word, daring her to speak.

# CHAPTER 13

## MIGRATION

IKAYA DID NOT smell the badgers until it was too late.

She should have known better. With Gaunt on her back, she made her way through the pine trees to the base of the mountain, where the flock of geese prepared for their journey to the other side. The winds rattled the trees, drumming the twigs against the branches. They needed to go faster. If they missed the flock, they would have to climb instead of fly. The bat, having clung to her for so long, could tell when she grew pessimistic. He would prod her along. *Wind!* he would say, as if she could fly like he once could.

Partly inspired, partly delirious, and mostly pissed off, Nikaya went faster. Which was exactly how mistakes were made. When she stumbled into the camp, she thought for a moment that she had gone in a massive circle and somehow arrived at the garrison. A badger emerged from a lodge constructed from sticks and leaves. Another appeared from behind a tree trunk, his long white snout twitching at the presence of intruders. A third approached from behind, cutting off their escape. Like the badgers that guarded the garrison, they had shaved the fur from their arms and carved menacing tattoos into the skin.

But these lean, angry creatures were better trained, more disciplined than the ones she left behind. Better equipped as well, judging from their supplies. Next to their lodge, a trio of rifles leaned against one another in a pyramid. A pot of stew smoldered in a fire pit filled with orange embers. Each badger wore a belt with a long hunting knife fastened to the hip.

The flock needed these mercenaries for protection. Whereas the bats earned a reputation as skinflints, the migratory birds could always bring exotic goods from warmer climates, like nutmeg, coconuts, oranges, and rum. Even better, they required the badgers' services for only a few weeks a year during the last leg of their journey, when they were the most vulnerable. A lovely business arrangement. Ah yes, behold the civilized world we have created in the wake of endless war! Nikaya could neither bribe them nor threaten them, nor make grand pronouncements about her status as the founder of Lodge City.

Without a word, the badgers pounced on her, separating her from Gaunt. The bat whined like a baby torn from its mother. Nikaya could not say if he merely acted, or if he meant it. For her part, she refused to give them the pleasure of seeing her beg. "We are here to speak to the birds," she said calmly, before one of the badgers sealed her mouth with the palm of his hand.

"You will," he said.

They trussed her to a log. When they finished, she lay on her side, hugging the wood, her wrists and ankles wrapped around it and bound. These badgers were smart. The log, about six feet tall and over a foot in diameter, was eastern hemlock, a flavor that would make Nikaya vomit if she tried to chew her way out. They tied Gaunt to the other side, once again cocooning his wings around her. His hideous face pressed into hers. They tore his goggles off to blind him. The badgers finished by tying a rope to each of their necks. If one of them struggled, the other would choke.

They loaded the prisoners onto a large wheelbarrow and rolled them deeper into the valley. Nikaya tried to speak gently. "We are not thieves," she said. "We did not resist you. We have a deal to make with the birds."

This time, the lead badger could simply yank on the rope around her neck to keep her quiet. It worked.

"You bring a bat in here," the badger said. "Acting like he's wounded. You think we're falling for that?"

"The geese are eating meat these days," another badger said, patting his belly. "Not just fish and bugs, either. And they're very hungry."

Well, at least someone would carry them to their deaths, rather than forcing them to walk. How convenient. For all she knew, the badgers would drop them in the middle of the flock, and the geese, with their tapered beaks, would pick them apart, nibble by nibble. Like getting flayed to death with hundreds of teaspoons.

Another badger raced alongside with a plastic tarp. They stopped to cover the wheelbarrow so Nikaya could not see where they were going. Once the covering was secure, Gaunt had the nerve to exhale in relief, and his terrible breath warmed Nikaya's snout.

The bat squeaked to her. *What say you to birds?*

"I'm thinking."

She would have to talk fast since the badgers had probably tied them to the spit on which they would roast. The bat did not seem to realize that.

The noise grew as they descended farther into the valley. There were thousands of geese honking and squawking at one another. Nikaya recognized the tone. Jammed together, hungry, tired, these birds would grow more irritable by the minute and would bicker over the pettiest slights. Gaunt twitched his ears as he tried to track the conversations. Nikaya snapped her head to the side, yanking his rope. He got the message: *Stay calm, stay quiet. Nothing we can do now.*

The wheelbarrow halted. Footsteps surrounded them. A flurry of wings slapped at the sides of the tarp. The badgers said something Nikaya could not understand. At some point, the geese must have shoved them aside and taken over, eager for some entertainment while they waited. These flocks had no leaders, no hierarchy—only couples and their surviving off-spring, families looking out for their own. Several rivals jostled the wheelbarrow until it tipped over. Nikaya landed on her ribs. Someone whipped the tarp away. A row of beaks appeared, exactly as Nikaya imagined. They nipped at her hide, probing it. Gaunt flinched each time their mouths clamped onto his wings.

Though the Change did not grant them fingers, it made the geese larger, more unwieldy. Fine black feathers covered their heads, matching their dark eyes and beaks. A white strap of feathers wrapped under their chins. The black plumage wrapped around their long necks and came to an abrupt stop at their breasts, giving way to brown and gray. As if someone had painted it on.

The geese fought over their quarry. A few of them began a dance in which they bobbed their heads, with their tongues sticking out. Several fanned out their wings and flapped them, kicking away clouds of dirt. Between the combatants, Nikaya spotted several weaker ones. One of them had a broken beak, with the top part missing. The tongue slipped out like a pink worm. That image grounded Nikaya. These were people like her. She could reason with them.

"I am Nikaya of Lodge City!" she screamed. The geese continued to march about. "I know you can hear me!" she added. A large male craned his neck above her and honked so loud that her ears rang. Gaunt whimpered.

"This is Gaunt of Thicktree," she said, searching for the words. "The proudest family of the Great Cloud."

*Good*, Gaunt squeaked.

". . . and Protectors of the Sacred Forest—"

The male clamped onto her arm and tore away a strip of flesh. The pain shivered through her entire body, compelling her to pull on the rope, thereby choking the bat. The smell of her blood sent the others into a frenzy. Feather and bone collided as the geese slashed at one another—for the hell of it, it seemed.

Pushing through the melee, the goose with the broken beak stepped in between the fighters. As she squawked at them, her tongue popped out of the unnatural hole in her face before sliding in again. She leaned over and bit into the knot in the rope. The broken beak did not function well, and Nikaya wondered if the other members of the flock helped to keep this one alive. At this perilous time of year, they needed every female they could get. Once the goose secured a tight grip, she pulled one of the knots free. As the bonds loosened, Nikaya and Gaunt rolled away from the log.

When the geese noticed what the female had done, they surrounded her, honking and flapping and stamping their oddly shaped feet. She responded in English, probably so Nikaya could understand. "Listen!" she screamed. "Listen! Listen!"

As the bird raised her wings, Nikaya noticed the remnants of cracked eggshells stuck to her tail feathers, most likely frozen onto her from endless days of flight in the jet stream. Nikaya had heard stories of mother geese whose nests were destroyed and who instinctively sat on the broken eggs while the yolk oozed out. Whoever or whatever destroyed her eggs had to break her face to do it. *What have you seen?* Nikaya wondered.

The goose was too proud to accept a word of thanks from a beaver. Instead, she shouted down the others, then nodded for Nikaya to continue.

"You deserve a better nesting ground than this," Nikaya said, clutching the wound on her arm. "Lodge City is not far from here. Well, it's not far for you. And your magnificent wings."

The geese tightened the circle. Nikaya suddenly remembered that these birds did not value flattery. Had she faced a tribunal of peregrine falcons, she would have had to spew praise for hours before they let her get to her point.

"We once discussed letting your flock use Lodge City as a base on your way north," she continued. "If you take me," she said. "If you take *us* over the mountains, we can build a whole nesting site. Safe from the wolves." Her engineer brain went into action. She pictured a field carved from the woods, where the geese could congregate and pluck the bugs from one another's feathers. And after they left, the beavers could use their droppings for fuel.

A few of the geese stopped and craned their necks in thought. Several others continued to lean forward like vipers ready to strike. Gaunt, huddled on the ground beside Nikaya and motioned to the ones who seemed ready to listen. She addressed them directly.

"How much are you paying these badgers, anyway?" she asked. "You think they're worth it?"

"Yeah, we're worth it, you old bag!" one of the badgers said.

Nikaya turned toward the voice. The badgers waited behind a row of geese.

"What do you do exactly?" she asked.

"Protection."

"Protection? Then how did you let two assassins get this close?" She bared her buck teeth. "I can take down a live tree in minutes. What do you think I can do to a bird's neck?"

In a moment so satisfying she could never have imagined it while in prison, the badgers' faces dropped. They turned to one another, completely helpless.

A plump male goose waddled toward her. He was older than the others, with a scuffed beak and a limp. In the air, he could fly like an angel, no doubt. On the ground, gravity weighed on him like everyone else. "You want deal?" the goose said.

The female with the broken mouth flicked her tongue again. Nikaya tried to ignore it.

"Yes. A trip over the mountains, and then Lodge City will be part of goose country."

The plump one turned to Gaunt. "Bats hate beavers. Beavers hate bats."

"Not anymore," Nikaya said, trying to place her body between them. "Lodge City is a haven. For all species. Beavers built it, but we share. Like we shared the ponds we created, before the Change."

Gaunt was right. This was what she was good at. *Lying.* It might still save their lives.

"What do *you* offer?" the goose said to Gaunt.

Squinting in the bright light, the bat twitched his head until he located the sound of his voice. He waddled over to her and extended his right wing, like a handshake.

*Nothing*, Nikaya thought. *He has nothing to offer.* Refuge in a cave, perhaps, but little else. Yet the bird extended his own wing nonetheless, brushing his feathers against Gaunt's limb.

"You want deal," the goose said to Nikaya. "Bats want friendship."

A murmur rippled through the birds. The plump goose quieted them with a loud honk.

"We know you," the goose said. "We know what you do. You betray the bats. You think you run away from this? You think you wash it clean? No." He made a show of shaking his head so that the beak flipped from side to side. Soon, the others joined in. All the beaks moved in unison. The female with the eggshells in her feathers lowered her head. Though unwilling to pile on, she knew the old bird was right.

"How many dead?" the plump one asked. "How many did your monster kill?"

Castor once gave her a number, long before he learned of her plot to use the spider to destroy the bats. It was unbearable, especially with little Nikki among them. Someone else figured the number to be higher, considering how many went missing after the attack. One or a thousand, it made no difference. She was beyond saving. Beyond redemption.

"Bat comes with us," the plump one said. "We carry him." He pointed his feathers at Nikaya. "Tie the beaver to a tree. When wolves come, they eat her instead of us."

Nikaya turned to the female goose. The bird hid behind her siblings. In her condition, she must have owed them her life, and therefore could not question their decisions. As the badgers seized Nikaya, she went limp in their arms, defeated, but finally able to rest. Of course it would end like this. The bats would win, and the other animals would forget all the good her people did.

The honking started as they hauled her away. For all their talk of friendship, these people were not above taunting a defeated enemy. Nikaya felt a vibration through the ground—a scuffling somewhere behind her. Cutting through the noise, a single voice screeched and wailed. The birds' fat bodies moved aside to make room. Gaunt stomped through the opening they created. Someone had returned his goggles to him, but they sat askew on his face after he'd hastily put them on. It made him resemble a helpless child pretending to be a grownup. But then he bared his fangs and pounded his good wing in the dirt. The circle around him grew larger as the geese tried to distance themselves.

Gaunt pointed to Nikaya. "She make . . . good deal," he said.

Nikaya had never heard him speak so many words in her language. "She make *fair* deal! You take. You *take*!"

"No deal with traitors," the plump goose said. Again, his people drove the point home by shaking their heads.

"You take deal. You *need* deal."

"Need," the goose said, dragging out the word.

"Yes! Need! Beaver served time. She . . ." He searched for the words. "She . . . shoveled. Shoveled the caves! She carry me!" He tried to mimic climbing onto Nikaya and tromping through the woods.

"We carry too much already," the plump goose said. "No more—"

"I carry!" someone said. Nikaya knew right away that it was the broken female, the one with the eggshells and the mangled face. Maybe the only person here who could fathom what Nikaya had gone through to get here. "We need deal," she said. She did not need to elaborate. Her condition spoke for her.

Still, the fat goose hesitated.

"War between our people over!" Gaunt shouted, looking right at Nikaya. "Over now!"

Realizing that he had no real control over this flock, the old goose glanced at his comrades. A lone bird honked somewhere, but his protest died out.

"Very well," the goose said. "The wind arrives today." He limped into the crowd, into the protection of his immediate family. The female followed him. Nikaya realized then that they were father and daughter. He would forgive her for challenging him, but probably not today.

Nikaya took all of this as a yes to her offer. So did the badgers. They let her go, sniffing in disgust. "Hope they don't drop your fat ass," one of them said as he sauntered away.

Gaunt approached, a walking blanket with his wings dragging behind him. He waited for her to speak while he straightened his goggles. She wanted to say thanks. But it was too hard, like relaxing a cramped muscle.

*Wind*, the bat said in Chiropteran. It would have to do.

"The water flows," Nikaya replied. It would also have to do.

LATER THAT AFTERNOON, while Nikaya and Gaunt napped in a ditch, one of the badgers dropped a pair of harnesses beside them. The clatter woke Nikaya first. Gaunt merely rolled onto his other side. All around them, the birds doddered about, still tired, yet anxious to fly. As the old goose predicted, a cruel wind gathered strength, sending feathers, leaves, and pine needles swirling in miniature tornadoes. The breeze carried away the scent of bird shit for a few seconds before it settled in again.

The harnesses, fashioned from hemp, must have come from a squirrel community. Nikaya could tell by the stitching, having seen much of their work in the days when she oversaw the barter system for Lodge City. The geese may have traded some exotic seeds from the south for them. Though originally meant for transporting supplies, here they would carry a fully grown person.

When Nikaya tried on the harness, slipping it over her heard like a vest, she pondered the insanity of this plan. What would stop the geese from dropping them at the first sign of a predator? They already spoke openly of using her as bait on the ground. Why not in the sky? Why not dangle her to a bird of prey? Until now, she could at least control the slow pace she took. Here, she trusted a disfigured, possibly deranged goose and her strange people.

The strangeness did not stop once the geese agreed to Nikaya's bargain. Rather than offer food or some other gesture of diplomacy, the geese continued milling around, honking at one another, treating the two intruders like new obstacles placed in their way. No songs to lighten the mood, no rituals to mark the occasion, no games to pass the time. So many days spent drifting on an air current allowed these animals to get by with little interaction, and virtually no signs of affection that Nikaya could see. On the ground, everyone was a nuisance, and the birds hoped to settle old scores from the previous season. Fights broke out among the younger ones while the older birds resorted to passive aggressive tactics, like shoving their enemies from behind or shitting on someone's outstretched foot.

A strong male goose emerged from the crowd, wearing his own harness, a badger at his flank. Nikaya knew right away that this bird—most likely another offspring of the old goose—would carry Gaunt. The badger helped the wounded bat to climb onto the goose and strap in. The bird honked at Gaunt, who responded with a squeak. *You okay? Yes!*

One by one, the geese pointed in the direction of the wind, like clumsy weather vanes. A few of them flapped their wings, loosening them, shaking away the rust. Powder drifted from the snowcaps. The failing sunlight refracted through the particles. Nikaya's last day on earth would at least provide a pretty sight.

Something tapped Nikaya's arm. She turned to find the female goose, ready to take her. Next to her brother, the female appeared small, frail, disheveled. Her harness hung loose from her breast. Part of the vest covered the shells encrusting her feathers. Nikaya decided then that she would not ask the goose what happened to her children. She remembered a proverb that almost all the species claimed as their own: "You are the master over someone who tells you their story." Perhaps she was getting soft in her old age, but she could not bear to hold that kind of power over someone like this. Without a word, she climbed onto the goose and clipped herself into the harness.

Another stiff wind pointed the geese in the direction of the mountains. Somehow, this flock knew down to the minute when this air current would arrive. The leaders, far in the front of the flock, lifted from the earth one row at a time. As they climbed the slope, they formed into a triangle, with the strongest serving as the tip. Nikaya's heart seized. She could do this. Because she had to.

To her right, the gander spread his wings, ready to lift off. Gaunt clung to him, peering around his thick neck with his goggles in place. He had never seemed so small to Nikaya before.

"Hey," she shouted. The wind stole her voice, so she screeched like a bat. Gaunt turned to her. His goggles reflected the orange sun.

She wanted to say thank you. She wanted to say sorry.

"I'll see you on the other side," she said.

The female goose coiled her neck so that she faced Nikaya. Her long tongue slipped out of the hole in her beak, then retracted. "You see your friend again," she said. "Promise."

When her row reached the front of the flock, Nikaya braced herself by wrapping her arms tight around the goose's throat. The wings spread out. Nikaya expected to rumble and bounce. Instead, with a hop and a light flick of her wings, the goose glided along with the air current. Below her, the dirt gave way to rock. As they got higher, they passed over a layer of pristine, perfectly white snow. A chorus of honking cut through the wind. Nikaya felt the thrumming in the goose's neck as she joined in.

They flew on the right arm of a great V formation, with Gaunt two spots to the left. The bat flapped his wings, pretending to carry the enormous bird beneath him. He turned to Nikaya, his fangs protruding—a terrible sight under normal circumstances, but this was how the bat showed his approval. He was flying again, something he must have thought impossible when this journey began.

As the flock cleared the first set of mountain peaks, they shifted so the V formations stacked on top of one another. Nikaya glanced above to see the bellies of the geese. Below, a column of wings swayed in unison, with the spiked mountaintops passing far underneath.

A new current of air bounced Nikaya in her saddle. The bird groaned in protest. Another blast of wind carried the voices of dozens of geese, honking furiously like little trumpets. Her goose veered away from the sound in perfect timing with the other birds in the squadron. While Nikaya hung on, she caught sight of two geese dropping from the formation, trailing feathers in their wake.

One of the birds gripped the other at the neck with its beak, and then ripped away a chunk of bloody flesh in midair.

"Eagle!" Nikaya screamed. "That's an eagle!"

The geese already knew. The formations split into smaller triangles, with the strongest flyers taking the lead. Gaunt huddled closer to his partner. He must have known what enormous targets they made, a fat goose carrying a defenseless mammal.

More screaming and honking, this time from below. Nikaya turned in time to see an eagle dive bomb a formation, knocking out the leader. The bird tumbled, its neck flopping about. The eagle slowed, spreading its pearl-colored wings, flecked with brown and gold. Though slightly smaller than a goose, his angular shape resembled a missile compared to his round, slow-moving prey. The eagle flashed his talons and caught the helpless bird, plunging his beak into the neck. The goose opened its mouth to scream, but nothing came out.

The formation closed in to seal the gap.

Nikaya spotted four eagles circling far above—high enough to gather speed. As they overtook the flock, one of the eagles tucked in his wings and dove. He collided with the bird to Gaunt's left, bursting it apart in an explosion of feathers. Again, the formation tightened, allowing Nikaya to fly right beside Gaunt.

Nikaya was no hunter, but she knew that these eagles wanted

to isolate the two big targets. Remove anyone who could protect them before swooping in. She tried to throttle the bird to steer her away from danger, but the goose would not comply.

"Hold the arrow," the bird said. "Hold the arrow."

Despite the Change, this flock stuck to the same instincts that kept their species alive. They would stay the course because breaking formation would get them all killed. Those who died would save the rest.

The mountains were too far beneath them for Nikaya to jump to safety. She riffled through the harness, checking all the pockets and creases, hoping to find something hard or sharp, anything she could use as a weapon. But when she spotted the birds of prey again, she knew it was too late. Another eagle, the biggest one, dropped from the circling birds and began his descent, a spear aimed right for her.

She bared her front teeth. If this eagle took her, she would get one last bite in before the predator snapped her neck.

The eagle slowed by fanning out his wings. His claws flashed. And then something enormous and shiny plowed into him. Nikaya covered her head as a shower of feathers flitted about her. One lodged in her mouth and she plucked it out. Over the goose's shoulder, she saw the two creatures struggling in midair. The eagle beat its wings yet continued to fall, ensnared in the claws of something much larger. This new predator had an enormous head, and a body made of three large bulbs. Its transparent wings refracted the sunlight, and then buzzed so rapidly that they disappeared.

"Alpha!" Nikaya screamed.

The insect's antennae twitched. The ant released the eagle. As the broken bird fell away, the Alpha ascended toward the V formation.

The geese continued their pace. They would hold the arrow. But there were more Alphas in pursuit. Nikaya counted seven.

Eight. The remaining eagles dispersed. The ants ignored them. Of course. They wanted fatter meat from prey that could not fight back.

The failing sunlight painted the Alphas gold. They formed a triangle of their own, with the tip headed right for Nikaya. But as they drew closer, she realized that they aimed not for her, but for Gaunt. All of them. She recalled the Alpha that chased Gaunt into the trees. Why did they want him? *Take me*, she thought. *He's nobody!*

She could only watch as the Alphas overtook the geese, hovering directly over them. Gaunt turned in his saddle and tried to swat the beast away with his good wing. But the lead Alpha gripped his tail with its mandible. He screamed.

It was then that Nikaya noticed the marking on the ant's abdomen. A brand, charred into the carapace. It said CULDESAC.

"You whorefucker," she mumbled.

She had seen this creature before. It had ransacked Lodge City, along with its siblings, on orders from the dog and the cat who betrayed them. And now here it was, having sprouted wings like some demon.

The mandibles clamped around Gaunt's waist. He flailed and screamed. The goose ignored him, his eyes blank as a puddle.

Nikaya unhooked her harness. She tapped the female goose on the shoulder. "Thank you!" she said. The goose responded by flicking her tongue, now dried out in the wind like a hunk of leather.

Nikaya turned in the saddle to face this creature, only a few feet away. She would make it. Her legs had one last jump in them. And so she leapt from the goose and landed on the Alpha's abdomen, the largest part. With Gaunt still crying beneath her, she bit hard into the insect's leg, puncturing the leathery armor and digging into the nerves and muscles. She let go, and the leg dangled from a few fleshy threads, leaving a taste in her mouth like oil and metal. The ant's jaw snapped at her. Nikaya shimmied onto the thorax and drove her front teeth into the base of the neck. The antennae shot straight out. The Alpha tilted to the side until the four bodies—insect, beaver, bat, bird—all tipped over and spun out of control. As they plummeted, the V formation closed ranks once more as if nothing had happened.

Gaunt unhooked his harness. The bird broke free and flapped away. They fell faster now, still clutching the stunned Alpha. In great pain, Gaunt flapped his own wounded wings, slowing their descent but not stopping it. Nikaya reached for Gaunt's shoulder and pulled herself on top of him. With the last of her strength, she kicked the ant in the eye, feeling a satisfying crunch. The claws let go, and the beast tumbled away.

Gaunt continued to beat has wings. Somewhere behind them, the Alpha crashed into the forest. Unable to hold them any longer, Gaunt could only steer between the trees as he glided. He scraped against set of thick branches, and Nikaya ripped away from his harness and fell. The ground came at her. She clenched her teeth and braced herself.

She crashed into the mud, knocking the wind out of her.

Her ears rang.

The wind dissolved into silence.

Then blackness.

Then nothing.

# CHAPTER 14

---

## THE MOURNFUL

*(UNOFFICIAL) LOGBOOK OF THE SUS AL-RIHLA*
*FEBRUARY 12*

*TONIGHT, WE MAKE A RUN FOR IT.*
*WE. US. MY SON AND I.*
*IN THE MORNING, WE WILL*

SHRIEKING HOWL CUT through the forest. D'Arc knew it well. She set the pencil in the crease of her logbook and closed it. Sitting in her tent, she blew out the lantern and tried to listen. Another howl rang out in response, this one closer. Soon, a chorus broke out, but with no harmony, only voices shouting at random. A panic in the dead of night.

The Mudfoot camp was under attack.

D'Arc shoved the book into her backpack and grabbed her sword, a weapon the wolves found amusing when she insisted on bringing it along for the journey. Outside of the tent, she heard twigs breaking, branches rustling. With her eyes still adapting to the dark, she unsheathed the blade and let the tip lead the way. Another rally began, this one far off. She recognized none of the voices. They came from everywhere, closing in. Whoever attacked them arrived with numbers, enough so that the element of surprise no longer mattered.

A form rushed past her, toward the intruders. Probably one of Mercy's guards, sent to check on the disturbance. More of them raced to the scene, barking and huffing. None of them asked her to help. She was not one of them. These warriors trusted only their own blood. She could give them all the milk she had, and it would never be enough.

Somewhere near the train tracks, a skirmish began. D'Arc held still and listened to the wolves snapping at one another, their bodies rolling in the dirt and slamming against the tree trunks. The noises got closer, surrounding her.

Until this moment, she had a plan. A lovely, perfect plan that made her belly tingle when she thought of it. Even the Old Man would have found no fault in it, though he would never say that out loud. In her logbook, she drew diagrams of the camp, showing where each marauder slept, along with the tent where Mercy and the child retired for the night. Before sundown, D'Arc had traced the mountains to see if any of them may have looked familiar from her days on the ranch. And sure enough, one of them did—a peak with a dead cell phone tower that leaned to one side after years of neglect. It became the north star on the map she drew. After she took her child, she would follow that star to her old homeland, the same one she was so desperate to flee a lifetime ago. The baby would see all the places where Sheba the pet, Sheba the myth, became D'Arc, the bedraggled survivor of both fire and water. The pup would never believe the stories, but he would memorize them all the same.

That was the plan. And if D'Arc wanted to salvage it from this chaos, she would have to become like the wolves. A marauder with fangs bared. She would charge the matriarch and kill her and take her child. This was her last chance.

D'Arc stormed up the hill, weaving through tree trunks and

ducking under branches. The top of Mercy's tent appeared as an unnatural straight line within the bumpy terrain. With the blade of the sword, D'Arc pulled the flap open. The tent was empty save for the thick scent of her son and the milk she fed him less than an hour before.

D'Arc dropped to the ground and inhaled so hard that some dirt flew into her nose. When she snorted it out, she detected the warm smell of a pup, along with the earthy scent of a wolf, mingled into one trail that headed uphill. D'Arc followed on all fours, arriving at a patch of grass that had been trampled. The wolf had gotten sloppy in her desperation to run away. D'Arc broke into a full sprint. "I'm coming," she whispered. She listened for her child to respond in her mind, but heard nothing. She wanted to hear him whine again about how he wanted to go home to the boat, sounding like the Old Man nitpicking everything.

D'Arc passed a swaying branch and another flattened clump of earth before she saw Mercy standing upright, clutching the baby to her chest. She clamped her hand around the baby's snout, probably to muffle his cries. The wolf turned to face her. *Oh, do you even know who I am?* D'Arc wondered. *Do you even know that you'll die here in this lonely place?*

D'Arc brought the sword to her shoulder and ran faster. Mercy, who must have thought D'Arc had come to help, remained still.

"He's not breathing," the wolf said.

D'Arc stopped. The blade lowered on its own. She realized that Mercy was not clamping the pup's mouth shut. Instead, the wolf was trying to fish something out of the baby's throat. The pup did not resist. His head flopped to the side like a doll.

"He chewed something," Mercy said. "Tried to get him to spit it out. Then the howling started. We ran."

"Put him on the ground," D'Arc said. Instead of obeying, the wolf stared at her as she holstered the sword. "On the ground," D'Arc said. "Do it."

Mercy rested the pup on his side. D'Arc took him, flipped him around so that he lay on his belly. He was so light and warm. A stubborn heart still beat inside of him like a pair of fingers drumming the ribcage.

The wolf whined like a dog. *Oh no*, D'Arc thought. *You don't get to show emotion over this. You don't get to love what's mine.*

"My fault," Mercy stammered. "My fault. My fault."

"No one's fault," D'Arc said. "Babies choke all the time." She realized too late how bad that sounded.

D'Arc slipped her fingers under the pup's belly. Her left hand became a fist; she wrapped her right hand around it. Like the diagram she saw in a veterinarian's textbook. D'Arc tugged upward, gently at first. The tiny body lurched with each movement.

"What are you doing?" Mercy asked.

By the fourth or fifth try, D'Arc's vision blurred, and she found herself on the tiny lifeboat again, slipping her newborns, Tristan and Nautica, into the water. Beneath the surface, the dead ones took on a ghostly appearance, their fur fluttering around their skin, their tails lifting. And then they would sink far enough where they would dissolve out of existence, a dream that only D'Arc would remember.

Another set of footsteps arrived. A human, judging from the sound. Maybe Augur. Killing the wolf had become too complicated. D'Arc missed her chance.

The baby still would not cooperate, so D'Arc lifted him nearly vertical and squeezed on his abdomen as hard as she could.

"You hurting him!" Mercy said.

"Quiet."

One more squeeze, and the pup coughed out the knobby joint of a bone. The child inhaled desperately before crying out. Once again, D'Arc could hear him, even if the wolf could not.

*Why are you doing this to me?* the child asked.

"It's okay, it's okay," D'Arc said, smoothing out the tuft of fur on his head.

*Not okay! Not okay! Where are we?*

A true explanation would only anger the child more, at a moment when he could give away their position.

"You said we safe," Mercy said to Augur. "This not safe."

"The Mournful are panicking," he said. "Their slaves are rebelling. Their allies are turning against them. I've seen it."

"You did not see *this*!"

"That's because—"

More Mudfoot arrived. D'Arc recognized them by smell, as they still carried the soil from the camp where she first met them. Mercy's sister came the closest. She stooped onto her front paws and lowered her head, her eyes fixed on the child.

"Come on," Augur said. "There's a stream. If we cross that, we can make it."

Mercy glared at him, then reached for the child.

*No,* the pup screamed in D'Arc's head. *No, I want to stay with you!*

She held him tighter. And that simple movement, that slight tensing of her muscles, triggered something in the wolves. The circle around her tightened. The fangs flashed. The vapor from their breath shot out like geysers. Even Urna, the damaged one, dug her claws into the dirt. These people were a unit, no different from the wayward ant colony she raised, before she learned how the cruelty of the world could carve out people's hearts and turn them into killers.

D'Arc let Mercy take the child.

*No!* the pup screamed. *No, please! Please!*

A horse whinnied somewhere. Mercy led them away from the sound. She ran upright while slipping the baby into her backpack. Then she dropped to all fours and bounded through the trees. Soon, all the wolves followed suit. The humans as well.

*Run faster*, the pup said. *Hurry!*

"I'm right behind you!" D'Arc said.

*Look out!*

Something hard and heavy blindsided her from the right, punching the air out of her chest. From the ground, she lifted her head in time to see Friar, the silent one, scowling at her, warning her not to follow. He darted off like a wolf, his tail lifting with each step.

They knew. They had figured out what she was trying to do.

D'Arc got to her feet, unsheathed her sword. *Fine*, she thought. *I'll hunt you all.*

She ran after them. The pack veered to the right. D'Arc did not see why until a marauder was nearly on top of her, a black, hulking form tearing through the trees, too fast for its enormous size. The Mournful knew how to hunt. Scare the prey with the cavalry, then pick them off on foot. D'Arc swung her sword, and it sparked against the wolf's scimitar. The force of it threw D'Arc off balance. She managed to prop herself on one hand. Looming over her, the wolf planted his feet and raised his weapon. A horrible smile shone in the scant light; his fangs were capped with molded silver.

The scimitar arced through the air, barely missing D'Arc as she rolled away from it. The blade sank into a pair of exposed roots. While the wolf pried it free, D'Arc took off again, her nose searching for the muddy scent. More shadows darted among the trees. She passed a marauder as he pinned one of the humans to the ground. It was Friar. The wolf chasing her lost interest and joined in mauling the prone human. Friar remained silent even as they shredded him. To protect the pack, Augur must have ordered him to his death. And he'd obeyed without question.

The stream babbled in front of her. The scent of blood and musk clogged her nose, making her eyes water. At the edge of the stream, cold mud overtook the grass, and the ground sloped downward. The water trickled through a jagged column of ice. D'Arc tried to jump over it, but her foot broke through the ice, sinking into mud to her ankle. As she pulled the foot free with a loud sucking sound, she noticed a shadow downstream, getting closer. A horse with a rider. Two more cavalry appeared directly in her path. Another rider blocked her escape. *Goddammit—* they'd used the sound of the water to mask their footsteps.

It was over. She was so cold, and so tired. Her soaked foot went numb. She gripped the handle, raised the blade, and dared them to kill her.

The first rider dismounted. The others closed in.

"It's her," someone behind her said.

D'Arc spun around to point the sword at the wolf who dared to speak.

"We're not here to hurt you," the rider said. He held his ground when D'Arc turned the sword toward him.

"Grieve wants to talk to you," the wolf said. His tone let her know what would happen if she tried to resist.

D'Arc lowered the weapon. The tip landed in the mud.

"Let's get on with it," she said.

FEBRUARY 13

*PLAN FAILED.*
*CAPTURED BY MOURNFUL FOLLOWING SURPRISE ATTACK ON*
*MUDFOOT CAMP.*

"What are you writing?" The wolf rider asked as he rocked in the saddle. "What is that?"

As morning broke, the rider appeared as a pitch-black shadow against a purple background. Each of the marauders who marched alongside D'Arc wore a stripe of blue paint from their ears to their noses, while the cavalry officer displayed more elaborate adornments: jewelry, weapons, war paint of every shade, elaborate carvings in his fur.

"It's a logbook," D'Arc said. She saw no point in hiding it. These people knew her. Grieve must have remembered their meeting the previous summer. She tried to recall what he said when he saw her with Mort(e). *This warms my heart,* or something like that. A smug warlord, riding the backs of his slaves.

"Let me see it," the rider said.

D'Arc handed it over. Writing while walking made the penmanship wobbly, and she suddenly felt a twinge of embarrassment. This faded when the rider flipped through the book upside down, shaking his head in disappointment like a schoolteacher. He tossed the book to her.

"A *log*book," he repeated. He had no idea what that meant.

She continued writing. One of the marauders peeked over her shoulder as she scribbled. She let him do it, knowing full well that he couldn't read it, either.

WEATHER: DRY AND COLD.
PERSONAL HEALTH: TIRED. PULLED OUT THE LAST STITCH FROM WOUND. SOME BLOOD, NOT MUCH.
APPROACHING MOURNFUL CAMP.

D'Arc nearly dropped the book when she saw it: a row of horses lying side by side in the grass, a fresh bullet hole in each of their heads. The Mournful did not wait for them to rebel. They executed the horses without a care about what would happen to all the meat.

As the mounted wolf passed the corpses, the horse kept his eyes straight ahead. The bodies of his people might as well have been random mounds of dirt. It was either a smart move, or a reflex beaten into him over many years.

In a nearby glen, the wolves gathered in front of a row of tents fashioned from animal skin. There, they stood on their hind legs in total silence, all facing the same direction. D'Arc could hear a single voice shouting. At first, she thought it was one of their officers delivering orders. But the voice grunted and shrieked, each sentence punctuated with the sound of something breaking. When one of the tents suddenly collapsed in a heap, the crowd split to give space to the wolf who did it. And there, in front of the very soldiers who would die for him, Grieve the All-Powerful stomped and cursed as he tore apart another tent in a blind rage.

"Traitors!" he shouted. "Every last one of them, a fucking traitor!" With his scimitar, he beat the leather hide of the tent into tatters. Two of his concubines burst out, bedecked in necklaces and jangling bracelets. They ran into the arms of his other mates, consoling one another in a way that suggested they were bonded in their hatred for him.

More wolves arrived from different directions. Among them, a wounded marauder groaned while his comrades carried him on a stretcher. Another group hung their heads in shame—whether real or fake, it got the point across.

Grieve turned to a pair of wolves—higher ranking marauders, judging from their war paint. "Find who's left. Bring only those who can still walk. Leave the others."

The wolves ran off. If there was anyone left to question Grieve's orders, they chose to remain silent.

When Grieve spotted D'Arc, he planted his sword into the dirt and tried to catch his breath. With his chest heaving, he seemed older and more worn out than she remembered. He pointed to the horse and snapped his fingers. The rider dug his heels into the horse's side and rode off into a nearby thatch of trees. D'Arc suddenly felt isolated without his massive presence beside her.

Grieve stomped toward D'Arc, his skull necklace swaying with each step. The crowd parted to let him through.

"You again," he said. "I told you to stay out of wolf country."

Dozens of eyes turned to her.

"I'm looking for my son," D'Arc said. "The Mudfoot have him."

"The Mudfoot have a lot of things now."

Grieve got right in her face. She held her ground, only because she thought that any hint that she would run would get her killed.

"Did you know?" he asked.

"Know what?"

Grieve laughed. "Of course you knew nothing. You're a mercy girl. Like my mates." He gestured to the concubines, who held one another and wept.

"The Mudfoot baited us," Grieve said. "As soon as we attacked their camp, our horses revolted. Two of the packs sided against us. They attacked from behind. This is all enemy territory now."

Grieve told her this with a wistful smile. This chaos may have finally allowed him to shed the civilized mask he had worn for years so that he could become a true wolf again. That was all the wolves could ever talk about—who was a real hunter and who was not and who would never be.

"Is there anyone left?" D'Arc asked. "Is there anyone left who can stop them?"

A gunshot startled her. It came from the trees. Something large and heavy fell over, thudding against the earth. The Mournful had executed their last horse.

Grieve did not even flinch. "No one's left," he said. "But, on the bright side, I managed to keep a promise to an old friend. For all the good it'll do."

"Promise?"

Grieve pointed at something behind her. She turned to find more wolves arriving from the skirmish. Six of them, with charcoal fur. And a seventh, trailing behind, with a white patch covering his face and neck. He slowed once he spotted her.

"Falkirk!" she said, and then immediately clapped her hand over her mouth. It couldn't be. It couldn't be real.

The husky embraced her, digging his nails into her skin hard enough to hurt. And she did the same as she hugged him, to prove he was there. He was thinner than she remembered and smelled of mud and sap, like a real wolf.

"I saw him," she said. "I saw our son. He's alive."

"A son," Falkirk repeated.

"All right, you're welcome," Grieve said. "We're moving now. Stragglers will catch up with us."

He ordered his underlings to take the tents they could carry and to burn the ones they could not. They would head for a region he called the Blue Hills. Falkirk and D'Arc stayed in place while the wolves scurried around them.

"I want to hear all about him," Falkirk said.

"I know," she said. "But we have to get moving."

"Yes. All three of us."

D'Arc pulled away.

"Mort(e)'s here," Falkirk said.

She felt neither relief nor surprise at this. The Old Man followed her in her dreams, so why not here?

"Let's get him—"

"Wait," Falkirk said. "He doesn't know."

"We'll tell him," she said.

"We can't. Not yet."

"Why the hell not?"

Falkirk let her go. "Because he's dying."

# CHAPTER 15

**████ ██ ████**

# TEKNI

**M**ORT(E) SLID ALONG the ocean floor, leaving a cloud of mud in his wake. With the light barely penetrating the deep, all the colors drained away, leaving a blue haze in every direction. He sucked in a mouthful of salt water that vented through the gills in his neck. He placed his hands there to feel the force of it, the slightly elevated temperature. But his hands had calcified into bony claws, with three ghastly prongs each. The breaths came slowly as he pushed the water in and out, the sound of it whooshing in his ear canals. The fish creatures closed in around him, speaking in their language of clicks and squeaks and whistles. He realized then that someone dragged him through the dirt. His scaly tail swayed behind him in the current, skimming along the rocks and coral. Smaller fish darted away in fear.

One of the Sarcops drew closer. The enormous eyes somehow glowed at this depth, resembling massive glass lanterns. A tentacle probed his armor, while another reached out with a smooth object. A rock, perhaps? No, this thing had no earthly business here. It was a mug, fashioned from clay. With a clicking noise, the Sarcops placed it right at Mort(e)'s lips. The clay felt oddly warm. *Wait*, he thought. *Wait, why have a mug at the bottom of the sea floor?* He wanted to giggle at the absurdity of it. But then it made him angry, and a tightness seized his heart.

With that, the murky surface evaporated to reveal a blue sky, lined on either side with pine trees. He was on a path, somewhere in the forest. Cold Trench fell away as it always did, leaving him weightless for a few seconds. But this time, the people around him remained as Sarcops. Giant monstrosities, dripping with seawater, leaving a trail of it in the dirt. Mort(e) lay on a sledge of some kind, with two of the creatures pulling it. His head rolled from side to side with each bump in the trail. The closest one walked beside him, extending the cup with a tentacle that glistened in the sunlight.

The clicking sound changed into a word. "Tekni," the Sarcops said. "Tekni!"

Mort(e) rolled off the sledge and landed face down. As he got to his feet, the creatures surrounded him, their tentacles uncoiled. He crouched into a fighting stance. "Leave me alone," he said.

One of the Sarcops raced to the circle and pushed its way through, this one shorter than the others. The creature held out its claws in a gesture that Mort(e) could not translate.

"Mort(e), it's me," the creature said. He knew the voice.

"Go away."

Two of the Sarcops whispered to one another. He heard the word *Tekni* again.

"Mort(e), you're safe," the short one said.

He blinked a few times, and the creatures became blurry, like thick storm clouds. His legs gave out and he landed on one knee, still holding his hands in a weak fighting position. The short one knelt beside him, extending its tentacles. Only this time, he felt fur instead of scales and bone. He blinked again, and a dog appeared before him, nuzzling her nose against his like a beaver.

"Sheba?" he said. "D'Arc?"

"You're okay, Mort(e)," she said. "I'm here." Her tone was flat, exhausted.

As he rested his chin on her shoulder, he saw that a pack of wolves surrounded them. The Sarcops were gone for now.

"Go ahead," D'Arc sighed. "It's over. He can walk. We'll catch up."

The wolves started to move, but slowly. D'Arc growled at them. "I said we'll catch up!"

The wolves mumbled to each other. Mort(e) noticed their freshly bandaged wounds. Some hobbled on canes. One of them wore a sling on a broken arm, where a patch of dried blood indicated that the bone must have poked through the skin.

Mort(e) leaned away from her so he could take a good look. She was leaner than he remembered. Her palms were rough with calluses. The scent of mud clung to her skin. She smelled like a soldier. After a minute, she helped him to his feet. He put his arm on her shoulder to stay steady. He licked his lips a few times as the taste of salt began to fade.

"Where are we going?" he asked.

"We're running away."

Mort(e) recognized the defeat in the way the wolves moved—the hunched shoulders, the glassy eyes. He'd fought alongside these people, years ago. Or he fought with their fathers.

"Of course we are," he said.

She let him lean on her. Before long, he could walk on his own. But he continued with his arm on her shoulder, in much the same position in which they often used to fall asleep. It was only a matter of time before the taste of salt returned and the Sarcops summoned him once again to the deep. He needed to enjoy this while he could. Whatever scraps of pleasure he could find in this mess, he would pluck them out of the dirt and hold them in his shaking hands.

• • •

*MY NAME IS Mort(e)*, he thought. *Mort(e)*. *Mort(e)*. His own name resembled a nonsense word, a sound that a drunk would make while trying to fight off a bout of nausea.

Without warning, he made a clicking noise in the deep well of his throat, mimicking the cry of a Sarcops. Or did he merely hear the sound in his mind? A brief glance at D'Arc beside him confirmed the worst. She stared at him as she would a stranger.

"Sorry," he said.

"It's okay."

Dr. Marquez had told Mort(e) to repeat a series of phrases to himself every time he emerged from one of his episodes. He started with his name, then moved on to the motto of the Red Sphinx that Culdesac had taught him: *Aim true, stay on the hunt.* Then he recited the names of the cats in his unit in the order in which they had died. D'Arc's name came last. He managed to keep all of this silent, though D'Arc noticed him struggling and grimacing when the words piled on top of one another. Slowly, his memories crashed in around him again. But like the tide reclaiming a stretch of beach, they came and went, came and went. At least he could breathe again.

Like a good soldier, he took stock of the situation.

Mort(e) and D'Arc joined the stragglers in the rear of the pack. Most of the wolves at this part of the caravan wore a single blue stripe on their tails, a sign of their low rank. The older wolves, who wore more garish paint, had ordered them to watch for any attacks from behind. These marauders-in-training would either fight off any enemies or provide a distraction as the rest of the wolves made their escape.

Not far ahead, two wolves pushed a motorcycle with polished chrome fenders. Its mint condition seemed so out of place in this caravan. Wolves always bragged about keeping their old ways until one of the leaders spotted something shiny. This bike must have run out of gas, and now two lowly soldiers had to push it. One of them kept turning to D'Arc, staring for a few moments. The third or fourth time he did it, Mort(e) realized that he was the husky, Falkirk, who'd talked him into coming here. And now the dog gave him some time alone with D'Arc. How nice of him. It was the least he could do after they had parachuted into wolf territory.

The Mournfuls had found them immediately after that. As expected, the older wolves explained to the younger ones that this was Mort(e) of the Red Sphinx, who fought alongside the pack during the war. At that point, Mort(e) could have easily told them to take Falkirk prisoner. The dog knew that and decided to take the risk anyway, which Mort(e) could not help but admire.

The caravan reached the remnants of a highway, where some of the wounded needed help getting over the crumbling concrete barrier. Mort(e) assisted an old, impossibly skinny wolf, who wore a hook for a hand. He must have been a great warrior a long time ago.

Once on the road, the caravan gained speed, though Mort(e) could not tell where they would go. The highway skimmed along the territory claimed by the Bounty pack, one of several who'd sided with the Mudfoot at the last minute. Grieve may have hoped to reach Earthblood territory this way, though many would not survive the trip.

And who was left from the Earthblood now that their cavalry had revolted? Mort(e) overheard the others talking about how the horses trampled their riders in a spasm of violence and savagery. With no blades or guns, the horses relied on the blunt force of their hooves, powered by years of resentment and despair. It must have been glorious for them, an experience they'd missed out on during the early days of the Change.

Beside him, D'Arc walked with her shoulders hunched, her tail lowered. Back on the ranch, she would act this way after they euthanized one of their Alphas. Sometimes, she would go a day or two without speaking. Mort(e) wondered if his presence here made her sad. If it didn't already, it would at some point. He was a burden to her, a chain around her ankle. He had already made the mistake of asking her what happened, how she got here. She told him that the Mudfoot held her captive, nothing more. *You would know,* she seemed to say. *You've seen war. You talk about it enough.*

"I jumped from the airship," he blurted out.

A tiny smile curled her lip. "I know. What was it like?"

"I don't need to do it again."

"The Chief told me about the time she did it. I was jealous."

Mort(e) laughed. "Of course you were."

She nodded. This was better. If he could get through to her, if he could make her remember the way things were, maybe he could get her out of here. Hosanna was lost. They had no choice but to run. They could leave in the dead of night, head west, far from all of this.

"Why do they call you Tekni?" she asked.

One of the wolves turned and looked at her when she said it.

"It's some legend they believe in," Mort(e) said. "Tekni is a spirit that lurks in the woods. He watches over the good wolves. Rewards them with a good hunt."

"And the bad wolves . . ."

"He punishes them. They get lost on the hunt, disoriented. Or he leads them off a cliff, or into some trap."

He realized what she was doing. She was trying to ease him back into the real world by getting him to tell one of his classic Old Man stories from the war. They had not seen each other in months. She'd left him behind and would not apologize for it. And yet she performed this act of mercy, a kindness he did not deserve.

"The Mournful had a young leader in those days, cocky as hell," he told her. "Grieve's older brother. He wanted to prove something. One day, he attacked a human outpost. The humans retaliated. Decimated the pack."

After that, Grieve begged the Red Sphinx for help. Grieve wanted to attack the humans again, but first he needed to take control of the pack himself. Culdesac told him that his cats did not get involved in internal squabbles. But Mort(e) saw an opportunity. The wolves had been unreliable allies until then. They killed their share of humans but could not follow orders, and often ruined entire campaigns with their guerrilla tactics. Bringing them on board full-time would make a difference. And so the Red Sphinx agreed to help in exchange for a pledge of loyalty and a troupe of marauders who would answer to Culdesac for a season. "My toy dogs," he called them.

"So Grieve's brother went for a stroll in the forest one day," Mort(e) continued. "And he ran into Tekni."

"Wait," D'Arc said. "You didn't . . ."

"We didn't lay a finger on him. But we did tell him to keep walking toward the sunset till he couldn't walk anymore."

"Not a finger," she said absently.

"Okay, a *few* fingers. But he was able to walk afterward."

He stopped, realizing too late that he should have simply lied. She did not need to hear another story like this. The distance between them widened as she drifted to the edge of the road, her gaze focused straight ahead. No, no! It couldn't be that easily lost, could it? Were things that fragile?

He closed the gap and tried to match her pace. As he tried to think of something else to say, they passed the body of a wolf, an older female who'd lain on the asphalt and gone to sleep. Mort(e) could smell the gangrenous wound on her ribs. The blood dribbled on her blue war paint. There would be more before they reached Earthblood territory.

Walking slightly behind D'Arc, Mort(e) reached out his hand

to her shoulder. She saw him but did not react. The hand awkwardly hung there before he withdrew it

A howl broke out among the caravan. Some of the heavily
painted marauders ordered their brethren to stop. It made no difference. If the wolves gave away their position with their song,
so be it. One of their elders had fallen, and they would mourn.

D'Arc arched her spine and pitched her head back. She
released a howl that lasted a few seconds before turning into a
wheezing sound. Then she began again. She must have learned
it from the Mudfoot. Her voice cracked, a desperate cry that
Mort(e) had not heard since the war. It was the kind of noise
he thought he had left behind, and here it was, rising from the
throat of the person he raised. The person he created. He realized that he would never fully accept that she walked this other
path of her own choosing. With each broken howl, another
sharp rock fell to the pit of his stomach, weighing him down. He
slowed his pace as D'Arc moved farther and farther away. Soon
he became lost among the canines. He was the only one who did
not cry out.

THE HIGHWAY EXITED into a college town that the humans had long
since abandoned. The Earthblood maintained these old settlements to mark the borders of their territory, one of the only wolf
packs to do so. Rumor had it that they used a ten-story hotel near
a ski resort as a major base of operations, and they painted it red
with blood. Every few years, they needed a fresh coat. So the
rumor went.

Near the highway ramp, a crater marked the former location
of a gas station, lost in an explosion. Deeper into the town, the
school's main building rose above the rotting husks of cottages
and shops. An intricate layer of vines climbed the brick walls,
curling around the decaying bell tower. At this time of year,
the vines lay dormant and brown, waiting for spring when they

would burst out in green again. The same vegetation tethered the hollowed-out cars to the ground, transforming them into elaborate flowerpots, with tentacles crawling across the seats and through the chassis. A row of bicycles, still chained to a rack, also fell prey to the vine. The windows of the administrative offices remained mostly intact, though they were layered in dust.

Earthblood she-wolves, their faces painted red, greeted the arrivals in the enormous courtyard. The older females resembled human grandmothers feeding their pets, while desperate, delirious canines reached out to them, begging for treats. The wounded were sent to the sports arena to receive treatment, and a line had already wrapped around the building.

Mort(e) turned away from the spectacle to find the only sign of the war in town: a Huey helicopter in an empty parking lot. He got close enough to see a human skeleton in the cockpit, still in a jumpsuit, with a rusted pistol in their lap and a jagged hole in the top of their skull. Most likely, the pilot ran out of fuel, landed here, and weighed their options.

Mort(e) may have passed through here with the Red Sphinx at some point. He could picture his comrades mockingly toasting the dead pilot. The memory—if it even was one—melded with all the others. He stood staring, mumbling nonsense to himself while the wolves raced past him, heading for the scent of meat.

A hand pressed against his arm. Too big to be D'Arc's.

"Mort(e)," Falkirk said.

Mort(e)'s tail straightened. "What? What is it?"

"I told the Mamas that you would pay them a visit."

"The Mamas?"

"The old dogs." He pointed to the courtyard. "They can give you a place to lie down."

"I'm fine."

"We've already had this argument. Maybe you don't remember."

Mort(e) did not.

"D'Arc and I are meeting with the elders," Falkirk said. "To decide what to do next."

Despite his exhaustion, Mort(e) forced himself to speak. "I should go with you."

"Talk to the Mamas first," Falkirk said.

Mort(e) watched the throng of wolves swirling about the courtyard.

"Don't worry," Falkirk said. "We're not leaving without you."

Falkirk patted him on the shoulder and walked away. Mort(e) watched him as he pushed through the crowd toward the main entrance, directly below the bell tower. The enormous doors opened to let him in.

Mort(e) entered the courtyard, where frenzied wolves fought over pieces of meat as soon as the Mamas handed them over. Two of the wolves tugged so hard on a piece of flesh that it flew from their mouths and flopped right at Mort(e)'s feet. It rested on the ground, crusted with dirt. A wolf scooped it away, which prompted another melee. One wolf rushed in so quickly he nearly knocked Mort(e) over.

The elder females scolded them. "There's enough!" one of them shouted. "Enough for all! Save your energy!"

The younger wolves stopped on command. Mort(e) smiled at the thought of these great warriors, these invincible marauders, who still needed their mothers' approval.

Mort(e) followed the wall of the gymnasium to the service entrance at the rear, where capsized dumpsters and composting piles of trash littered the parking lot. A gang of young wolves gathered there, maybe fifteen in all. Fresh blood stained their lips. They had arrived here first, gotten the healthiest slices of venison, and now relaxed with full bellies. One of them, the smallest, sat in the middle while another painted his coat with a handmade brush. The young wolf had passed his first test on the way to becoming a full-fledged marauder, and thus earned a new set of markings.

"Tekni!" the wolf called out drunkenly. Mort(e) smelled moonshine. Some of the wolves passed the bottle behind their backs so he wouldn't see. The wolves always claimed they stayed away from the stuff, but no species could resist entirely.

The circle opened to welcome him. Mort(e) figured that these young warriors had been instructed to show deference. The Mournful in particular liked the ceremony of rank. But after a day's march, with the world ending all around them, these exhausted wolves ignored the protocols.

"Tekni," the baby of the group said again. "Tekni, Tekni, look." He clumsily pointed to the painting on his fur, showing a pitched battle in bright red, orange, and blue. It would wash away in the rain, and he would touch it up again, like a human fixing their makeup.

"Shhh," one of his comrades said. "Quiet."

"What?" the wolf said. "What, I wanna show 'im something."

"Tekni, we're sorry," another said. "Jovan here is drunk, likes to run his mouth."

"*Jovan* asked us for the markings!" yet another said. "It was *his* idea!"

"Yeah, yeah!" more of them chimed in. "He thought he was being funny."

"It's not bein' funny!" Jovan said. "It's in honor of—"

"Shut *up*!" one of his friends said.

Mort(e) got closer. "Let's see it."

They fell silent.

Jovan pointed to an image of a dog on his chest. A white dog, holding what appeared to be a stick, charging into a forest. It was D'Arc. Upon closer inspection, the stick had a nice curve to it. The wolves' ability to paint on fur astonished him. He had not seen artistry like this since the war.

As he leaned in closer, someone tried to distract him by shoving a bottle of moonshine in his face. "Try some of this!" Mort(e) pushed it away.

"Just let me show 'im!" Jovan insisted. He traced a line to his ribs, the part of him that would display most prominently when he ran on all four feet. The painting depicted a group of wolves standing in a circle. Their spiky fur and red eyes indicated a sinister intent. Even more ominous, they surrounded a smaller creature, a puppy that reached out his hand to D'Arc.

"Sheba the Mother," Jovan said proudly. "To the rescue!"

"That's enough!" another wolf barked.

Mort(e) straightened himself. With their snouts lowered and their eyes drooping, the marauders had transformed into meek puppies, hoping to regain their master's favor.

"Congratulations on your promotion," Mort(e) said.

"Thank you!" Jovan said. As Mort(e) turned away, someone hit Jovan on the back of the head. "Hey!" the wolf barked.

"I told you to shut up!" someone said. An argument began. Mort(e) left it behind, making his way across the courtyard, through the chaos of the new arrivals. The Mamas shouted to him to join them, to get something to eat.

"Fill your belly, kitty!" one of them said. Mort(e) sauntered right past. For the first time in days, he felt like his old self. No hint of salt water in his mouth, no sound of lapping waves chugging in his ears. His senses sharpened, and movement around him slowed until he could see the individual hairs on the hide of each wolf. They must have smelled it on him, this new sense of clarity, for they cleared a path even as they fought for the last scraps of meat.

Two guards waited in front of the main building, leaning on the Roman columns, where the steps rose to an archway and a pair of glass doors. When they spotted him approaching, they whispered to each other. These wolves enjoyed a higher rank than the others, judging from the sidearms dangling from their leather belts.

"I'm sorry, Tekni," the larger one said, extending his palm. "The elders are meeting."

"You gonna shoot me if I try to walk in?"

The smaller one puffed out his chest, prompting a snicker from Mort(e).

"Please, wait out here," the larger one said.

Mort(e) gestured to the gun. "How fast are you with that thing?"

The guards glanced at each other.

"You've already let me get too close," Mort(e) said, emphasizing the last word by climbing one more step. "It's too late to draw."

The larger one suddenly found his courage. "No it isn't."

"Show me."

The wolf squared his feet. It was one move too many. Before his fingers could tap the holster, Mort(e) shot his fist out and drove his knuckles into the smaller wolf's throat. With his other hand, he grabbed the wolf's pistol and spun him around, finishing with one arm over the guard's neck, the other pointing the newly acquired gun. The larger wolf, still squared and ready to draw, had managed to pull his own weapon halfway out of its holster.

"Now," Mort(e) said, "you can either let me in, or we can tell Grieve what just happened. All three of us."

The glass doors opened to a lobby with a dusty marble floor and rotting paintings of pudgy men on the walls. An earthy scent seeped through the next set of doors, smelling like the bottom of a ditch after a rainstorm. Mort(e) grabbed the handles and swung them apart, revealing a large hall that formed the heart of the building. On the high ceiling, a freshly painted star chart set Polaris at the northern corner of the room. The floor, astonishingly, was covered in an elaborate earthwork sculpture, complete with grass, stacks of rocks for mountains, pools of water for lakes. In order to move forward, Mort(e) needed to climb the miniature terrain. He noticed small model houses, packed tightly together, along with an enormous model of the city of Hosanna, built beside a river, a wooden bridge stretching across it. Ringing the city were wooden stakes poking out from the dirt, organized by color. Red for the Earthblood; blue for the Mournful; green, yellow, and orange for the smaller packs. And surrounding them all stood stakes with dark brown paint, some of which had received a new coat only hours before.

Mort(e) stood atop a three-dimensional model of wolf country and its surrounding territory. Some Earthblood elder must have demanded it so he could seem important while planning out another senseless raid, another pointless skirmish over land that they would lose within a season anyway. The wolves who constructed this map room enjoyed a level of sophistication and comfort that most of their people would ridicule. What kind of a hunter had time to make something like this?

To the north of Hosanna, a tiny gathering of wolves and dogs huddled in a square. Grieve, Harrek the White, Falkirk, and D'Arc. Three more guards lingered in the other corner, near the edge of the forest where the bears lived. At the center, a cylindrical object carved from wood rested on the ground. Mort(e) recognized it as the *Vesuvius*. On the other side of the river, a capsized cylinder marked the crash site of the *Upheaval*. The Earthblood tracked the airships' movements through a network of eyes on the ground and in the air. Falkirk probably gave them even more intelligence.

Only the guards noticed Mort(e) enter, and by then it was too late. Mort(e) lifted the model *Vesuvius* and flung it at Hosanna. The resulting bang echoed off the walls. All the people in the room jumped, but Mort(e) took note of D'Arc in particular. Her ears perked, and her hand shot right to the pommel of her sword. Her face sank when she saw him stomp through Hosanna like a giant. He gave the tower in the middle a swift kick, sending it flying far out into the wilderness.

Grieve at least had the decency to find it all amusing. Mort(e) remembered that grin, the same one the wolf had showed years earlier when Culdesac agreed to get rid of his brother.

"I asked you to wait outside," Falkirk said. He shut his mouth as soon as he saw the look in Mort(e)'s eyes.

"Forget it," D'Arc said, waving him off. She watched Mort(e) for a moment, much like she did before the Change, when there were no words to confuse them.

"He knows," she said.

BEHIND THE MAIN building, a dried-out fountain moldered among the fallen bricks and other debris. The stone basin had cracked and crumbled in several places, and rust had sealed the metal hose shut. In the center, the severed feet of a discarded statue were fused to a pedestal. D'Arc sat on a section of the basin she deemed secure while Mort(e) paced around her.

"I don't owe you an apology, Old Man," D'Arc said.

"You lied. You said you were never with Falkirk."

"It was my way of saying that it was none of your business."

"I told you," Mort(e) said. "I told you that these pets from Hosanna would—"

"I know what you told me," she snapped. "I've thought about it every day. Every day since I left, I've had your voice in my head lecturing me."

"Oh yeah? Was I right about anything?"

"A few things. And I know how important that is to you."

As Mort(e) turned away, he spotted two young wolves peeking around the corner, eavesdropping. The two vanished when he caught sight of them.

"I can't make you understand," D'Arc said. "But when I left—when I set out on my own—I was trying to do something good for once. Something that would create rather than destroy."

Mort(e) snorted.

"Don't laugh!" she said. "We've had enough of the war. I sat out most of it, and I know you'll never forgive me for that."

"I never said that."

"You didn't need to." She stood. "I was trying to do something new," she said. "Maybe I could help make things better, in my own way."

A flurry of desiccated leaves scraped along the fountain.

"I was trying to avoid becoming like you," she said.

Mort(e) stopped pacing. "How did that work out?"

She folded her arms. "Don't you even want to know about them? My children? I had a chance to get one of them back until you messed it up."

"Tell me."

D'Arc extended her arms and cupped her hands. "They were so small."

She told him their names. The first, Tristan. The second, Nautica. And a third, with no name, whom she held and lost, and then held and lost again. The universe tugging the child away from her each time she grasped for him.

"They're your children too," she said. "In a way."

A lightness swelled in his stomach as he remembered a vision that the Sarcops bestowed on him: Sheba's first litter of pups, lost to the war. Three little ones, calling him a name that no one would ever use for him.

Papa.

*Papa, over here! Papa, come find me!*

"Mort(e)," D'Arc said. He realized that he had moved several feet without realizing it. Another hallucination. At least it was a good one this time.

"There are more important things going on right now," D'Arc said. "Harrek is leading his people west. A few of us are going east. To fight."

"It's suicide, then."

"It's suicide if I don't go. Only slower. I know you understand *that* part."

In frustration, Mort(e) sat on the lip of the fountain. "These wolves can see the future," he said. "So I've heard."

"I've been inside their camp," D'Arc said. "I know how they operate, how they move."

"Even so. How long before the humans bomb all of it to hell?"

"Falkirk says it'll be soon. That's why have to move now."

Mort(e) knew then that he could not convince her to walk away, cut her losses.

"I can help," he said weakly.

"Mort(e)," she said. "You're not well. I'm sorry you came all this way. It wasn't for nothing—the Mournful saved my life. But I can't . . ." She pulled her hand away and covered her mouth with it. "I owe you everything, but I can't bring you with me."

Mort(e) said nothing.

"Don't fight me on this," she added. "Please. Grieve and Harrek are on my side. They say you can go with them. You are still the Ten-ki."

"*Tek*ni," Mort(e) corrected.

She crouched before him and rested both hands on his knees.

"I love you, Old Man. I want to introduce you to my son one day."

Mort(e) would never see her son. He knew that now. She would bring the pup to a grave, a mound of dirt with a stone on top, and tell him whatever stories she still remembered. In his time left, Mort(e) needed to find meaning in that.

Before he could say something, the taste of salt water flooded his mouth. *No, not now*, he thought. *Not here, please.*

"Are you all right?"

"I'm fine. Let me sit here for a bit."

"We'll be in the war room," she said. "Falkirk and I leave in the morning."

"I'll see you off."

She patted his shoulder. "Don't just see me off. The Mamas are serving dinner tonight. Our last good one for a while. Come talk to me."

"Okay."

Mort(e) nodded, his gaze on the ground. The frozen earth softened to the muddy ocean floor before changing back. The hallucinations mocked him at this point.

When he looked up again, D'Arc was gone.

# CHAPTER 16

## THE TRAITOR

HE PUP WOULD not stop crying. Maybe because he knew the truth.

Walking upright like a human, Mercy tried jamming one of her sore, dry nipples into his mouth. The pup coughed out the first one, then bit hard on the second. Out of frustration, he grasped for her tooth necklace and tugged on it. She pulled it free from his grasp and flipped the tooth over her shoulder, where he could not reach it.

The other wolves, who had marched beside her all day on this trail, closed ranks around her. Her head poking over their shoulders negated their camouflage, which made them nervous, especially Carsa. The older wolf brushed against Mercy's leg a few times, but would not demand that Mercy travel like a wolf. Mercy had already snapped at Carsa when she suggested letting the pup walk. This was not the time to train him. The young one would walk when he was ready. Not before.

The sound of the river trickled through the trees, carrying a wet smell. After going uphill for so long, the trail at last eased downward again. The pup did not seem to care and continued screaming. Helplessly, Mercy scanned the forest once more for the wet nurse, the mongrel dog from Hosanna. The pup behaved when the nurse suckled him. But in the two days since the attack, the young one howled constantly. Each cry condemned Mercy for finding him on that beach, for taking him, for passing him off as her own. She imagined her own children, Rove and Herc, sniffing the baby's head, wrinkling their noses at the scent. They never would have accepted this pup as their brother.

The scouts had gathered at the edge of the river. The group split apart to make room for Mercy when she arrived. She lowered to her front paws and slid the pouch to her shoulders, where the baby continued protesting in her ear. She dipped her front paw into the water, to feel the familiar icy shock.

The rear guard of the humans arrived last, their boots squishing in the mud. Augur acknowledged Mercy with a bob of his chin. Crossing would be her decision. They had barely said a word to each other since the attack, when she forded this same river in the dead of night while on the run from the Mournful, the pup screaming in her ear the entire time. Today, after receiving word that the battle had ended, they returned to the scene of the ken-ra. There, they would seal their alliance with the newly joined wolf packs before pressing on to Hosanna. Augur no longer needed to see the future. Instead, the future came barreling toward them, an avalanche that uprooted everything and carried it along.

Urna pushed her way past the others. She, too, had barely spoken to Mercy while they took refuge in the hills. But now, faced with the river again, Urna pawed in the mud, drawing a line that pointed downstream. Carsa and Creek mimicked her. They wanted to find a bridge somewhere, or at least a narrower bottleneck.

Finding another way would take too long, and Mercy wanted to rest. She wanted time to think—and to remember.

To make her intentions clear, Mercy splashed the water three times. They would not merely cross the river. They would swim with the current. It would shave hours off their journey. The cold would sap their strength, and the pup would cry louder. But they would move faster.

Mag barked in protest, and then the pack drowned him out with angry barks of their own. The humans remained quiet. Perhaps Augur told them to give the wolves their space after all they had endured these last few days.

Carsa barked at something in the water. Mercy turned to see the carcass of a marauder floating downstream. Another Bounty wolf, judging from the faded green stripe painted on his spine. The body collided with a rock and spun in a shallow whirlpool before continuing its journey.

Mercy would not wait for the others. After listening to the pup's mewling, she could not bear to debate with them. So she trundled into the water. The chill numbed her. Once her feet lost contact with the riverbed, she could no longer feel her tail. Her anger kept her warm.

The others followed. The pup turned his head to Carsa, no doubt begging for her to get him out of here. The little one had learned how to give orders before he could speak.

Mercy focused on the body floating far in the distance. After a few seconds, the pup faced straight ahead and saw it. At last, he was quiet, either out of fascination or terror. She may not have been his real mother, but Mercy would teach him about the real world, about the real future that awaited. The cruelty that no language could describe. The emptiness that no glory in battle could fill. He would see it all firsthand, and it would make him one of her people whether or not his heart pumped their blood. *Cry now*, she thought. *While you still can.*

THE WOLVES AT the train station gave the Mudfoot a decidedly different welcome this time. Bounty wolves, painted green. Mournfuls in blue stripes, bedecked in jewels. Opa with their spiked collars. They howled, stamped their feet, danced about. The few with rifles fired them into the air. The movement of bodies warmed Mercy's fur, still dripping from the river.

Something sharp pierced the bottom of her foot. When she flinched, the pup let out a worried sound, and she soothed him by rubbing her nose against his. She lifted her foot from the ground to find something white lodged into the skin. She pulled it loose. It was a tooth, a wolf fang, sharp enough to draw a small bead of blood. Mercy stopped and noticed droplets of red spattered on the walls, along with a few shiny pools of it gathering at various spots throughout the station. A few patches of grass were stained red or white where the painted warriors fell in the skirmish. The bodies were all gone. She stopped wondering and instead chose to be grateful for it.

It was at this point that Augur felt comfortable enough to walk beside Mercy as they followed the train tracks into the station. His deerskin tunic and pants were still dripping from the river, but his boots were dry, as he had tied them around his neck when he swam. In all, he acted as if he had simply taken a bath. If all humans could adapt like this, they would have won the war.

More wolves streamed in, so many that they made space by climbing onto the roof of the station. When Mercy reached the train tracks, her eyes followed the metal beams all the way to the forest. There, a train engine, painted bright orange, emerged from the tree line, gliding along the metal slats, pulling more cars behind it. Many of the wolves broke ranks so they could reach out and touch the metal. The pack leaders let them do it, knowing full well that most of them had never seen anything like it.

On top of the engine sat a troupe of humans with pale skin, almost pink in the sun. Despite the cold weather, they wore no shirts, only deerskin pants and thick leather boots. While one of them appeared to be operating the train from the inside, their apparent leader—a bald man with broad, sculpted shoulders—straddled the front of the engine like a Mournful riding a horse.

This astonishing machine, far larger than the piece of the airship that landed in wolf country, represented the Bounty pack's tribute to Mercy the Merciful. It was the reason they met here—the wolves and the humans.

As the train pulled into the station, its wheels screeching, Urna counted the cars out loud. Four silver cars followed the engine. Mercy could see the cushioned passenger seats through the windows. Near the end was a wheeled metal platform carrying an enormous truck on top, the largest Mercy had ever seen. With its round shape, it resembled a beetle curling into a ball to protect itself. By then, Urna had lost count and needed to start over.

A Toqwa woman emerged from the train station. Fresh blood glistened on her tunic, though it appeared to belong to someone else. As the screeching changed pitch, she covered her ears with her hands and whined like a dog, something that would always sound strange to Mercy. The woman waved Augur over. She gave a hand signal, wrapping her two index fingers around each other. It meant *friends.*

"They're here already," Augur said. He took Mercy's hand in his and led her to the station. The woman bowed her head as Mercy passed.

Inside, shafts of light pierced through the holes in the roof. Posters with smiling humans peeled from the stone walls, and a billboard with plastic numbers attached to it showed the last scheduled trains to arrive and depart from over a decade before. In the middle of the floor, the Toqwa warriors gathered around a wooden table. Another human lay on it—a man. His scuffed boots stuck out from between the bodies. He wore the same outfit as the humans who rode on the train. A ragged wound opened his torso from his hipbone to his armpit. Despite the human physiology, Mercy recognized the cut—definitely from a Mournful scimitar.

A pair of humans tried to stanch the bleeding with pieces of cloth. The fabric turned red each time they applied it, layer after layer. Wolves entered the room, carrying steaming buckets with boiled rags, the most sanitary bandages they could find.

While they tried to patch the man's side, a Toqwa woman stood over him, holding a quill in one hand, a rag in the other. A clay bowl of black ink sat next to the man's head. The woman dipped the quill into it and dabbed it on his cheek, producing a blob of ink and blood with each little poke. With the rag, she wiped the fluid away and started again. An image formed around his eyes and mouth—a wolf mask, given only to the elite Toqwa warriors.

Though dazed, the man gave Augur an enormous smile when he saw him. The tattoo artist continued her work.

By exposing his belly, the man showed deference to the higher-ranking member of the pack. In his condition, he could do little else. With a gentleness of a pup, Augur traced his other finger around the growing tattoo.

"We brought it," the man said. "The mission was a success."

Augur took the man's hand, lifted it to his own chest, and squeezed it.

The man weakly motioned to his face. "I told them that I needed to get a Toqwa mask before I die."

The woman glanced at Augur and nodded.

"Please see to it—" A sudden wave of pain overtook the man. He bit his lip to get through it. "Please see to it that my men . . . receive the same honor."

"The honor is ours," Augur said.

The woman pierced the skin right above the eyebrow, tapping again and again as the blood rose. Rather than show any pain, the man shifted his gaze to Mercy and her pup. His face softened. No matter how old they became, these humans could sometimes resemble children.

"This is our future," the man said. "The little prince."

Mercy hesitated to get any closer. Augur gave her a look that said it was all right. She slid the pup from her back and cradled him. Fully awake now, the little dog remained still as the man reached out and rubbed his index finger under his chin. A dog knew when another creature was suffering. The man's eyes drooped shut as the woman dabbed another blob of ink into his skin. He may have died in that exact moment. The woman continued with her task anyway.

Augur released the man's hand. "Let's see what they brought us."

Outside, the stench of blood nearly overpowered Mercy. Near the entrance, on the concrete platform, two humans and two wolves pulled apart a fresh deer carcass with their teeth. With no fangs, the humans used their hands to peel away the flesh, while the wolves could simply thrash the pieces away. Urna instinctively reached for a morsel that had landed a few feet away, leaving a wet streak.

Augur led them along the platform, past the train cars, each one an impossibility. Enormous, shiny machines, larger than any tree trunk and smoother than the most weather-beaten rocks. Standing atop the engine, the bald man signed a greeting to Augur. The other wolves who crowded the platform stepped aside as they headed toward the rear of the train.

Augur pointed to the large vehicle sitting on the flatbed car. "It's a trash truck," he said. "That's how much garbage they used to have," he added. "They needed huge vehicles to move it from their homes to ours."

Mercy noticed that the rear of the truck could seal itself with a steel bar that pressed the hatch closed. She turned to Urna to get her reaction, but her sister refused to go any farther.

A few feet closer, Mercy realized why. The greasy, fishy smell of the rahvek returned, more potent than before. It leaked from the rear of the truck. The great door, with its cylindrical metal arm, sealed in a new supply of the potion. Mercy inhaled so deeply that the cartilage in her ribcage popped. Suddenly a blast of wind sucked away all the sounds around her, leaving her in a vacuum. She saw Augur as a child again, surrounded by his wolf family, wearing the hide of a skinned deer to keep him warm in the snow. In a hazy blur, her mind traveled far into the future, where the forest hummed with life again, and the song of the wolves rang out at dusk. She flew above the trees, carried on the wind. Her tongue fell from her mouth and instantly dried out in the breeze.

Just as quickly, she crashed into the present, and all the sounds of the platform returned with a whoosh. The force of it made her rock to the side a bit, but the pup's whimper reminded her to steady herself. Augur was in the middle of speaking—something about this being the last of the rahvek.

"But we don't have to worry about that anymore," he said. "The future we have been building will be here soon enough."

Mercy glanced at her sister, who stood obediently along with the other wolves, like a pet dog.

"Are you all right?" Augur asked.

She wagged her tail.

"You felt it, didn't you?" he said. "You stepped outside of time."

"Yes."

"It calls to us now. We are all connected. No one else can understand. But they will."

The pup stirred against her chest. He did not care about stepping outside of time and all of that. He simply wanted more milk.

"Wet nurse," she said.

"I'm sorry," he said. "The one we brought with us—I had to get rid of her."

"Why?"

He stroked his chin. "I couldn't see what would become of her. It was a blank space, nothing more. Which means I couldn't trust her. Better to get rid of her now, rather than regret it later."

Mercy remembered the first time she took the rahvek, and how it twisted Augur's mind, incapacitated him. Any deviation from the future he expected made him nervous.

"Don't worry," he said. "She's gone now. And my people are looking for another wet nurse."

Mercy realized that everyone on the platform waited silently for her to speak to them. They had come so far. She needed to say something.

"Need rest," she said to Augur. She turned and headed for the station. Augur followed. He knew not to push her after so long a journey. As Mercy passed the crowd, she expected Urna to follow, or to call to her. Instead, her sister kept her gaze on the truck, as if it contained everything she feared. Wex could jump out at any second. Or opening it could release the Damnable to this place and reduce everything to ash and dust and decay. But Augur was right. No one could truly understand. They simply needed to obey for a little longer. After that, they could all be wolves again.

THE ENGINEERS TINKERED with the train late into the night. Mercy fell asleep to the noise with the pup cuddled in her arms. Augur spooned with her from the other side, his muscular triceps squeezed around her ribs. The guards formed a perimeter around them, and the breeze carried their scent to her nostrils, making her feel safe.

Some time later, a grinding noise woke her, like a giant screwdriver eating its way through steel. Her heart jumped. Still half-asleep, Augur held her tighter.

"They're fitting the engine with some armor," Augur breathed into her ear.

Though it taxed her mind, she decided to speak in the human language. Any wolflike gestures would wake the baby.

"Tell me what you see," she said. "In days to come."

"I'll fill one more canister. The last one. The truck will remain on the train. Everything should be—"

"No," she said. "Tell me what it will be like. When all this over."

He had told her enough times. Under the night sky, it would sound like a lullaby.

"I see green where there was once gray," he said. "I hear singing where there was once silence. I smell fur, and mud, and hot breath. Like I do now. Only it's everywhere. And the smell of our packs, human and canine, mingle in the air forever."

He asked her what she would do once Hosanna fell.

"When we go back," she said, "I show the child the hook."

"The hook?"

She held out her paw and bent the fingers. "Where the river bends. My brothers and sisters hunt there."

"I see."

"We run there as pups. To become wolves."

Mercy was the slowest in those days. Her older brother picked on her, told her she would be an omega. Urna was still whole then. She would defend her sister, sometimes with a growl, often with her teeth and claws.

Three gunshots thundered in the distance, coming from the station. Mercy tried to sit quickly, but Augur's arm held her in place.

"Don't worry," he said.

How could he say that, after the attack the other day?

"I must see," she said.

"No. Stay here with me. We are safe."

"Safe from what?"

He had an answer for everything. This time, his lips tucked themselves between his teeth.

"You see this?" she asked.

"I don't see everything. It's probably some of the guards doing some target practice."

Some primal instinct told her to investigate. She stood, making sure to hold the pup steady. She shifted him around to her backpack so she could run on all four feet. Somehow, through all the marching and swimming, this maneuver had become second nature. Or the baby had grown used to it.

She trotted past Mag, who immediately let out a loud bark, summoning the other guards to follow.

They ran single file alongside the tracks, past the train and through the station, where several packs of wolves slept in the courtyard. A few of them lifted their heads to see what was going on.

The tracks curved into the overgrown grass, where a team of guard dogs shouted and barked. Mercy could make out their silhouettes on the horizon. The sentries at the perimeter had captured an intruder.

No. They had stopped a deserter. The smell gave it away.

"There are more of them," one of the guards said. He was a giant Bounty wolf, with green paint glistening on his face. "Follow the scent. They're injured. Can't get far."

Mercy approached the scrum of wolves who piled on the deserter. She could smell that this was a female who could not bear children, a scent she had grown accustomed to in Mudfoot country. With so many guards surrounding her, the deserter stopped struggling.

"You gonney," one of the Bounty wolves said to her, aiming his pistol. "Traitor! You and the others."

"What happened?" Mercy asked.

"They stole one of the canisters. The others got away with one. This one fell behind."

The wolves stepped away so that Mercy could see the deserter.

As they spread out, Mercy's guards crouched into their fighting stances, hind quarters lifted, teeth bared.

It was Urna. Blood dribbled from bite marks on her neck and front paw. A random swipe of a claw had torn part of her ear off. The pup awakened and began to cry softly at the sight of this wretched animal.

Mercy turned to Augur. The human stood far outside of the circle. For all his talk of becoming more like the wolves, he knew to stay out of this.

He also knew—or must have known—that whatever was about to take place could not happen any other way.

"Where is canister?" Mercy asked her sister.

"Gone," Urna said.

Mercy stood over them on her hind legs. She expected Urna to cower in fear, as this was exactly what Wex would have done. But her sister remained still.

"You know what the canister holds?" Mercy said.

"It holds tomorrow."

Tired of speaking the human language, Mercy jerked her head forward and huffed. It signified a simple question: *Why?*

Urna replied with a howl that began with a whooping sound and faded into a long hiss. Mercy knew it well. It was Dregger's warning signal. If the two sisters ever needed to run away from danger, they would call out this song and meet at the nearest high point.

Urna howled again and again. The pup tried to mimic her with a high-pitched song, a sound of pain and regret.

Mercy turned to the Bounty wolf and stuck out her hand. The wolf placed the gun in her palm. The weight of it made her hand drop to her hip.

In the years to come, in the great paradise that she saw in her visions, she would tell herself that she never would have done any of this had she known what it would cost. She would also tell herself that her sister died long ago, and that it was the Damnable betrayed her pack, not this creature before her.

Urna let out a last howl that faded in a broken voice. Mercy raised the gun and fired. The bullet caught Urna at the base of the neck. She slumped to the earth. Mercy fired three more times into the torso, until the body stopped jerking with each round. Steam rose from the wounds.

Mercy handed the gun to the wolf. "Put her on train," she said. They would bury Urna at the hook in the river, where, really, she died a long time ago. One day, the yellow flowers that bore her name would grow there again.

As Mercy walked away, her guards formed a wide halo around her, with old Carsa taking the lead, the twins Mag and Quick in the rear.

The pup let out Dregger's howl a few more times, then fell asleep.

# PART IV
## STALEMATE

# CHAPTER 17

## A FAIR FIGHT

ALKIRK SPRINTED THROUGH the forest, gripping the barrel of his rifle. Behind him, a wolf named Loder—one of Grieve's lesser sons—tried to keep up.

The trail forked around an enormous red oak with fresh wolf tracks imprinted on both paths. A war party hunting for prey, following the howls of their leaders. The size of the prints and the long strides between each one told him everything he needed to know.

Falkirk slapped the bark with the palm of his hand and turned to Loder. "Which way?"

The wolf bent at the waist and propped his hands on his knees. His tongue hung so low that Falkirk imagined it would fall out of his mouth. Falkirk had never met a wolf who was out of shape before, especially one so young, but this marauder panted and staggered like a pothound on his last legs. Despite Grieve's disappointment in this one, he nevertheless spoiled Loder with gifts stolen from the human world, including a motorcycle—which he clearly had spent too much time riding.

"I said, which way?" Falkirk repeated.

"To the left, maybe?"

A gunshot thudded in the distance. Definitely from the right path.

"Or the right?" Loder said.

The clap of another gunshot ricocheted through the trees. Falkirk ran toward the sound.

"Stop!" he screamed. "Stop shooting!"

The trees thinned, and the loamy earth gave way to exposed rock. Emerging into the light, Falkirk arrived at the top of a sharp cliff, where a group of wolves took cover behind a row of boulders. Near the edge, something poked its head over the trunk of a fallen tree. Bullet holes riddled the bark, leaving a pile of sawdust on the ground. The person behind the trunk lifted a claw over the top and fired a pistol. The bullet whizzed past Falkirk's ear. He dropped to all fours and crawled.

The wolves taunted their prey. "How many bullets ya got left, partner?"

"Can't bury you here," another said. "We'll hafta toss you off the cliff!"

Falkirk wriggled his way to Grieve. The wolf sat against a boulder, loading shells from his bandolier into the breach of a sawed-off shotgun. For all his bluster, for all his posturing around the females and bullying, Grieve truly relished battle. It was not an act. Who could ever dethrone someone like this? Who would *want* his job?

When Grieve noticed Falkirk approaching, he grinned. The little skull on his necklace grinned with him. "Oh, look," he said. "The husky's here to save us."

One of Grieve's ass-kissers laughed beside him. It was probably his full-time job.

Falkirk crawled closer. "Grieve, listen to me."

"Father!" someone shouted. It was Loder, running upright toward their position like a complete moron. A gunshot inevitably followed, and the bullet skimmed the rocks and rustled the branches. Loder dropped to his face, shivering.

"Stay down, you fat slob!" Grieve said. He turned to his lieutenants. "There's no way he's mine. His mother must have fucked somebody's pet dog."

"Who's firing at you?" Falkirk asked.

"Some crazy bat. Can't fly, must be wounded. But he managed to steal one of our guns."

Another shot. Falkirk covered his ears as the wolves responded with their own volley. In the silence that followed, a cloud of smoke slid over them before floating off the side of the cliff.

"Is he with someone?" Falkirk asked.

"Yeah. A rat."

Falkirk shimmied over to the edge of the boulder and tried to peek around it without getting his face blown off. The bat could hardly hide with those ears poking above the rock. Falkirk saw no sign of another.

"Are you sure it's a rat?"

"No, and I don't care."

Falkirk waved Loder over, but the trembling wolf stayed in place.

"Tell him what you told me!" Falkirk said.

Only twenty minutes before, at the edge of the university town, Falkirk had overheard Loder talking with some of the wolves, the ones who were almost certainly forced to be friends with him, thanks to his status as Grieve's son. Loder mentioned how the patrols picked up two intruders: a bat and a beaver. When Falkirk heard this, he grabbed the wolf by his necklace and demanded to know where. The others made no move to stop him. They seemed to draw some amusement from watching this spoiled brat get pushed around for once.

"Father," Loder said, "I saw it myself. That's a beaver with the bat."

"Like hell it is! I saw it. Too scrawny."

"Yeah, beavers are fat like you!" someone shouted.

"I told the marauders, but they didn't believe me," Loder said.

And Falkirk knew why. Bats and beavers hated each other. Nothing could change that. No matter what was left after the Mudfoot destroyed everything, those two species would fight over it.

"One of the first places the Mudfoot hit was a bat recon post," Falkirk said.

"Yeah, on the other side of the mountains."

"The recon post had a jail cell. With beavers in it. Let me talk to them."

Grieve slammed the last shell into the breech. "*Talk*," Grieve said. "The pet from Hosanna wants to negotiate. Look where that's gotten us."

"If they made peace with each other, they can make peace with you."

"Maybe they already made peace with the other wolves. *Lots* of people have."

He kept his unblinking gaze on Falkirk, to remind him of all the dogs from Hosanna who joined the Mudfoot cult. Ignoring it, Falkirk surveyed the cliff, hoping to find a place where he could sneak around the shooter. He couldn't risk luring the bat out from his hiding space. One of these trigger-happy marauders would likely shoot both of them.

"I could climb down the side," he said. "Then climb up right behind the bat. Maybe I can disarm him."

A few of the marauders glanced at one another. They preferred a straight fight. Though Falkirk wondered if they were simply afraid to climb it themselves.

"Sure, give it a try," Grieve said. "But don't die. I don't want your baby-mother poking me with her sword tonight."

Another random bullet cracked against the boulder. Falkirk

didn't even realize he had dropped to the ground, hands on his head, until he spat out a clump of frozen dirt.

"You sure you want to do this?" Grieve asked.

Falkirk brushed some dead grass from his coat. "Don't worry. I'm not afraid of heights."

FALKIRK ARRIVED AT the base of the cliff a few minutes later, after finding an offshoot of the trail that led into the ravine. Though the cliff rose a good thirty feet into the air, it sloped gently, enough to give an inexperienced climber a chance. Falkirk cracked his knuckles, gripped the cold stone, and got to work. When the wind scraped along the side, he held on and waited for it to pass. Near the top, where the breeze whistled at a lower pitch, he heard more gunfire, more taunts from the wolves. The last thing he needed was for the bat to actually get lucky and hit someone. Including him.

His muscles aching and his fingertips rubbed raw, Falkirk waited at the summit for another volley. This time, a pair of bullets whined off the rocks, spinning madly into the ravine behind him. He peeked over the top to find the bat huddled behind a boulder, his head swiveling as he tracked the marauders getting closer, trying to flank him. On the ground, the bat resembled a half-assembled doll, with an emaciated midsection and wings folded against his exposed ribs. A crack ran through his left goggle. His teeth flared out like sharpened white sticks, and Falkirk wondered if this creature could fully close his mouth.

To the left, huddled behind a hunk of granite, lay a shriveled rodent. A female beaver, barely breathing, prone on her side. Her eyes glistened like black marbles as she stared out, away from the promontory, perhaps hoping to somehow fly away from all of this.

With his heart pounding from his stomach to his neck, Falkirk lowered himself below the ridge to give himself a moment to think. A beaver stuck out here with a bat. The Lord worked in mysterious ways. Sometimes, God's hand scattered everyone at random so they could either find their way back, or carve out a new path.

Falkirk pulled himself up again, ready to face the bat. And as he rose, his snout bopped against the cold steel of the gun. The bat held the pistol awkwardly in the long fingers at the tip of his wing, the bones encased in stretchy leather. His ears twitched, letting Falkirk know how foolish it was to think that he could sneak behind a bat. Behind him, the beaver rolled over to her stomach, propped herself on a weak hand. She squinted and clicked her enormous teeth.

"Another doggie joined the Mudfoot," she said.

"I'm not Mudfoot. I'm here to help." *God, let me help someone.* He'd watched the soldiers at Cadejo die from a distance. He'd watched Ruiz bleeding out on the deck. Something had to go right for once.

The beaver crawled closer, dragging her flat tail. She sniffed him.

"You're here to help," she mumbled. "I've heard that before."

Falkirk's foot slipped, but he held on and dug his toes into a more solid crevice. The bat squeaked at the sudden movement. He shuffled closer, gun still raised.

Despite his shortness of breath, Falkirk forced out the words. "You're . . . you're the matriarch." He turned to the bat. His jaw fell open. "And you're—"

"Gaunt of Thicktree," she said. "Proudest family of the Great Cloud. Protectors of the Sacred Forest."

And then, something he never could have imagined: she squeaked at the bat—a full sentence in Chiropteran, albeit with an accent, and an octave too low. The bat said something in response, then backed away from the edge to give Falkirk room. The husky dragged himself onto solid ground and took a sitting position. He held his arms in a cactus position to show that he meant no harm.

"I remember you," the beaver asked. "You're Sanctuary Union."

"No," Falkirk said, lowering his gaze. "Not anymore."

"We need to speak to someone from Hosanna. We . . . have something. Something they need."

"You're injured," Falkirk said.

"It's worse than that, I'm afraid."

The bat let out a sad whistling sound.

A barrage of bullets pinged off the rocks. Falkirk and Gaunt both flattened themselves on the ground. The matriarch hardly moved.

"You were saying," the beaver said.

"Hold your fire!" Falkirk shouted, his breath blowing out a puff of dust from the earth.

Gaunt crawled to the boulder to fire a few more shots. Falkirk grabbed him by his broken wing, the skin slippery in his paw. The bat spun around, his face so twisted with rage that he resembled a demon. He jammed the barrel of the gun beneath Falkirk's chin.

"We're not your enemy," Falkirk said. "You want to get something to Hosanna, I'm your only chance."

The bat glanced at Nikaya. The beaver waited.

"You may have lied to me once," Falkirk said. "But I never lied to you."

Nikaya tried to speak, but was seized by a rattling cough. She braced herself on her hand to keep from keeling over. When she finally steadied herself, she stared at the bat for a moment. Falkirk expected them to squawk in their broken Chiropteran. Instead, they used some unspoken language, the kind born of desperation and familiarity. Their time out here had changed them into wolves.

Gaunt withdrew his gun, folding it into his wing. Falkirk

rolled away from him and crawled to Nikaya, who slumped onto her stomach.

"We'll get you some help," Falkirk said.

"Of course you will."

Falkirk rose to his feet and waved his arms. "It's over!" He shouted to the wolves. "They're surrendering! We need some help over here!"

He knelt beside Nikaya as the footsteps approached. Gaunt placed his pistol on the ground and huddled beside the beaver. With her undersized paw, she clutched the tip of his wing. The bat made a humming noise.

Nikaya tried to draw a breath. "You have to . . . get this bat to Hosanna. Everything . . . depends on it."

The wolves surrounded them. Gaunt bared his teeth when they arrived. But when Nikaya squeezed his claw, he grew calm again.

"See!" Loder shouted. "I told you!"

Grieve slapped him on the ear. Loder glared at him. "Good job," Grieve mumbled. The young wolf looked to the others for affirmation, but the sight of the dying beaver left them transfixed.

"You're a good puppy," Nikaya said. "I remember. I trust you."

The bat continued to hum. The wolves kept quiet and listened.

THEY CARRIED NIKAYA on a tarp into the map room. Lying emaciated on the fabric, she resembled a pile of dust pushed into the corner of a room. One of her tiny hands dangled off the side. The other rested on her belly as it rose and fell with each desperate breath. Gaunt insisted on following behind them as they carried her, but he needed to lean on Falkirk to walk. His wing wrapped around Falkirk's shoulders, a warm second skin.

Nikaya's eyes lit up as she entered. No doubt she had heard of this place. Now, with the end so near, she finally got to see it.

A hand grazed Falkirk's elbow. It was D'Arc, leaning over him, her mouth agape at the sight of the matriarch. "What's going on?" she whispered.

"The beaver wishes to speak."

Gaunt confirmed this with a squawk.

More wolves entered. Harrek the White and his entourage lined the walls. Grieve ordered his officers to the other side. Even on this imaginary landscape, the wolves would segregate themselves.

From her stretcher, Nikaya pointed to a cluster of wooden sculptures that straddled one of the rivers. A bridge constructed of sticks stood next to a waterwheel that someone had toppled over. Together, the models created a startlingly accurate depiction of Lodge City. The wolves placed her on the ground, spreading out the tarp. She reached out her hand and rested it on the waterwheel.

"What is this?" Harrek grunted. Falkirk shushed him.

Gaunt slid from Falkirk's arm and crawled to Nikaya. Everyone leaned in closer to hear them as the beaver and the bat whispered to each another.

"We escaped from the garrison near Thicktree," Nikaya said.

Gaunt said something else in her ear. She translated. "And you've heard the rumors about the Mudfoot being able to see the future. The rumors are true."

"How?" Grieve said. Falkirk could hear the jealousy in his voice, the kind that only a person who has held power for too long would have. Despite his conquests, he still needed more. It was a permanent arms race.

More Chiropteran whispered between the bat and the beaver. The conversation grew heated. Nikaya emphasized a point by gripping the bat's wing and shaking it while she spoke. Finally, the bat turned to Falkirk and D'Arc. As he approached, he reached under his wing and pulled out a metal canister no larger than his claw. He raised it to Falkirk's chest. The wolves gathered around as Falkirk accepted it. Some of them huffed at the insignificance of this object—a little human bauble, another shiny object to distract a pet.

"This is what they call the rahvek," Nikaya said before descending into a coughing fit. "It's a truth serum."

"It makes you tell the truth?" Grieve asked.

"It makes you *see* the truth," she said, trying to catch her breath. "The truth about what is to come."

Falkirk began to unscrew the lid. Gaunt stopped him by slapping his leg with his wing.

"Don't," Nikaya said. "Even a whiff of it will make you forget what day it is."

Falkirk screwed the lid tight, then wiped his hand on his belt.

"You must have known about it," she added.

Falkirk rotated the cylinder and found a serial number etched into the side. 120718. Only Hosanna would use something like this. The humans loved serial numbers.

"The flood," Nikaya said. "The flood washed away a lot of things. It couldn't wash this away."

Falkirk felt all the eyes in the room watching him.

"There were some weapons projects," he said. "I mean, I heard rumors."

"Rumors."

"Colonial biotech, they called it. Nobody knew how it worked."

"Somebody knew," a voice called out. The attention shifted to the door, where Mort(e) leaned on the frame. He looked frail, wobbly, with sagging eyelids, and patches of hair that needed some grooming.

Gaunt cried out a greeting in Chiropteran. Mort(e) nodded.

The beaver also recognized him, and a fire flashed in her beady eyes. It took a few seconds before she finally blinked away her rage.

Mort(e) eyed the canister. "A team of humans smuggled this stuff out of Hosanna last month."

"Ah," Nikaya sighed. "That's the best part."

Breaking into a strange, jerky dance movement, Gaunt flapped his wings and snapped his jaw open and shut. Startled, the wolves backed away to give him space.

"Whatever this *bio*tech is," Nikaya said, "the Alphas are searching for it too."

"Alphas?" Grieve said. The wolves murmured.

"I've seen them," D'Arc said. The room quieted as she explained that her ship had been tracking Alphas in the Atlantic. Nikaya described her own encounter with them in the mountains, while Gaunt acted out the attack by flapping his wings and pouncing on the ground. He must have thought that this made it sound scarier, as if anyone needed the reminder.

"I'm supposed to believe that the ants can smell this stuff from miles away?" Grieve said.

"The Queen could see outside of time," Mort(e) said. "Everyone who comes into contact with her gets a taste of it. When someone enters that world, it ripples outward. They're drawn to it. Like I was. It's the reason why we're all here."

"So the ants think the Queen is calling them."

"It's worse than that." Mort(e) turned to D'Arc. "You said they had wings."

"Yes . . ." A wave of horror washed across her face as she spoke.

"They think it's mating season," Mort(e) concluded.

"The Mudfoot would not bring the ants back," Grieve said. "They're bastards, but they're not *that* crazy."

"They don't know," D'Arc said. "The human who's with them—Augur, from the Toqwa pack. He tells them that the Mudfoot will rule again in peace. But he never said anything about the Colony."

"Suppose we tell them."

"It won't do any good. They don't trust you. Why would they?"

Grieve paced the room. His skull necklace clacked when he stopped at the model of Hosanna, where the sticks in the ground represented the troops protecting the city.

"Let's get to the point," he said. "Where do the Mudfoot attack?"

Gaunt shuffled over to the model train sitting at a station near the western frontier. He rolled it along on its tracks, through the dead towns, and straight into the heart of Hosanna. Returning the train to the city was part of the peace agreement. It would show that the Mudfoot spoke for all the wolves now.

"It's a Trojan horse," Nikaya said.

"It doesn't make any sense," Falkirk said. "Even if they made it into the city, what would they do?"

"Kill the Archon," Grieve said. "Seize the capitol."

"No," D'Arc said. "They don't need any of that. They're bringing our son. When the dogs see him, they'll rise up."

"Exactly," Nikaya said. "We have to stop them now, before they take the train line!"

Everyone went silent. One by one, the wolves looked to Grieve to respond.

"Oh, you poor thing," he said. "You're too late. They already captured the train line."

Nikaya glanced at Gaunt. Falkirk expected them to speak in Chiropteran. But the gaze they held said everything.

"It's not too late," Falkirk said. "We still have the *Vesuvius*. If we can get word to them, we can . . ."

He stopped talking when Gaunt plucked the model of the airship and tossed it into the blue part of the map. Right in the middle of the Atlantic. It lay there like a dead fish.

"*Vesuvius* is gone," Nikaya said.

"What do you mean it's gone?"

"Went out to the ocean. Never to return."

"How do you know that?"

Nikaya translated as the bat spoke in her ear. "The wolf packs have wanted to destroy the *Vesuvius* for years. Take that off the board, and it's a fair fight."

A few of the marauders nodded. It made sense to them. It was all part of a military calculation, a fresh movement of chess pieces. Falkirk nearly dropped the canister as he recalled his first officer, Ruiz, calling him a traitor with what may have been his last breath. There must have been other traitors onboard. And now the ship could be at the bottom of the sea for all Falkirk knew, while he stood here, so unworthy and scared and small.

D'Arc placed a gentle hand on his elbow. It stopped him from screaming. "Can we get word to Hosanna or not?" she said.

"What good would it do?" Grieve said. "The Mudfoot have already tricked us into attacking once. For all we know, they're using the train as bait."

"You lose one battle, and you quit!"

A collective gasp sucked the air out of the room. Enraged, Grieve reached over his shoulder to pull the scimitar from its sheath. D'Arc gripped the handle of her katana. No one moved. A smile stubbornly stretched across Grieve's face. He pulled his hand away from the sword and tiptoed to D'Arc, holding his hands out. She let go of her own weapon.

"Mort(e), you sure know how to pick 'em," Grieve said, still staring at her.

"My son is out there," D'Arc said.

"I know. I got lots of sons out there myself. Some of them I never even met."

D'Arc refused to crack a smile.

"You call it quitting," Grieve said. "There's no quitting. No victory, either. For us, there's only survival. We pick up what's left after each battle and we carry on. Like it was before the Change."

"You created this mess," D'Arc said. "The Mudfoot asked you for help, and you turned them away."

"Hosanna created the mess. Ask them how the occupation went. They thought they could choose what kind of blowback comes next."

"You did their dirty work. You turned on your own people."

"Of course I did."

D'Arc looked around, to see if anyone found this honesty shocking. She was alone.

"I am no human," Grieve said. "You do not have to read between the lines with me. I saw an opportunity, and I took it. Why do you think your government chose to work with me?"

Grieve surveyed the map, all the mountains and valleys of the known world. "The Mournful will go west in the morning." He turned to Nikaya, who no longer had the strength to sit straight. Instead, she lay on her back, ready to sleep.

"I thank you, matriarch," Grieve said. "You saved us."

Nikaya tried to swallow. Some spittle gathered at the corners of her lips.

As the Mournful filed out, the Earthblood began to argue among themselves, their voices echoing off the walls. Harrek tried to calm them, though Falkirk could tell that the old wolf would eventually choose to follow the Mournful. This was what they knew. And Hosanna hardly gave them a reason to risk their lives again.

With the canister in one hand, Falkirk peeled away from the crowd and walked over the *Vesuvius* model, sitting only a few feet from the island of Golgotha. He considered plucking it from this painted ocean and taking it with him. But he did not know where he was going. And besides, this ship no longer belonged to him.

# CHAPTER 18

## THE LODGE AT THE EDGE OF THE WORLD

PAIR OF YOUNG Mournful carried Nikaya across the campus, past the chapel and the parking garage and the remains of the stadium. D'Arc and Gaunt followed, the bat barely able to keep pace. It was midday. No shadows. Moss covered every structure, turning everything so green that it hurt to look at it.

"Water," Gaunt said in his high-pitched English. "Water! Water!"

"We heard you," one of the Mournful said. "We're almost there."

The water they hoped to find trickled out of a concrete drainage pipe. In the warmer months, after the snow melted, it would become a creek. For now, it produced a sad little stream in the grass. Gaunt had requested a river. The matriarch deserved to die beside one. The Three Goddesses would use it to carry her spirit away.

"This is all we have," the Mournful said. "Unless you want to walk another four miles."

The bat's face became a mask of teeth as he screeched every foul word that his language could produce. As the wolves set the beaver on the grass, Gaunt demanded that they lift her again, and take her to the river. The wolves began to lose their patience with him. The younger one barked at Gaunt when the screeching got too loud. D'Arc prepared to get between them if a fight broke out.

"Stop," Nikaya groaned. "It's okay."

The wolves left without a word. Gaunt continued to yell at them, screaming a new sound that barely registered in D'Arc's ears. The bat scrunched his nose as he tried to figure out how to say it in English. Finally, he shouted, "House!"

"House?" she asked.

"Beaver house!"

Nikaya started to cough again. As D'Arc knelt beside her and stroked her coarse fur, the bat waddled over to a tree and broke off one of its branches. He carried the branch in his mouth and dropped it beside her.

"More!" he shouted. "Beaver house!"

By then, the Mama wolves had arrived. Like good dogs, they sensed that someone among them had fallen ill, and gathered around for comfort. D'Arc had never seen a wolf do this. But she had no business acting surprised. She did the same thing when her own master took a sick day or broke up with a girlfriend and spent the weekend on the couch. All her people did this because that was how they stayed alive.

One of the Mamas, a very old wolf with white fur around her eyebrows, carried a bowl of broth. She knelt beside the beaver, lifted her head and tried to get her to drink. After a few sips, Nikaya turned her head away.

The entire time, Gaunt strutted around, repeating his demand for a beaver house.

"What are you talking about?" D'Arc said.

"He wants a lodge," the old wolf said. "Isn't that right?"

"Yes," Nikaya said.

The wolves gathered sticks from the nearby clutch of trees.

First, they layered them on the dirt near the stream. Then they gently lifted Nikaya and laid her on top. Even in her weakened state, she reached for the closest branch and began chewing on it. Working around her, the wolves propped the other sticks so that they leaned against one another, forming a cocoon around the beaver. The wolves were so patient they let Gaunt act as if he directed the entire operation, because they could sense that he needed this even more than Nikaya did. Their good will rubbed off on Nikaya. She weakly smiled at what must have been the saddest excuse for a lodge she had ever seen.

When Falkirk arrived, he asked them what they were doing.

"Beaver house," D'Arc said.

More of them gathered, including a few Earthblood marauders, painted from head to tail and armed with knives and clubs. It was probably everything they owned, all that they would carry with them into the west. Gaunt hummed a song and Nikaya matched the tune with her raspy voice. Soon the Mamas began their own music, a low-pitched growl that D'Arc could feel vibrating in her guts. She tried to join them, but her throat could not create the sound.

An Earthblood commander walked by and saw what the soldiers were doing. He chastised the younger wolves and ordered them to get on with preparing for the march. Then he turned to the Mamas. "And who said you could waste time with this beaver? She's a war criminal!"

"So are you," the oldest Mama said.

"We don't take orders from you," another Mama said as she placed a branch over the lodge.

The commander walked away without saying another word.

There was nothing left to do but sit and wait. Gaunt lay beside Nikaya with one wing wrapped over her chest. The wolves waited at the mouth of the lodge, continuing their song. They made space for D'Arc and Falkirk.

"I don't deserve this," Nikaya said. She started coughing again. The bat squeezed his wing around her, pleading with her to be quiet.

The wolves kept singing. They were not here to judge.

"I told myself for years that I regretted nothing," she said. "But the Three Goddesses . . . they humbled me."

A twig broke somewhere behind them. D'Arc turned to find Mort(e) approaching.

"Is my son still alive?" Nikaya said.

"He is," Mort(e) said.

"They're rebuilding the dam in Hosanna," Falkirk said. "Beaver-style."

Nikaya turned away from them so she could picture it.

"I never thanked all of you," she said. "For saving my people. I thank you now. They will be worthy of it. Even if I'm not."

She blinked a few times. Then she began a new song, whispering it. D'Arc leaned in to hear, but could not make out any of the words. The bat sang along in Chiropteran, while the wolves continued to moan in a lower pitch.

"Gotta get ahead of those wolves," Nikaya said. "Stay ahead of 'em." She drifted into her delirious song again.

Falkirk tapped D'Arc's arm. "She's right," he whispered. "We need to get moving." D'Arc waved him off. She wasn't there when they buried the Chief. They could stay a few more minutes.

It happened quickly. The beaver wheezed out each line of her song, softer each time. The animals around her, sensing the end approaching, lowered their voices to match the volume of the trickling stream. Nikaya got stuck on the last line: "You and I will be the only light." She repeated it again, each time throwing in names of her people. Castor. Tracer. Kerdigan. Nikki, little Nikki. People who needed to forgive Nikaya. People who would one day meet this bat she saved, a mortal enemy turned into a friend.

Finally, the beaver tilted her head upward. Her jaw relaxed, and her lips peeled away from her giant orange buck teeth. Her eyelids fell shut. The only sound remaining was the bubbling water.

D'Arc leaned against Falkirk's shoulder. He rested his snout on top of her head, between her ears.

(UNOFFICIAL) LOGBOOK OF THE SUS AL-RIHLA
FEBRUARY 18

WEATHER: OVERCAST. NO BREEZE, BUT DAMP.
PERSONAL HEALTH: TOO TIRED.

WOLVES ARE LEAVING. THE EARTHBLOOD HAVE AGREED TO
TAKE GAUNT TO A NEARBY BAT CAVE ON THEIR WAY WEST. WE
ARE AMONG THE LAST ONES LEFT.

1432 NIKAYA DIES.

"GOTTA GET AHEAD OF THOSE WOLVES," SHE TELLS ME.

AT LONG LAST, after weeks of racing against time, D'Arc's fatigue gripped her tightly and squeezed out any energy she had left. She had barely slept, had eaten only scraps. The freshest water she drank came from melted snow in her mouth. After giving birth, her piss felt different when it exited her body, sometimes making her wince as it forced its way out. The healing wound on her side still itched as it sealed into a pink lump. Blisters rose on the fingers she was never meant to have, threatening to burst open the next time she held her sword. Everything was struggle and regret, leading to more of the same.

While D'Arc leaned on Falkirk, her head rising and falling with each of his deep breaths, Gaunt finally let go of Nikaya and crawled from the makeshift lodge. The bat stretched out his good wing, then the injured one. He noticed her watching and curled his arms closer to his body. D'Arc imagined what it was like to have wings so she could fly to her pup, then far away from here, to where it was warm again.

She sniffed the air and realized that Mort(e) was gone.

"I wanna see that little canister," she said.

Falkirk pulled away from her.

"What?" she said.

"You know what. That thing's dangerous."

"I just want to see it." She wanted more than that. She wanted to hold it in her hands to see if she had the guts to try it. The future had to be better than this.

Falkirk's canvas satchel sat on the grass beside Gaunt. D'Arc told the bat to open it and bring the canister to her. "No, don't do that," Falkirk said. But it was too late. The bat had already begun rummaging through the bag.

"We might be better off destroying it," Falkirk said. "So it doesn't—"

Gaunt let out a tortured screeching sound. He emptied the satchel onto the ground. The canister fell out, along with a tiny knife and a plastic water bottle. He tossed the bag away and continued cursing in Chiropteran.

"What's wrong?" Falkirk said.

Gaunt handed him the canister. Falkirk spun it around in his hands. "That's not it," he said.

"What?" By the time that word tumbled from her mouth, D'Arc noticed that the canister was merely a pipe with a metal cap. The same size and weight, fashioned to take the rahvek's place long enough for the thief to get away.

Falkirk stood. "The Mournful," he said. "Those guards who built the lodge. They made the switch."

D'Arc pulled her sword free from its scabbard. Everything

came into focus. Her nose tracked the scent of the wolf pack on the wind. She broke into a run.

"Wait!" Falkirk shouted.

Somewhere behind him, Gaunt screamed in his native language.

Falkirk caught her by the arm. She stopped and raised her sword over her shoulder. Falkirk did not flinch. "You saw what it did to Mort(e)," he said.

"Are telling me that there's a price to pay if I use that canister?" she asked. "We're way past that. All of us."

She knocked his hand away. It fell to his hip. His nostrils dilated as he picked up the scent of the Mournful. He nodded in that direction.

"Fine," he said. "They went that way."

AS THE PAIR sprinted through the campus, the Mamas shouted to them from their butcher tables. "There's plenty of food! Take for your journey! Take some, puppies!" Blood stained the front of their coats. Hungry, wounded wolves waited patiently in line for their share. One of them barked at the two runners, and soon the rest of them followed suit. D'Arc figured that it was a warning. These wolves were thick as thieves. The Mamas wanted the Mournful to know that the two interlopers approached.

Beyond the library and the athletic fields, a row of cottages marked the border of the school property. From there, the two dogs hacked their way through the woods, hoping to catch the Mournful on the highway. In their haste, the wolves had grown careless, leaving behind scat and urine, broken twigs, and clods of fur.

The sun dipped over the hills. In the failing light, dozens of eyes turned to them from the road, blinking like fireflies in summertime. The barking began and quickly devolved into growling and grumbling, a warning to stay away. By the time D'Arc and Falkirk emerged onto the road, the wolves had swarmed around them, pawing at the earth with their front claws. Falkirk kept his rifle pointed in the air. D'Arc held her sword close to her body, the blade shimmering by her ear.

Maybe it would all end here, with crazed dogs on both sides, shedding this dream of walking like humans. Until then, she still had words to speak.

"Is your leader too much of a coward to face us?"

The growling lowered, though only slightly.

"What, no one can answer? You need permission?"

Falkirk chuckled. "Good one."

She pointed the tip of the blade at a random wolf, one with more war paint than actual scars, a pretty boy who probably hadn't seen a real battle. "How about you. Talk to me! Where's Grieve?"

The circle constricted as more wolves snuck behind them, cutting off their escape.

"Grieve!" D'Arc shouted. "You owe us! I will tell everyone what the Tekni told me!"

Amid the barking, a bewildered wolf whispered the name Tekni. D'Arc heard the word pass through the crowd, like a little treasure that everyone wanted to touch.

"Make up your minds already!" Falkirk said.

The barking died out. The wolves lowered their snouts to the ground, revealing an enormous form approaching on two feet. Despite running away in shame, Grieve wore a fresh coat of paint on his fur, and his necklace rattled with a brand-new deer skull placed between the human ones. His harem of she-wolves made a show of pawing at him, begging him to stop. They must have rehearsed it as a way to curry favor. As Grieve entered the clearing, he stroked the fur of the nearest marauder, like a human petting his dog. He carried with him the arrogance that created this world, the vanity that could never be destroyed, only handed from one tyrant to another.

"I see why Mort(e) likes you," Grieve said to D'Arc. "And why he doesn't like *you*."

Falkirk nodded. He took it as a compliment.

"Give it back," D'Arc said.

"I'll have you know that Mort(e) came to us for help already. I took the rahvek with his blessing."

"I don't care about his blessing."

Grieve stroked his chin. "So this is your plan," he said. "To charge right at us and demand your little trinket."

D'Arc placed her sword in its scabbard and lifted her hands. "Everyone, listen to me, please," she said. "That canister is the only way we can defeat the Mudfoot. And your leader here wants to keep it for himself."

"I'm keeping it for us."

"And who's going to use it?" Falkirk said. "You saw what happened to Mort(e)."

"Oh, that's it, isn't it?" D'Arc said. "You'll have one of your subjects take it."

She let this linger. A few of the wolves looked at one another.

"The humans did the same thing with their prophet," D'Arc said. "He didn't even know his own name in the end."

Grieve loomed over her now. "I told the Tekni that I would spare you. And I have. But I don't have to do it again. Now leave."

D'Arc laughed. "You have learned nothing. Those horses were willing to die to free themselves from your rule. What about the people who have suffered far more?"

She hovered her hand over the sword to remind him that she was still dangerous.

"We're the only ones left doing the right thing," she said, loud enough for all of them to hear. "You can help us, and maybe get your territory back. Or you can run away."

"Nice speech," Grieve said.

"I got another one," D'Arc whispered. "It's about how you betrayed your brother. Wanna hear it?"

Grieve's ears drooped. He instantly became like a pet dog waiting for his master to hit him with a newspaper.

"I wanna hear her plan!" someone shouted. A lone wolf stood over the others, who remained cowering on the ground. He was shorter and fatter than most, with a crooked face and a stubby tail. An omega—or close to it.

"Sit your ass down, Loder," Grieve said.

"These people risked their lives to come here. And they want to fight!"

A murmur made its way through the crowd. Grieve acted as though he expected this distraction. "You dogs from Hosanna will never understand," he said. "We are a pack. We would die for one another."

A few of the wolves nodded in agreement.

Grieve flicked D'Arc on the shoulder. "Everyone else is outside the pack. A potential enemy."

"You didn't answer my question," D'Arc said softly. "Who can get rid of you quickly and benefit the most from it?"

Everyone turned to the harem. The four she-wolves stood side by side, each doing their best to appear innocent and sweet.

"And what happens to your sons when you're gone?" Falkirk added.

"That's enough," Grieve said. "Your plan—get on with it."

"We have to get ahead of them," D'Arc said. "If we get to the train and find out what they're up to, we can stop them. We just need to see further into the future."

"And what if you see them winning?"

"Then nothing changes. They take Hosanna, and you keep going west."

Grieve jammed his hand into a pouch that hung from his belt. He pulled out the canister, which looked as thin as a stick in his fingers. "I never decided if I really wanted to see the future," he said. "Pack leaders rarely die in their sleep."

"Give it to her!" Loder shouted. A few others stood with him now. In a few minutes, there would be more. D'Arc could feel it.

Grieve stretched out his hand and let D'Arc grip the canister. But he would not let go—not yet. "You say this could kill you, and yet you want to use it."

"If you're ready to die, you can keep it," she replied.

Grieve let go. D'Arc pulled the canister to her chest. It felt oddly warm.

"Thank you," she said.

"You still *refuse* to understand," he said. "If this goes right, then I'll take the credit. I can't see the future, but I can take a guess."

D'Arc placed her hand on his arm, perhaps the only time someone had touched him willingly in a long time. "I'm thanking you anyway."

Grieve looked at Falkirk as if to ask what was wrong with these females. The husky responded with an icy stare.

"The world is changing," D'Arc said. "Even you can be a beacon of light for your people."

Grieve tried to conceal his laughter. "Go ahead, drink the potion," he said, turning his back on her. "You're already crazy."

As he walked away, Grieve called one of his lieutenants over. "Show them the way," he said. "Then get them out of here." He then joined his harem. The females comforted him by rubbing their hands on his shoulders and ears.

"Did you say 'beacon of light'?" Falkirk whispered.

"You heard me," D'Arc said.

# CHAPTER 19

## THE PASSENGER

T WAS TOO late. The ice caps had melted and the oceans flooded the rivers and bays. All the land was submerged, and the fresh water was tainted with salt. This was the real world now, nothing but endless sea, flat and blue and shiny, stretching to the impossible curve of the horizon. The world Mort(e) had left behind was the dream. The dry land, where the mammals squabbled over bits of dirt, had blinded him for too long. A tempting illusion. Only here, in the sea, was he truly awake.

But unlike before, he could now travel between the two worlds. He could control it. Not even a god could do this. Not even the Queen. Something had finally broken, some membrane had finally been pierced. He may have been finished with the dream, but the dream was not finished with him. He needed to go back. One last thing to do before he answered the call of the ocean and sank beneath the surface forever.

All it took was a tilt of his head and a deep gulp of water. With that, he emerged again, bursting through the skin of the sea. Above, the purple sky glowed with stars, most of them so small they coalesced into a white cloud. Mort(e) found himself in the rowboat again, his hands gripping the oars, with black pine trees swaying on either side.

He remembered boarding the boat that afternoon. But that simple word, *remember*, no longer meant anything to him. Not when he could move in and out of time, in and out of the past. He figured that a late-stage EMSAH patient must have experienced this same sense of freedom at the very end, as the virus blossomed and performed its final act. Culdesac and Tiberius had lied to him all those years ago. They said EMSAH was a curse, a plague. Mort(e) had learned to fear it as he did all the unknown things from his days as a pet. *If you see something, say something*, they always said. Oh, but they couldn't have known what it felt like. The Queen bestowed this gift to the brain as it fizzled out. She kept this promise to her chosen ones, whether they spoke to her through the translator or drank potion from a vial or became infected with what the animals called a disease. For all their loyalty to her, the Queen's own daughters proved unworthy. Only the uplifted animals would see the world as she saw it.

The boat scraped against a protruding rock. Mort(e) steered away from the bank and into the center of the river. This awkward little vessel forced him to sit backward, and after miles of rowing, his neck had grown sore from turning toward the bow. He raised the oars and listened to the water dripping from them. In this position, the boat resembled an Alpha with wings. After some time, he turned again and saw the bridge spanning the river, maybe thirty feet high. Against the indigo sky, the bridge formed a perfectly straight line, a black monolith with enormous arches cut into the stone.

Mort(e) pulled in the oars and let the current carry the boat. At the base of one of the arches, the flowing water bubbled and gurgled, echoing off the stone. The humans had repurposed this structure to support a train. A century earlier, their horse slaves dragged carts from one side to another. But the endless wind and rain over the decades had weakened the bridge. The train would have to grind nearly to a stop and creep across, engines cut. Anything faster could rattle another piece of mortar loose or dislodge another bolt or screw. One of these days, the structure would collapse on its own, another human-made marvel surrendering to nature. Until then, the wolves needed it. And here, a sneaky cat could climb aboard under cover of darkness.

As the boat passed under the bridge, Mort(e) grabbed onto the ancient bricks at the base of the arch. He kicked the boat away and watched it continue on its journey downstream. Above him, the wooden beams supporting the tracks formed a grid against the sky. He loosened the straps on his backpack to give his arms a more room to move. After digging his toe into a foothold, he began to climb. The rushing water drowned out the sound of his nails scratching the mortar. At the top, he gripped the edge of one of the beams and pulled himself over.

While lying in between the steel tracks, he rolled onto his side and sniffed the wood. He ran his palm along it until a splinter pricked him. The train had not passed here yet. He would have felt it.

He searched for a loose board. After all these years, some of them must have shaken free of their rusted bolts. Near the middle of the bridge, one of the boards wobbled under his weight. The end of it had rotted, which allowed him to move the wood at an angle, wide enough for him to slip through. Luckily, this gap appeared right above one of the stone arches of the bridge. He shimmied through the opening and found a perch on the edge of the arch, where his feet could dangle over the water. When he sat straight, his head poked through the gap in the boards. He placed his ear on the steel beam and listened. No sign of a train yet. It sounded like a seashell, only with a metallic hum.

His time in the war prepared him for long waits in uncomfortable spaces. Only now, instead of passing the time with memories or mind games, he slipped out of the dream world again. The waters rose around him. The bridge sank. The clicking vibration traveled through his brain, along his spine, and into his heart. The blood pumped in rhythm with the sound. He would wait here until the dream called him back. Hopefully for the last time.

WITH THE SURFACE now miles above him, a current carried Mort(e) across the sunken forest, where the trees turned to seaweed and the flocks of birds became schools of fish. Ever since the war, the animals loved to see the grass overtaking the towns that had never belonged there in the first place. Every building that collapsed, every highway that disappeared provided another victory in a conflict that would never end. Mort(e) got to see the land not as it was meant to be, but as it deserved to be once every glacier melted and every dam broke, all the evil drowned and flushed away.

Mort(e) descended into a valley where the kelp hung from the surface in towering strands, like a forest suspended from the heavens. On the ocean floor stood a boxy structure, completely alien amid the weeds. The structure consisted of a house connected to a garage, with fencing that enclosed everything in a neat rectangle. Though he had never seen it from above, Mort(e) knew this to be the ranch where he had lived—where he dreamed another life.

The Sarcops chorus clicked in his ear. *See again*, they said. *See no more. See again, see no more.*

They did not have a word for goodbye.

Mort(e) moved through the open gate of the fence, heading for the house. For the first time, he took notice of his true form, with his fur shed, and his scales hardened into knobs. Tentacles sprouted from his back and propelled him through the water with a twirling motion. Despite his fish body, he kept his whiskers. The Sarcops were not without mercy, though sometimes it came across as a sense of humor.

A lamp switched on inside the house, sending a shaft of light into the murky water. Mort(e) swam closer. Impossibly, the inside of the house remained perfectly dry. A protected air pocket. The almond-colored felt couch, the wooden bookshelf lined with paperbacks, the cracked mirror, all of it remained as he'd left it when he journeyed to Hosanna a year earlier. Something moved inside the house, casting a shadow across the wall. When Mort(e) reached the window, he saw Sheba hunched over the fire, poking it with a metal rod. Bright orange embers escaped from the flames and floated into the chimney. She seemed younger than he remembered. This was the Sheba from the ranch, before Lodge City and Hosanna and all the rest took her away. Satisfied with the size of the fire, Sheba stood and set the metal rod against the wall. Like a good dog, she sensed an intruder at the window.

*See again, see no more.*

Mort(e) rushed to the door. A tentacle, acting on its own, slithered out from his body and twisted the knob. Sheba pounded on the glass. She barked at him, acting as if she did not want him to enter. He responded in the Sarcops' language. *You do not understand*, he clicked. *It will be all right. I am here.*

The knob turned, and a great force pulled the water into the room. The air pocket vented through the entrance and the chimney. The last of it blew out the window, ascending to the surface in a giant silvery bubble. Mort(e) burst into the house as the water rose to the ceiling. The dog was gone. The lighter objects tumbled out. A coffee mug collided with a candlestick. The blackened firewood spun outward from the hearth. The roof collapsed. With the cracked beams falling around him, Mort(e) pulled himself free and floated high above the wreckage. A cloud of mud spread over what remained of the house, burying it so that no sign of the ranch remained.

The song of the Sarcops went quiet in his head. They offered him a brief respite while he watched the ocean reclaiming his former life. It came for everything eventually.

A new sound began, a high-pitched squeal of metal scraping metal. It came from the surface. Mort(e) turned away and swam upward. As he got higher, the pressure dropped, and the light grew brighter. The sun became a perfect white disk, rippling in the waves.

Mort(e) broke the surface to find himself leaning against the rail, still seated in his perch on the bridge. The sun approached slowly through the trees, creating fingerlike shadows that stretched across the tracks. Mort(e) needed to blink a few times to realize that the sun was in fact the front headlight of the train engine. He took note of the shifted stars and the brightening skyline to the east. A few hours had passed.

The train, completely shrouded in darkness, came to a dead stop. The brakes squealed. Mort(e) nearly jumped from his hiding place. The thing he wanted, the treasure he'd chased from Hosanna, had finally arrived.

There were people on top of the engine. They slid off the sides and landed on the edge of the tracks. A moment later, they appeared, three wolves in all. Grieve warned him this might happen. The wolves would act as scouts, checking the bridge for any defects. Anyone who wanted to operate this behemoth would need to make sure the bridge would support its weight.

Two of the wolves carried sledgehammers on their shoulders. The third one held a crowbar. Once they made it past the first arch of the bridge, they tapped the rails and beams to listen for any weaknesses in the foundation, any crumbling mortar or hollow wood. While the wolves with hammers made their noises, the one with the crowbar used the sharp tip to scrape the side of the bridge that faced upstream. Only a few granules crumbled away and fell into the river. This arch would hold. The wolf waved his comrades on.

Mort(e) eased his way onto the edge of the arch and lowered himself over the side, holding on with his fingertips and his rear claws. He imagined himself as a six-pound housecat again, clinging to a curtain or the armrest of a chair, light as a feather, hoping his master would not see him and chase him away. But then, unable to resist, he turned and gazed into the churning water below. If he simply let go of this stone—let go of this dream—he could return to where he belonged. He told himself that he would go there soon enough. The water would wait.

The wooden boards squeaked as the wolves walked above him. The vibrations from their hammers traveled through the stone and into his wrists. Mort(e) held his breath to keep the vapor from escaping his lungs. An ugly snout poked into the gap in the boards. The nostrils sniffed something. A breeze came along at the right moment to throw off the scent. The wolf continued with his inspection, with the others following behind.

Sometime later, after Mort(e)'s fingertips had gone numb, the engine switched on again. A new tremor shook the bridge as the train began to roll across. By leaning to the side a bit, he could see the beastly machine pushing its way out of the forest. As the train crept along, the passenger cars came into view. A dull yellow light glowed through the windows. Behind that, a flatbed emerged from the trees with a massive garbage truck loaded on top. Mort(e) remembered it well: the one that got away.

The front grill of the truck, with its headlights and pointed snout, resembled a large animal with a human face. A metal sphinx mocking him with its riddles. Whatever lurked inside had the ability to warp the space around the vehicle, like hot air rising from asphalt. The wolves *must* have seen it. A person could step into that vortex and be carried off to their destiny—or to an infinite number of destinies in an infinite number of futures. All time converged here, in this man-made contraption originally designed to haul the humans' garbage. It called to

Mort(e) now. All the answers resided within. All the questions tormenting him would at last grow still.

The train gathered speed. Mort(e) stuck his head through the gap in the rails. The breeze tousled his fur. But as the flatbed car approached, he could hear only the beautiful song of the Sarcops, a purring that spoke in every language. The car passed above him. He reached toward it, and his hand tingled as it entered the warped space around the vehicle. He caught hold of a metal box—most likely the braking mechanism. He pulled himself up and hung from the bottom of the car, finding enough room to keep from scraping along the boards. When it was safe, he would climb onto the flatbed. But for now, he needed to take in the strange aura of this object. His past as a housecat and his future as some hybrid creature collided in this tiny pocket. He had no regrets, no fear for what would come. While hanging on to this instrument of death on a suicide mission, Mort(e) had finally experienced the most peaceful moment of his life.

# CHAPTER 20

## THIS IS NOW

ALKIRK AND D'ARC walked on opposite sides of the motor-cycle, each of them gripping a handlebar. A lantern dangled from the brake lever, which made their shadows stretch and shrink and spin all around them. Taking the bike through the forest was the quickest way, the wolves said. Get the bike through the trees and to the highway, then drive like hell, and they had a chance of intercepting the train at an abandoned town nearby. If they hurried, they might even get to it before Mort(e) did. But with each tree root and divot that slowed their pace, with each mud patch that sank the wheels to the hub, Falkirk knew they were losing time.

Another puddle splattered mud on the chrome fender. Etched into the metal was the name LODER. To help the two dogs, Grieve had confiscated the bike for them. A Harley Softail Springer, with a converted Colonial engine that ran on plant matter. The rat mechanics at the academy used to salvage motorcycles like this. They could not ride the heavier bikes themselves, so they set them aside for Falkirk. When it came time for a test run, the rats would form a line along the riverfront highway, first thing in the morning. As he streaked past them, they would yell, "Skydog likes to fly!"

The path ahead at last sloped downward, allowing them to

roll the bike more easily. By this point, the muscles in his arms had constricted into tightly coiled ropes. He could not stop panting, and soon his tongue dried out in the frigid air.

"When we find our son," he said, "what should we name him?"

She did not answer.

"You said you never gave him a name," he added.

"That's right," she said. "I was busy. But really . . ."

He gave her a chance to think about it.

"Tristan and Nautica died right after I named them," she said. "They never even learned their names. I don't think I ever said them out loud."

"You think that if you name him, it could—"

"Yes," she said.

"I'm sorry to ask this," he said, "but did you name . . . your other children?"

"The humans would say no. But I remember how the pups smelled. Each of them has a different scent to me. Those are the names. The human language doesn't have words for it."

"I can still smell Amelia and Yeager," Falkirk said. "They would wrestle in the dirt outside of our house. That's what I remember."

Falkirk smelled it in his dreams. Sometimes he would be in the woods, calling their names, the scent growing stronger. He decided not to say any of that out loud.

"This might not be the best time to ask," he said, "but would you ever want to live in a regular house again? After this?"

To avoid the question, D'Arc used her shoulder to nudge the rear tire over a rock.

"I cried when I first realized I was pregnant again," she said. "I recorded it in my logbook. One day, my bunk started to feel really tight. The mattress felt like a brick. I had this crazy urge to steal pillows from everyone else's bunk. I grabbed a bunch of towels from the shower and lined the inside with it. My bunkmate Verasco asked me what I was doing, and I snapped at her. I said, 'Get away from me!' I've never yelled at anybody like that. She was terrified. And so was I."

"My mate did the same thing," Falkirk said. "She wanted to bring a bunch of leaves and sticks into the house."

"The ship's doctor called it nesting," D'Arc said.

"Right," Falkirk said. "I told my mate, 'You're a dog, not a bird.' She didn't think it was funny."

With a grunt, D'Arc rolled the tire over the rock. It immediately struck another one, starting the process over again.

"After I came clean and told the captain, I was almost . . . euphoric," she said. "I imagined the baby being born in the Azores, or on the coast of Africa, or some other place. And just when I started to feel good about it, *boom*. I was in a lifeboat in the middle of nowhere."

She went quiet for a few seconds. Falkirk knew better than to ask her for more details.

"So I guess I'm not ready to talk about a house," she said. "Not yet."

At some point, she would drink the rahvek. Maybe she would see the house where they would live. Or maybe she would see nothing but inky blankness, a void where a future could have been.

"We're almost to the highway," she said.

After another hundred paces or so, he spotted the concrete barrier, covered in moss and ivy and stained from years of neglect. On the other side, the asphalt had burst open, surrendering to tall stalks of grass. In another few years, there would be little left. But it was flat enough for a Harley.

"There's a log on the ground," D'Arc said.

Falkirk did not see the log until he nearly tripped over it. D'Arc suggested using it as a ramp to get the bike over the barrier. While wondering if his eyesight had begun to fail, he propped the hunk of wood onto the concrete, then climbed over to the other side. Instead of helping, D'Arc remained in place, her snout raised.

"What is it?" Falkirk asked.

"Nothing," she said. "Nothing."

Together, they pushed the motorcycle up the log and lowered it onto the highway. When D'Arc hopped over the wall, the canister, fastened by a loop to her backpack, jiggled free and hit the asphalt. Falkirk picked it up.

D'Arc held out her hand.

Instead of giving it to her, he pulled the canister close to his chest and stepped away. "We haven't agreed on who's going to drink this stuff."

"*I'm* drinking it," she said.

"He's my son too," he said. "Am I going to tell him that you sacrificed yourself?"

"You might have to. None of this is easy."

"No," he said. "I wasn't there for my family. When the Colony took them. The family that raised me told me it would happen."

Somewhere far away, the wind carried his mother's voice. *The white takes you*, she said.

"You're not the only one with regrets," D'Arc said.

She was right. But so was he. He turned away quickly, unscrewed the cap, and brought the canister to his mouth. The rank, fishy smell invaded his nostrils like a swarm of insects. He coughed. *Do it*, he thought. *Hold your breath and do it.*

Before he could drink anything, something flashed in his eye. He held the canister like a telescope, peered inside, and saw the bottom, a shiny metal disk with a tiny drop of the rahvek gathered at the base.

"I'm not taking any chances," D'Arc said. "I drank it before we left."

"You thought I was going to steal it."

"And now I know you were."

Falkirk lowered the canister until it clinked on the handlebar. "You took *all* of it?"

"Start the engine," she said, gazing past him like a blind person. "We don't have much time."

WITH THE SUN long gone, the entire world collapsed into a single ball of light emanating from the front of the motorcycle. The broken road streamed toward Falkirk. The encroaching forest had reclaimed large sections, leaving a winding path ahead. He swerved around the bumps and potholes as best as he could. He took his chances with the stalks of grass, which let out a little *thwips* as he mowed them down.

A crooked, faded road sign flashed and then vanished. He caught the number: exit 96. Two more to go—assuming Grieve gave them the right directions.

The front tire hit a stick at full speed, sending a jolt through Falkirk's body. He gripped the handlebars and steadied the bike. D'Arc barely moved. Her arms stayed tightly wrapped around his waist, as they had been for nearly an hour now. Falkirk let go of the handle and tapped her hand.

"Hang in there," he said.

She lifted her snout from his shoulder. "Falkirk?"

"I'm right here!"

She whined in his ear like a puppy. "I can't . . ."

"Stay with me," he said. It sounded stupid, but he needed to shout something.

He felt her heart thumping on his spine. He relaxed his wrist, easing the throttle. The bike slowed.

"No," she said into the wind. "No, keep going."

He turned the handlebar again. The engine roared and the front tire lifted for a brief moment.

"Are you in pain?" he asked.

A pause. "Not yet."

"What do you see?"

She squeezed him tighter. "This is now," she said. She squeezed a handful of his fur. "This."

"Right," he said. "This is now." With his left hand, he gripped her arm. She responded by biting his neck. He suddenly remembered doing this exact thing to her during their brief time together, a memory that still surfaced at the most inappropriate moments. She clamped harder, and he gritted his teeth through the pain. "You're right here with me, D'Arc! This is now!"

She let go of his neck. Her head slumped against his shoulder blade. Falkirk felt a trickle of blood weaving through his fur. It could have been worse.

He didn't know if he should keep her awake or let her rest. Either option seemed too dangerous.

In her fever dream, D'Arc whispered something that died out under the growl of the engine.

"What?" Falkirk said.

"Wolf," she said. "Wolf."

Two pairs of glowing dots floated above the side of the road. Two wolves, their pupils capturing the headlight's glare. As the bike sped past them, the dots streaked across Falkirk's peripheral vision like tracer bullets.

"Are there more?" he asked. "Do you see more ahead?"

"Not yet."

A new sign flashed. Exit 98. Another abandoned stretch of road leading to some lost human settlement. Grieve told them they would have their best chance of boarding the train here—if such a feat were even possible. "What exactly do you expect to do if you get on the train?" he had asked them as he handed over Loder's motorcycle. D'Arc insisted that the wolves would not expect such a move. Falkirk could only hope that the rahvek made her say that, rather than some crushing desperation.

He turned onto the ramp. The road elevated, lifting him high enough to see the entire town. On the horizon, the first hints of sunlight burned a hole in the clouds above the collapsed roof of a church. The buildings and houses that remained were covered in moss and weeds, and a full-sized tree had pushed through the main street. On top of the train station, a clock tower was frozen at 12:30. And on the very edge of the town, the train lumbered through, its metal skin slicing like a knife through the green and brown surroundings. It was headed for the station, with no signs of slowing.

"No," Falkirk said.

They had hoped to camp here and rest, maybe find a hidden spot in the station where they could board the train undetected. But they were too late. The best they could do was follow and hope that the engine could not reach its top speed.

As he watched the train, Falkirk noticed pair of headlights blinking in the rearview mirror. A crew of marauders was tracking them.

Falkirk cranked the throttle, and the motorcycle jolted forward. The exit ramp dumped them onto a four-lane road where streetlights still hung over the intersections. The road ran parallel with the tracks, a block away. At each corner, he glanced to his right and saw the train rolling through the town. In the dull sunrise, a shard of light glowed on the top of the passenger cars like an arrow on fire.

D'Arc squeezed him so tight that he could hardly breathe. "We have to get on that train."

"*On* it? No, it's too late for that."

Her claws dug into his skin.

"We'll follow it," he said. "We'll figure something out on the way."

"No!" she said, her voice raspy. "We have to get on!"

She barked, the way any dog would when an intruder invades their home. This wasn't D'Arc speaking. It wasn't even Sheba. This was some primal language, a grunting that signaled something worse than danger.

"What is it?" Falkirk said. "What do you see?"

"Get us on that train," she said, and then barked again. "I don't care how. Just get us there. It's the only way."

Falkirk took the next right and sped toward the train tracks. A row of houses and driveways streamed past him while dead powerlines zipped overhead. At the end of the road, the last car on the train lazily rolled through the intersection, leaving a void in its place.

D'Arc gasped for air, as if gravity had collapsed on top of her.

"Talk to me," Falkirk said. "What's going on?"

"There's too many of them . . ."

"Too many wolves?" He knew that already.

She searched for the word while her teeth grinded. "Too many futures. There are all these paths to take. They all point outward from here. I see all of them."

"Focus on the train, then," Falkirk said. "Focus on where it's going."

Falkirk swerved left onto an unpaved service road that led out of the station, running alongside the tracks. A rusted chain-link fence separated the road from the rails. As the train gathered speed, Falkirk weaved around a fallen telephone pole and a dead tree, both painted green with moss. He caught up with the last car on the train, a metal passenger coach with oblong windows. Something moved inside. They must have heard him. And now they could see him.

D'Arc had been quiet for a few seconds. He turned to see her reaching for the train, her hand coming dangerously close to the fence. Falkirk jerked the bike to the left to keep her from slicing her fingers off.

"What are you doing?" he said.

"Falkirk," she said, on the verge of tears. "Hurry."

In another half mile, the train would pass under a bridge.

"Look out!" D'Arc screamed.

A muzzle flashed from the train car, and machine gun fire clattered in his ear. Bullets whizzed overhead. He eased the throttle, and the train began to pull away.

"No!" D'Arc said. She reached for the handlebar and tried to accelerate. Falkirk batted her hand away.

"We have to find another way," he said.

"There is no other way," she said. "Look."

She nodded behind them, where a truck pulled onto the road, shooting gravel as its tires spun. A wolf stood in the rear of the pickup, aiming a rifle. He slapped the top of the cab to urge the driver to go faster.

"Tell me what you see," Falkirk said. "Is it our son?"

"It's everyone," she said. "If we don't stop this train, they all die."

The road terminated at a hill covered in dead grass, which formed the base of the bridge. Falkirk scanned the fence, hoping to find a gap in the chain links. If he tried to turn to the left, he would go straight into another stretch of forest, where he would have to abandon the motorcycle and most likely get caught by the marauders in the truck, if not some other hunting party.

More of them waited on the other side of that hill. Not just wolves, but lost dogs like him, like his brother. It might be a husky like Wendigo who finally ended this journey for him, sending him into the white forever.

Falkirk twisted the handle forward.

"Yes," D'Arc said. "Keep going. This is how we get on the train. I can see it."

"See what?"

The engine drowned out the sound of gunfire from the train.

A few bullets sparked against the fence, while others splashed in the dirt. Falkirk overtook the train and its rear gunner. More wolves moved about inside the car, searching for a spot where they could take aim. One of them tried to kick out the window, but managed to make only a few cracks.

The road ended, and the tires slipped a little in the dead grass. But the bike was going too fast now. It was simple physics. Falkirk held on tightly as the bike ascended, and the train fell away. Angling the handlebars, he pulled back as the bike launched over the bridge. Weightless, they cleared the two-lane road and hung for a frozen, breathless moment above the train.

Gravity caught them. The bike dropped, the rear tire connecting with the metal first. Falkirk turned the handlebar to the left to keep from gliding off the top, but this forced the motorcycle to tip over. As he tried to brace himself with his leg, he let go, and the motorcycle slid away from him, tires spinning madly, the engine smoking. With D'Arc still holding on to him, he slammed his palm onto the metal and dug in with his feet. They came to a stop right at the edge. The bike tumbled over the side, hit the ground and flipped over in the dirt, its front wheel bent from the impact.

Falkirk breathed. He patted his ribs and his leg. Nothing broken, though everything would be sore in the morning, if he survived that long. An enormous dent in the roof showed the path the bike had taken. D'Arc lay beside him, huddled against his fur, her eyes sealed shut.

The marauders would arrive any second. Falkirk reached for the gun in his holster.

"How many futures are there now?" he said.

Without pause, without any emotion, she answered him: "Two."

# CHAPTER 21

## BACK AND FORTH

'ARC SAW EVERYTHING. All that there was, and all that there could be.

LIKE A BIRD flying over Hosanna, she watches as the train enters the city. The metal serpent slithers into a concrete maze, its venomous head painted bright orange. The people gather in the streets, on rooftops, the crowds surging to see the wolf queen and her child. Flags wave, showing a burgundy pawprint against a white background. The dogs separate into packs, howling in praise of their savior as she at last arrives on a chariot stolen from their enemy. For their part, the humans take their places along the barricades and wait, hardly moving, barely acknowledging one another. By returning the train, the Mudfoot succeed where the other packs have failed. They honor the terms of the ceasefire. And now the humans will listen.

D'Arc walks among them, trying to peer over their heads. A human child runs toward her, bumps into her hip. He holds a doll made of rags, a stuffed wolf that an older relative must have made for him. He wants to talk to her, but his friends chase him away. A woman tells them to slow down before they trip and fall.

D'Arc blinks and finds herself at the checkpoint, a rifle in hand. The weight of it startles her. She nearly drops it. The human guard beside her notices but says nothing. A barricade of barbed wire and logs blocks the path of the train. Behind it, a row of concrete cylinders adds another layer. Pillboxes and sniper nests, manned only with handpicked human soldiers, surround the train as it arrives. Mercy the Merciful has come in peace, but Hosanna has prepared for war.

The train slows. The brakes squeal, a sound that the citizens of Hosanna can hardly remember. This is, after all, another reclaimed relic, a tool from a more civilized time that will help the humans be human again.

Something moves inside the cabin of the front car. A door slides open and a man emerges, wearing fresh deerskin, a grotesque tattoo shading his face. He climbs the ladder and rises to the top of the engine so everyone can see him, even the crowds watching far behind the barricade. Despite their preparation for this moment, despite their training, the guards react in their own quiet ways— shifting their stances, tightening their aim, sneaking a glance at their comrades. This man-wolf represents everything that has gone wrong with their peaceful experiment. He is the claw of the great ant Queen, plunging into the city's chest and ripping away its heart.

The female wolf emerges beside him, skinnier than expected, smaller. But strong, with defiant eyes, pointed ears. She holds a furry bundle at her chest. And as she climbs the ladder to stand beside the man-wolf, she raises her child, the future leader who was never meant to live. The pup unfolds and flops open, his tail dropping to the wolf's knees. A grin opens from ear to ear, spiked with white fangs. D'Arc waits to hear his thoughts in her head. But they do not come. As she sinks into the emptiness of this moment, a lone howl begins somewhere in the crowd. Another voice joins, then another. Soon, almost every dog joins the song. Their pack has arrived.

A single bullet could end this. Another path for the future to take. But the humans do not fire, and the path closes. Of all the wolf packs, the Mudfoot have kept their promises and delivered on their threats. The dogs of Hosanna have seen the rumors coming true. All the bullets in the world cannot stop what will happen next.

The humans frantically search the train, checking for weapons and bombs. The Toqwa warriors and the Mudfoot marauders exit their respective cars and climb on top while the humans rummage through, barking their military codes. "Clear," they shout, their boots stomping the decks.

"Clear."

"Clear."

It takes a long time. The Mudfoot and their allies remain still and calm. The humans sweat. A stain spreads on the commanding officer's jacket from his armpit to his ribs.

When it's over, the barricades lift. Two bears roll away the concrete cylinders, opening a path for the train to enter the city and make its way to the station. The passengers return to their cars. As the train rumbles forward, the howl from the crowd becomes a roar. The train crosses a small river, where people of various species cheer from canoes and makeshift rafts. The spectators have been waiting for more than a day. On land, fights break out as the dogs try to push their way to the edge of the tracks. A game of zagga spontaneously begins, forcing a circle to open among the onlookers. Several of the flags collapse in the chaos, but more rise to take their place.

On the platform, the newly installed Archon waits, his hands folded at his belt. Here, the roof of the station shades the concrete island where the passengers will disembark. At the far end, severed pillars point sharply into the air, the remnants of a Parthenon-like structure mostly destroyed in the war. This place was never meant to receive a train again, and yet the oncoming locomotive generates a breeze that swishes the Archon's robe and flutters his salt-and-pepper beard. The bodyguards squeeze in tightly around him. More soldiers arrive, flooding the platform.

D'Arc is so close to him that she can feel his heartbeat, yet no one sees her.

The breeze from the train grows stronger. The Archon blinks. The bodyguards shuffle. The old wheels of the train scrape and squeal as the engine gathers speed. Some of the people in the crowd cheer louder. But the rest know something is wrong. They know that the train is not stopping.

Not a single one of the dogs loyal to the Mudfoot are anywhere near the station.

Two pairs of hands grip the Archon by the shoulders and arms, dragging him away. The train roars through the station, past the pillars, heading south along the river. A metal click cuts through the noise. The three cars in the rear disconnect from the engine and roll freely. Their brakes engage and they grind to a stop at the edge of the platform. Some of the soldiers scream to stay away, while others rush to the scene.

The flatbed with the trash truck on top sits in between the other two cars. D'Arc witnesses the explosion in slow motion. The blast shreds the metal, splitting the truck open like the skin of a molting insect.

Everyone in the crowd cowers, some dropping to the ground. After a few seconds, they realize that they are still alive. The bomb is a dud. Either it failed, or the wolves intended it as a message to their canine allies in the city. Many of the onlookers laugh out loud. Black smoke billows from the fissure in the trash truck, carrying the scent of burnt oil and grease.

In the distance, the train streaks along the river, wobbling on the old tracks. A few rogue soldiers take potshots, if for no other reason than to blow off steam. The officers let them do it for a while before ordering them to hold their fire. The train's horn blows, one final taunt as the wolves return to Mudfoot territory.

It's over. The people are safe.

But more paths to the future suddenly close, never to open again.

A NEW BREEZE brushed through D'Arc's fur. She opened her eyes and found herself on top of the moving train, lying on her side. She could still hear the soldiers from her vision firing blindly.

Falkirk knelt beside her, screaming something, but she could not hear what he said.

The gunshots snapped in her ear. Much closer now.

D'Arc rolled her head to the other side, toward the rear of the train, just in time to see bullet holes puncturing the roof of the car. Someone was inside, pointing a machine gun at the ceiling and firing in a zigzag pattern from one end of the car to the other. The rounds punched through the steel in tiny smoking volcanoes.

D'Arc scuttled to the front of the coach and slid over the edge, landing on the small platform above the coupler. She unsheathed her sword. The metal door clicked and slid open. A wolf with blue face paint stepped out, gun raised to his chin. D'Arc blinked as the muzzle fired a round right over her head. Above the wolf, Falkirk hung over the side, gripping the handle of a knife. The blade sank into the base of the wolf's neck, above the collarbone. He tried to turn to see who had stabbed him, but the movement wedged the blade even deeper. Falkirk withdrew the knife, and the wind threw a skein of blood against the metal wall. The wolf fell into the space between the cars and vanished into the blurring tracks.

Falkirk jumped onto the platform, landing to the right of the door. He peeked inside the car, then immediately took cover. A volley of bullets sprayed from the door, ricocheting off the next car. Falkirk removed a grenade from his belt and yanked the pin. As an act of mercy, he stuck his hand out so the wolves could see. The gunfire stopped. D'Arc leaned in to see one brave wolf charging right at them, a young one with no war paint. Falkirk lobbed the grenade, and it bounced off the wolf's chest. As it clanged on the deck, the wolf finally realized the danger. He turned and ran. Falkirk slammed the door shut.

The blast blew out the windows in the coach. D'Arc smelled burnt plastic and fabric before the wind sucked it away.

"Where's our son?" Falkirk said.

"At the front. Four cars away."

D'Arc held the sword so that the blade rested on her shoulder. She nodded to the door of the next train. Falkirk removed another concussion grenade.

"Last one," he said.

He opened the door and tossed it in. Someone inside shouted, but the door slid shut and silenced him. A thud followed, like a hammer against the hull. The door popped open an inch, releasing white smoke.

"So we fight our way through," he said.

"It's our only chance," she said. "They didn't see this coming."

"And what do *you* see?"

She allowed the image of the train station to bleed into her field of vision again. "I see nothing but . . . animals. Tearing one another apart. Like it was before."

No more talk of compromise. No more treaties or diplomacy. They would cut their way through this human contraption or die trying.

Inside the car, two humans lay on the floor by the baggage rack. A dazed Toqwa warrior knelt in the center aisle. The fire alarm on the ceiling blared and then went out. With blood dripping from his ears, the warrior gripped the seat rests and got to his feet. When he bared his teeth, the tattoo mask stretched into a hideous, scowling wolf. He pulled a cutlass from his belt, the handle beaten and weathered. Behind him, the door slid open, and more humans formed a line in the aisle, brandishing clubs, their wolf tattoos sneering. Near the front of the train, a spear rose above the others and poked the ceiling. All at once, they stampeded toward D'Arc, their footsteps rumbling on the deck like a boulder.

D'Arc lifted her sword and ran straight into the maelstrom.

SHE STANDS ON the platform in Hosanna again, completely still, when the first scream pierces the air.

*No*, she thinks. *Enough of the future. I need to stay here.*

Her mind will not listen. She has to see it again. Until it becomes the present.

The exploded trash truck continues to vent its thick smoke into the sky. The humans who had rushed the train now drag one of their own away from it. Clad in their camouflage uniforms, they each take the limb of a man who convulses and squirms. Someone calls for a medic as they set the man on the concrete. He pulls one of his hands free and tears at his jacket. His comrades try to keep him from bashing his head on the ground. More soldiers arrive to keep the crowd away. When one of them falls to his knees, his body jerking about and his hands clutching his throat, someone finally asks, "What's happening?"

D'Arc spins around to see more people, animals and humans, falling into seizures. A cat kneels on the pavement with her hands around her neck, choking, trying to cough something out that will not let go. One of the bears at the checkpoint claws at an old telephone pole, and, when this fails to knock it over, he rams it with his shoulder again and again. When D'Arc completes her revolution, she sees one of the dogs overcome with rage. He bounds over the first row of spectators and latches his long jaw onto a human's neck. The people scream—but not in shock.

With incomprehensible grunts, they egg him on. And then they pounce, moving as a single organism toward their prey. The soldier disappears in a mass of bodies. A trickle of blood streams out from the scrum before gathering in a crack in the cement.

Both the humans and the animals move on all fours, convinced that the space in front of them is their territory, under attack. The air grows thick with blood and musk. D'Arc turns to find a human racing toward her, spittle dropping from his lips. His torn shirt flaps about, barely hanging on to his shoulders. She raises her hands in time to grab him by his neck. She wrenches him to the side and cracks him in the face with her elbow. She blinks and his red face suddenly bears the wolf tattoo. Another blink, and he is the raging man again, driven mad. D'Arc stands in two places at once, in the present and in the very near future.

The smoke from the explosion descends on her. She inhales it and knows right away what it is. The Toqwa have created a new batch of rahvek, more potent than before. She feels it in her blood, in her muscles, in her spine. It will make everything young again. It will put things back as they were. A sudden, irreversible cure for the Change, infecting all of Hosanna, breeding a new supply of prey for the Mudfoot and their allies.

Someone grabs her from behind, a creature covered in black fur. She slashes at it while fending off the human with her other hand. Falkirk barks beside her, behind her, above her, though she cannot see him. Like a starving feral, she sinks her teeth into her enemy's furry hide and jerks her head left and right while the taste of iron floods her mouth.

She no longer cares who will win the war, who will be the latest to gain control of a lost city. She can no longer hear the scuffle and the clashing swords from the train car. The present fades. The blood in her mouth is all that exists, from the beginning of time until the end.

With her jaws chewing through flesh, crunching into the marrow of a man's spine, she twists her head the way her people have done for millennia, without being trained. The vertebrae snaps in her mouth, one by one, and then the meat hangs limp like a sleeping child.

# CHAPTER 22

## THE PATH DIVERGES

URNA'S BODY LAY on the floor of a passenger car, facing the wall. Mercy sat on the scratchy blue carpet, fiddling with a loose thread while the pup sniffed at Urna's tail. When the pup tried to lick one of the wounds, Mercy tugged him away.

Outside, the trees flew past while the hills beyond remained eerily still. It was some kind of optical illusion. The wheels beneath the car clicked at regular intervals. *Kuh-kik. Kuh-kik. Kuh-kik.* A sound that the forest could never produce. She and Urna spent days following the rusty train tracks that cut through Mudfoot territory. The older wolves told her that the tracks carried a monster made of steel. Mercy had nightmares about a creature crawling on the lines to snatch her away. When she told Urna about it, her sister laughed. They were stories to scare children, Urna explained, nothing more.

Mercy whispered her sister's name. She wanted it to be the pup's first word. But the young one soon lost interest in the body, choosing instead to flick a loose bolt he found on the floor. Since Aunt Urna would not play with him, he would have to entertain himself. Mercy admired his pragmatism, his stubborn refusal to dwell on the past. For him, for all rulers, the past would rot, as it should.

She scratched behind his ear. He tilted his head to allow her to dig in deeper. She smiled, flexing muscles in her face that had lain dormant for a long time.

A tremor vibrated through the deck. The train wobbled, throwing off the steady *kuh-kik* sound for a second. Mercy's heartbeat throbbed. The pup stopped with the bolt squeezed between his lips. Did they hit something? Did something hit them?

The front door slid open. Augur entered, tying his pelt over his shoulders. He crouched in order to get a better look out the windows.

Mercy whimpered, a sound that pleaded with him to tell her what was happening. He blew a puff of air that inflated his cheeks. *Stay here*, it meant. As he hurried past her, he reassured the pup with a pat on the head.

Mercy felt the train curving to the right. She followed Augur to the rear door, with the young one tugging at her ankle. As Augur reached for the latch, he balled his hand into a fist, his veins bulging into blue snakes. He collapsed to one knee.

Mercy grabbed his wrists and pulled his arms around her neck. He trembled while the pup barked at their feet.

"Someone is . . . interfering again," he said.

Over her shoulder, Mercy eyed her sister's corpse. Had Urna given the rahvek to someone? Someone who wanted to see the future? Who would want that kind of power? Who wouldn't?

"Everything was a straight line a few seconds ago," Augur said, gasping. "Now I see a web. A cloud. A . . . blizzard."

She tried to hold him. But he broke free of her grasp, crawled to the door, and banged his forehead on the metal, rattling the frame. She barked at him.

"What do you see?" she said.

Before he could answer, the latch turned on its own and

the door slid open. Creek stepped halfway inside. Seeing the human on the floor, the young wolf glanced at Mercy for an explanation.

Augur forced himself to his feet. A red welt bloomed just beneath his hairline.

He was scared. She could smell it.

"Intruders," Creek said. "Two dogs."

"I know," Augur said.

The pup curled around Mercy's ankle, oblivious to what they said. She pried him away from her leg and handed him to Creek. "Wait here," Mercy said. "No one comes through."

While squirming in Creek's arms, the little one cried out to Mercy as she stepped outside with Augur. The door closed, sealing in the pup's wailing.

Augur gathered himself. Despite the wind and the cold, a trickle of sweat slid along his neck. He pinched the bridge of his nose.

"They're too late to stop this train," he said.

She watched him, trying to determine if he said this to her, or to himself.

"Nothing can stop it," he added. "But they can still hurt someone. Including your son."

The door to the next car hung open. Mudfoot marauders stood in the aisles, awaiting orders. Carsa towered over them, the old wolf's gray coat sticking out. Mercy barked to get her attention. Carsa nodded. She gathered the others and headed for the exit. Whoever was coming toward them would soon face a pack of wolves, as well as the Toqwa soldiers in the next coach.

Mercy motioned to the roof of the car. Augur immediately understood. She wanted to climb on top, to see the entire train as it made this long turn to the southeast. Mercy went first, planting her foot on the handle and pulling herself up. She slapped her palm on the roof at the exact moment that the windows on one of the cars blew out, releasing white smoke. A rifle fired in response before going dead. Mercy heard shouting and barking, more doors slamming, windows shattering. One of the passenger cars was pockmarked with bullet holes, each one piping with soot.

Beyond that, the flatbed with the trash truck remained intact. The intruders had left it alone, choosing instead to work their way to the engine.

"They won't get far," Augur shouted over the wind. "But they could decouple the train."

The whistle in the locomotive blew, a signal to anyone watching from the surrounding countryside that the train was under attack. Soon, the fires would rise on the hills, and word would spread to Hosanna.

Mercy had seen enough. She needed to join the others. A pack leader who hid inside a steel contraption did not deserve her station in life. She brushed Augur with her tail and ran along the roof to the gap between the cars, where she jumped over. Below, Carsa's enforcers streamed through the doors, swords drawn. Her people knew how to stalk prey out in the open. This bottleneck made Mercy nervous. But then she saw one marauder slash his scimitar against the doorframe as he passed through, leaving a deep dent in the metal, and she knew that these intruders could not fight their way through.

She pressed on to the next car, the one filled with Toqwa warriors. Judging from the gunshots reverberating through the hull, the intruders had arrived at a stalemate here. A window burst open as a bullet flew through. Metal clanged against metal. A human screamed. Smoke leaked from the holes in the roof. A cloud lingered inside, fogging the broken windows.

Directly below her, on the narrow platform, a canine

warrior, armed with a sword, slashed at one of the Toqwas. It was a female, with crimson spattered from her chest to the tip of her nose. A set of human fingernails had raked across her snout, leaving four wet lines in her fur. At first, Mercy thought it was some crazy wolf with no pack. But then she smelled the blood. This was no wolf. It was—

"You," Mercy whispered. The wet nurse with the sword had returned. And she knew how to use it in a confined space. When the Toqwa swung his club, the blade deflected it, cutting out a hunk of wood that flipped away in the wind. The movement exposed the man's ribs. The dog elbowed him, dropping him to one knee. Another swing cut through his shoulder, the blade so sharp it exposed the bone and muscle before the wound had a chance to bleed. The club fell between the cars and exploded under the wheels in a shower of splinters. The dog kicked the man in the chest, lifting him off the side of the train. He landed in the gravel and vanished.

When the dog readied herself for the next opponent, she spotted Mercy looming over her. The dog's lips parted to reveal a set of tightly clenched fangs. Her fingers stiffened around the handle of the sword. Her brow knitted into a bolt of muscle. Somehow, this gentle creature, this plaything for humans, this gonney, had turned herself into a monster, boiling over with hatred. This dog had come to kill her.

Someone stepped out of the doorway below. Another dog—a husky—firing a rifle into the car as he retreated. He saw Mercy and raised the barrel, the muzzle a perfect circle between his bright blue eyes. A hand grabbed Mercy's shoulder and pulled her away as the rifle fired. She landed on her tail with Augur beside her, his arm draped over her chest for protection. Mercy sat up and saw the two dogs retreated inside the car, sealing themselves inside.

The tracks edged along the side of a highway. A truck drove

parallel with the train, gathering speed as it belched smoke from its tailpipe. While one wolf drove, another was perched in the pickup, aiming a mounted machine gun at the train. He waved to Mercy.

She pointed to the car where the intruders had fled. Then she ran her fingernail across her throat.

The wolf aimed the gun and fired. Yellow flashes burst from the muzzle, followed by a sound like an insect flapping its wings. *Bup-bup-bup-bup-bup.* Shells flipped off the side of the truck, tinkling on the asphalt. The rounds shredded the hull, bursting out the other side. The gunner swept from front to back, stopping before he hit the trash truck on the flatbed. Part of the roof sank as the bullets sliced through the walls. The gun went dead as the last rounds emptied from the chamber.

The wolf reloaded. Mercy raised her hand, signaling him to hold off. On the platform below, a pair of humans awaited her orders. Mercy flicked her chin toward the bullet-riddled passenger car. That was all they needed. The first human broke the window, reached inside, and unlocked the door. Once it slid aside, the Toqwa warriors piled in, with more wolves following. Mercy could taste blood in the air, as strong as an open wound on a deer. She could not contain herself. She needed to join them. She prepared to climb down, but once again Augur's hand grabbed her shoulder.

"Wait," he said, wincing in pain.

She exhaled through her nostrils, a sound that demanded more information.

"Look," Augur said.

The compactor on the trash truck slowly opened like the mouth of an enormous fish. A fluid thicker than water gushed out and splashed along the sides of the car.

In the driver's side window, a furry head leaned out to see

what was happening. Another stowaway. But not a dog this time. A mountain lion, perhaps, judging from the ears and whiskers. Or a mere housecat. Either way, he knew how to operate the vehicle.

Something inside the compactor moved. Layers of skin unfolded, then stretched forth in eerie, slithering appendages, like great serpents. The creature's head emerged from beneath the lid of the compactor. Two enormous eyes blinked. A mouth opened to a vortex of white teeth. A three-pronged claw hooked onto the lip of opening.

Augur had tried to prepare Mercy for this, in the event that she came face-to-face with a Sarcops. It took only a dozen of them to destroy half of Hosanna. But no description of fangs and tentacles by the firelight could do justice to this alien, this abomination. Prepared or not, Mercy knew a hunter when she saw one. This beast was ready to strike.

As the creature emerged, Mercy noticed the plastic tubes stuck to its skin, drawing blood. That was how Augur's precious rahvek was made—by siphoning it from the living tissue of this perfect killing machine. The Sanctuary Union must have invented this mobile torture chamber for this very purpose, to sedate the creature and contain it while drawing away its life. The Toqwa were going to return the Sarcops to the city as a gift as soon as they collected their own share.

A hail of bullets struck the compactor. In a panic, the gunner truck had opened fire again. To get closer to the train, the driver swerved off the road onto a grassy patch.

"No!" Augur shouted. "Hold your fire!"

Though dazed from its long slumber, the creature homed in on its attacker. A tentacle shot out from the compactor and whirled around the wolf's neck. Another wrapped around his ankles. Together they lifted the wolf from his perch in the pickup. The gunner tried to hold the stock of his weapon, but the tentacles pulled him away. Mercy could feel the wolf's fingers break. The tentacles stiffened, changing from slithering pythons to two slim branches. In a great burst of red mist, the tentacles ripped the wolf's body in half at the waist before dropping the two mangled pieces alongside the train.

The Sarcops oozed out of the truck, a deformed child birthed from a metal womb. Rather than opening the door to the coach, it punctured the metal and slithered into the hole it had made. Despite the roaring wind and the clicking tracks, Mercy heard the first man scream, along with the second and the third. The roof suddenly bulged as the creature lifted one of the warriors and broke his skull against the ceiling. The only intact window remaining became shaded with a coat of blood. At the front of the car, the warriors formed a stack of bodies as they tried to retreat. A man on top of the pile yelped as something grabbed him and pulled him inside.

"We can stop this," Augur said, as calm as a drop of rain rolling off a leaf. "But you have to come with me. Now."

A dreadful screeching sound began as the roof of the coach split open, ripped asunder by the tentacles. Bodies lay draped on seats, spread-eagled in the aisle. Huddled in the far corner, the husky and the wet nurse held each other the way Mercy and Augur did, with the world tearing itself apart around them. The Sarcops had let them live.

"Come on!" Augur said. "There's still time."

Mercy turned to follow him to the front of the train. When she did, the city of Hosanna appeared on the horizon, the first time she had seen it. The morning light reflected off the smooth glass of a skyscraper, creating a second sun. Windmills of every shape spun on the rooftops—some round like sunflowers, others with three enormous propellers, shaped like the wings of a swan. All of it formed into a sea of metal and brick where a green valley should have been. Every path that the rahvek revealed—even the ones that scraped at Augur's mind—led here, on this single track into the future. These people trying to stop her could never understand. Their journey would end, one way or another.

# CHAPTER 23

## WELKOM

**M**ORT(E) OPENED THE door and stepped out of the driver's seat. The train had entered a straightaway, cutting between another town and the highway. Here, the houses were more densely packed together, many of them with rusted vehicles still parked in the driveways. On the rooftops, people of all species had gathered to watch the train enter the city limits. A dog with a pup on his shoulders waved like an idiot, like some toy with the string pulled. On the roof of an office building, a family of rodents lifted a sign that read WELKOM in giant red letters.

Something landed on the flatbed only a few feet from Mort(e). It was a hunk of bread, freshly baked as far as he could tell. Bread. For wolves. These fucking people.

Mort(e) could not remember a train zipping through his neighborhood before the Change. And yet, if he had read the maps correctly, the house where he grew up and fell in love could not be far from here. Something must have remained from the quarantine. Perhaps the Queen had decimated everything except his master's home and the little square of sunlight where he spent most of his days. It would be a nice spot to fall asleep and never wake.

Behind the train, a great cloud gathered in the streets. More trucks and cars and motorcycles appeared, disturbing the dust that had caked this suburb for over a decade. As Mort(e) suspected, signal fires burned in the hills. A chorus of howls rolled along, barely audible over the clatter of the train. All the wolves would descend on the city now. It was what the wolves and their sycophantic puppy allies had always wanted. A straight fight. How many of these gawkers knew about it? How many of them prayed for this day to come?

*Fine*, Mort(e) thought. *Let's die together.*

He turned to the front of the train and saw the full devastation of the coach where the Sarcops had cut through the humans. With the roof torn off, the broken walls jutted upward in ragged spikes and valleys. Most of the bodies overlapped in the center aisle. A human sat in one of the seats, his hands folded in his lap, his head spun completely around, the neck purple and swollen. The only survivor would not last much longer. He leaned against the wall under the fire alarm. With his spine broken, the man lazily covered a puncture wound on his stomach. The tattoo on his face became like that a sad dog waiting for scraps from the dinner table.

Strangely, the doorframe remained intact. Rather than hop over the sharp metal, Mort(e) slid the door to the side until it broke free of its moorings and flopped onto the first row of seats. Across the aisle, D'Arc and Falkirk huddled beside the baggage rack. She had pulled her knees into her chest. He placed his arm around her neck, as if she would float away if he let go. The wind carried their voices away. But since they kept repeating themselves, Mort(e) eventually caught their words.

"This is now," Falkirk said.

"This is now," D'Arc replied.

"This is now."

"This is now."

When Mort(e) and D'Arc lived on the ranch, they would find themselves in this exact pose whenever one of them had a bad dream. His nightmares brought him back to the war; hers showed glimpses of her old life, of the children she'd lost. He would comfort her in this same way, mumbling nonsense in the dark until she started snoring again.

From the front of the train came the sound of twisting metal. D'Arc flinched, and Falkirk covered her ears. The Sarcops had ruptured another car, working her way to the front.

Mort(e) knelt before the two dogs. He expected D'Arc to act surprised. Instead, she watched him as she did on the first day he saw her, with the expressionless eyes of a young pup.

"I've got good news and bad news," Mort(e) said. "Good news: I think I've figured out why the fish-heads let me live."

"That Sarcops looked at us," Falkirk said, still shaken. "It looked right at us and kept going."

"I told her to," Mort(e) said. "You're welcome."

"I know what the bad news is," D'Arc said. "You found a bomb on the trash truck."

"That's right," Mort(e) replied. "And I can't—"

"You can't disarm it," D'Arc said, finishing the thought for him, like she did whenever she got annoyed on the ranch.

"We could decouple the cars," Falkirk said.

"That won't matter," D'Arc said. "We're almost to the city."

"So we can't stop, and we can't turn around," Mort(e) said. "We need to run this train *through* the city, then carry it out the other side."

"Will that work?" Falkirk asked.

D'Arc craned her neck, as if searching for a ball that her master had thrown across the yard. "It could," she said.

"You drank it, didn't you?" Mort(e) said. He could smell it. And feel it.

"Yes," she said. Her tone warned him against asking any follow-up questions.

A noise to his right. Through the open doorway, he saw a pickup riding next to the tracks, its fat tires flinging gravel as they accelerated. When the driver matched the train's speed, three humans jumped onto the flatbed, each armed with a rifle. Toqwa warriors, sporting fresh deerskin leather shirts, cut low at the neck, with leggings and shin-high boots. The first man to hop on had a bright bald head as smooth as an egg. He motioned to the trash truck and his two minions inspected it, one of them aiming his rifle into the driver's seat, the other peering inside the empty compactor. He took a sniff, then recoiled at the fishy scent.

When the bald man turned toward the shattered coach, Mort(e) recognized him. It was the Jerk, the leader of the humans he encountered in Hosanna. Oh, and look: the Toqwa had rewarded him with a wolf tattoo on his face. No going back to Hosanna for this human. Mort(e) had to admire that. The other humans huddled with the Jerk to receive their next orders. The tall one with the weak, hairless jaw was Slinky. The boxy one beside him was Meat.

"Get to the front of the train," Mort(e) said to Falkirk. "Find the human. Kill him. I'll hold off these wolf boys."

"You don't have to do that," Falkirk said. "We can figure out—"

"I'm not sacrificing myself, husky," Mort(e) said. "I'm using you as bait."

Falkirk waited for D'Arc, but she already understood. A straight fight in a tiny space would get at least one of them killed. Better to attack from behind, like the Red Sphinx taught him.

While Mort(e) peeked out the door, D'Arc and Falkirk prepared to sprint to the next car. Mort(e) unsheathed his knife and held it with the blade pointed outward. He twirled his fingers at Falkirk, and the dog handed him another knife, which Mort(e) held blade down. One for slashing, one for stabbing.

Mort(e) positioned himself behind the broken door. With a nod, he signaled to his friends to run. They took off through the aisle. The humans on the flatbed shouted something. The Jerk came through first, passing right by Mort(e), raising his rifle and firing. The dogs had already made it to the next car. Slinky barreled through after him, taking a position behind a row of chairs and taking aim.

Mort(e) listened for Meat's heavy footsteps pounding against the metal. When they reached their loudest, he stuck out the blade at ankle height. On the front of Meat's left leg, connecting the shin to the top of the foot, was an extraordinary tendon, a piece of flesh that the humans had evolved to help them stand upright. The knife cut through this band of tissue with an audible snap. Meat yelped before landing face-first in the aisle. Mort(e) did not allow him to react. He sank his other knife into the vertebra at the base of the human's neck. Slinky turned to the noise behind him, only to find Mort(e) seizing him at the waist and collar and tossing him toward the wall of the coach. His hip slammed violently against the metal. He tried to grab something to keep him on board, but his hand gripped the torn metal and fell away. If he landed in the right way, he might live.

The Jerk, kneeling in the aisle, tried to swing his rifle around. Mort(e) threw his knife. The human raised his weapon, and the blade clanged off the stock of the rifle, knocking the weapon out of his hands. Mort(e) charged. The human grabbed Mort(e)'s wrists, and the two warriors became locked in combat, grunting and snarling. The Jerk pulled Mort(e)'s hands apart, propping him up like a crucified figure, his chest exposed. Mort(e) had never encountered a human so powerful.

The man smiled. Mort(e) could smell the rahvek on him. With two pistols on his belt, all the Jerk needed to do was grab one and fire. But he wanted to toy with Mort(e) first.

"You're old and weak," the human said. "I saw it on the bridge. You thought you were the future, and you were wrong."

Mort(e) tried to pry his wrists free, but the human's grip only tightened. He tried to kick the man in the chest. The human anticipated the move, and drove the tip of his boot right into Mort(e)'s stomach. The impact rippled, turning his muscles to liquid. He fell to his knees. The Jerk kicked him again, this time square in the face. Mort(e) rolled with the first one. The second blow caught him in the temple. Blood leaked onto his tongue, a welcome respite from the salt water.

The Jerk readied for another kick. As he shifted his weight, Mort(e) shot upward like a piston and bit into the man's neck, sinking his fangs so deep that he could feel the pulse throbbing in his mouth. With a thrashing of his head, the flesh pulled free, and a warmth dribbled from Mort(e)'s chin to his chest. The human let go of Mort(e)'s wrists and fell backward, landing in the aisle with his hands shaking over the glistening wound. Mort(e) allowed the hunk of meat to fall from his fangs. It landed on the man's shirt, a bright red lump, warm to the touch. Stupidly, the man groped the piece of him that had been torn away, as if he could paste himself together. His mouth, spattered red like a clown's mask, tried to gulp the air.

Despite all of it, the Jerk wasn't afraid. Mort(e) had killed enough humans to know the smell of fear. Leaning over the dying man, he saw the reason why. The gaping wound shrank at the edges like an iris constricting. This was what the rahvek could do. With his windpipe knitting itself together again, the man swallowed a breath of air. He laughed in wonder at this miracle unfolding, a gift that only the chosen could enjoy.

The laughter stopped when Mort(e) yanked the pistols from the man's belt. Two Glock 19s, nice weight to them. The expression on the Jerk's face was priceless. *Don't you want to see?* he seemed to say. *Don't you care?*

Mort(e) did not. He emptied the handguns, the shots clapping in his ears. As the body wriggled from each round, the shells flipped in the air and collected at his feet. When the breaches popped open, Mort(e) dropped the guns in the aisle, the barrels still smoking. He took the man's rifle and made his way to the front of the train, passing the other fallen warriors.

To enter the next car, he carefully stepped through the hole that the Sarcops created when she punctured the hull. Another hole appeared at the other end. Mort(e) crouched to peek under the seats. No one was here. Despite all their supposed bravery, the wolves and their human allies could run away faster than anyone else. Some of them must have jumped off the train. On his way through, the light streaming into the broken windows suddenly went dark. It was a tunnel, a sure sign that they would reach the city limits any minute. He tried to shake off the strange pressure building in his ears. As the train emerged, the light changed again—now, a sunny morning had become overcast. On this side of the tunnel, Mort(e) could hear gunshots coming from the city.

He pressed his face against one of the windows. Outside, columns of smoke blotted out the sun. The tracks curved toward the bridge leading into Hosanna. There, a row of military vehicles, along with fencing and concrete pillars, sealed off the city. A crowd of people rushed the barricades, so many that some of them plummeted from the bridge, either shot dead or shoved aside by their comrades. Despite the distance, Mort(e) could tell that these rebels were all canines. They bounded over one another like mutts fighting over a piece of meat. And there were more of them coming from behind—from *inside* the city.

Mort(e) arrived at the next car, the last before the locomotive. He checked his rifle, switched off the safety, opened the breach to see the rounds inside. Strangely, the door was halfway open. The Sarcops must have gotten bored with simply plowing through. He imagined her knocking first, then opening it like a civilized person.

A buzzing sound like a thousand insects scraping their legs

together emanated from the doorway. Mort(e) positioned himself behind it and peeked inside.

The Sarcops occupied the aisle, her scales undulating and convulsing. She pitched her head back to release a scream. A stabbing pain shot into Mort(e)'s eye like an icepick trying to work its way through the bone. He fought it off by digging his fingers into the stock of the rifle. At this proximity, her pain became his.

The Sarcops was stuck in place somehow, unable to control her body. Two of her tentacles clung to the ceiling. The other two extended to her right and her left, where they wrapped around the necks of Falkirk and D'Arc. The two dogs clawed at the tentacles as they coiled more tightly.

At the front of the train, the human, Augur, held out a plastic device, some kind of audio speaker. The noise it created drove the Sarcops mad. She may have forced all the Toqwa and Mudfoot to leap from the train, but she would go no farther.

Beside Augur, the mother wolf wagged her tail. A tooth dangled from a leather string around her neck, yellow and shiny.

The Sarcops yanked the two dogs toward the aisle. D'Arc collapsed to her knees, choking. Mort(e) tried to aim, but the moving bodies made it impossible. He needed to get closer.

The Sarcops leapt onto the ceiling and stuck there, a pulsating mass of scales and claws. She pounded her head against the metal, denting it. Mort(e) felt it each time, a pair of knuckles on the inside of his skull.

He couldn't take it anymore. He slipped through the opening, charged past his friends and underneath the monstrosity above. The wolf barked. Mort(e) dropped to one knee and took aim. Augur darted to his left as Mort(e) pulled the trigger. Mort(e) tracked him in the rifle's sights, but the man moved too fast. With each flash of the muzzle, he changed positions. Dropping the device, Augur vaulted the first row of seats. A bullet flew past his shoulder and pierced the window. He leapt to the next row, balancing on the headrests. Another bullet cut through his leather shirt but did not hit his body. *No*, Mort(e) thought. *Impossible to miss at this range!* Still, the man kept coming. He gripped the luggage rack and swung into the aisle, allowing yet another round to pass right under his armpit. When he landed a mere two feet away, Mort(e) knew it was over. The human lunged for the rifle and grabbed it. As Mort(e) resisted, Augur used his momentum to smash the stock into Mort(e)'s chin. The room sparked. Mort(e) let go, tumbled away from the human, and regained his footing. He swung a fist, and the human dodged it. With his other hand, Mort(e) withdrew his knife, still warm with blood. He cut an arc through the air. Augur ducked beneath it and jabbed him in the stomach. As Mort(e) doubled over, an uppercut cracked one of his teeth. He collapsed. In a crab walk, he backed away from the human. Mort(e) glanced at the Sarcops for help, but the creature flattened itself against the wall, terrified. She released D'Arc and Falkirk, who staggered to their feet.

Augur relaxed from his fighting stance and folded his arms. An invitation to try again. No human had ever shown such disrespect to the Red Sphinx.

Mort(e) sprung to his feet. The movement triggered a stabbing pain in his side that made his right leg go limp for a second. A broken rib, most likely. He turned to D'Arc and Falkirk. They knew what he wanted.

The three of them stormed through the narrow aisle. Mort(e) reached Augur first. His first swing missed badly. His second connected, but it was a glancing blow. The human rolled with it and slammed the heel of his palm in the exposed space on Mort(e)'s side. He knew right where to strike. Mort(e) collapsed into the seat. Falkirk took his place, slashing at the human and missing. His claws dug out a hunk of fabric in the nearest seat. Augur kicked the back of the husky's knee, then elbowed him in the snout. A jet of snot and blood ejected from Falkirk's nose.

D'Arc jumped over the husky and swung her sword in a great vertical swipe, pinning the blade into the carpet. It passed so close to Augur that Mort(e) expected his nose to simply drop off. But the man stomped his heel on D'Arc's wrist before she could raise the sword again. The weapon fell from her hands. When she reached for it, the train swerved to the right, and the hilt rolled away. Augur stepped on the blade and slid it behind him.

Either out of sympathy, or to mock them, the human gave them a few seconds to consider their predicament. The audio device lay on the floor behind him, still blaring.

"It almost worked," Augur said.

He turned away from them and headed for the front of the train, a sacred place that they would see but never reach themselves. Their long journey ended here.

The door opened. A pack of wolves poured into the car, a roiling mass of fur, fangs, and claws. Mercy's personal bodyguards, fouling the car with their earthy stench. Four of them circled their leader. They clawed the carpet and flashed their teeth. One of them, an older female with a white muzzle and a missing ear, crouched at the top of the aisle, awaiting orders. A fresh cut bisected the space between her eyes. She must have escaped from the Sarcops only a few minutes earlier.

The human stroked the wolves' fur as they paced about. Mort(e) recognized the numbness in Augur's dark eyes, the smug loosening of his jaw and cheekbones, the untroubled brow. Humans like him never knew fear or want because the world was rigged in their favor, and they never needed to imagine otherwise.

Augur nodded to his mate, the female wolf with the fang for a necklace. The others waited. With a single bark, she would order her servants to tear these intruders apart and chew the bones to pulp and lick the blood drops clean.

# CHAPTER 24

## THE GHOST

MERCY INHALED THE scent of her people, and soon it over-powered the stale air trapped in the metal tube. Carsa and Creek. Mag and Quick. Each part of a whole. Everything became simple again. The world split between her pack and the enemy, the way it had always been while she pretended to be a diplomat, a peacemaker. A mother.

The train entered the heart of the city, where the skyscrapers blocked the morning sun. By then, the rebels had received the signal that the train was under attack. It was their job now to clear the barricades and get the train through so it could deliver its payload. Augur had warned her that skirmishes would break out on every street. Once the shield was lifted and the skin exposed, this giant blade would slip between Hosanna's ribs.

At the other end of the car, the three intruders prepared to fight. This was the best Hosanna could do: a wet nurse, a fake wolf, and an old cat with no claws. Mercy laughed inwardly at the last one. They sent someone who resembled the Tekni legend that the older wolves would talk about. But this imposter was too short, too scrawny.

Behind them, the fish monster lay still, its oily, flexible body splashed against the floor and the wall. Augur had switched off the device—the pacifier, he called it. The creature stirred. It may have had the strength to fight, but the device drained its will. Mercy recognized defeat when she saw it, like the blank stare of a doe surrounded by predators.

With the wolves forming a wall in front of him, Augur reached out to scratch Mercy on her head. He gave her a look that asked for her permission to do away with these invaders. He had stayed true to his word. Despite his power, despite the flaws of his species, he viewed her as a partner, something many of her fellow wolves would never do.

With a quick, high-pitched bark, she gave the order without taking her gaze off Augur. Her bodyguards charged the intruders. Whatever happened next would never last long.

As she turned to watch, a monstrous squealing sounded in her ears, and a great force lifted her from her feet. Everyone in the car hung suspended in the air. Carsa, the lead attacker, appeared to be falling backward down the aisle. The two dogs and the cat flung forward, as if shoved from behind. Mercy's fang necklace levitated in front of her face.

She collided with the wall at the front of the car. The force of it crunched her ribs, expelling air and spittle from her mouth. Augur hit the wall and dropped to a sitting position. The train stopped.

Someone had pulled the brake. Someone in the locomotive—another intruder. She knew enough about this machine to understand that. Outside, the concrete landscape was still. A monolith of brick and glass blocked one side of the train. She heard shouting and gunfire mingled with the throbbing in her skull.

Augur placed his head between his knees and pressed his palms to his temples. A choking sound clogged his throat.

"Someone . . . interfering again," he said.

Before Mercy could reach for the door handle, it clicked on its own, operated from the other side. The hatch slid open. A furry creature stepped inside, walking on two feet. It turned away from Mercy, and its tail flipped her in the face. On purpose, she imagined. This creature—this wolf—towered over Augur, still sitting against the wall. In its hand it held a piece of metal with a red plastic knob on the end—a lever from the control room, broken off to create a weapon. A drop of blood fell from the tip and absorbed into the carpet.

For the first time since this began, Augur gazed at something unexpected, something he could not have seen coming. The terror manifested in his slackening jaw, his parting lips, his hands rising to fend off the inevitable. The wolf plunged the weapon into his chest, so deep that only the plastic knob remained. The wolf turned to Mercy. It was a female, her body covered in puncture wounds, the blood having dried and crusted into the fur.

"Urna?" Mercy said. She had never seen her sister stand on two legs before.

Urna eyed her in a way that blamed her for every terrible thing that had ever happened in the world. The truth suddenly dropped into place. Urna did not merely steal the rahvek. She drank it. She must have seen all of this, along with a thousand other futures, and this was the only way to stop what was happening.

Creek descended on Urna first. The others followed. Snarling, Urna fought back. She was no omega. Those days were over and would never return. Mag yelped as Urna bit into his leg. The others tried to get hold of her, but she proved too slippery, too strong.

The scrum moved deeper into the aisle. The three intruders retreated, unsure of what was happening.

"Mercy," Augur said.

She rushed to him. His blood-soaked hands pried the lever from his chest. She motioned to help, but he shook his head no.

"Get your son," Augur said. "Now."

With Urna still holding her own against four marauders, the two dogs and the cat were trapped on the other side of the battle. They knew where Mercy would go next. The wet nurse led them toward the exit in the rear. They would get to the engine from the outside.

Mercy bolted through the door, stepping across the gap and onto the locomotive. Inside, she followed a narrow hallway, with plastic walls that hummed with the sound of the engine. A set of bloody pawprints on the linoleum floor showed Urna's path from the control room. A small flight of steps led to the compartment at the very front of the train, where a set of windows wrapped around the face of the car. Beneath that, the controls spread from one side of the compartment to the other in a giant horseshoe shape, covered in buttons, knobs, switches, dials, and levers. Seated at the controls, one of the Toqwa women leaned against the head rest, her ponytail flipped over the front of her deerskin tunic. Blood dribbled from a puncture wound in her neck. Her red hands indicated that she must have tried to stanch the flow before passing out.

Mercy found the pup shivering at the human's feet. She crawled over to him, nudged her paws beneath his body, and rested her snout on his spine. She knew then that he must have hated her the way that only a child can hate a parent. She had dragged him through too much, all while telling him to be grateful that he had not seen what she had seen. It was the same mistake every generation made with the young ones.

*Please*, she wanted to say. *Please, it's almost over. Trust me.*

Something heavy slammed onto the nose of the locomotive. Mercy scooped the child away from the control panel. A pair of hairy feet stood outside the window. Their owner leaned down, peering inside the cabin. It was a dog, a brown mutt, holding a rifle. A gunshot forced him to take cover against the hull. He fired a few times in response. More dogs surrounded the engine.

The brown dog rapped his knuckles against the window. "Come on!" he said. "We're leaving, come on!" He pointed to a sealed door to her right. She turned the knob and it creaked open. A breeze blew a puff of smoke inside. The pup squirmed in her arms, demanding to stay inside amid the shouting and gunfire.

Mercy stepped out and dropped nearly two feet. The train had almost made it to the stone slab of the train station, maybe a quarter of a mile away. Here, the tracks cut through an abandoned railyard, an expanse of palm-sized granite rocks, rotting wooden beams, and stubborn stalks of grass poking toward the sun. Old train cars rusted on the parallel tracks. She had never visited a city before and would probably never set foot in one ever again. All the right angles, all the metal and glass, plastic and paint. Her siblings told her to fear this place, but the sight only made her angry. The humans cut this land from the forest, and the forest would reclaim it, one way or the other.

As Mercy exited the car, a group of dogs formed a phalanx around her. Across the railyard, a trio of human soldiers exchanged fire with them from behind the rusted hulk of a boxcar. A bullet grazed the top of the train. One of the dogs grabbed Mercy's shoulder and forced her to kneel so they could shield her.

"Get ready to run," the dog said.

A fleet of pickup trucks rumbled through the railyard, each with machine guns mounted in the rear. While the gunners provided cover, the lead vehicle wheeled beside Mercy. The dogs hustled her into the pickup as more gunfire erupted, this time from a concrete barrier that sealed the railyard from the highway beside it. One of the dogs slumped onto her shoulder. The pup cried. He batted his paws against the dead soldier until Mercy shrugged the dog away.

Once inside the pickup, she let out a desperate howl, the signal she used when she needed her bodyguards to protect her. Despite the deafening noise, three wolves tumbled out of the passenger car: Creek, Mag, Quick. Carsa came last, carrying Augur on her back. There was no sign of Urna. Mercy did not wish to know either way.

The wolves raced to the pickup. Once they got on board, they lifted Augur and dropped him so that his head landed in Mercy's lap. She slid her arm across his chest and took hold of his bloody hand. He closed his eyes, in great pain but fighting through it.

One of the dogs pounded on the roof, ordering the driver to accelerate. Carsa leapt onto the pickup halfway, and the others pulled her aboard. Suddenly, her spine went stiff. She tried to yelp but only gurgled. With her eyes fixed on Mercy, the old wolf tumbled out of the pickup as the driver sped away.

"I'm sorry," Augur said, his eyes still closed. His mind was right again. And so he saw all of this before it happened.

Running after them, the wet nurse and the husky barked and hollered. A cloud of dust billowed across the railyard, hiding the attackers from Mercy's sight.

# CHAPTER 25

## THE SNAKE

ALKIRK RAN ALONGSIDE the stalled train. The truck carrying his son gathered speed, blasting a plume of oily exhaust in his face. When it hit a bump, the vehicle bounced like a child's toy rolled across an uneven carpet. After clearing the train, the truck swerved onto the tracks, its massive tires rolling over the wooden beams. One way or the other, this would lead the wolves to Mudfoot territory. They would shoot their way out of this trap and leave their weapon behind.

More trucks rolled past him. One of the rear gunners shouted, "Get on!" while sticking out his hand. In the confusion, these Mudfoot loyalists assumed that every dog here was on their side. Falkirk realized then that Mort(e) had disappeared, which may have saved their lives. As the last truck passed, a spray of bullets pinged off the side of the train. Human soldiers emerged from their hiding spots, behind empty train cars, concrete barriers, metal switchboxes.

Realizing they were caught in the middle of a street battle, the two dogs ducked beneath the train and fled to the other side of the railyard, racing down the grassy hill toward the river, where a barbed-wire fence prevented them from going any farther. The bullets found them again, splashing the dirt and pebbles a few feet away. Falkirk tucked into a ball and covered his head. They were pinned here, and their son had disappeared in a cloud of dust and smoke. Beside him, D'Arc lowered her head, looking too tired to cry. With as much tenderness as he could manage, Falkirk placed his hand on her shoulder and eased her below the cover of the hill.

She rested her head on her forearm. "I saw us saving him," she said. "I swear I saw it."

"I know you did," Falkirk said.

He searched for a way out. They could hop the fence and jump into the water, if it came to that. But on the other side, more fighting erupted in the old apartment buildings that had survived the war. Snipers blew out windows and picked off targets in the streets. Soldiers tried to position themselves on nearby rooftops to return fire. This was no coordinated attack. The word had spread to every canine with a grudge, every dog who saw the wolves as their true allies, every stray who remembered eating scraps before the war.

Ruiz was right. He had seen it all during the occupation. Despite all the dire warnings, the wolves would never invade. Instead, they would ask their sleepers in Hosanna to create havoc. They wouldn't need training—or even official orders. Just a whisper here, a nod there, a few signals in the night disguised as random howls. Those who rebelled to blow off steam would cause the same amount of damage as the zealots who wanted to live as wolves. The same thing must have happened on the *Vesuvius*. Ruiz may have survived the bullet wound only to die while defending the ship from traitors.

More soldiers swept in from the station to drive out any marauders who remained. Falkirk fumbled for his old Sanctuary Union identification badge. If he flashed it in time to the right person, he might live through this. But the soldiers racing to the railyard were young, all human. Red-faced, glistening with sweat despite the cold, with enormous eyes that rarely blinked. Falkirk knew the look.

He nudged D'Arc. They followed along the embankment, using the hill to hide their movement. They made it to a freight car that had been tipped onto its side and left in place for many years. The rust had eaten through the roof, and the smell of corroded metal wafted from the holes. Falkirk tried to see around the corner, but the smoke hung in the air, shrouding the chaos from the other side of the river.

"We have to get that bomb out of here," D'Arc said.

"I know," Falkirk said. "Do you see a way?"

"I'm trying." Her head jerked back and forth like someone watching a tennis match. He knew right away that she could see multiple scenarios in which they broke cover and tried to reach the train, each one ending in their deaths. "No," she finally said. "There's too many of them."

A break in the smoke revealed more soldiers swarming into the railyard. Two of them helped a wounded comrade, while several others checked under the stalled train for any stragglers. Another soldier knelt by a corpse, feeling the neck for a pulse.

"What if I tried talking to them?" Falkirk said.

Her face went blank. "It depends on what you say."

"Obviously!"

Again, she ran it through her head, all the scenarios that her mind could handle.

"Quickly," he urged her.

"Find the leader," she said. "Get their attention. Be kind. Speak slowly."

"That's it?"

"If I tell you more, it won't happen."

His heart lurched as he realized that D'Arc never told him *when* the bomb would detonate.

Two soldiers—young men with maybe half a chin between them—turned their attention to the overturned freight car. They split apart, taking opposite ends so they could corner whoever waited on the other side.

Falkirk wanted to ask D'Arc which one would give him a chance to speak. But there was no time left.

"Over here!" the human shouted.

"Sanctuary Union!" Falkirk said, emerging from behind the train car. "I'm with Sanctuary Union! Special Operations!" He held out his identification. The human aimed his rifle, ready to shoot a hole through the ID card. The man's visor tilted low over his dark eyes. He pressed the stock of the rifle against his freshly shaven cheek.

The other soldier rounded the corner. D'Arc remained still, letting her sword drop to her feet. Falkirk put his hands high over his head and slowly lowered to his knees.

"There's a bomb on that train!" he said. "We have to get it out of here!"

The man motioned with his rifle for Falkirk to drop the ID badge. He flicked it to the human. The badge landed right in front of the man's boot.

"What's the worst thing you can eat at the academy cafeteria?" the soldier said.

"Wouldn't know," Falkirk said. "I'm still alive."

The man lowered his rifle to his hip. With his face revealed, Falkirk could see the smooth skin around his eyes and mouth, not a wrinkle or a crease. So young, like so many of the human soldiers. Another child who knew nothing but war.

More of them arrived, led by a woman with two lieutenant's bars on her helmet. Given how this day had gone, she may have taken command a few minutes before, after the traitors killed her captain.

The lieutenant plucked the ID badge from the dirt.

*Be kind*, D'Arc had said.

"I don't care what you do to me," Falkirk. "But we have to get that train out of here."

She pocketed the card.

"It has the rahvek on it!" he said.

"The what?"

"Ask one of your commanders. They know what I'm talking about."

The humans whispered to one another. Despite their inexperience, they knew enough about animal hearing to keep their voices extremely low. Falkirk could hear their dry mouths clicking, and little else.

A tremor shook the gravel where Falkirk knelt. He checked on D'Arc, who remained calmly seated while a soldier aimed a rifle at her. But she must have felt it too.

About fifty feet behind the lieutenant and her men, the train began to move. Someone had disengaged the brakes, allowing the wheels to turn. The lieutenant must have sensed something but did not react until a few soldiers came running. "It's moving!" one of them shouted.

The engine kicked on, grinding the wheels against the rails. The lieutenant ordered her soldiers to pursue—though she clearly had no idea what they could do to stop it.

"Let it go!" Falkirk said.

An abandoned truck sat on the rails, blocking the train's path. Despite its slow speed, the engine struck the vehicle with horrific force. The truck twirled out of the way, its tires bending on their axles, the hood crumpled against the windshield. One of the soldiers raced to the flatbed and hung on to the side. Thinking better of it, he jumped off and tumbled in the gravel. After clearing the platform at the station, the train descended into a tunnel that led under the city like a snake retreating into its lair.

A soldier ran to the lieutenant, saluting awkwardly. She

twirled her fingers in a signal that meant *get on with it.* "It was a cat!" the soldier said.

"A what?" the lieutenant asked.

"A cat was driving the train!"

D'Arc snickered. It unnerved the man who guarded her. "It's your messiah," she said. "You saw him."

The man pursed his lips in embarrassment. "I mean . . . he was the same color, but . . ."

"So it's true," D'Arc said.

"What's true?" the lieutenant asked.

"The prophecy. Your messiah has finally come to save you."

# CHAPTER 26

## SARCOPHAGUS

**T**HE TRAIN EMERGED from the tunnel, somewhere to the south of the city. The throttle pointed to the front of the control panel. A quivering dial showed the speed topped out at seventy miles per hour.

The woman who once drove the train remained in her seat, facing the ceiling, her neck opened like a second mouth. Mort(e) wiped his hand across her face to close her eyes—not out of kindness, but because they seemed to follow him around the cockpit.

He went to the side window to watch the city as it fell behind. He hoped to spot the dam, but it was too far away. He could only imagine Castor and the rest of the beavers rebuilding once again. Maybe they would write a new song about the crazy cat they once knew. At the Grumpy Beaver, they would belt out the Ballad of Sebastian while slapping their tails and spilling their Lodge City Specials on the floor.

As the train crested a hill overlooking the forest, a new country spread out before him, the same as every other territory conquered and reconquered since the war began. As he did in his youth, he leaned against the glass and marveled at the world that awaited him if he dared to find it. He could rename this place if he wanted. Might as well. One day, some other warrior would come stomping through to rename it once again.

But what to call it? His only brush with creativity had come when he decided on his own name. And that was only because he could hardly spell. The Sarcops words bouncing around in his brain could barely be pronounced, let alone painted on a sign. So he went through the names of people he knew. "Sheba" was too on the nose, even for him. The other members of the Red Sphinx came to mind. Maybe Tiberius. Or Culdesac. Right, that made sense.

"Dead end," he said, tapping the dead woman on the shoulder. "What do you think of that?"

He leaned on the control panel as the train entered the forest, where the tree limbs scratched the sides of the engine, their tips bursting with green buds. In another few weeks, the leaves would sprout to drink in the sunlight. New life that he would not see. If he timed it right, maybe a tree would grow on the spot where he finally lay on the grass and went to sleep for good.

With that depressing thought, the taste of saltwater returned. *Of course*, he thought. *They let him enjoy the view long enough. It was time.*

He followed the scent to the rear of the engine room and into the first passenger car. His foot squished in a patch of blood on the carpet, now cold and beginning to stick. From there, the red streak in the aisle showed where the wolves dragged their human friend out of danger. Claw marks tore open the seats, and the foam stuffing spilled out like organs. To his right, the female wolf with the patchy fur lay on her side, bleeding out from multiple wounds. An omega if he ever saw one. Her rib cage rose and fell, and a tear bubbled in her eye. She lacked the energy to blink it away. In the darkness of her pupil, that tiny black spot, Mort(e) recognized the permanent gaze into the unknown. She had stepped outside of time, like he had. Anyone who dipped a toe in that whirlpool found themselves carried off in it, circling again and again past the same set of events before finally going under.

She wheezed. He wanted to give her water, but he had none. Her thirst became his. And surely she could taste the salt building in his mouth, adding to her misery.

"The human," she said, her voice struggling. "The human was right."

"You're certain?"

"I see it," she said. "Like . . . Augur did. I see the wolf queen. And her prince. And . . . peace."

The train wobbled. The wolf groaned as her weight shifted. Mort(e) reached out and held her hand. The saltwater in his mouth drained away for a few seconds, replaced with the scent of a fertile deer running for her life. Like a ripe fruit hopping through the forest. Another chance to live for this tired, broken wolf and her pack, now long gone.

"I see you," she said. "In the . . . tomorrow."

"I doubt that."

"You will be reborn."

"Oh, you're one of those."

"No." She struggled. "You happy again. In the time you have left. Like me."

Mort(e) could not say that he was happy. Then again, how would he know?

"Thank you," he said.

She acknowledged him with a blink. Her chest sank with one great exhale, and then did not rise again. Her hand slipped from his and rested on the floor.

Mort(e)'s ear twitched at a sound coming from his left. He turned to see the Sarcops looming over him, her tentacles slithering along the seats. Cracks had formed in her scales. She needed to get to the water.

A tentacle reached out and landed on his shoulder, then brushed his whiskers against his cheek. She spoke to him in her language. "Cross into the cold water," she said. The Sarcops had no words for *thank you*. But this was something better. It meant good fortune. For them, the frigid depths signaled food, life, safety, family. A chance to live.

Outside, the trees cleared away. A wide, blue expanse filled the windows as the train crossed a bridge. The Sarcops' gills flared out like a pair of hands opening. She turned and headed for the rear exit, her tentacles trailing behind her.

"Wait," Mort(e) said in their language. "I want to go with you."

The Sarcops ignored him. She stepped outside into the howling wind and straddled the gap between the two cars. A forty-foot drop would get her to the river.

"I want to go with you," he repeated.

The Sarcops turned to face him. "You are not a fish," she clicked.

Mort(e) tried to think of a snappy comeback.

"Stay," she said. "Be at peace."

Mort(e) lowered his gaze to the floor. "Peace," he said in English. "I'm not sure if I—"

She was gone. He ran to the doorway in time to see her splash into the river. The bridge ended, and the forest blocked the view, swallowing everything again.

He leaned on the doorframe for a while.

As the sun climbed over the trees, Mort(e) noticed a terrible stench. Not even the wind could disperse it. An unnatural decay, mingling human-made chemicals with decomposing plants. The trees thinned out to a random few, stunted and sickly. Shiny puddles dotted the ashen earth. This was the dead zone, the Damnable, the place that turned the wolves mad. A fitting place to die.

Mort(e) made his way to the flatbed car. As the last surviving member of this rolling sarcophagus, he made sure to reverently step over and around the fallen warriors clogging the aisle. He looked away from the ones who fell faceup. In death, lips would curl, gazes would wander. A tongue could pop out. No one should see them like that, no matter which side in this war they chose.

At the shattered passenger car, which had been reduced to a platform with a jagged wall, Mort(e) found an empty seat facing the rear. He sat and stared at the flatbed, where the trash truck swayed. The bomb inside would cause no damage out here. No way to kill what was already dead.

He leaned into the headrest and watched the sky. *A convertible train*, he thought. For all their ingenuity, how come the humans had never come up with that? D'Arc would have laughed at the idea, right before scolding him for asking something so ridiculous.

"Old *Man*," she'd say, dragging it out.

He heard her voice next to him, the breath tickling his ear.

Old Man.

Old Man.

Sebastian.

# PART V

# REVELATION

# CHAPTER 27

## AN EARLY SPRING

HEY PUT A muzzle on her, a device that Hosanna had supposedly outlawed in the name of peace and tolerance. Someone—most certainly a human—had made it from the hide of some poor soul, another violation of the law. The sharp edges cut into D'Arc's snout. The humans forgot many things from the days before the Change, but keeping dogs in their place never went away.

Two days had passed since Tranquility arrested D'Arc and Falkirk. After the train left, the soldiers did not believe her when she revealed her identity. She demanded that they contact Grissom, the former chief's assistant. The humans claimed that no such person existed.

It did not take long for them to recognize Falkirk. Before the *Vesuvius* disappeared over the Atlantic, it sent a warning to Hosanna about its captain going rogue. They took him away for questioning. It was the first time that D'Arc saw true fear in his blue eyes. His ears drooped. But he held himself together. "Don't worry," he told her with a trembling voice as they marched him away.

They used an empty trailer as a holding cell while they decided what to do with her. To keep her still, they tied a rope around her neck, and then connected it to her wrists and ankles, forcing her to sit with her head between her knees. With the doors closed, the light penetrated through the tiny gap in between, a single bright line from floor to ceiling. The inside smelled like fresh bread at first. By the end of the first day, when they fitted her for a muzzle, the scent had congealed at the top of her throat, like wet mud. The only relief came in the morning and at night, when a soldier opened the door and slid a tureen of bean soup toward her. After she finished, they would lead her by a rope to the side of the trailer, where she would relieve herself. It was then, while acting very much like a pet on a leash, that the hopelessness of it all crashed around her. Her son was gone, carried off to the same fate as all the others. As the rahvek wore off, a numbness trickled into her mind, draining into her muscles and bones, leaving her awake but trapped in a dream.

On the afternoon of the second day, the engine started. Inside the trailer, the noise sounded like a lion roaring. Officers shouted orders nearby. More engines switched on. She heard a heavy vehicle rumbling beside the truck, spewing a greasy exhaust that seeped through the gap in the door. After two days of waiting, something was finally happening.

The doors opened. The sunlight blinded her. Two men shoved Falkirk into the trailer and shut him inside. He wore a muzzle meant for a much smaller dog. The leather dug into his skin. His left nostril struggled to open as he breathed. With his hands and ankles bound, he fell onto his side. She wriggled over to him. With or without the muzzles, there was no need to speak. She held his cold hands, exhaling on them to make them warm again. After a while, his tail wagged, albeit with caution. He must have known. He must have figured out that she had ordered him to chase that train despite seeing him die in so many different versions of the future. Maybe they would talk about it someday. But as he lay here, the father of her last living child, she realized that she needed to keep this to herself. No, they would never speak of it. This secret, like so many others that made up a person's life, would lurk in the background. It would occasionally skim the surface before sinking once more. She would have to live with that.

The trailer began to move. D'Arc held herself in place while the vehicle did a U-turn and then exited onto a highway. More vehicles rode beside it, forming a convoy.

With the truck's tires purring underneath them, D'Arc cradled Falkirk's head on her lap, stroking the hair between his ears. She hummed the song of the beavers. After the first verse, he recognized it, and hummed along with her.

AT LEAST TWO hours passed before the convoy left the highway, moving single file through what must have been a narrow street. The asphalt ended at a lumpy dirt road, which rocked the trailer so much that D'Arc became nauseous. Finally, the vehicle stopped. The two dogs waited while the humans ran about barking orders, moving equipment. Troops marched in formation alongside the trailer.

Someone fiddled with the lock. Falkirk sat straight. The doors opened to a row of soldiers, all wearing gas masks with large glass goggles, like an insect's eyes. They pointed rifles at the two prisoners. One of them approached the rear bumper of the trailer. He outranked the others, judging from the chevron on his shoulder and the handgun on his belt. He motioned for D'Arc to get closer, and she scooted toward him. With a gloved hand, he plucked the St. Jude medal from her chest. The chain dug into her neck as he scrutinized the engraving.

As he let go, she at last recognized this human. The nametape on his chest read JACKSON—*Carl* Jackson, a field officer for Tranquility. He commanded the city's patrol units. The last time she saw him, he'd sported a goatee, with thick locs tied in a bun that dangled over his shoulders. He had since shaved his head and face, leaving his chin and scalp perfectly smooth.

"So," he said, his voice muffled. "One of you fell out of the sky. The other washed in with the tide. Is that right?"

He must have known that they couldn't answer.

"It's them," Jackson told the others. "That necklace used to belong to the Chief. She gave it to this dog."

The soldier beside him seemed genuinely disappointed to hear this.

"Now get those goddamn muzzles off them," Jackson said. One of his underlings handed him a pair of breathing filters. Jackson tossed them onto the deck of the trailer.

"We brought you here because you might be able to tell us what the hell is going on," he said.

The soldiers hurried to untie the two prisoners. When the muzzle came off, D'Arc opened and closed her mouth to regain feeling. She felt it when Falkirk pulled the contraption free, dropped it to the floor, and kicked it away. The straps left behind an imprint. She pushed past the soldiers and rubbed his face. He winced at first, but then lifted his tail to show that he was okay.

The humans led them outside onto a crumbling two-lane highway, where a row of troop transports and other vehicles were parked along the shoulder. The road cut through a barren, open space, an expanse of dirt the color of ash. The wind carried a lifeless scent, almost like wet concrete. A smattering of dead trees remained standing amid the wasteland that had once been a meadow. Others had collapsed, their trunks petrified, their roots clawing their way out of the broken earth. The wolves at the Mudfoot camp had warned her about this accursed place. Nothing would grow here. The poison in the water had killed off the children and the elderly. The grass had turned brown, then crumbled and blew away in the breeze. It was a forgotten country that gave birth to another war.

D'Arc and Falkirk followed the soldiers toward a defensive perimeter consisting of ditches and sandbag forts. More troops arrived to dig trenches and mount machine guns behind the barricades. In the middle, a green tent with a table inside served as a command post. For the first time since her arrest, D'Arc saw nonhumans among the soldiers, including a few dogs who passed sandbags to one another in a line. She wondered what they had to do to prove their loyalty.

The landscape elevated slightly. Near the top of the slope, the train tracks emerged from another clutch of dead trees before veering away over the hill. Here, the train had dislodged from the rails, moving too fast for the curve. It plowed through the earth, leaving a deep scar in the clay before coming to rest in a twisted heap.

D'Arc stopped when she saw it.

"Come on," Jackson said, waving her toward the tent.

She turned to Falkirk. The husky's jaw dropped.

The train cars were piled onto one another at odd angles. Bird patrols circled above, taking photos and scanning the area. Strangely, impossibly, a new forest had sprouted from the debris. Healthy trees, bustling with shiny green leaves, burst violently through the wreckage. The shattered train cars resembled hatched eggs, with the trees as their offspring. The explosion had scattered the rahvek throughout the soil, creating an oasis amid the wasteland.

And it was growing. D'Arc could feel the vibrations through the earth. Roots expanded underground, forming a spiderweb of cracks in a slow-moving tremor. A new ecosystem had grown within a matter of hours. The Colony held so much power. While the Mudfoot saw this power as a weapon and nothing more, a crazy cat with a death wish was able put it to better use.

"Old Man," she said.

Using stakes and yellow police tape, the soldiers marked off a trail from the perimeter to the crash site. Four people in bright white hazmat suits returned from the wreckage, walking single file, each carrying metal briefcases. One of them had a tail which bulged against the artificial fabric. As the group approached, the soldiers cleared out of the way.

"Collecting samples," Jackson said.

The four scientists disappeared into another trailer, some kind of mobile laboratory.

In the command tent, a private handed Jackson a piece of paper with an aerial photo of the crash site. He slapped it on the table beside another image taken an hour earlier.

"Come look at this," he said, waving them over. The image revealed the desolate landscape, with the train tracks to the north, the riverbank to the south. In the middle, the day-old forest bloomed like a desert flower.

"The device exploded first," Jackson explained. "About a mile from here. The train carried the chemical. Dusted the ground. Then it slipped the rails and landed here."

Falkirk leaned in closer, his finger tracing the outline of the new vegetation. "Is it . . . ?"

"Yes," Jackson said. "It's getting bigger."

He handed Falkirk a pair of binoculars.

"I'm told you took a really big risk to get on that train," Jackson said. "You're gonna tell me why."

D'Arc didn't know where to start.

"I'm asking you because Tranquility won't tell me," Jackson said.

Falkirk tried to take a stab at it. "It was a weapons program," he said. "I don't think it even had a name." He explained that the Toqwa got their hands on it, used it to disrupt the peace talks and divide the wolf packs.

"But what *is* it?" Jackson said. "What are we dealing with here?"

"It's a chemical passed down from the Queen," Falkirk said.

"Is it viral? Is it airborne?"

"It doesn't matter," D'Arc said.

Jackson squinted at her. His human underlings backed away as if she carried some contagion.

"What we're dealing with," she said, "is the Queen's way of making sure the war keeps going forever. She leaves her mark on us. It warps time and space. Draws people in until they start fighting over something that will only get them killed."

"You're saying she's, like, a ghost?" Jackson said. "She's haunting us from beyond the grave?"

He was close. But he wasn't quite right.

"She's a god," D'Arc said.

"So we're doomed to repeat things," Jackson said. "Tell me something I don't know."

She remembered what the Old Man told her about his encounter with the Sarcops.

"We *can* say no to her," D'Arc said. "We could always do that."

Jackson folded his arms as he pondered this. The bug-eyed goggles reflected the overcast light.

One of the bird patrols overhead squawked a few times. Jackson yanked the binoculars out of Falkirk's hands and stepped out of the tent. He tracked the birds' movement, then scanned the field beyond the wreckage.

"Sir!" someone shouted.

"I see it," Jackson said, sounding exhausted.

A row of dark forms appeared at the top of the hill. Marauders— both human and canine—poured over the ridge. In only a few seconds, they surrounded the wreckage, all while barking and howling. D'Arc had heard this pitch before. They taunted the soldiers, hopping about to give the illusion that they had no fear. While most of them walked on all fours, those who stood straight brandished their weapons, their full war paint, and their jewelry made of teeth and bones.

A cat in a machine gun nest turned to Jackson, desperate for the order to fire. His sharp ears poked over the top of his ill-fitting gas mask. But then his slit eyes fixated on something coming from the west, from behind them.

The bird patrols honked out a warning before darting off in the same direction, their feathers dropping like snowflakes.

Jackson lowered the binoculars.

"D'Arc," Falkirk said. "Are you all right?"

Her hands had balled themselves into fists. She couldn't breathe. The mask felt like a hand clamping her face, squeezing tighter and tighter until she tore it off and spiked it on the ground.

"No!" Falkirk said.

And as he retrieved the mask, he must have heard it too. A complete, perfect silence. The wolves had stopped howling.

D'ARC'S BODY SWAYS. Something carries her. She knows right away that she has fallen away from the field and its mysterious grove. She has tumbled out of the present and landed in the future again.

The brim of a straw hat blocks her vision. She lifts the brim. D'Arc straddles the thorax of an Alpha on a late summer day, with blazing heat, blinding sun, and dry grass everywhere. Ah, this is not the future. The past, then. Her past on the ranch, where she takes her herd for a daily walk. My ladies, she calls them, marching in single file, leaving the exact same tracks. Abdomens bobbing, antennae probing. None of it meant to be, all of it happening anyway.

She hears a scuffle somewhere in the rear of the herd. One of the older ants has tripped. She pulls the reins on Gai Den, her strongest. The ant stops, and the rest obey. She dismounts and races to the injured Alpha. On the insect's hide, a brand marks her as SUGAR. They're all named after the Old Man's friends from the war. This ant has long since passed her lifespan. Cracks have splintered through her exoskeleton. When D'Arc arrives, the antennae probe her. One of them has broken, leaving it shorter than the other.

Euthanizing these older ants typically requires two people. One to hold her, the other to deliver the killing strike—a sharp point at the base of the skull. Instant death. This one seems ready. Despite having no face, no expression, the ant's calm demeanor, her stillness, tells D'Arc what she needs to know. *It is okay. You have been good to me. It is time to rest.*

She has a knife. She can do it. Too far to call for the Old Man anyway. He has already warned her about Sugar. *Every season, more of them will leave us.* Still, she needs to wait. She needs to sit with Sugar, resting her head on the beast's armor.

A breeze rustles the leaves.

The herd waits.

The sun inches across the blue void.

D'ARC BLINKED. SHE knelt on the ground, propped forward on her hands. The St. Jude medal dangled below her nose. When her palms went numb from the cold mud, she knew she had returned to the present. For now.

The noise grew around her, filling in the silence. The soldiers took cover in their barricades and ditches. Pistol in hand, Jackson waved them on. His mouth moved, but D'Arc could not make out the exact words.

Something tugged at her arm. She managed to tilt her head to see Falkirk urging her to follow him. Her body felt so heavy. It still needed to catch up with the present.

"They're here," Falkirk said.

Before she turned, she already knew what she would see.

Cruising beneath the clouds, in a triangle formation so perfect it resembled an arrowhead, a group of flying Alphas approached, at least twenty strong and descending rapidly.

D'Arc wanted to call them a flock, but that wasn't right. A pack? A brood? There was no name for this. Their wings beat so fast that they became invisible, leaving only the sleek armor, like misshapen torpedoes.

"Quarantine!" one of the cats shouted. "It's a quarantine!"

"No," Jackson said. "Do not fire! Do *not* fire!"

"Hold your fire," another officer called out.

Jackson dropped his binoculars and aimed his handgun. Like so many other commanders in so many other wars, he took a guess and immediately doubted it. D'Arc could not blame him.

Falkirk shielded her body with his. He faced her because he could not bear to look at them.

The Alphas passed right over, their wings buzzing in D'Arc's ear. A breeze followed, so strong that it nearly knocked Falkirk on top of her. The rifles pivoted to follow the insects as they headed for the train. There, the smarter wolves had already broken into a run, while the ones with something to prove, the ones with so little to lose, barked in defiance. They thought they were protecting some newly conquered territory. But here, *they* became the trespassers on land that was more than sacred, more than holy. The lead Alpha picked out the loudest canine—not even a wolf, but a brown dog—and landed on top of him. D'Arc felt his bones snap.

The Alphas cut through the pack. They snatched the fiercest marauders, the same ones who'd fought their way out of Hosanna. The wolves' pack mentality worked against them here. They tried to flank the Alphas like they would with any prey. But the ants would shake them off, then pin them with their jaws. With a quick thrashing motion, the ants broke their enemies, leaving them as furry bags of blood and shattered bone.

The markings on the ants' skin gave them away. These were D'Arc's Alphas. The rahvek had called them to become like their true mother, the Queen.

"My God," Falkirk breathed in D'Arc's ear.

One of the wolves in full battle gear charged at them with a scimitar. His blade came to a dead stop on an Alpha's hide. As he lifted the sword again, the ant coiled and struck him like a viper, leaving a bright red gash from the wolf's chest to his hip. Another strike. The ant clamped the wolf at the neck and shook her head violently. The sword flipped through the air and sank into the earth blade-first, the hilt wobbling.

It was that image—of a primitive weapon torn from their enemy—which prompted a wild cheer from the soldiers of Hosanna. They lowered their rifles and pumped their fists. In a show of loyalty, the dogs made the most noise, letting out a howl to match the primate-like hooting of the humans.

"How do you like it?" a human shouted. "How do you like it now?"

"Give that ant a hug!" someone said. "She wants to play with you!"

It had finally happened. The Mudfoot had gone too far, and Nature had corrected them. It must have felt so good for the humans to see this. They must have believed that they earned this somehow. The tables had finally turned. "That's what you get!" someone said.

With Falkirk's help, D'Arc stood. The ants continued to swarm, picking off the marauders. A few armed wolves opened fire from the edge of the field, but it drew the insects' attention. The ants made the snipers regret it.

"Our son's out there," D'Arc said.

Falkirk let go of her and walked toward the perimeter, right behind a wall of sandbags. A row of soldiers cheered on the ants each time they dispatched another wolf. Like a human at the end of his rope, Falkirk ran his fingers along his scalp as he watched the carnage. He had told D'Arc about his own experience with the quarantine—about a feeling of helplessness, of inevitability as a force he could not control tore apart everything he knew.

Falkirk turned to her, extending his arms, ready to embrace her and shield her from all of this. Such a sweet dog.

D'Arc did not have time for any of that. She ran past him, shoved the soldiers out of the way, and vaulted over the barricade. The laughter and the cheering faded behind her as she raced across the field, so fast that she floated over the earth.

# CHAPTER 28

## ALLEGIANCE

**ITH THE PUP** riding on her back, Mercy tried to shake Augur awake. The human lay on a pallet made from deerskin and two polished branches. A blanket of bear hide kept him warm. His eyes danced beneath his lashes. Despite all the screaming around them and the barely healed wound in his chest, she had never seen him so calm. He must have dreamt of someplace far from here. Or some time far removed, or a time that could never be, a path long since covered over.

She nudged him again with her snout and whined in his ear. One of the flying monsters streaked overhead. The pup began to cry. Mercy couldn't believe it had taken him this long. The marauders had formed a protective wall around her, but it would not hold. And for every wolf that tried to fight them off, there were two or three more who remained still, paralyzed by their fear of these demons. The most vicious predator could behave like prey when confronted with a creature that showed no remorse.

Creek and Mag appeared at her side, both panting. Creek jumped around in a panic, hoping this would stir Mercy to run.

Mercy snapped her jaws a few inches from Augur's face. The man awakened. He grinned upon seeing the pup.

Mercy grabbed his collar and pulled him upright so he could witness it all: the monsters dropping from the sky, the shattered bodies, the wounded trying to limp away. She expected his lip to curl and his brow to knit, a sign of distress that their species shared. Instead, his face softened with relief.

"You see *this* coming?" Mercy demanded.

He leaned on her shoulder as he got to his feet. As the wolves ran away from the slaughter, Augur moved forward, arms outstretched. For two days, they had dragged him to their territory as he teetered on the edge of death. Mercy thought she had lost him, that his spirit would drift into the woods and rejoin his people. But here, the human swaggered as he did when she first met him.

One of the creatures swooped above. Augur's tunic flapped in the breeze. The insect hovered in front of him, its abdomen pulsating. Someone had burned a marking into the ant's skin, a word in the human language. Each ant wore its own unique brand, though Mercy could not read them.

The head tilted. Was it afraid? Did it recognize him?

Creek yipped in Mercy's ear. *Please*, he was saying. *Run away!* But the same force that drew in this human called to her as well. She had tasted this same power. So much suffering had brought her to this barren field. She needed to know what it could really do.

Two more of the ants stopped attacking, hanging suspended around Augur. He became a planet with three misshapen moons orbiting, his gravity pulling them closer. A fourth and fifth joined while the other insects flew high above.

Mercy stayed outside of the circle. The pup tightened his grip on her shoulders. She brushed him with her cheek to keep him calm. He squirmed, feeling like a sack filled with warm water. She realized too late that he wanted out of the backpack in which she carried him. Before he slid face-first into the dirt, she caught him by the neck with her jaw. When he responded by scratching her, she squeezed harder, compressing his scream into a growl. Her own mother had done this to her. All the young ones needed to learn the hard way, and it could take longer for this half-dog.

Still, he insisted on getting away. His tiny hand reached toward the swirling mass of insects surrounding Augur. The ants revolved around the human faster now, creating a whirl-pool of dust. And through blurring bodies, Mercy saw the bright white fur of the wet nurse. While the wolves retreated, this dog ran toward her on two feet. She was afraid, like all Hosanna's pets. Yet she kept putting one foot in front of the other. Her dog friend, the fake wolf, chased after her, shouting her name, some-thing Mercy had never learned. "Dark, wait!" he said. He slipped the gas mask from his snout and gazed at the flying creatures.

All of the ants formed a cloud around Augur. Mercy felt the crowd gathering behind her. A few of the wolves could not help but lower to the ground in a show of submission.

When Augur turned to face the two intruders, the cloud turned with him. And with each step he took, the swarm lurched along, as if connected by strings to his outstretched hands. The wet nurse backed away.

Augur lowered his arms. He gave the wet nurse a chance to contemplate her last few seconds in this world. To her credit, she seemed ready. The soldiers from Hosanna waited behind their barricades, unwilling to intervene.

In a quick jerking movement, Augur stretched out his hands toward the dog. All at once, the ants flew at her, like stones tossed from the top of a hill. They landed in front of her, forming a wall at first, then piling on top. A dome of insect bodies grew, the abdomens writhing.

"No!" the husky screamed. He grabbed the nearest ant's leg and tried to wrench it free from the pile. The creature snapped its hindquarters like a whip and flung him away. He landed hard and skidded across the dirt. On his stomach, the pathetic dog watched in horror as this mobile colony executed the spy from Hosanna. He must have known that they would come for him next.

Their hunger satiated, the ants on top climbed down from the pile. Like the mouth of some massive animal, the dome opened, revealing the space where the dog had waited for death. A furry body lay on the ground, amid the tracks left by the insect's claws. The husky moaned when he saw it.

The body moved. The dog had curled herself into a ball. And now she rose, surrounded by her would-be executioners.

One by one, the ants lifted off and flew in Augur's direction. Shaking, he held out his palms, ordering them to stop. They continued past him.

They were coming for Mercy.

And suddenly, the wolves who had gathered around her dispersed. She and the pup stood alone. Strangely, the young one stopped crying. As she cradled him, he bounced in her arms and reached out to the creatures, these demons with hinges for mouths. The first landed to Mercy's right, the second behind her. The pup gave a friendly bark. *Hello*, he said. He had no idea what they could do.

One of the ants lifted onto its hind legs and clamped its claws onto the pup.

"Please," Mercy said. As if the monster would understand.

The ant pulled the dog from her grip. She did not fight, as a wolf should. As a wolf *would*, if this pup really were her son. And every canine here saw it. Every wolf who renounced their pack, every dog who defected from Hosanna. They saw her simply let go of the future of the Mudfoot.

She waited for the ant to end it. The insect probed her, its antennae grazing her neck. The jaw opened and closed. Then the ant held the pup tight to its thorax, fluttered its wings, and lifted high above her. The others followed, leaving a dusty breeze behind them.

*Your name is Mercy,* Wex had told her. *For that is what I give you.*

The swarm once again flew past Augur. For all his power and prophecy, he was nothing to them now.

The ant landed before the wet nurse. Gently, it handed the pup to the dog. The young one curled against her and plugged his mouth onto one of her teats, his eyes closed. While the pup drank, the dog licked his head, letting out a satisfied moan each time.

"I know," the wet nurse said. "I know."

Still in shock, the husky stumbled over to her. He wrapped an arm around her neck and stroked the pup's fur. Mercy saw it now: a real family, born from this madness.

The wolves, hundreds of them now, left Mercy's side to surround the wet nurse named Dark. Even the Bounty warriors, covered in green war paint, lowered their snouts to the earth. The only one who remained at her side was Augur, the defeated human.

Dark marched over with the husky following and the ants flying above, ready to strike.

Augur got closer to Mercy. He placed his hand on her shoulder. She shrugged it off. She wanted to face this dog on her own.

Dark stood before her like a human, taller than Augur. She cradled the young one against her chest. "Run away," she said. "Both of you. Run away and never come back."

The pup glared at her, then returned to his suckling.

A chorus of barking began. The dogs who had worshipped her as a god now snarled and paced about, marking a boundary she could no longer cross. She searched the crowd for her bodyguards. They were gone. The Toqwa as well.

The barking grew louder. As she started to walk away, her toe brushed something. Lifting her foot, she saw a flower with bright yellow petals stubbornly pushing out of the clay.

*Keep going!* the barking said.

These were urna flowers, her sister's namesake, like little suns bursting from the ground. She sniffed for more of them, and their sweet smell invaded her nostrils, so thick that she sneezed. Dozens of the flowers had sprouted, reclaiming the dead earth. And mocking her while they did it.

"This is what you saw?" she asked Augur.

"I told you," he said. "I saw the land at peace. And I saw spring. This is the spring we were promised."

She looked toward her homeland for the last time. The hills had shaded over with green. A new forest stretched its roots, lifting the dead soil. This time, she let Augur place a hand on her shoulder. He was still with her. That part of the prophecy remained perfectly clear.

The wolf and the man turned to the west. Toward the real future.

# CHAPTER 29

████████ ██ ████████████

# DÉTENTE

*(UNOFFICIAL) LOGBOOK OF THE SUS AL-RIHLA*
*MARCH 25*
<u>*WEATHER*</u>*: OVERCAST.*

*DAY 2 OF EXPEDITION.*
<u>*0600*</u> *BROKE CAMP. PROCEEDING TO DESTINATION AT N 39 40*
*53.1. W 075.*

"ARE YOU READY?" Falkirk asked.

D'Arc could not yet answer. And anyway, the answer was no. It would always be no.

Having hacked their way through the woods, they emerged onto an exit ramp of a highway. According to the signpost, the humans had given this road the number 495. The three wolves who escorted them this far promised that the bridge would appear around the bend. And so it did: a flat concrete platform, bleached white under the sun. The brown water underneath flowed so slowly that one could have mistaken the river for a lake. Steel towers that once held electrical wires guarded either side like the skeletons of enormous beasts.

In the middle of the bridge, the representatives from the

Sanctuary Union waited. Over a month had passed since the attack, and they chose this spot to talk peace once more. D'Arc and her party made it on time. The Hosanna delegation had arrived early. She wondered if this constituted some psychological tactic on their part.

Three wolves of the Opa pack marched in front of D'Arc so the Hosanna delegation could see their full war paint and jewelry. Swords dangled from their hips; long rifles bounced on their shoulders. Quay—the wolf who saved D'Arc's life once—took the lead, wearing the silvery feather of a patrol bird in her fur. Another wolf displayed a necklace that included the jawbone of an adult boar, a prize meant to intimidate other marauders.

The Archon himself stood in the middle of the Hosanna delegation. The wind rippled his black gown. His long white hair bounced stiffly in the breeze. With his thin fingers interlaced at his waist, he resembled a clergyman at the steps of his temple, welcoming the flock inside.

Jackson lurked behind him, wearing a camouflage uniform. D'Arc realized that she did not get the chance to see the man's face in their last encounter. Without his gas mask, he seemed older than she remembered, thanks to the white whiskers on his chin. Upon seeing the marauders, he rubbed his trigger finger against the pad of his thumb, centimeters from his sidearm. A soldier to the last.

Representatives of other species joined them. D'Arc recognized Grissom, the silent feline. He gave no indication that he recognized her, which strangely felt right. A German shepherd and a stag eyed her, though the deer acted uninterested. He impatiently clicked his hoof on the asphalt.

Two smaller, furry creatures stood off to the side: Gaunt the bat, wearing wraparound goggles, and Castor the beaver, squatting with his tail flat behind him. Hosanna certainly could have done worse than these people. But D'Arc got the feeling that the delegation brought along her old friends to remind her of what was at stake for this meeting. As if she, of all people, did not know.

A row of troop transport vehicles blocked the other side of the bridge. The soldiers formed a line across, holding their rifles diagonally across their chests.

For a few seconds, the river gurgling around the pillars of the bridge provided the only sound.

"Are you injured?" Jackson asked D'Arc.

"No."

"And your son?"

"He's safe."

Jackson nodded. "But are you . . . okay?"

"I'm not being kept against my will, if that's what you're asking."

The delegation stirred.

"As for the rahvek," she added, "I don't know yet what it will do to me."

"We have doctors who can help," Jackson said.

"There are more pressing matters."

"Indeed," the Archon said, his voice surprisingly deep for such a weathered man. "I need to know if you speak for the wolves. For all the wolf packs surrounding Hosanna."

"I speak for now," D'Arc said. "Jackson, you saw it."

"I did," Jackson said.

After Jackson had ordered the retreat from Mudfoot territory, the wolves gave D'Arc a new title: Aneega. It literally meant water, but they used it to mean Protector, Life-Giver. Pack leaders who took in strays often earned this title. D'Arc insisted that her leadership would last only a brief time. At the next ken-ra, a council of wolves would take over. A generous wolf is a strong wolf, she often heard.

"Why, though?" the Archon asked. "Why take this on?"

"You tell me," D'Arc said. "It's your prophecy."

A hint of a smile appeared on the man's face.

"Think of what would have happened if I hadn't done it," she added. "That should answer your question."

She let that stew for a few seconds. All their prophecies of the Warrior saving them and the Mother sheltering them had come true. What more could they want?

"There will be no more attacks," D'Arc said. "There will be peace. But only if we earn it."

"Let's get to your demands, then," the Archon said.

"The border stays where it is," she said. "We keep Camp Echo and the Northern Reservoir. You took those in the occupation. The wolves are simply taking them back. You know they're not worth fighting over."

The Archon folded his arms, making his hands disappear into his baggy sleeves. She took this as consent.

"The Mudfoot took in too many people," D'Arc said. "More than a pack can handle. We sent some west. If they want to live as true wolves, they can do it elsewhere. As for the rest: you should pardon them. Let them return."

"That I cannot do," the Archon said. "They betrayed us."

D'Arc turned to Falkirk.

"We understand that," he said. "But we also understand that your electrical plant needs to be rebuilt. Along with the ship-yard. The beavers can't fix all of it."

Being a good beaver, Castor of course could never admit such a thing. But they all knew it was true.

"Let the dogs return," Falkirk said. "They can help rebuild. Let them earn your trust."

"Still not good enough," the Archon said. "It's a generous offer, but I owe it to our people to keep them safe."

"I'll go," Falkirk said. "And I can bring at least a hundred with me. If it goes well, more will come."

The Archon fidgeted with his collar as he considered the

offer. It meant something to have the captain of the *Vesuvius* join in the reconstruction. Falkirk convinced D'Arc of this a few days before. A penance, he called it. For abandoning his post. The husky's sense of honor had remained intact through all of this.

"One season," Falkirk said.

"The defectors can return," the Archon said. "As for the known murderers and saboteurs—they're wolves now, as far as I'm concerned. They can't come back."

D'Arc agreed that this made sense. The angriest dogs would have no interest in helping Hosanna rebuild anyway. In seven days' time, the workers would gather at the border so that Tranquility could identify them and let them into Sanctuary Union territory.

Once she worked out the details, D'Arc glanced at Falkirk. This was really happening. She'd left him nearly a year before. Now he would leave her, though he promised to return.

"I must say something unpleasant," D'Arc said. "It would be unfortunate if the father of my child had some kind of accident during his time in Hosanna."

"He won't," the Archon said. "I'm not letting your dogs into the city just to start another fight."

There was more to discuss. More trades. Hosanna agreed to send farmers into wolf country to show the hunters how to grow crops they could eat. In the meantime, the wolves would purchase carcasses from the morgue in exchange for the highly prized pelts of fallen marauders. It was a ghoulish trade that would nevertheless keep the peace. Meanwhile, the wolves would let Tranquility restore their communication towers in the formerly occupied territories. If the bears or any other species attempted an invasion, the wolves would act as a buffer, and they would warn Hosanna immediately. An armistice now could lead to a much-needed alliance in the future, should the situation arise. For all the hope bound in this summit, the world remained a cruel place. Old enemies would have to trust each other—or at least pretend they did.

Those were the easy parts. The Archon saved the most difficult question for last.

"The ants," he said. "I have to ask."

"They've already built a hill," D'Arc said. "Digging out tunnels. But you knew that."

"And you expect us to take your word for it that they're not dangerous," the Archon said. "That they're simple farmers. Like us."

"That's right. Because that's how I raised them."

"You told Jackson that the Queen wanted the fighting to go on forever."

"The Queen has no say in this," D'Arc said. "Send your scientists if you must. Observe. Do some studies. But do not interfere. The only way we break this cycle is by learning to live together. That is what victory will look like."

"Put yourself in my position," the Archon said. "I have to go back to Hosanna and explain to people why I trust you."

"You trusted her when you used her as a prop," Falkirk said. Everyone turned to him. "You asked everyone to believe in the prophecy about the Warrior and the Mother. And now you can't do it yourself."

"You think *this* is the prophecy?"

"It's better," Falkirk said. "She's still the person Michael said she'd be. But now you have to share. With the wolves and the ants."

The Archon must have liked this explanation, though he did not say it. Instead, he approached D'Arc. Quay tapped the hilt of her cutlass, but then thought better of it and remained still.

"Walk with me," the man said.

The two delegations waited while the Archon led her to the edge of the bridge. They leaned their elbows on the guardrail. To her surprise, this man of God pulled out a cigarette, most likely hand-rolled by beavers. Shielding it with his palm, he struck a match, lit the tip, and inhaled. His fingers trembled in ecstasy. He must have loved a nice smoke before the war. She knew then that this thankless job had been thrust upon him. When he offered her a puff, she gently declined.

"I appreciate what you did," the Archon began. "Without a leader, the wolves would have split apart again. We'd be right back where we started."

"Yes."

"But I have to tell you," the man continued. "A lot of our generals want us to roll the dice. Invade wolf country again. Because they think you're bluffing. Or you're simply wrong."

"I might be."

He took a knowing drag on his cigarette. "You might be. But if this is our best chance for peace, then I have to give it a shot. Even if the warmongers don't like it."

He tapped the cigarette with his thumb. Ashes broke from the tip and floated toward the water. "Do you think that one day, we can get along without the threat of annihilation?"

"No," she said. The Archon raised his bushy eyebrows. "Not us, I mean," she added. "It's too late for our generation. But maybe our children will get it right."

The Archon smiled. "That reminds me," he said. "Did you give your son a name?"

"Rev."

He squinted at her. "Is that short for something?"

"Revelation."

The Archon laughed uneasily. "Hey, why not?" he said.

His cigarette had burned to a nub. He flicked it, sending it end over end into the water. "Maybe our children *will* get it right."

He placed a hand on her arm, long enough for her to feel the warmth in his palm. It was his human way of saying that he believed her.

"Before we leave, my friends have something to give you," the Archon said. He gestured toward the others, and they walked over.

Gaunt spread his wings to reveal a long, narrow object wrapped in cloth, pressed against his chest. Castor took it and handed it to her. She unwound the fabric to find the scabbard of her sword underneath. When she pulled the blade free, it emerged polished and sharpened, brighter than the day she found it.

"Thank you," she said. "Your mother . . ." She realized that she did not know what to say.

"I know," Castor said. "Gaunt told me all about it."

She clipped the sword to her belt. "The Old Man," she said. "He was grateful for what you did. And he was sorry."

"It's all right. I understand now."

"Your nephew. Did he . . . ?"

"He'll live."

A weight slipped from D'Arc's shoulders. She gazed at the forest, the Old Man's burial ground. He was everywhere, in all the ditches and streams, the roots and the soil. She wanted to believe that this place could hear Castor's words and find some peace. The forest answered with a strong breeze. Gaunt pulled in his wings to brace himself. He must have felt it.

"Seven days," D'Arc announced. "Our dogs will leave from Camp Echo. You can escort them into Hosanna from there."

The Archon's fingers nervously twirled a cigarette that was no longer there. "We'll be ready. Good luck to you."

"Good luck to *us*," D'Arc said.

As she headed for the tree line, Quay and the other guards gathered in formation around her. The muscles in her chest loosened. She could breathe normally again. Diplomacy could be more frightening than warfare, but she would learn.

Something brushed her tail. It was Falkirk, playing with her tail like a dog would, to let her know that things would be all right. The stern guards tried to ignore him. D'Arc was still mad at Falkirk for suggesting this compromise with Hosanna, which would take him away for months. All the same, she used her tail to playfully swat his hand away.

# CHAPTER 30

━━━━━━━━━━━━  ■  ━━━━━━━━━

## UNDAUNTED

FALKIRK PUT ON his welding gloves. Before him lay the starboard hull of a freighter, an enormous hunk of metal lying flat on the shipyard dock. The bolts had been removed, and the supports had been severed with cutting torches. A row of heavy trucks had joined together to drag the piece free from the sunken ship and onto the dock, using the largest chains that Falkirk had ever seen. Once the hull was in place, water spilled from the sides, pouring out of the divots and flooding the shipyard.

"Torches," someone shouted. The overseers repeated it. "Torches! Torches!"

The dogs formed a line at the edge of the hull. One hundred and six dogs stayed at this camp alone—a penance camp, as the Archon called it—each hoping to earn their way back into Hosanna again. In the guard towers overlooking the shipyard, soldiers watched them with binoculars, their rifles ready in case the torches gave the dogs any ideas.

Falkirk motioned for Angel, a young pit bull who slept in the bunk beside him. On days when they removed a big piece from the water, Angel acted as Falkirk's assistant. Here, the young ones would learn from those with more experience. Older dogs like Falkirk would set a good example so they would not be led astray again. While Angel handed over his blowtorch and goggles, Falkirk staked out a spot near the corner of the hull. He cranked the knob on the torch until a sharp blue flame formed at the spout. It took only a few seconds for the flame to make the metal glow red hot. Once it reached a shade of bright orange, Falkirk moved the torch in a wide arc, slicing away the hull into a smaller chunk. When he finished, the piece fell away and hit the concrete with a pinging sound that echoed off the wall of the old customs house. Angel pulled the metal away and slid it behind him, where other dogs collected it and loaded it onto a truck.

The row of cutter dogs acted like termites chewing away at a piece of wood. Orange sparks shot out from their torches. The air shimmered with the rising heat, and Falkirk, having the thickest coat, began to pant. In another hour, the sun would crown over the skyline, making the work even more difficult. He would fight his way through. Every piece of metal they hauled away represented progress and another step closer to home. To D'Arc. To his son.

This was day thirty-nine of his penance. Finally, he had to do something besides moving equipment from one end of the shipyard to the other or fixing the barracks where the penitents slept. The sunken ship, the SUS *Undaunted*, sat half-submerged in the water, a gift from the Mudfoot. By destroying it, they clogged the port, making it impossible for the larger ships to dock. For weeks, the best engineers in Hosanna had tried to recover the ship. Divers patched the hole, pumped out the water. But as the ship rose, the hull ruptured again, breaking the vessel into several pieces and worsening the situation. From then on, the penitents referred to it as the *Daunting*. Rather than waiting for heavy machinery to do the job, the overseers ordered the dogs to remove the debris in any way they could. Somehow, destroying the ship felt like a more suitable task for the penitents. They were here because they chose to destroy rather than build. It made sense to let them hack away at this giant steel sea creature until they worked the anger and the regret out of their systems.

Falkirk adjusted the flame and readied for another cut. The last piece he removed was still on the ground. He turned to find Angel gazing in the opposite direction.

Falkirk lightly elbowed him in his chest. "Wake up!" he said.

At the entrance of the shipyard, about fifty yards away, a row of soldiers formed a line at the metal fence. Among them was Colonel Thornton, the lead overseer for the penance camps. Standing beside her, wearing his black robe, was the Archon, his narrow face fitting almost perfectly between the bars. A breeze fluttered his wispy white hair.

"Is that a council member?" Angel asked.

"It's the leader of the council," Falkirk said.

"The fuck is he doin' here?" someone to his right said.

The relentless hissing of the torches began to die out as word spread through the penitents.

"Let's go," one of the humans shouted from the guard tower. "Get back to work!"

Falkirk remembered his promise: to set the right example for the others. He pushed the flame against the metal and watched it change from red to bright orange.

"What's going on?" Angel asked.

Falkirk needed to concentrate. Moving the flame too slowly warped the metal, spilling blobs of molten steel on the ground. Moving too quickly would require him to start over.

"Why are they here?" Angel said.

"I don't know," Falkirk said.

The piece fell away and dribbled on the concrete. When Angel reached for it, Falkirk whispered in his ear: "When you bring the next load to the truck, ask Vera. She might know."

Vera drove one of the supply vehicles. If anyone needed quick information on the outside world, she would have it.

Angel acknowledged him with a grunt as he pulled the piece of steel away. Falkirk felt a strange combination of terror and euphoria upon seeing the leader of Hosanna here. Anything new amid this dreary routine could at least provide a distraction, if not point to a way out of this place.

Falkirk stole a last glance at the Archon before the soldiers escorted the old human from the site. The Archon wagged his finger, issuing orders while Thornton bowed her head and nodded. Falkirk knew the look of a leader faced with a decision. Something was happening. Something was coming.

THAT NIGHT, AFTER lights-out, whispers drifted among the cots, bouncing off the canvas ceiling of the tent. Every so often it would get too loud, and the older dogs would shush everyone quiet. Then the noise would build again.

Angel tried his best to explain what Vera had told him: that the council planned to bring more penitents later that week. They wanted the *Daunting* removed from the water as soon as possible.

"They're gonna go back on their word," a mutt named Geiger said. "They're gonna get us to do all this work, and then kick us out."

"Really?" Angel asked.

"No," Falkirk said. "This is something else."

One of the old codgers shushed them.

"Pssst," someone said. It was Hicks. "Pass this along. Overseers are going to offer double shifts tomorrow."

Angel, who lay between them, began to relay the message. "Overseers are offering—"

"I heard him, Angel," Falkirk said.

"Quiet," another dog whispered. "Guards are right outside. I want to sleep!"

Falkirk whispered the message to Geiger, who huffed in response, as if he already knew.

As the hissing died out, Falkirk rolled over and imagined himself in a place that smelled like dirt, leaves, and grass. But when he drifted to sleep, his dreams carried him to the dock, where he tried to pull the *Daunting* from the water using a single chain. When the chain snapped, he leapt into the water to retrieve it. He found the links piled at the bottom. He pulled the chain free of the dirt and kicked his legs. The surface drew closer. At the exact moment when his chest felt ready to burst, the chain tightened, jerking him backward. He felt the ship lurch a few inches, but he could go no higher. If he would simply let go of the chain, he could breathe again. *No*, he thought. *No, I can do it.*

Falkirk snapped awake. The dogs around him snored, sounding much like his brothers and sisters in the pen where he was raised. As he settled in once more, their breath became synchronized to the sound of the water lapping against the riverbank. When he fell asleep this time, he plummeted into a blackness so silent and deep that he thought the entire world had collapsed onto itself.

THE NEXT DAY, during the morning roll call, Thornton and the overseers told the penitents what they expected to hear. Optional double shifts would begin immediately, with volunteers getting an extra day off at the end of the week, along with extra rations. "The Archon wants this fixed," Thornton said. "We're behind schedule."

To speed things along, they decided to use explosives on the *Daunting* to break it into smaller pieces more quickly. They needed divers to plant the bombs, and to attach chains to the hull. After the detonation, the chains would pull the loosened debris from the water. The dogs who served as engineers in the Colonial war shook their heads at this. It was too dangerous.

Why risk a drowning or an accidental explosion when they could clear the port the hard way by the summer?

The overseers had little patience for all the questions and complaints. "You want your citizenship back, this is the price," Thornton said. "If you don't like it, you can go back to the wolves." She resorted to this threat whenever the dogs complained about the work. They were penitents, not prisoners. At any point, they could sign a document renouncing their loyalty to the Sanctuary Union, then try their luck in the wilderness beyond. So far, no one from this camp had quit, thanks in part to peer pressure from Falkirk and the other dogs who remembered the Change. If this agreement collapsed, then everything he did here would be wasted.

A few dogs wondered aloud why Hosanna wanted *this* dock cleared. The river offered plenty of places for a ship to land. Falkirk asked himself what a military commander would prefer, and the answer became obvious. Unlike the other docks, this shipyard enjoyed the comfort of a cement barrier and a steel gate blocking it from the city. Tranquility could hide something in here or quietly shove it out into the river if it came to that.

Falkirk kept that observation to himself.

He decided to plow ahead. They all had work to do. Falkirk not only agreed to the double shifts, but also volunteered to plant the explosives. This required him to go through a crash course in diving, using a homemade frogman outfit similar to the ones that humans invented over a century earlier. It consisted of a jumpsuit, a metal bulb where his head would fit, and a hose connected to an air supply. Several of the dogs announced that they would never go near such a thing. Angel nearly passed out when he saw it.

On the morning when Falkirk and two other dogs planned to make the dive, a fight broke out in the barracks. Angel and three other penitents had some disagreement over who would get to organize a zagga tournament, triggering a brawl that left one of the dogs with a broken arm. It was a pointless argument, since the guards would have never allowed them to play. Angel and the others were sentenced to solitary confinement—an especially cruel punishment for a pack animal. Falkirk begged the overseers to discipline Angel *after* he helped with the dive. For all of Angel's faults, his fear and loyalty could keep Falkirk alive. He would pull Falkirk to the surface the second the humans started to panic. The overseers reluctantly agreed.

That afternoon, Angel helped him zip up the suit. He fastened the helmet onto a metal ring on the collar. A single glass portal allowed Falkirk to see straight ahead, but with no peripheral vision. Nearby, the other divers climbed a ladder into the water and vanished into the murky depths, their hoses snaking along the dock.

Falkirk noticed Angel smiling, despite having a cut on his snout from the fight.

"What is it?" Falkirk asked, his voice echoing in the metal chamber.

"Got some more news from Vera," Angel said. "It's nothing. I should tell you after the dive."

"Tell me now."

"Nah, it's not that big a deal," the pit bull said, guiding him toward the ladder.

Falkirk placed his weighted boots onto the rungs and awkwardly climbed into the water. As he broke the surface, the tension pressed the suit against his fur like a second skin. In the training, the water made him feel weightless. But here, he felt heavy as a boulder, ready to sink to the bottom. He forced himself to breathe.

"Tell me what you heard, Angel, and I'll see if I can get you a break on the solitary."

"Aneega is coming here."

The words almost knocked Falkirk off the ladder and into the water. "D'Arc is coming to Hosanna?"

"She's coming *here*. To the shipyard."

"Why?"

"Hey!" one of the overseers shouted. "Hurry up. You're wasting your air supply."

Falkirk ignored him. "Why?" he demanded.

Angel laughed. "Does it matter?" He patted the helmet. It was enough to push Falkirk under the surface. As he sank, the battered hull of the *Daunting* rose all around him, much like it did in his dream. *You can't stop me*, he thought. *You can't keep me here. I'll take you apart bolt by bolt if I have to.*

THE ANCHOR CHAINS—EIGHT in all, with links the size of a man's arm—emerged from the water inch by inch. Dump trucks pulled the chains along a concrete ramp at the edge of the dock. The bulkhead for the engine room rose from the depths like the carcass of a sea creature. It was the last piece of the *Daunting*, the final obstacle to getting out of the camp. The engineers decided against using explosives on this part of the ship—doing so would scatter the remaining debris and create more work. Because the chamber remained largely intact, they figured they could siphon out the water with a pump and lift out the bulkhead whole.

In the driver's seat of one the trucks, Falkirk rested his elbow on the window frame while his right hand gripped the steering wheel. One of the overseers signaled to the drivers to keep going. Falkirk tapped the gas pedal, feeling the weight of the chain holding the vehicle in place. Angel sat beside him. At this last stage, he could do nothing else but watch.

"Check it out," Angel said.

The enormous gate opened at the entrance to the shipyard, letting in a crowd of people, escorted by Tranquility soldiers.

Several of them wore the robes of the council. They had come to see the raising of the final piece, which would reopen this shipyard. Maybe D'Arc had come too.

Falkirk could smell the forest once more. It was so close. He pressed the pedal again. This time, the wheels stalled, and the chassis let out a sad creaking sound. The overseer demanded that they keep going. Falkirk stuck his head out the window.

"What is it?" Angel asked.

The water frothed around the bulkhead. Some of the engineers shouted. Off to the side, a trio of humans frantically worked on the pump.

"Something's wrong," Falkirk said. "The pump is choking. Too much water."

Something must have compromised the hull on its way to the surface. Judging from all the bubbles, it would flood in minutes and start to sink again.

"Take the wheel," Falkirk said as he opened the door and slid out.

"Whoa, whoa, wait a minute," Angel said. He continued shouting Falkirk's name as the husky walked away.

Falkirk waved his arms, trying to get the engineers' attention. The overseer stepped in his way.

"Get back in the truck," the man said behind his reflective sunglasses.

"They need another pump," Falkirk tried to explain. "That thing can't—"

Before he could finish, a chain broke loose from one of the trucks. It slithered along the ground, heading toward the water.

"Look out!" the overseer shouted.

The chain caught the wheels on the pump, and the entire apparatus pitched onto its side, tearing free from the hose. The machine fell into the water with a splash.

With the pump gone, the bulkhead began to sink again. The remaining chains lifted from the ground, the metal groaning from the strain.

Falkirk followed the chain to the concrete ramp and dove into the churning water. All the shouting went dead around him as the liquid filled his ears. The pump sank below him like a submersible. Falkirk tilted his body entirely upside down as he grabbed the handle. The weight of it pulled him deeper, even as he righted himself and kicked toward the surface. The pressure squeezed his lungs. He grunted, and a burst of bubbles left his mouth, floating away. He kicked harder, pulling with both hands. Above, humans and dogs jumped in after him. Finally, he began to rise. He let out a giddy laugh. More bubbles. His tail swished beneath him, propelling his body.

Slippery human hands gripped his arms. He broke through this quiet world into the air, where the voices barked and screamed all around him.

"Get the hose!" he gasped. "Get the hose back on."

Together, they lifted the pump and rolled it onto the dock. Falkirk flopped beside it as a human reattached the hose. The pump kicked on again, but nothing happened. On his knees, Falkirk slapped the machine, and a torrent of water shot out of the other side.

Delirious, he got to his feet and limped toward the trucks. "Do it! Hit the gas!"

Angel gave him a thumbs up. The wheels spun, releasing the acrid smell of burnt tires. This was their only chance. If the pump failed, if the chains broke, the bulkhead would sink, and all of this would amount to nothing.

The links rattled as they slid across the yard. Near the entrance, the soldiers formed a line to keep the civilians from getting too close.

Dripping wet, Falkirk turned to see the bulkhead rise. It made contact with the ramp. The chains gave a final tug, and the steel beast tipped over and smacked onto the dock like a great whale, defeated after a long battle.

The penitents let out an incredible roar, followed by howling so loud, so sincere, that even the overseers smiled when they heard it.

Falkirk melted to his knees. He did not have the energy to shake off the excess water.

Someone stood over him, blocking out the sun. He lifted his snout to see their silhouette. A hand reached out. It was her. D'Arc. Her tail wagging, her sword clipped to a belt. Her fur was slick and clean, with some black lupine war paint on her brow and ears.

Her bodyguards filled in the space around her, with Quay standing at D'Arc's side. "He looks like he's gonna pass out," she said.

Falkirk stood and wrapped his arms around D'Arc. She was so warm. Her heart beat so strong against him. She was real. This time, he would not awaken in a tent full of strangers.

"You made it just in time," he said.

"No. You *finished* just in time."

He gave her a look—tilted head, with the ears going floppy.

"Let me show you," she said.

Holding his hand, she led him around the crowd of workers, around the engineers and the overseers, one of whom patted Falkirk on the arm as he passed. At the edge of the dock, the council waited, surrounded by guards. Castor and Gaunt stood among them. Grissom stood on his own, away from everyone else. He folded his hands and bowed when he spotted D'Arc. She returned the gesture.

Falkirk noticed that more people had assembled outside of the shipyard, forming a cluster along the chain-link fence.

The Archon waved Falkirk over, toward the edge of the pier. The others made room.

Far downriver, an object approached, something neither Falkirk nor anyone else had ever seen before. At the front, a ship led the way, its entire crew waving from the bow. Behind the ship, towed with cables, floated something that resembled an iceberg, with several shiny, craggy peaks that reflected the sun. And all around this flotilla, propelling it, were long, flexible paddles, swaying in the water.

No, not paddles, he realized. Tentacles. Like the flagella of some enormous bacterium.

"What in the world is that?" he asked.

"The future," D'Arc said.

THE *AL-RIHLA* QUIETLY made its way to the shipyard, making a perfect turn into the space that the dogs had spent months trying to clear. On either side of its hull, the Sarcops tentacles undulated in unison. The creatures had fastened themselves to the metal and pushed it forward like the oarsmen of an ancient human vessel. The ship had sustained heavy damage at sea. Only a single windmill remained on deck, and an enormous hole, large enough for a car to fit through, punctured the port side. Water sloshed in and out of it. Though the crew had sealed the breach in time, the damage had clearly disabled the ship.

The object it towed barely fit into the dock. While the iceberg shape dwarfed the *al-Rihla*, it rested atop another vessel, about the same size as the ship. Falkirk's mouth fell open. D'Arc squeezed his hand. This was the *Vesuvius*, or what remained of it. Falkirk remembered Gaunt flinging the object across the giant map room, declaring it lost forever. The balloon had collapsed, crinkling into a shape like crushed tinfoil. That left the canopy as the base.

"It's like one of those popcorn pans," the Archon whispered

to a cat beside him. "Remember those things? You cook 'em on the stove?" He mimicked holding a pan by the handle and waving it over a flame. The cat did not seem to understand.

The two vessels came to a halt as the *al-Rihla* dropped its anchor. The dock workers attached a gangplank. As the crew members disembarked, D'Arc grew more excited. She hopped on one foot and waved. The gangplank emptied the crew into the middle of the crowd, where the Archon and his council greeted them with hugs and handshakes. By the time they reached Falkirk and D'Arc, the crew seemed disoriented from all the jostling.

"Harlan!" D'Arc said. A middle-aged human saw her and nearly tripped over his own feet. She hugged him while he gaped in disbelief. More of them followed, and they all had the same reaction. The ship's cook. The lead scientist. Even a bear named Moab, who did not wish to be hugged, but got one anyway.

On the deck of the *al-Rihla*, Falkirk recognized the aquamarine jumpsuits of the crew of the *Vesuvius*. A lump formed in his throat. He positioned himself behind D'Arc, where he could simply nod to them as they passed. Now was not the time to plead his case. Maybe some other day, if ever.

His heart pounded as they clustered on the gangplank, eager to touch land again. The ordeal that brought them here must have decimated the crew. O'Neill limped on a pair of crutches, her frayed hair barely held together in a ponytail. Bulan the orangutan waddled along behind her. Unoka came next, standing a full foot taller than the others. His smile conveyed the happy bewilderment of a survivor who has blocked out the terrible things he endured. And behind him, the last member of the *Vesuvius*, acting captain Ruiz. Falkirk nearly fell over when the man appeared. After what happened, he did not deserve to see his first officer alive again. Ruiz's face had thinned; his hair had gone gray. The new captain of the *Vesuvius* survived a betrayal, a bullet wound, a mutiny, and a crash landing in the water. In Ruiz's distant stare, Falkirk saw the months of hardship and grief where the man's resolve had taken root.

D'Arc must have sensed Falkirk's unease with all of this. As the crew of the *Vesuvius* passed through, she gave them gentle handshakes. Either out of mercy, or fatigue, they gave Falkirk the same tired head nod, an acknowledgment that fate tossed them out into the sea and brought them back for reasons they may never learn.

Ruiz would not acknowledge him at all. Falkirk understood. On a better day, in a better world, he would have told Ruiz how proud he was, how Ruiz deserved to be the captain.

The crowd suddenly went silent, as if the volume had cut out on a loudspeaker. Captain Vittal of the *al-Rihla* made her way across the plank. A small woman, she wore her full ceremonial uniform, complete with epaulets, medals, and a cap over her white hair.

Two animals escorted her. One of them resembled a cat, with golden fur and a thick tail that ended in a tuft of brown hair. An enormous mane covered his ears.

"Yo, that's a fucking lion," someone behind Falkirk said.

Following the lion was a leathery beast walking on all fours. The creature rose onto its hind legs. Everyone in the crowd gasped at how tall it stood. Two impossibly large ears splayed out. This was an elephant matriarch, larger than any bear Falkirk had ever met. The gangplank dipped in the middle as she made her way across.

A pair of hands gripped Falkirk and shook him. "They made it," D'Arc said, nearly in tears. "Do you see? The Sarcops took them across the ocean."

Vittal saluted the Archon. She gestured to the guests from Africa. "Gajavu," she said, pointing to the elephant. The trunk lifted from between the two tusks and extended to the Archon's face. The man did not know what to do until Vittal mimicked a handshake. The Archon nervously palmed the underside of the trunk. In response, the nostrils expanded and contracted. The Archon had no choice but to interpret it as a friendly sign.

Vittal motioned for the lion to step forward. With his amber eyes glowing in the sun, the giant cat leaned in to the Archon. He offered his paw, large enough to pulverize the human's tiny hand.

"Mufasa," the lion said in a voice so low it could have been a bass drum.

That name meant nothing to Falkirk. But the Archon—who until now maintained a solemn demeanor befitting of his post—burst into giddy laughter. "I'm sorry," he said, holding his hand over his mouth. "It's just—wow. Mufasa."

While the Archon made small talk to cover for his indiscretion, Vittal caught sight of D'Arc and began to work her way through the crowd, giving quick handshakes to the council. The captain nearly knocked D'Arc over when they embraced. After they untangled themselves, Vittal held both of D'Arc's hands. "Your children?" she asked, her voice quivering.

"I lost two," D'Arc said.

"I'm sorry."

"But one survived."

"One," Vittal repeated. She stepped in front of Falkirk and eyed him up and down in a way that humans were not supposed to do with animals anymore. "You're the father?"

"I am," Falkirk said.

D'Arc reached into a pouch on her belt and pulled out a notebook. Falkirk had seen it before: the unofficial logbook of the SUS *al-Rihla*.

"My final report," D'Arc said. "For your records."

Vittal flipped through the pages, dumbfounded at possessing such a holy object.

"I followed your advice as best as I could," D'Arc said. "We both did."

Vittal did not seem to remember.

"Beacons of light," D'Arc reminded her.

Vittal smiled. "Right. Beacons of light in the darkness."

"Guiding the other ships home," D'Arc added.

By this point, the formal diplomatic ceremony had become a party, with people of every species hugging and laughing. The guards let the spectators on the street enter through the main gate. These were the people who had survived to rebuild this place once more, to do it right this time. And behind the noise of hundreds of voices, the song of the Sarcops hummed through the crowd like distant foghorns. Falkirk recognized it as a message of peace—but also as a warning, a reminder that what they held in their hands right now could easily slip away.

# CHAPTER 31

## SANCTUM

**THE HOWLING BEGAN** as soon as D'Arc crossed the border and only grew stronger as she and her bodyguards left the highway and entered the woods. Quay had told her: someone was always watching in wolf country. More voices joined in as they passed Camp Echo, coming from opposite directions, far off in the hills. At the river, where the new forest mingled with the old, the howling came from all the points on the compass.

"How do they see us?" D'Arc asked.

"They don't," Quay said. "They watch the trees sway. They hear the twigs breaking. The bugs swarming. And then they wait for the wind to carry your scent. *Everyone* knows your scent."

The wolves meant well. The same song that warned intruders served as a greeting for her. D'Arc could get used to this, if she put her mind to it. She had grown accustomed to far stranger things in the last few weeks.

Near sunset, they at last arrived at the abandoned vineyard, where the mansion served as her command center. The grapes grew wild here, overtaking the rotten wooden posts. The Spanish tiled roof gave the illusion of a faraway place that never saw winter. With no city and no capitol building, a sturdy farmhouse in a clearing would have to do. D'Arc intended it as a more inviting place than a police headquarters, or a corporate campus, or a factory farm that had once processed meat. The wolves regarded houses as strange, unnatural objects, having spent so many years sleeping in caves and ditches. They would enter only when she commanded them to do so. The rest of the time, they stuck to the growing wilderness beyond, mapping out the hills, flattening new trails. Before the day ended, a few more of them would most likely leave. Those still hungry for war would find it somewhere beyond the frontier. For the rest, the miracle surrounding them would compel them to stay. Protecting this new forest would become their sacred duty. Besides, in the coming months, many of them would be carrying babies, which rendered war an increasingly foolish prospect. Quay had already picked three marauders who could father her children, though she had yet to settle on one. And when Falkirk returned—after wrapping things up at the pier—D'Arc would have to fend off the female suitors who considered him an exotic arctic wolf.

As D'Arc entered the main gate, walking on two feet, the guards greeted her with lowered snouts and wagging tails. A few of them went through the trouble of rolling onto their backs, getting leaves and pebbles in their fur, a performance that always made D'Arc uneasy. Someday, when the time was right, she would relinquish her power to the pack elders. It would get messy. Some would not understand and would fall into the old ways. But if the ants could change, if the bats and the beavers could change, if even the humans could change, then so could they.

Two guards opened the large wooden doors. D'Arc stepped into the foyer and then the dining hall, with its long table and wooden chairs, and an empty wine rack at the far wall. When the humans had evacuated many years before, they knew exactly what to take with them.

In the doorway, D'Arc's bodyguards awaited her orders.

"Find out about how the fields are coming along," D'Arc said. "See if you can pull together some more volunteers to help."

Quay nodded. She sent one of the other guards to the new farm, where the former hunters worked the soil with plows and shovels.

"And I want to know as soon as the scouts spot the husky," D'Arc added. She tried to think of something else since the wolves appeared so eager to receive new orders, but Quay lifted her hand to put a stop to it.

"Please rest, Aneega," Quay said. "See your little one."

D'Arc embraced Quay, resting her head on the wolf's snout for a few seconds. Then she closed the door and leaned on it to recover her strength.

She took the spiral staircase to the third level where the master of the house once lived, which now served as her personal quarters. She followed the light to the end of the hall, past the study with its musty smell of books, and into the main bedroom. The hardwood slats creaked as she entered. With the room completely silent and the king-sized bed empty, she knew exactly where to find her son. In the padded rocking chair facing the window, her little Revelation lay curled between two pillows, resembling a pillow himself. She eased herself next to him. Without opening his eyes, he crawled into her lap and rested his ear on her chest. *Missed you*, he said in her mind. She pulled him in tighter.

He fell asleep here as he often did: staring at the countryside, where the forest continued to grow from its focal point at the crash site. The tree line rose higher each day, and the hills and meadows grew green under the spring sun, with blotches of yellow and purple indicating new patches of flowers. In the center, the ants crawled about their mound. With their mating season over, the ants lost their wings again, and set about digging their tunnels and harvesting plants for their underground stores. Some days, entire swaths of trees collapsed and then vanished into the mound, which Rev could watch for hours on end.

A breeze puffed the curtains. She stroked his fur and let his warmth seep into her own. D'Arc turned to the bed. She listened for movement coming from under the mattress, but could hear nothing. So she clicked her tongue a few times.

"Come on out," she whispered. "It's okay."

Two tiny feet emerged, covered in white fur, with a whiskered face leaning over them. A pair of green eyes peered at her, slit vertically in the middle.

"It's me," she said. "Come on."

A creature that no one had seen in over a decade crawled out from under the mattress. An orange cat the size of a loaf of bread, with white fur around his maw and his underside. His stubby tail popped out last, sticking straight in the air. He had been found like this not far from the crash site, wandering about and sniffing the grass. Though lost, he did not seem to have a care in the world. All his worries had been wiped clean, all his regrets left buried in the dirt, consumed by the roots of the trees and released into the air as oxygen.

With his nostrils twitching, he reached his front paws onto the chair and sniffed at Rev. The pup stirred, and then settled again. Without a sound, the cat hopped up next to him, draping his body over D'Arc's leg and tucking his head into Rev's neck. D'Arc ran her finger under his chin. He tilted his head to give her more surface to explore. With each stroke, his eyelids drooped until he fell asleep.

The sun dipped behind the trees. As the sky cooled from orange to purple, D'Arc felt herself dozing off, her arms wrapped around her pack.

# CHAPTER 32

## THE STORY OF SEBASTIAN AND SHEBA

FTER HE TOOK his new name, after the animals rose up and overthrew their oppressors, after there was talk of prophecies and saviors, after the seas rose and the old empires fell, the great warrior Mort(e) became a simple house cat, known to his companions as Sebastian, the only name he could ever remember having.

He could not recall the exact circumstances that brought him here. He remembered padding through a wooded area while his paws turned brown from the mud. The dew on the grass and the tree bark compelled him to sniff everything. When the Alphas found him, he fled into a thicket and cowered there, not realizing that they, too, could locate him through scent. Despite their massive size, they appeared all at once, with virtually no sound. When one of them reached for him, he tried to bat the antennae away. Rather than force him to come out, the insects waited patiently for him to grow calm again.

Before long, his curiosity got the best of him. He emerged from the bushes and sat on his hind legs while pawing at an antenna as if it were a toy. The insect let him do it until he grew bored. Gently, like a mother cat lifting her kittens, the ant took him in her jaws and placed him onto the back of one of the other creatures. They marched single file, forming a new path through the forest. The swaying made Sebastian sleepy, and he promptly slipped into darkness with his head bouncing on the ant's flexible shell.

He dreamt of things that could never be. The hills on fire. Metal flying machines streaking across the sky. Terrible screaming in the night. Eventually, his dreams placed him on the floor of a house, beside a window, where a square of sunlight warmed the carpet.

He awoke in a bedroom and immediately set about exploring the place. The old mortar hid many secrets, as did the musty wine cellar, the layers of wallpaper, the dusty bedsheets, the darkened closets where overcoats and suits hovered like spirits above him. It would take a lifetime to map out the entire mansion.

At the end of that first day, Sebastian heard someone speaking at the bottom of the stairs. While he waited in the hallway, the voice got closer, rising to the third level of the mansion. He retreated to the bedroom and waited. When the door opened, a dog entered, standing on two feet. He knew her name was Sheba. The word simply formed in his mind, so clear that it had its own scent. A much smaller dog appeared at Sheba's ankles, hiding behind her. Sheba smelled like the square of sunlight from his dream. When he approached her, she lifted him to her chest, whispering gently. *I know you*, her affection seemed to say. *Where have you* been?

He purred. *Don't worry. Don't be sad. I am strong. I will not leave you.* She made a wheezing sound in her throat. He frantically licked her chin until her tail wagged again. As she set him on the bed, the pup jumped onto the mattress and crouched into a fighting stance. Sheba whispered to the young one, and the pup grew calm. He crept closer, letting Sebastian rub his cheek on his legs to get the scent buried in the pup's fur. To reciprocate, the pup gave him kisses so sloppy and forceful that they nearly knocked him off balance. Sheba seemed pleased with this.

From that morning on, the days dissolved into one another for little Sebastian. As the pup grew stronger, Sebastian followed him around the house, into the overgrown vineyards, past the wolves who guarded the hallways and entrances. At one window, they watched the ants tending to their hills. At another, they saw the dogs and wolves working the land, turning over the soil so that the wet smell traveled on the wind. In the sky above, flocks of birds returned from their winter homes, on their way to nesting grounds to the north. Sebastian understood that some things ended while other things began, and all of it would repeat again and again. His simple mind could not ponder it beyond that, and anyway, something new would always grab his attention before long.

In the evenings, Sheba would return, exhausted from the work she did during the day. She would sip tea and let both her son and the cat rest in the chair with her. She whispered to Sebastian. He would tell her about his day, using meows of differing lengths and pitches. Sometimes, she seemed to understand him. He was sure of it. Oh yes, she knew that there was a world to explore and a home to protect. The love they created here did not have to remain locked inside the walls, where it would shrivel and die. Instead, it could build and build until it overflowed and washed over the land. And then long after they were gone, what they created and shared would still live.

As always, the thought drifted away once it took up too

much space. It would return to him when he needed it. For now, these were his people, and he belonged with them. This was home. Everything was now, in the present moment, and it was perfect. He was safe here. There was nothing else to life. There didn't need to be.

# ACKNOWLEDGMENTS

IT HAS NOW been twelve years since I had a strange dream about sentient animals taking over my hometown by force. That image stayed with me for months until I started writing a novel, thinking the entire time that my Animal Farm on steroids epic would most likely never see the light of day. But writing a draft with no expectations turned out to be the easy part. The real work began when I shared the book with the many, many people who helped it along on its journey.

First, I'm grateful to my agent Jennifer Weltz, who helped to shape this series, and found a great partner in Soho Press. At Soho, I was fortunate to have fellow novelist Mark Doten overseeing this project for nearly a decade, and his effort, passion, and insight turned this from a quirky idea based on a dream to a real novel. I am grateful to the team at Soho, which included Bronwen Hruska, Rachel Kowal, Rudy Martinez, Paul Oliver, Juliet Grames, Erica Loberg, Janine Agro, and Steven Tran, among others. Thank you so much for the work you do.

Kapo Amos Ng designed the beautiful covers for this series. I've never met this man, but if he called me and asked me to hide a body, Goodfellas-style, I think I have to say yes at this point.

I'm lucky to have a supportive family, and I'm grateful for the enthusiasm and encouragement they've given me. My friends Brian Hurley, Jane Berentson, and Michael Hennessey have been champions of my work for a long time, even when they were reading some very rough first drafts. There are a few people—some I've met electronically, others I know in person— who have helped to promote this series, including Eric Smith, Maria Haskins, Katelyn Phillips, Rick Kleffel, Kelly Justice, Paul Hammond, Kenya Danino, Justin Wolfson, Jeff Wong, David Barr Kirtley, James Scott, Jenny Doster, Jenny Keegan, Kelly Caldwell, and Anna-Lise Santella, among many others. (Seriously, let me know if I left you out.) And I am eternally grateful to Ashley Wells for encouragement, understanding, advice, and patience.

If you're holding this book many years from now, take a look at the publication date and know that most of the work was done during a very difficult time for everyone involved. That fact makes me even more grateful, and more aware of how publishing is a collaborative process. I wrote these books in part to explore what it means to see the humanity in people who are different from you, people you were raised to distrust, dismiss, or hate. I hope this surreal time has encouraged you to find some empathy, as well as its active form: kindness. Thank you for reading.